JERUSALEM'S
QUEEN

THE SILENT YEARS

JERUSALEM'S QUEEN

A NOVEL OF SALOME ALEXANDRA

ANGELA HUNT

BETHANYHOUSE
a division of Baker Publishing Group
Minneapolis, Minnesota

Published by Bethany House Publishers
11400 Hampshire Avenue South
Bloomington, Minnesota 55438
www.bethanyhouse.com

Bethany House Publishers is a division of
Baker Publishing Group, Grand Rapids, Michigan

Printed in the United States of America

Library of Congress Cataloging-in-Publication Data
Names: Hunt, Angela Elwell, author.
Title: Jerusalem's queen : a novel of Salome Alexandra / Angela Hunt.
Description: Minneapolis, Minnesota : Bethany House, a division of Baker
    Publishing Group, [2018] | Series: The silent years
Identifiers: LCCN 2018019154 | ISBN 9780764219344 (trade paper) | ISBN
    9780764232787 (hardcover) | ISBN 9781493416073 (e-book)
Subjects: LCSH: Salome Alexandra, 139 B.C.–67 B.C.—Fiction. | GSAFD: Christian
    fiction. | Biographical fiction.
Classification: LCC PS3558.U46747 J47 2018 | DDC 813/.54—dc23
LC record available at https://lccn.loc.gov/2018019154

This is a work of historical reconstruction; the appearances of certain historical figures are therefore inevitable. All other characters, however, are products of the author's imagination, and any resemblance to actual persons, living or dead, is coincidental.

Cover design by LOOK Design Studio
Cover photography by Aimee Christenson

Author is represented by Browne & Miller Literary Associates.

18 19 20 21 22 23 24   7 6 5 4 3 2 1

In the Christian Bible, one turns the page after Malachi and finds Matthew as if only a few days fell between the activities of the prophet and the arrival of Jesus Christ. In reality, however, four hundred "silent years" lie between the Old Testament and New, a time when God did not speak to Israel through His prophets. Yet despite the prophets' silence, God continued to work in His people, other nations, and the supernatural realm.

He led Israel through a time of testing that developed a sense of hope and a yearning for the promised Messiah.

He brought the four nations prophesied in Daniel's vision to international prominence: the Babylonians, the Persians, the Greeks, and the Romans. These powerful kingdoms spread their cultures throughout civilization and united the world by means of paved highways and international sailing routes.

God also prepared to fulfill His promise to the serpent in Eden: "I will put animosity between you and the woman, and between your descendant and her descendant; he will bruise your head, and you will bruise his heel" (Gen. 3:15).

For God never sleeps, and though He may not communicate as we expect Him to, He can always speak to a receptive heart.

Our sages commanded that one should not teach one's daughter Torah because the minds of most women are incapable of concentrating on learning, and thus, because of their intellectual poverty, they turn the words of Torah into words of nonsense.

Moses Maimonides, *Mishneh Torah*,
"Laws of Torah Study," 1:13

Chapter One

They are all here, gathered like vultures around my bed, watching with long faces and occasionally bending near to listen for my breathing. Hyrcanus studies me with wet eyes; Aristobulus is not present, undoubtedly intent on working mischief outside Jerusalem. His wife, whom I have never liked, smiles at my bedside, ready to fly to her husband once I am gone.

HaShem, can I not stay a little longer? My sons are not at peace with each other, and I worry their animosity will destroy the peace of Judea.

I close my eyes and the room goes silent. When I open them again, the daughter-in-law at my side frowns.

I shift my attention to the others. Such beloved faces! Here is Simeon ben Shetah, who takes my hand and pronounces a blessing on my head. There is Honi the Circle-Drawer, who pushes his way past Simeon to see me. I try to smile at him, but my lips do not respond as I would like.

The distant sound of mournful music seeps into the room. The figures around me soften in a hazy glow, and my friends and family are replaced by loved ones from long ago. My father! My sister, now a woman as beautiful as I expected. My mother, who smiles at me with pleased surprise. And Uncle, standing erect, his hands folded, wearing a look of satisfaction. I see Alena and Avigail and Ezra Diagos—

"Mistress?"

I blink at the sound of Kissa's voice. My eyelids flutter, and with an effort I focus on the oval face hovering near mine.

"Honi Ha-Meaggel would like to pray with you."

I nod, or try to, and as the circle-drawer reads, the beloved words lift me from my surroundings and distract me from my visitors.

> "I will lift up my eyes to the mountains—
> from where does my help come?
> My help comes from Adonai,
> Maker of heaven and earth.
> He will not let your foot slip.
> Your Keeper will not slumber.
> Behold, the Keeper of Israel
> neither slumbers nor sleeps . . ."

I look down on the palace courtyard that has filled with my people, many of whom are weeping. The air vibrates with the ululation of mourners. Men and women are beating their breasts, asking HaShem to bless my journey . . . *as I have blessed Israel.*

Their words are a balm to my soul. Thanks be to HaShem, He listened to the prayer of a fatherless girl and granted her most earnest desire: to matter in a world where women were often chattel, overlooked and forgotten.

And then He made her queen.

CHAPTER TWO

Shelamzion

I covered my eyes, unable to look at the dead man on the table. Thus occupied, my hands could not protect my ears, which had filled with the sound of Mother's frantic wailing and the mourners' rising ululation.

"My husband," Mother cried, her voice trembling. "And my beautiful girl! How can I lose them both in one day?"

"Hush now." Avigail pulled my mother into her arms. "Ketura Desmona may yet live. We will know nothing until they find her."

Mother shook her head. "She is gone. HaShem has taken her from me."

The mourners wailed on cue, and Mother burst into fresh sobs.

Overcome by the sights and sounds of grief, I crouched lower in the corner, willing myself to disappear. No one looked in my direction because I was the second daughter, the plain one. I was only Shelamzion.

"So sudden," Avigail said, releasing my mother. The old woman, our closest neighbor, picked up a piece of wet linen, wiped it over my dead father's chest, and shook her head. "Ittamar was a fine man. HaShem blessed you with a fine husband, a prosperous man, and now He has taken him away."

"Blessed be the name of the Lord," another neighbor murmured, determination in the straight line of her mouth as she scrubbed between the dead man's toes. "He gives and He takes away."

"But to take him—like this!" Mother sputtered, looking from one neighbor to another. "He was fine this morning. He broke his fast and went riding with Ketura, and before I could even visit the well, my husband returned to me, dead! And my daughter—my pride and joy—what has become of her?"

A newcomer caught Mother's arm. "A swift death is a mercy, and my son said your husband died instantly. Apparently the horse reared, and Ittamar fell backward. Your daughter must have been thrown from the saddle."

"So where is she?" Mother shrieked. She stepped to the window, threw open the wooden shutters, and looked into the courtyard as if expecting my nine-year-old sister to materialize outside the door. "Where could she be?"

"Poor, proud Ittamar." Avigail's hands drifted to the corpse's forehead. "Why did you have to insist on a horse? Would not a mule have served you as well?" The other women did not reply but kept washing the body.

Though I was but a child of six years, I knew the old woman had raised a valid point. Most of the villagers in Modein rode mules, if they rode at all, yet Father had insisted on riding a horse. And not just any horse—his mount had to be a stallion, the finest money could buy, and it had to be a proud beast, and lively, with a wild streak to intimidate less-skilled riders.

That insistence, born of pride, had probably cost Father his life. The skittish stallion often fidgeted when a rider climbed onto his back and frequently kicked at any passerby who happened to startle him. Mother often spoke of how untrustworthy the animal was, yet Father only laughed at her fears.

He was not laughing now. And Ketura? Where was my sister?

Before sunset, Father would take his place in the family tomb, and Mother and I would face life without him. I would miss his twinkling dark eyes, his booming laugh, and the work-worn hands that had always patted my head with gentle affection.

A sob rose in my throat, and I barely forced it down. Mother was already mad with grief; I did not want to distract her and cause her further pain.

Now she walked around the room, her hands in constant motion—pressing against her forehead, clinging to the table for support, tugging at the neckline of her tunic. "What will we do?" she asked, glancing around the room. "Ittamar's parents are dead, and he has no brothers. His sisters have married into other families . . ."

"The people of Modein will be generous," Avigail said, "as they were generous with me when my man died. The Law commands them to leave grain and fruit for the needy."

"But I don't want to be poor!" Mother looked from one woman to the other, searching for answers they did not have. "All I have are a few wild horses, and no one will want to buy them after this. I have daughters to feed, unless—" Her voice broke as she looked at the small stool where Ketura usually sat at meals. "Ketura!" Her anguished voice spilled out the window as she turned toward it, frantically looking for my sister.

"Tend to your husband!" Avigail's voice cut through the mourners' cries. "Half the village is out searching for your daughter. They will find her soon."

Reluctantly, Mother left the window and stepped to the table, then looked at the dead man and broke into fresh tears. "What a fool I married! He should never have taken Ketura with him on that animal."

This earned her a sharp look from Avigail, but I had no time to wonder about it, because a strong voice suddenly called from the street: "Sipporah!"

Mother lifted her head, and for an instant the worry lines between her brows melted away. "Did they find my beautiful girl?"

She flew to the window again, and from the sound of her anguished cry I knew they had not found my sister alive. Mother took several steps backward and crumpled to the floor, tearing at her tunic as the air trembled with the agony of her grief.

A man from the village came through the doorway with my sister in his arms. Without speaking, he laid Ketura's body next to my father's, and the women in the room lifted their voices in another chorus of unspeakable loss.

The cause of death—later they would say it was snakebite—did not matter. All I could hear was Mother wailing that with her husband and beautiful daughter gone, she had nothing, so she might as well join them in the grave.

⌇⌇⌇⌇⌇⌇

Two days after we buried my father and sister, a man riding a fine horse entered the village. I saw him come through the gate, and some deep-seated intuition told me he had come to see my mother.

"Who is that?" one of the other girls whispered, pointing to the stranger at the center of a dust cloud.

"Someone important," another girl answered. "He wears elegant clothing."

I left my jar at the well and hurried home. Mother had not done her chores since the funerals, so I had been fetching water and doing my best to grind the grain. But my arms were not strong, and my efforts were far from satisfactory.

I passed several houses, each sitting behind a courtyard. In each courtyard a woman stood and peered toward the well, where the stranger had dismounted to water his horse.

"Well-bred animal," one woman remarked.

"Expensive tunic," another said.

"He looks familiar," called the woman across the street. "I've seen him before."

"He is one of the high priest's sons." Avigail's mouth curled in a smile. "Distant cousin to Sipporah. Mark my words, he has come from Jerusalem to see her."

"He can't go in the house," the first woman said, her voice flat. "He won't. Sipporah will be unclean until the Sabbath."

"As will we all," Avigail said. "But we can still speak to him."

"Sipporah!" The woman who lived next to our house turned toward our door. "Someone has come to see you."

I reached our home just as Mother stepped into the courtyard. Her face was pale, her head uncovered, and her eyes still puffy. She looked around, then asked the air, "Who would come to this house of sorrow?"

Without speaking, all the women turned toward the well, where the well-dressed man had left his horse. He was moving down the dusty street, saying nothing, and studying each woman he approached. Finally he stopped at our courtyard gate.

He did not ask permission to enter but dipped his head in a respectful nod. "Sipporah, wife of Ittamar?"

Mother squinted at him. "Could it be John Hyrcanus?"

"Cousin." He greeted her, his deep voice resonating with concern. "How sorry I was to hear about Ittamar and your child. I know your heart is heavy, but I have come to extend what comfort I can. I want to assure you that we will never ignore your needs. My family will be your family, and you do not need to fear the future."

Tears glinted in Mother's eyes. "I have suffered a great loss. Ittamar is gone, and Ketura—she was the most beautiful girl in Modein. She would have been a lovely bride for some fortunate young man. She would have been fit for a prince."

The visitor inclined his head. "Yes, the last time I spoke with Ittamar, he remarked on your eldest daughter's beauty. But you have another daughter, yes?"

Mother blinked, then nodded. "Salome Alexandra."

"Ittamar said your youngest daughter was exceptional, as well. He said she was clever."

Mother blinked again. "Clever?"

"He said she taught herself to read. That she was advanced beyond her years and studied Torah with him, memorizing as easily as a scholar."

Mother gave him an uncertain look. "He said that?"

"He did. So when I heard about your tragedy, I knew I had to come and offer our help. We will be happy to take care of you and your daughter."

"You are too kind." Mother murmured the words absently, and I could tell she was still thinking about what Father had told this man.

"Nonsense. I'm sure Ittamar would do the same thing if the situation were reversed."

I tilted my head and considered the stranger's words. While my father had been a good man, I could not imagine him offering to take care of this powerful man's family. They would probably laugh at his offer, a tribe of lions scorning help from a mouse.

"I will send a wagon for you after the Sabbath," John Hyrcanus went on. "Henceforth, you and Salome will be under my guardianship. We have a place for you, so you need not worry about anything."

That promise, bestowed so easily, seemed to fill the shadows in the courtyard and brighten Mother's face. Looking up, somehow she found the courage to offer him a weak smile. "May HaShem bless and keep you, cousin, until we see your wagon coming through our gate."

~~~~~~~

Though grief lay heavy on my mother's heart, throughout the next week she did her best to prepare for our move to Jerusalem.

She gave away my father's clothing and sold our goats to the neighbors. She sold Father's wild horses to a trader. She packed up our few tunics and sandals, putting all our possessions into wooden trunks and woven baskets.

When we had finished packing, we had little to occupy our time as we waited for John Hyrcanus to send a wagon. Mother sat in the nearly empty house and wept while I wandered through the village, pausing at the gates of the neighbors' courtyards and silently saying good-bye to the sights and sounds I had known since I was old enough to walk. The village of Modein, small though it was, encompassed my entire world, and I could not imagine anything outside it.

As I wandered through the dusty streets, the other mothers called out condolences and assured me they were going to miss me. "Take care of your mother in Jerusalem," I heard time and again. "Don't let her forget us."

While we waited, I sat by the fire pit and thought about all the things my father had taught me. From the Tanakh he read portions of the Torah, the writings and the prophets, and frequently the Scriptures mentioned the word *Savior*. "My God is my rock, in Him I take refuge," David wrote, "my shield, my horn of salvation, my stronghold and my refuge, my Savior— You save me from violence."

I had never endured the hard things David suffered, but as my childish lips repeated the Scripture I had memorized, I realized that John Hyrcanus was a sort of savior to Mother and me. With Father gone, we faced a life of poverty and want until John Hyrcanus, son of Simon the high priest, left his home in Jerusalem and came to little Modein with his promise to save us.

But that promise vanished when two sweaty riders stopped at the well and broadcast a terrible report: Simon Maccabaeus, son of Mattathias the righteous priest, had been most foully murdered, along with his two eldest sons, Mattathias and Judah.

Simon had been the last of the five brothers known as the Maccabees, and the first of the Hasmon family to be proclaimed Israel's "leader and high priest forever, until there should arise a faithful prophet."

As a child, I did not understand the full meaning of those words, but I had heard the name *Simon* enough to know he was important to everyone in Judea.

Mother went silent at the somber news, and the village of Modein sank into a grief that eclipsed the mourning of my father and sister. The sons of Mattathias, I heard people say, were *our* people. Simon had grown up in Jerusalem, but his father and his brothers had launched their war against the Seleucid invaders in Modein. The neighbors around me had watched and prayed with Judas Maccabaeus, who led the army of Israel, and they had traded and worked alongside Johanan, Eleazar, and Jonathan. Along with Mattathias, they had sacrificed their husbands, fathers, and sons to win their freedom from pagan tyranny.

Simon, Mother reminded Avigail, had been our high priest for only seven years. "He should have died in his bed," she said, weeping. "He should have led us until his death as an old man."

"Even more horrible," Avigail replied, "is the betrayal! They say Ptolemy, his own son-in-law, planned the murder."

Confused, I tried to make sense of the wailing I heard from every house. I tugged on Mother's tunic and waited until she looked down at me. "Ima, was Simon our king?"

She shook her head. "Simon was our leader and high priest."

"So who will be high priest now?"

She looked at Avigail, her brows lifting. "What do you think? With the two older sons in their graves, the high priest must be John Hyrcanus."

Avigail frowned. "I am surprised they did not try to kill him, as well."

16

"Maybe they did. Maybe . . . he was somewhere else when they sought to kill him. Maybe he was here . . . with us." An odd look settled on Mother's features—surprise, puzzlement, and a touch of fear. "I am being foolish. Surely we are too small to matter in such dealings."

Avigail smiled. "HaShem uses all things to work His will— even small things." She peered at me. "Never forget that, Salome Alexandra. Even a girl as small as you is not too small to matter."

The corner of Mother's mouth twisted at that suggestion, but the mention of Hyrcanus had turned her thoughts to other matters. Her face clouded. "My cousin may not send for us now. He will mourn his father and brothers, and he will move his family into the high priest's house. His life is about to change completely . . . I would not be surprised if he forgot about us."

I tugged on Mother's tunic as hope filled my heart. "If he forgets, can we stay here? Can we get our goats back?"

Mother gave me a swift tap on the shoulder and told me to run along.

As I wandered through the village, I realized that Mother was not the only person talking about changes in Judea. The news that John Hyrcanus would become our high priest seemed to stun the village almost as much as the news about Simon being killed. "Hyrcanus has not been trained," the men protested as they led their sheep and goats out to pasture. "He was never meant for the priesthood."

"Is he not a Levite?" others countered. "And was Simon not his father? The hand of HaShem will be on his life, and surely even this is the Lord's doing."

When I returned home, I found Mother sitting by the window and chewing on a fingernail. She would not tell me why she appeared anxious, but when Avigail came to visit, Mother did not mince words. "I thought we would be all right," she said, her hand at her throat. "John Hyrcanus promised to take us in, but how can he do that now? The high priest and the leader of Israel will have no time for poor relatives. He will have far more important things on his mind."

"A priest looks after HaShem's people," Avigail said, her voice low and soothing. "If John Hyrcanus made you a promise, he will keep it. You must be patient and give him time."

"And when we run out of grain, what then?" Mother's eyes snapped. "Am I to beg by the well? Perhaps I should resort to thievery and steal one of my kinsmen's lambs."

"Patience, Sipporah," Avigail counseled. "HaShem hears the cries of the widow and the fatherless. He will take care of you as He took care of Hagar in the desert. As He took care of me."

He would be our savior.

I looked at Mother, hoping to see relief in her face, but all I saw was a cloud of fearful desperation.

Chapter Three

Kissa

I saw the cook coming, noticed the large wooden bowl in her hands, and winced. She was watching the contents of the steaming bowl, not her feet. Because I had no time to move in the narrow space where I was not supposed to be, I flattened my body against a stack of crates, willing myself to be as small as possible . . .

My effort failed. The cook's left foot struck my heel and down she went, spilling hot soup all over herself, the floor, and me.

I yelped in pain and squirmed away, but not before the cook spotted me. Her face went red as she released a scream of equal parts agony and anger. As other servants appeared in the doorway, the cook shook herself like a wet dog and reached for me.

"I'll kill you," she said, her hand closing around the back of my neck. "Worthless child! Why didn't you speak when you saw me coming?"

"Because," I shouted, "I was afraid the noise would startle you and you'd drop the soup on me!"

She did not care for my answer, of course, and I knew I

would never be able to convince her that I had tried to get out of her way.

As my skin blistered, she pushed me forward. I stumbled beneath her iron grip and fell into the courtyard, where nearly a dozen slaves had gathered to investigate the commotion. They watched, wide-eyed, as the cook stood above me, wet, furious, and sputtering in Aramaic. I glanced over my shoulder as someone tossed her a strip of linen. She wiped the hot soup from her skin, wincing as she did so.

"I ought to string her up and let the buzzards pick her bones clean," she said, her cheeks blood red. "Never have I seen such a stupid girl. Always in the way, and she eats far too much. Too weak to carry a basket of fruit and too thin for beauty. I ask you, why should the master keep her around?"

"If he doesn't want me around, why doesn't he send me back?" I yelled.

"Stupid girl," the cook said, glaring back at me. "Do you think our new master even knows who you are?"

Several slaves shook their heads, as if they could see no reason for my existence. But one young woman lifted her chin and said, "She may have a temper, and she may not please you, but she is the high priest's property and he would not appreciate losing her. I do not think you should harm this child, or you may pay dearly for it tomorrow."

The cook, whose hefty arms had begun to blister, glared at the young woman, then scowled at me. "The new master hasn't arrived yet. So it's not likely he would miss a skinny Egyptian girl."

"I would miss her. And I might tell the master about the cook who thought nothing of killing one of his slaves."

I looked up, eager to see the face of the angel who had defended me, but I could barely see her through the crowd. Her words, however, had their intended effect on the angry cook.

"So I won't kill her," the cook said. "But I will beat her because I'm her overseer. I'll teach her not to lie on the floor if it takes my last breath. Switch!"

She held out her hand, and almost immediately one of the young boys placed a thin reed on her palm. She bent it as if testing its strength, then looked at me.

"Remove the tunic," she commanded. "By the crud between Seth's toes, you will remember this lesson until your dying day."

Though I protested, two stableboys lifted me from the ground and yanked at the shoulders of my tunic. I clung to the front of the garment, holding it against my chest. The tallest of the boys turned me so that I stood with my exposed back toward the cook.

"One question," the young woman said. "If she is not to lie on the floor, where is she supposed to sleep?"

The question resonated among the observers, and I nearly turned to see the cook's reaction. We slaves did not have the luxury of beds and slept wherever we could find a bit of empty floor. Most of the slaves had claimed favorite spots on the property, but I was a recent arrival and had not yet found a place where I would be out of the master's sight and out of the cook's way.

In this land so far from my home, I had found nothing but trouble and a never-ending sense of restlessness.

"She can sleep anywhere," the cook replied, her voice still ragged with fury, "so long as it is not in my kitchen."

Then I heard the switch rend the air and felt its sharp cut upon my back. "One," the cook said, and the switch sang again. "Two."

On that day I learned two things: the importance of staying out of the cook's way, and how to count to ten.

⌇⌇⌇⌇⌇⌇

"You, girl. Come here."

I rose from the cold ashes of an abandoned cook fire, the

sleeping spot I'd claimed as my own. I thought no one had noticed me, but the chief house slave had sharp eyes.

I walked toward her, head down, moving slow. Perhaps she had some new work for me to do, something to take me away from the hot kitchen. Such work would be welcome, for I had not been outside in over a week.

The woman's bony hands caught my shoulders and pulled me forward, then pinched the flesh of my upper arm. "A little dirty and thin, but nothing a good scrubbing won't remedy," she said, her eyes narrowing as she glanced at another slave by her side. "She's the right age, and that's what matters. Didn't the master say he wanted a girl of nine or ten years?"

"Eleven." I lifted my chin. "I have lived eleven years. Mama said I was eleven when she told me good-bye, and a full year has not passed since I left Egypt—"

"No matter," the house woman said. "Tell the master you are ten and make him happy. That is the most important thing."

I did not understand what she meant, but the second woman took my arm and led me away. She released me once we reached the courtyard. "I am Gaia," she said, glancing at me as we walked, "and I am the mistress's handmaid."

"What does the mistress—?"

"We have no time for questions." Gaia walked me through the courtyard and stopped at the stone trough where the servants watered the livestock. Without warning she ripped off my tunic and bade me step into the murky water.

I squealed as the cold liquid touched the scabs on my back.

"Hush, girl. Don't act like a child." Gaia pulled a rough sponge from her skirt. "Now you must be still and let me scrub you. If you want to improve your lot in this house, you'll need to be clean and presentable. You will also have to tame that tongue of yours."

I bit my lower lip and remained as upright as possible as she ran the sponge over my neck, back, and trembling limbs. Then she dipped a linen square into the cold water and brought it up to wipe my face and chest.

"Your hands," she said. "Let me see your nails."

I thrust out my arms, displaying pudgy fingers and cracked, gnawed fingertips. I had no fingernails to speak of, for as soon as they showed even a bit of white, I peeled off the papery growth.

Gaia frowned as she studied my hands, then sighed. "You had better take better care of yourself, but whatever you do, keep your nails clean. The Jews are always washing their hands."

She gestured for me to step out of the trough, so I did. She grabbed a horse blanket from a rail and wrapped it around me. "Come," she said, turning toward the house. "We will get you a new tunic and take you to see the master. Then you will understand how your life is about to change."

I had never been inside the master's house. Though a slave should keep her eyes downcast when walking, I lifted my head and stared as Gaia led me through the tall columns at the building's entrance. The cool and colorful floor tile cooled my bare feet, and golden accents on the column delighted my senses. Bright bits of glass formed an intricate floor design in the center of the entry, and in the hallway beyond, servants in flowing tunics moved soundlessly through the space, their sandal-clad feet gliding over the amazingly beautiful designs.

"Come, girl, and don't gape." The sharp edge in Gaia's tone spurred my feet to walk faster. I followed her down a long corridor that led to an open room at the side of the house. The fragrance of fresh flowers perfumed the air, and servants wielded fans to keep the scented air moving. Yet the beauty of the room went far beyond floral arrangements. I also saw two lovely ladies, whom I assumed to be my master's wife and her friend or relative. They were talking to a tall man, who wore a simple linen tunic. He had to be John Hyrcanus, the Jews' high priest and a man of great authority.

Gaia approached the trio and bowed. "Master. If I may—"

"What is it, Gaia?" the first lady interrupted.

Gaia rose and addressed her mistress. "I found this girl among your servants. Will she be acceptable for the master's purpose?"

The tall man looked at me, and so stunned was I by the power in his gaze that I forgot my place and stared. John Hyrcanus was a good-sized man, thick through the body and shoulder, with black hair spilling onto his forehead above an even blacker beard. A blunt nose dominated his face, and behind it, two dark eyes raked over me in an appraising glance.

"She'll have to learn proper manners," he said, lifting a brow.

Gaia turned and gave me a sharp look, which reminded me where and who I was. I fell to the floor and pressed my forehead to the polished tiles.

"Humph," the master replied. "Age?"

"Ten," Gaia answered. "But who can know for certain?"

"From which miserable corner of the world did she come?"

"Egypt, I believe."

"Egypt." He repeated the word in a thoughtful voice, then sighed. "How fitting that the country who once enslaved the children of Jacob now sends slaves to us."

"Whenever a child is sold as a slave," Gaia said, a slight tremor in her voice, "it is almost always because the parents are too poor to support them."

I felt a rush of heat fill my face, but I dared not look up to see how—or if—her words affected the master.

"How did this one come to Jerusalem? And have her stand—I can see nothing of her while she's on the floor."

Gaia turned to me. "Rise, child."

The high priest's voice had sent a shiver up my back, but I managed to stand erect and keep my head down.

"I heard she was purchased from a traveling trader," Gaia said. "The cook wanted a child to help her."

"Does the cook still want a helper?"

"Yes, but not this one. Apparently this girl is not skilled enough for the kitchen." Gaia gave a wavering smile. "You can speak directly to her, if you wish. She speaks Aramaic and a little Greek."

I spoke a little Hebrew too, and my native tongue, but I did not want to appear immodest.

"Girl," the master said, his sharp eyes locking on mine, "are you well behaved or will we have to beat you?"

The shiver traveled up my back and neck again. "I do not like beatings, sir."

"So you will do your best to avoid them?"

"I will."

"Good." A brief smile flashed in his beard. "In a few days I will be giving you to a young relative who is coming to live with us. She is younger than you, and you will be her handmaid for as long as she requires your service. You will obey her in all things, do you understand?"

I stared in amazement. The situation he described sounded a hundred times better than my present position, though anything would be better than washing vegetables, sweeping ashes from the hearth, and being continually scolded. The cook did not like me, but—a girl! A young girl and I could be friends.

A tiny kernel of happiness took root within me, one that could very well replace the anger that had smoldered there ever since leaving Egypt.

"Thank you, master." I couldn't stop a smile from flooding my face. "Thank you so very much."

My master turned to Gaia. "See if you can teach her some

of the things a handmaid is expected to know. She has only a few days to learn."

"Yes, master." Gaia bowed, then turned and escorted me away. And in her sidelong look of appraisal I thought I glimpsed a faint shade of jealousy.

⌇⌇⌇⌇⌇

I slept that night in a quiet hallway, until early the next morning when Gaia shook me awake. "Up, girl," she said, her tone sharp. "I've a lot to teach you, and I have to do my own work, as well. So rouse your lazy bones and come with me."

I blinked the cobwebs of sleep away and sat up in near darkness. Gaia held an oil lamp and was already dressed. I forced myself to stand.

"Every morning, the first thing you must do," Gaia said, speaking only after I had stood erect, "is fetch water from the well. You must always have a pitcher and basin ready for the moment your mistress wakes. She will want to wash her face and rinse her mouth. Then she will relieve herself in the basin, and you must carry it out of the house and dump it behind the barn."

Without waiting for a response, Gaia pivoted on her sandal and led the way down the stairs. I moved quickly to keep up with her long-legged stride.

A few minutes later we reached the well in the center of the courtyard. I stood silently as Gaia dropped a bucket into the opening. She pulled up the rope, then poured the water into two glazed containers that dangled from a pole. When she had finished, she turned and placed her fingertips over my lips. "I am going to take you into my mistress's room to show you how this must be done. If you make a sound, if you so much as sneeze in my lady's room, I will beat you myself, do you understand?"

Terrified by the flaming light in her eyes, I nodded.

"Follow me, then, and mind your step."

Gaia slipped her shoulders beneath the pole with the containers, bent her knees and stood, taking the weight onto her thin frame. She walked toward the master's house, moving steadily so as not to spill a drop of the precious water.

I followed, coming no closer than her shadow for fear of disturbing her. We entered the house, soundlessly crossed the marble-tiled entry, and climbed the stone staircase. Then we slipped into a spacious chamber, where gauzy curtains twirled and twisted in a breeze from the window. I glimpsed a bed in the center of the room, with two enshrouded figures on it.

Feeling like an intruder, I lowered my gaze and followed Gaia to the far side of the room. A small but beautiful table stood next to the wall, accompanied by an upholstered bench. Gaia bent her knees until both clay vessels stood on the floor. She then set the pole down, lifted one of the vessels, and poured water into a beautiful white pitcher on the table.

Holding my breath, I watched as she crossed the room and went to another table, a sturdy, heavier type. She emptied the second vessel into another pitcher, then jerked her chin toward the door and led the way out of the room.

"You may have realized," she said once we were halfway down the stairs, "that the beautiful table belongs to our mistress. The other table belongs to our master. They both require water in the morning."

"I am going to serve a girl," I said, thinking aloud. "I will not have to pour water for a man."

"Is that what you think?" Gaia lifted both brows. "In a few years your mistress will have a husband, and when that time comes, you must serve both. Do not fail to serve those your mistress loves, or she will be unhappy and sell you in the slave market. Would you like that?"

I don't think Gaia meant to be cruel, but a tremor of mingled alarm and horror shot through me at her words. With difficulty I swallowed my fear and shook my head.

"Your job is to perform the services your mistress needs before she knows she needs them."

I took a deep breath to calm my heart, which had begun to beat double time. "How is such a thing possible?"

Pity filled Gaia's eyes. "You are only a child, but you will be surprised at how quickly and how well you will come to know your mistress. One day you will know her better than she knows herself."

I did not see how such a thing could be possible, but Gaia had years of experience. "Is it . . . is it like that with you and your mistress?"

The slave pressed her lips together for a moment, then turned and stared toward the horizon as if watching something I could not see. "I have served the lady Alena since I was about your age, and if the gods are willing, I will serve her until the day I die."

I heard no bitterness in her tone, only resignation. And as Gaia walked away, I wondered if I would feel the same way about the girl who would soon arrive.

～～～～

The next day, Gaia taught me how to curl hair, steam wrinkles out of a tunic, and tie a *himation*—the long, colorful mantle fashionable women wore over their sleeveless *chitons*. "You must ask your mistress how she wishes to wear the himation," Gaia said, holding the fabric strip in both hands. "Sometimes she will wear it over one shoulder secured with a brooch. Sometimes she will tie it around her hips, or drape it across her chest and fasten it with a pin. Sometimes she will wear it like a shawl, and other times she may use it to cover her head."

"Why would a woman wear it at all?" I asked, wondering why

free women wore so much clothing. We slaves wore simple tunics and were probably much more comfortable in the dry heat.

Gaia lifted her gaze as if imploring the gods for help. "Silly girl." She smiled. "Women wear them because they wish to display their wealth and sense of style. These fabrics are expensive. The more himations a woman owns, the wealthier her husband."

I said nothing as my gaze drifted toward the overflowing trunk in our young mistress's chamber. Dozens of himations lay jumbled within it, and a mound of linen chitons filled another. A third chest, a smaller one, held gold pins for our lady's hair and silver brooches to adorn her clothing.

Gaia pointed out a box of silver pins with pearls attached to the end of each pin. These, she told me, were for securing a woman's hair after it had been set and curled. Pearls were a true mark of wealth, even more valuable than gold or silver because they were more difficult to obtain.

Over the next few days I learned how to clean a lady's garments; how to rub her shoulders and feet to bring pleasure, not pain; and how to heat stones so they could be placed in a lady's bed to warm it or ease pains in her inner parts. "At certain times of the month, your lady may experience pains here." Gaia patted her abdomen. "You should heat stones, wrap them in linen, and place them in her bed. She will lie with her belly close to the stones, and the heat will bring relief."

Overwhelmed by Gaia's instruction, much of which hinted at a mysterious womanly world I knew nothing about, I sought out a quiet corner in the barn. I finally slipped into the stall of a gentle mare and curled up in the corner, out of the way of her hooves. The fresh straw made a comfortable bed, and the earthy smells reminded me of Egypt . . . and home.

For the first time in many nights, my throat did not burn with resentment when I thought about my parents and the awful men at the slave market.

The mare looked over her shoulder and whickered as if asking why I had come. But she did not seem alarmed and made no move to kick me.

"Perhaps you and I shall become friends," I told her as I closed my eyes. "Because I could surely use one in this strange place."

CHAPTER FOUR

Shelamzion

Two months after we buried my father, Mother returned the pots and clay bowls she had borrowed from neighbors and threw out the flowers I had placed in the window. Then, with a quivering chin, she opened the trunk that contained our belongings and pulled out the tunics that had belonged to Ketura. As tears flowed over her cheeks, she carried them into the courtyard, dropped them onto the packed earth, and set them ablaze. While I watched, she went back into the house and returned with Ketura's sandals, which she also tossed onto the burning pile.

Avigail saw the smoke and came running outside.

Her face twisted in consternation as she watched from her courtyard. "What are you *doing?*"

"I am burning Ketura's belongings," Mother replied in a calm voice.

Avigail stared at me as if I might have an explanation. I didn't.

"Your younger daughter might have worn those garments," Avigail pointed out. "Or you might have given them to the poor."

Mother folded her arms and sighed heavily. "John Hyrcanus

has sent word. We are leaving as soon as the wagon arrives from Jerusalem." Her voice trembled. "I . . . I want to start a new life, and these things only remind me of my loss."

"You are so fortunate," Avigail went on, "to have such a kinsman! He reminds me of Boaz, who redeemed the widow Ruth—"

"And married her." Mother blinked as if an idea had just occurred to her, but then her brow furrowed. "You do not think he intends—"

"I am sure he has a wife already," Avigail assured, apparently following Mother's thought. "He is doing this because he is a kind and generous man."

"Is he?" Mother bit her lower lip and looked at me. "Or does some other reason lie behind his generosity?"

"Perhaps HaShem sent him to save us," I said, offering what I considered a perfectly logical explanation. "HaShem sent Moses to lead our people out of Egypt. He sent Jehoahaz to save our people from the Arameans. Why wouldn't He send the high priest's son to deliver us from being poor and alone?"

"See how she knows the Scripture!" Avigail beamed at me. "That is a girl who listened to her father."

"Indeed," Mother murmured. "But I hardly think the Almighty God would send anyone to help a woman and child." Then she went back into the house where she would remain until it was time to go.

Avigail gave me an understanding and compassionate smile. "I hope you like Jerusalem, Shelamzion," she said, using the pet name my father had given me. "I hope you won't forget Modein. Important leaders have come from this village. Indeed, a great life can come from small beginnings."

She had no sooner finished speaking than we heard a commotion from down the street. We turned and saw a wheeled vehicle approaching, a cart drawn by two horses and guided by two servants. Only a wealthy man could afford such an extravagant conveyance.

Avigail leaned over the courtyard wall. "Sipporah! Your wagon is here."

When Mother opened the door, I saw that her hands had begun to tremble. "Are you sure?"

"And who else would it come for?" Avigail smiled when the wagon halted outside our gate.

One of the men jumped down and halted when he saw Mother. "Sipporah, widow of Ittamar, John Hyrcanus has sent us for you and your daughter. Now that the period of mourning for both families is over, the high priest invites you to become part of his household. You are a kinswoman, and neither you nor your child will go wanting."

Mother swallowed hard even as something that looked like relief crossed her face. "The high priest is most generous," she said, "but I would not want to cause him or his family any difficulty."

Puzzled by Mother's restrained reaction, I turned to Avigail. "Why did she say that? She wants to go to Jerusalem."

Avigail pressed her finger to her lips, then bent over the wall to reply in a low voice, "She does not want the people here to think she was eager to leave. Do you see?"

I nodded, though I felt a long way from real understanding. The adult world seemed a confusing and difficult place where no one said what they truly meant.

"Are we going, then?" I asked.

Avigail squeezed my shoulder. "You are, little Shelamzion. Trust HaShem with your future and never doubt that He will take care of you."

~~~~~~~~

The high priest's house was nothing like our home in Modein. First, it was called a *palace*, not a house. Second, I thought such a holy person would live in a building that looked like the Temple, with richly colored blue curtains and golden bowls at each entrance. I pictured John Hyrcanus wearing his sacred tunic and breastplate as he welcomed people to his home, and eating at a table fashioned like the altar used for the morning sacrifices.

Our old house had been firmly situated in a neighborhood, with a family to the right and Avigail to the left, a courtyard in front and a garden in back. The single room held a mattress for Mother and Father and, in the corner, sleeping mats for Ketura and me. A large table stood under the east window, a surface where Mother worked to prepare meals, grind grain, and stitch the garments we wore. Opposite the table, embers from a small fire glowed in a depression in the earthen floor. Mother cooked on this fire during the day, and at night Father had used light from the glowing embers to read the Torah to me.

The high priest's house in Jerusalem, however, appeared to be many houses, not just one. It stood by itself in the Upper City, away from the small houses of regular people. A tall stone wall surrounded the place, with wide iron gates that opened to let visitors enter. Beyond the gate was a wide courtyard paved with flat stones, and several buildings stood at the edges of the courtyard—one was clearly a stable, another a place for guards. A small brick building with a smoking chimney appeared to be the kitchen, which stood some distance away from the other structures.

Straight ahead of us I counted at least three buildings, or perhaps they were all palaces. The doorway of the center building yawned directly before us. So after climbing out of the wagon, Mother and I approached it with caution. The elaborately carved doors stood open, and when we hesitated to enter, one of the men who had brought us from Modein nodded and urged us forward.

My heart thumped against my rib cage as we ventured into the house. My eyes drank in the spectacle of the amazing floor—so many colors and patterns! Some artisan had taken great pains to create a picture with shiny tiles. The peacock spreading his plumage beneath my feet was so realistic he seemed to wink at me.

"Oh," Mother whispered, and I looked up, having never heard such awe in her voice. The high priest might have been a kinsman, but no one on her side of the family had ever lived in a place like this.

Overwhelmed, we stood in that glorious vestibule until a servant in a plain linen tunic approached and bent slightly at the waist. She asked Mother her name and smiled at the reply.

"Sipporah? Let me fetch the mistress. She is expecting you."

The servant hurried away while I continued to marvel at the extravagance around us. Mother locked her hands behind her back as she surveyed the room, obviously struggling to appear as if she visited palaces every day.

We waited for what felt a long time, and then I heard the soft rustle of fabric. A beautiful young woman appeared on the stone staircase, trailed by a girl about Ketura's age. Was this another servant?

Definitely not, I decided, as the young woman drew closer. She wore jewelry, which few people wore in Modein, and her skin was as pale as parchment, so she did not work outdoors. And she was young—younger than my mother, and far younger than John Hyrcanus.

"Cousins," the woman said, coming toward us with her graceful arms extended. "I am so happy to meet you. I am Kefira Alena, but most people simply call me Alena." She smiled and squeezed Mother's hands, then released her and transferred her attention to me. "My husband was right—your daughter is a charming little girl. What do you call her?"

"Salome Alexandra," Mother said, lifting her chin. "Her father called her Shelamzion."

"The peace of Zion." A dimple appeared in the woman's cheek as she looked back at Mother. "I like the name. I know the fashion is to give our children Hebrew *and* Greek names, but since no one uses both names in ordinary conversation, I fail to see the sense in it."

Mother looked away as a blush stained her cheek. She was not accustomed to such rapid conversations, such beautiful women, or such luxurious surroundings. For a moment I felt her embarrassment—even as a child I could sense why she did not feel at ease in this place.

"Listen to me, prattling on without a thought for your comfort." Alena turned toward the grand doors, and for a moment I thought she would tell us to go back to Modein. She smiled instead. "Come, I will show you the house we have prepared for you. My husband is determined that you shall live here with us, and your little girl will lack for nothing."

She led the way out of the building, and as we crossed the dusty courtyard I looked up at my mother. She had furrowed her brow and compressed her lips, a sure sign of irritation. But the high priest's wife had been more than kind to us, so what had aggravated my mother?

In the corner of the courtyard, not far from the gate, stood a small stone house with a porch, tall Greek columns, and a carved door similar to that at the massive entrance of the palace. Mother's irritation vanished when Alena led us over the porch and opened the door. "Welcome to your new home."

The high priest's palace had awed me, but this smaller house—and the knowledge that Mother and I were going to live there—stole my breath away. Polished tile covered the first floor, the walls were plaster, not mud, and the painted ceiling rose high above our heads. Elegant columns supported a balcony overlooking an open area, and a graceful stone staircase stood against the wall.

Alena brought her hands together. "I do hope this place will be comfortable for you. We want you to be happy here in Jerusalem."

I was ready to throw my arms around the woman in sheer gratitude, but Mother was not quite so eager. "Why?" she asked, abruptly turning to face our hostess. "Why would you do this for us? And why does your husband care so much about Shelamzion? She is no prize."

Alena's mouth opened, and her lovely face went the color of a rose. "My—my husband asked me to make these arrangements," she stammered. "We are more than willing to help you now that . . . now that you are alone with a child to raise."

"But you are doing so much. You could have simply sent food or arranged to send a few talents—"

"You are family."

Mother's tense mouth relaxed into a wry smile. "Your husband's father was my grandfather's brother. So we are not the closest of kin."

"All the more reason why we should remain involved with each other." Alena stepped forward and slipped her arm around Mother's waist. "Families should not allow themselves to be torn apart. HaShem has blessed the Hasmonean family, and my husband wants to be sure we use His gifts wisely."

Mother narrowed her eyes. "I still don't understand why—"

"Look—here comes someone I want you to meet."

Alena stepped back as a woman and a girl approached. I focused immediately on the girl, who looked older than me, and darker. She and the woman wore simple tunics, and the woman led the girl by the hand. They crossed the front porch and stopped at the threshold, then bowed before Alena.

"As the master commanded," the servant said, "I have brought you the slave called Kissa."

"Thank you, Gaia. Both of you may rise." When they did, Alena bent toward the child and lifted the girl's chin with two fingers. "Kissa, do you understand what a handmaid does?"

Kissa nodded.

"You may speak, child."

"Yes, mistress. A handmaid obeys her mistress at all times." The girl spoke common Greek, though she had darker skin than any Greek I had ever seen—but not many Greeks came to Modein.

"Do you understand what must happen if a handmaid does not obey her mistress?" Alena tilted her head and adopted a sorrowful expression. "I would hate to see you get a beating. Please assure me that you will not disobey."

"Never, mistress." The girl's round eyes gleamed with sincerity, and I believed her with all my heart.

Alena stepped aside, leaving a clear space between me and the girl. "Kissa, meet your new mistress. This is Salome Alexandra, and it is your master's wish that you serve her for as long as she desires your service."

The girl's eyes widened, and I am sure mine did, too.

Beside me, Mother gasped. "You are giving Shelamzion a *slave?*"

"A handmaid." Alena spoke like a woman who presented slaves to children every day. "You will be grateful, believe me. These two will keep each other company, and Kissa will be a good companion for your daughter. She speaks fluent Aramaic, adequate Greek, and a smattering of Hebrew."

Mother's frown deepened. "I still don't understand—"

"Do not question good fortune." Alena smiled and extended her hand toward the stone staircase. "Go choose your bed-chamber. I will assign a slave to help you make this your home. If you would like furnishings brought from your former village, tell one of the servants in the courtyard, and he will fetch them for you. If you need anything else, let me know. We want you and Shelamzion to be happy here."

I barely heard her words. My mind was still reeling from the realization that I had been given a girl—an *interesting* girl, and one who was not likely to monopolize my mother's attention as Ketura had.

The girl before me was tall and thin, with dark hair, slanting brows, and black eyes. Her skin was the color of burnished metal, and her face as smooth as a marble statue. Her gaze rested on me, alight with curiosity, and I looked at her with outright awe. She was alien, older, and different—and she belonged to me.

I tried out her name on my tongue. "Kissa."

She dipped her head in a bow. "Yes, mistress?"

"I only wanted to say your name."

For a moment we stood and examined each other, then she smiled. In that instant I felt an unspoken agreement pass between us. She would be my servant, and I would be her mistress, but we would also be friends. Until life forced us apart.

My polite smile split into a grin. I looked around, anxious to leave the women and explore the house with my handmaid.

Finally, Alena took her leave. Mother closed the door, then leaned against it and swiped a tear from her eye. "If only Ketura were here," she said, speaking to the air as she looked at the balcony and the ornate pillars. "This is the life my little beauty should have enjoyed."

Leaving Mother to her memories, I grabbed Kissa's hand, and we ran to the staircase, leaping up the steps and racing toward new possibilities.

CHAPTER FIVE

Kissa

I wasn't sure what to make of the girl who grabbed my hand and took me up those stairs, but I knew one thing: she was glad to have someone with her. Though I did not know what sort of child she was—she could have been glad to have someone to tie to a post and torture with biting ants—her smile was wide and friendly and her nature seemed pleasant.

On the other hand, I had met people who seemed harmless at first, but then time and circumstance revealed darkness in them, a love of distress and pain . . . so long as this was experienced by others.

After we raced up the stairs, the girl peeked through the balcony posts and watched her mother wander aimlessly around the lower floor. Then the woman left the house, probably hoping to find someone who could explain how things worked in the high priest's palace. I thought it odd that the woman did not say anything to her daughter before leaving, yet the girl did not seem to notice the oversight.

When the mother had gone, the girl dropped to the floor, crossed her legs, and looked up at me. "Aren't you going to sit?"

I dropped faster than a dead donkey. If I obeyed this girl, if I did what I was supposed to do, maybe the gods would smile on me and send me home.

"You are Kissa," she said, studying me.

I nodded. "And who are you?"

"Shelamzion. That's what Father called me, and he loved me best."

I took pains to maintain a blank expression, reminding myself to remember those words. "Does your mother have a name?"

"Ima." The Hebrew word for *mother*.

"What do other people call her?"

The light of understanding filled the girl's eyes. "Sipporah."

I nodded again, then tilted my head. "May I ask you something else?"

She nodded.

"You promise you will not become angry?"

She laughed. "I promise."

I decided to trust the child. Since becoming a slave, I had learned not to speak unless spoken to, and then not to say anything about myself. But from household rumors I had heard that my new mistress was a village child, so she might not know about proper behavior for slaves.

"I was wondering," I dared to ask, "how old are you?"

Shelamzion held up her right hand and touched each of her fingers, then added her left thumb. "Six years. My sister was nine, then she died."

Bound by my habit of silence, I did not reply at first. But if I were going to be on good terms with this girl, common sense told me to befriend her. Children could be cruel and petulant, especially spoiled children. Though this one did not seem spoiled, she was young, and might come to despise me . . .

Unless I taught her to trust me. And to do that, I would have to talk to her. As one girl talked to another.

41

I forced a smile. "I did not know you had a sister."

"I don't, not anymore. She died with Father."

"That is sad. What happened?"

As the girl lifted her wide gaze to the ceiling, I saw the sheen of tears in her eyes. "They went riding. People say the horse saw something like a snake, and Father and Ketura fell off the horse and died. They were brought home, the women washed them, and we put them in the cave. We gave away most of our things, and now we are here."

I pressed my lips together and sighed. "I am sorry about your father and sister."

"So is Mother. She loved Ketura more than anything. She said my sister would marry a powerful man and make us great. But now Ketura is with Father, and we are with John Hyrcanus." The girl's lower lip quivered. "I miss Father. I miss studying with him."

I smiled, grateful for the insight into my young mistress. "I will study with you," I told her. "Every night, if you like. But you will have to teach me, because I know very little."

My new mistress leaned toward me. "How old are you?"

"I have lived eleven years," I said. "I think."

She smiled. "I hope we will be friends."

Despite the warning voice in my head, my heart warmed at her expression. While I could use a friend in this place, I could not forget the great gulf that existed between slaves and masters. The sort of friendship she had in mind would be impossible, but perhaps we could define our relationship ourselves . . . for as long as we were paired with each other.

Shelamzion rose to her knees and caught my hand. "Can you help me learn my way around? I know this is supposed to be our house, but it is so big! What if we get lost?"

"In truth, I have never been inside this house. I have been helping in the kitchens."

Shelamzion giggled. "Then we will get lost together. Can we go outside?"

"If you wish." I stood and lifted a warning finger. "We must not get in the way. The master does not like slaves who make things difficult for other slaves to do their work."

"We will be careful," Shelamzion promised, taking my hand. She laced her fingers through mine and pulled me toward the stairs. "I want to see everything."

"I don't know everything," I protested, trying not to lose my balance as I followed.

"Then take me to the places you do know," she said, her small sandals slapping against the stone steps. "And we will learn together."

As my young mistress and I explored the stables, the cookhouse, the henhouse, and the garden, I wondered if the gods had finally smiled on me. Thus far I had found no comfort or friendship in the high priest's house, but finally, unexpectedly, I had been granted an easy job and a friendly mistress. This girl might learn to keep me in my proper place, but until that time my life would be far easier and I would sleep in peace and safety, not worrying about being scalded by hot soup, trespassing on another slave's territory, or being stepped on by a horse.

And if I did my job well, who knew what might happen? My parents' gods might finally hear their prayers and send me home.

When my little mistress became tired of exploring, I suggested that we sit in the shade of a terebinth tree. She agreed and eagerly followed as I led her to a spot where we could rest unmolested. I sat on one of the bulging tree roots, facing the house, while Shelamzion sat and turned toward me.

"Thank you," she said, her eyes crinkling as she grew serious. "Now you must tell me about yourself."

43

I blinked. "What do you want to know?"

"Where were you born? Who is your father? What happened to your mother? Did your uncle send you here? Did your father die? Was he a farmer? Did he raise horses?"

I took a deep breath, stunned by the avalanche of questions. "I was born in Egypt."

"Is that near Jerusalem?"

"It is far away. A journey of many days."

"How did you get here?"

"I walked. With other people." I closed my eyes, resisting the memory of that torturous ordeal. Several months before, a slave dealer had put shackles around my wrists and dragged me and a dozen other slaves to Judea. I walked over hot sand in papyrus sandals so thin my feet blistered, and my wrists still bore scars from the cruel iron bracelets. But that was not the worst of it—the most horrible aspect of the journey had occurred each night, and memories of those hours still haunted my dreams.

But I would not speak of those things to this innocent child. No one—not even a slave—should experience those horrors. If I were to see that slave trader at this house, I would find a knife and plunge it into his heart.

Shelamzion regarded me with a serious look—a look I had never seen on the face of another child. "You seem sad. Do you miss your parents?"

I nodded.

"Where are they?"

"Probably in Memphis."

"You don't know for certain?"

I shook my head. "They could be dead."

"I am sorry. What was your mother's name?"

I squinted into the sun, trying to summon the face of the woman who had dressed me in a plain tunic and cut my hair short. By then she was half starved and desperate enough to sell her only child for food.

I looked away from my earnest mistress. "My mother was called Oseye."

"Was she sick?"

"She was hungry."

"Why didn't she eat?"

"She had no food."

"Why didn't she ask someone for something to eat?"

I blew out a breath. "She had no one to ask. Please, miss—I don't like to talk about my past."

"Sorry." Shelamzion pressed her lips together as pain glowed in her own eyes. "I know how sad feels. I was sad, too, when Father and Ketura died. So was Mother. Mother is still sad . . . because Ketura died, and not me."

I was startled by her admission. Could a child sense such a thing? I had not spent much time with the girl's mother, but no decent woman would admit such a thing to her daughter.

"You . . . can't know that," I said, hoping to ease the girl's sense of loss. "Your mother would be sad if you died, I am sure of it."

"I'm not." Shelamzion pushed a wayward curl from her face, then hugged her knees and studied a root pushing up the earth at our feet. "When I grow up, I will have children and I will never, ever love one more than the other. It is not fair."

"You are right, mistress. But life is not always fair."

"It should be." Her eyes met mine. "I am not beautiful like Ketura."

"Not so. You are a pretty little thing—"

She shook her head. "Do not say that. Friends should always tell each other the truth."

I dipped my chin in an abrupt nod. "You are right."

She drew a breath and began again. "I am not beautiful,

but my father loved me. He taught me to read the Torah and said I was a smart girl. Father said HaShem makes us all different, and we are to be who HaShem meant us to be. As it says in the writings, 'You fashioned my inmost being, You knit me together in my mother's womb. I thank You because I am awesomely made, wonderfully; Your works are wonders—I know this very well.'"

Shelamzion's shoulders slumped as she finished, and I knew she must have worked hard to memorize so many words. "Did your father ask you to learn that?"

She nodded. "He said studying Torah and the writings and the prophets would make me wise. He said most fathers taught Torah only to their sons, but since he did not have a son, he would teach me as long as I wanted to learn. Since he is no longer here to teach me, perhaps you can help me study."

I did not know what to say. Despite living in the high priest's house for several weeks, I did not understand what the Jews believed or why they believed it. I *did* know they worshiped an invisible God, they were strict about obeying his Law, and they washed their hands several times a day.

"I do not understand the Jewish God," I admitted. "And what I hear of your Law confuses me. If you want me to help you study this Torah, you will have to teach me first."

"We will learn together." She placed her hands over mine, her eyes shining with earnest innocence.

"How did you come to live here?" I asked, nodding toward the main house.

She relaxed and released me. "The high priest is a kinsman. Mother says I should call him my uncle."

"*Is* he your uncle?"

"Well"—she shrugged—"Mother says John Hyrcanus is my grandfather's . . . wait. I get confused. His grandfather was my great-grandfather's brother."

I lifted a brow. The connection seemed weak to me, but the Jews were a peculiar people.

Shelamzion propped her chin on her bent knees. "Do you know him?"

"Who?"

"Uncle."

I snorted. "He is not my uncle; he is my master. I don't know him, but I have met him. He told me you were coming and said you would be my mistress."

Shelamzion clapped in delight. "We shall be great friends. I did not want to leave Modein, but now I am no longer afraid. You will sleep with me in my room, won't you?"

"My place is outside your door," I said. "That is the way things are done here."

"No." She lifted her chin. "You shall sleep by my bed, on a soft pallet. And we will tell each other stories every night until we fall asleep. And I will tell you secrets and you will tell me secrets, and we will never, ever tell anyone else."

I felt a wry smile creep onto my face. Gaia would probably admonish me for encouraging this sort of intimacy, but why should I keep this girl at a distance? She seemed to like me, ignorant though I was. I saw nothing objectionable in her. Perhaps we *could* be friends for a while . . .

If the gods were good to me, we might be friends until it was time for me to leave.

CHAPTER SIX

Shelamzion

Throughout the next several weeks, Kissa and I filled our days with exploring the high priest's palace. Kissa took me into the workrooms and pointed out which slaves were hard workers and which were lazy. She identified the best cook and the women with the sharpest tongues. She showed me where servants dyed the fine linen used in the high priest's everyday tunics and where they grew the herbs and vegetables for his table.

At the end of every day, Kissa and I returned to the house where I lived with my mother. She had finally stopped questioning our good fortune and seemed content to live quietly in Jerusalem. Blessed by our kinsman's generosity, she allowed Alena to fill the house with furniture and fabrics I had never seen in Modein. Gauzy silk curtains separated the rooms on the lower floor, and fine linen curtained our beds. Every night I lay down on a mattress as soft as lamb's wool.

Kissa slept in my room on a mattress she would unroll and place at the side of my bed. The first proper bed I had ever enjoyed had wooden legs, an elevated platform, and a painted headboard. Mother's bed was even finer, and she slept in a separate room so she wouldn't be kept awake by the sound of giggles coming from me and Kissa.

Even though we had been blessed, Mother did not seem truly happy. She rarely smiled and spent most of her time sitting quietly or sewing garments she never finished. And at night, if I chanced to walk by her door, I often heard her weeping.

Once Alena asked if Mother and I were content, and I told her I was as content as I could be. "But Mother," I added, "weeps at night and does nothing all day."

Not long after that, Mother and I were invited to dine with the high priest and Alena. Not every night—not when they had important guests, and not when Uncle was away with the army or occupied with important affairs—but whenever Uncle and Alena planned to eat alone, Mother and I were invited into the house. We went to the *triclinium* where couches were arranged along three sides of a massive table. After Uncle and Alena joined us, servants brought trays of food, and we ate until we were about to burst.

During those extravagant meals I often felt my uncle's gaze on me. I suspected that he watched to see if I could behave myself in fine company. So I took pains to imitate Alena and to be mindful of my uncle's furrowed brow. More than once I caught him looking askance at Mother, who ate and drank as she always had, smacking her lips and frequently dropping food onto her clothing or the couch. Realizing that her clumsiness displeased our benefactors, I took care to avoid such behavior.

Alena proved to be a useful model in other ways, as well. I watched how she walked, held her head, and gestured. I observed how she treated the slaves and tried to imitate her firm yet gentle voice. She was clearly a different kind of woman, and life had certainly treated her better than it had my mother. Perhaps, I told myself, I would be wise to follow Alena's example.

Though my mother suffered in comparison with Alena, I

did not despise her. She remained what she had always been, a woman in love with her firstborn daughter, a mother who would never see me as anything but a girl who did not measure up to her sister.

But Father had seen something in me, and I would do all I could to make him proud. For I was certain that somewhere, somehow, he was watching everything I did.

Once, after a long day spent exploring with Kissa, I ran into the triclinium without checking to see if we had been invited to join Uncle and Alena for dinner. I found the high priest at the table but saw no sign of Mother or Alena. Three serious-looking men occupied the dining couches, and after a moment of embarrassment I stammered an apology and attempted to back out of the room.

But Uncle would not let me go. "Friends," he said, smiling at me, "this is my niece, one of the few girls in the Hasmonean family. Salome Alexandra, say hello to my guests: Simon, Apollonius, and Diodorus."

I bowed my head. "I apologize, Uncle. I did not know—"

"Stay, Shelamzion. Come sit beside me and eat your fill."

Even more embarrassed now that all four men were looking at me, I sat on the edge of Uncle's couch and carefully took a pigeon breast from the tray.

I glanced up, saw the patronizing smiles of the three strangers, and quickly lowered my gaze. Uncle believed children should not speak unless spoken to, so he would be pleased so long as I ate quietly.

"So," my uncle said, returning his attention to his guests, "let us rehearse our plans. You shall depart for Joppa on the morrow. After you sail for Rome, practice your speeches. We have no room for error—you must present your case well, for the Romans place great emphasis on oratory. We must remind the Romans of our existing treaty."

"All thanks to Judas Maccabaeus, blessed be his memory," Simon said. "If only he could see how the past threatens to repeat itself."

Apollonius shifted on his couch. "I am more concerned about our losses. Gazara, Joppa, Pegae—since your father's victory over those territories, those cities have filled with Jews. What will happen to them now that Antiochus Sidetes possesses those towns?"

"All the more reason for you to travel quickly and quietly," Uncle said. "Do not draw attention to yourselves in Joppa. And make haste on your return—we cannot let the Seleucids gain the upper hand." With great tenderness he placed his palm on the top of my head. "For the sake of our little ones, you must convince the Romans to support our cause." He cleared his throat. "Otherwise, may HaShem bless your journey, and may He speed you back to us."

I glanced up, wondering what he meant. He returned my look and gave me a smile tinged with sadness.

Over the next few months, I began to understand more about the night I stumbled into Uncle's dinner. I had unknowingly discovered Uncle at work, and over time I began to realize what his work entailed.

I knew about the high priest's duties—I had observed the high priest Simon every time we traveled to Jerusalem for the feasts of Passover, Pentecost, and Tabernacles. As a child, I understood that my father worked with horses, other men raised crops or sold goods, and the high priest offered sacrifices in the Temple.

But my uncle did so much more, and the second part of his job involved ruling Judea. He did not call himself king like the heads of other nations, but he did talk to a great many advisors and priests about how to keep our people and our land safe.

Some kings, Kissa informed me, coveted the land of other nations, so sometimes my uncle had to be involved in the business of war. And Judea had been at war ever since Uncle became the high priest.

One of the adults always ordered Kissa to take me out of the room when they began to discuss the danger beyond the city walls, but even children have eyes and ears. Though Kissa and I left whenever we were dismissed, we did not go far. We remained close enough to hear the adults' worried voices, and eventually I learned that we were fighting Seleucia, an empire that had nearly destroyed Israel before the Maccabees decided to resist and fight. Our current enemy, the Seleucid king Antiochus Sidetes, wanted to conquer Judea again. He especially wanted to regain valuable territory he had lost when Uncle's father defeated him in battle.

Due to the war, Uncle began to be away from home more frequently, and from the look of distress on Alena's face I knew the war against Sidetes was not going well. Remembering the three men Uncle sent to Rome, I began to pray that they would be successful on their trip. I didn't know exactly what they were expected to do, but judging from the serious expression on Uncle's face that night, I knew their mission was important.

When the dry days of winter arrived, we began to see smoke above the northern horizon. A few days later we inhaled the foul odor of death.

Sidetes had advanced to the walls of the Holy City. Jerusalem had come under siege.

I heard the unfamiliar word from a woman on the street, and when I asked Mother what it meant, her face went pale. "Siege," she said, her voice a rough whisper, "is something that would never happen in Modein. Why did I agree to come here? We should have stayed in our little house."

I asked Kissa if she knew what *siege* meant, and she shook

her head. "But I know it's bad. I've heard talk about children dying in a siege."

Though my mother meant to shield me from war, how could she when war had come to Jerusalem? I noted Uncle's lowered brow, heard him bark commands, and counted dozens of soldiers coming in and out of the high priest's palace.

I knew things were truly serious when Mother said Uncle was moving to the Baris, the tower fortress at the Temple. Kissa and I waited in the courtyard until we saw him enter his chariot. I ran forward and caught the edge of his tunic. "Please, Uncle," I begged, "don't leave us here to die from siege!"

The hard look on his face softened. "Shelamzion, do not fear. I am leaving this house so my presence will not draw the enemy to you. Here you will be safe, safer than anyone in Jerusalem. So do not be afraid; HaShem is your strength and shield."

He patted my head, then picked up the reins of his chariot and urged his horses forward. I stepped back to watch him go and felt Kissa's arm come to rest on my shoulders.

Comforted by her company, I caught her hand in mine.

I tried my best to be brave, but how could anyone not worry when the man at the center of your universe had just ridden away?

CHAPTER SEVEN

Kissa

The night John Hyrcanus left the high priest's palace, Shelamzion and I went to bed at sunset as usual, yet neither of us could sleep. I tried singing, but my throat had tightened with worry so that my voice came out scratchy.

Finally, Shelamzion said I should stop. "Your singing is sweet," she said, obviously trying to be kind, "but your song does not fit my feelings."

"And what are you feeling, miss?"

"I am feeling . . . dark. Like when I wake in the night and cannot see anything. Or hear anything. I know I'm all right, but danger seems to be waiting for me."

"I know that feeling," I answered, closing my eyes against a premonition of impending doom. "I have felt it many times."

"So let's talk about something happy," Shelamzion said. She fell silent for a moment, then clapped. "I know! Tell me about your fondest wish."

Grateful that she could not see me, I made a face in the darkness.

"Kissa? What is your fondest wish?"

"I don't know," I said. "Tell me yours."

"That's not fair, I asked you first."

"I can't think of anything."

"Sure you can. If HaShem came to you like He did to Solomon—"

"I don't know this Solomon."

"You don't?" My mistress heaved a sigh. "Long ago, Solomon reigned over the kingdom of Israel. HaShem came to him in a dream at night and said, 'What should I give you?' And Solomon said, 'I am but a youth. I don't know how to go out or come in. So give Your servant a mind of understanding to judge Your people, to discern between good and evil—for who is able to judge this great people of Yours?' So Adonai said, 'Because you asked for this thing—and have not asked for long life, nor asked for riches, nor asked for the life of your enemies, but asked for understanding to discern justice—behold, I have done according to your words. I have given you a wise and discerning mind, so that there has been none like you before you, nor shall anyone like you arise after you.' And then HaShem said He would give Solomon riches and long life, as well."

I smiled. "That is a nice story. For a moment I forgot to be afraid."

My mistress chuffed in exasperation. "So what is your fondest, most secret desire? Is it money? Nice clothes?" She hesitated, then whispered, "Do you want to be free?"

I blinked in surprise. Every human wants freedom—the ability to wake when you want, do what you please, and go where you will. But I had lived long enough to know that, although freedom is something everyone wants, it is also hard to attain. Even the high priest, with all his power, was not truly free. Responsibilities and care filled his days, and I knew he did not want to be hidden away at the Baris while his beloved wife remained at home.

If Shelamzion was clever enough to appreciate a slave's yearning for freedom, maybe she would understand my truest and deepest desire.

"I want," I said, keeping my voice low, "to go home and find my parents. I want to see them, tell them how much I miss them, and feel their arms around me. I was crying when they sold me, and I want to tell them not to feel guilty. That I understand . . . they did what they had to do."

"But you said they were dead."

"I said they *might* be dead. But what if they still live?"

The bedchamber swelled with silence, and for a moment I thought my mistress had fallen asleep. But then I heard her hiccup, and when I sat up, I discovered she was sobbing.

"I—I—am sorry," she said, hiccupping. "I wish I could take you to Egypt. I would—if—if I could."

"Do not worry." I sat on the edge of the bed, slipped my arm around her shoulders, and squeezed. "You are kind to feel that way, but I do not expect you to grant my desire. Only the gods could make such a thing happen." I pushed damp hair away from her face and smiled, hoping she could see the shimmer of my teeth in the darkness. "Aren't we only pretend-talking? I thought this was a game."

She hiccupped again. "Yes."

"Then what is *your* desire, miss?"

I heard nothing but pebbly sounds from a wagon in the court-yard. Then Shelamzion shifted to face me. "I want to have two babies and love them both the same."

I laughed. "That is not a secret—you have said that many times."

"Then I want . . . to *matter*. To be important to someone. Maybe lots of someones."

"You are important to your mother."

I heard the brush of her hair against her tunic as she shook her head. "Not really."

"You are important to your uncle. He brought you here, didn't he?"

"He barely knows me, so how could I matter to him?"

I pulled away from her. "I do not know what you are talking about, but if you wish it, then may it be so." I slid off her bed and landed on my pallet. "All right then. You are talking nonsense, so I am going to sleep. Good night, little mistress."

"Good night." I heard the rustle of her blanket as she lay back down, and the sound filled me with peace. What an odd child she was! Perhaps it came from being born into a family of priests.

But no matter. Her little game had worked—we were no longer thinking about war and danger, and we were both ready to sleep.

CHAPTER EIGHT

Shelamzion

War is hard for everyone, but it is particularly hard on mothers, children, and animals. Even those of us in the high priest's palace suffered as Jerusalem entered a time of starvation. We had more food than most families, but we also had more mouths to feed: animals, servants, guards, and family members.

Antiochus Sidetes and his men surrounded Jerusalem completely, establishing seven different camps. The pagan king ordered some of his soldiers to dig a deep trench around the city while others built siege towers, each as tall as three houses stacked atop one another. Groups of soldiers dragged heavy battering rams to the entrances to the city, where they pounded on our gates for hours. "Oh, my aching head," Mother cried nearly every afternoon. "It throbs with every thump of those battering rams!"

Though Uncle had made sure our home was provided for, we did not eat as well as we had before the siege. Servants brought us fewer foods, and we ate smaller portions. Mother told me that outside the city, our enemy feasted on grains, vegetables, fruits, and animals stolen from the fields of Judea. Inside the city, people scrambled for bread and shriveled fruit that before the siege would have been fit only for animals.

If not for Kissa, I would have been unaware of how the ordinary people were faring. Every day she spent time with the other slaves, who frequently ventured out and told her what things were like outside our gates. She shared this news with me, though I suspected she spared me the worst reports.

"The elderly and the very young are dying," she told me one afternoon. "They are unable to search for food, so they grow sick and die. They say the streets are crowded with carts carrying the bodies of old people and children."

I gasped. "Where do they take them?"

Kissa blew out her cheeks. "To burial grounds outside the city walls."

"But the enemy is outside the wall!"

She shook her head. "The enemy is not *that* close or our soldiers would be able to drop stones on their heads or kill them with spears. The enemy remains far enough away that we cannot harass them."

But we were doing our best to bedevil the enemy. One night at dinner Alena told us that Uncle was sending out raiding parties in the dead of night. His raiders had one objective: destroy the wooden towers and battering rams. "John told them to inflict as much damage as they could," she said. "And they are doing their best."

Those reports cheered us, but burned and broken catapults could not ease our hunger and thirst. We ran short on food and water, and the heat sapped our remaining strength. A haunting silence replaced the happy gurgle of the huge fountain in the courtyard. Kissa and I did not spend our days playing or exploring, but instead lay side by side on the tile floor in Mother's house, seeking coolness wherever we could find it.

One afternoon in late summer, a dark cloud blew in and blocked the sun. Wondering if this might be some sort of sign, I went out to the courtyard with Kissa. We stood with lifted gazes until lightning cracked the clouds and thunder answered. A sudden downpour dropped from heaven, drenching us and making water dance in the tiled fountain. We twirled in the rain, and I looked up to see Alena smiling at us from her open window.

"See?" I told Kissa. I opened my mouth to catch raindrops on my tongue. As water ran down my cheeks, I grinned at her. "I told you HaShem answers our prayers!" Though the rain was a welcome respite, the siege continued on.

We did not see Uncle often during those days, but he did come home to visit his wife. Another afternoon at the end of summer, Kissa and I heard angry voices from an open window. I shuddered at the sound, because any sort of arguing made me uneasy.

"The master is angry," Kissa said, stating the obvious.

"Alena is upset, too," I added. "What could he have done to displease her so?"

We learned the answer the next day. Mother came into the house, her face flushed and her brows lowered.

"What's wrong, Ima?"

"We have to leave." Her wide eyes met mine. "Your uncle has issued an order: in ten days, anyone in the city who is not a soldier must go. Anyone who is not . . . useful."

I stared at her, unable to believe what I was hearing. "But we are his family. Why would he make us leave?"

Mother released a bitter laugh. "*He* is not making us leave. *Alena* says we must go. She insists that if other women and children have to leave their homes, then she will go, too. She is already packing a wagon."

I looked at Kissa, who had squinched her face into an expression of horror.

Mother looked angry enough to beat Alena with a switch. "Where will we go?" I asked.

"Back to Modein," she said, walking toward her room. "And we are never coming back here."

With John Hyrcanus and his commanders safely sequestered in the Baris fortress, Alena led the members of the high priest's household through the palace gates and onto the street. Though she could have ignored the plight of the common people, she draped her himation over her hair and ventured out on foot, leading the way for the rest of us.

As I followed, I couldn't decide whether or not I still admired her.

I could not see the point in leaving a safe, comfortable place simply to be like almost everyone else in Jerusalem. To further complicate matters, Mother seemed set on going back to Modein, where people ate on the floor instead of a proper dining couch. I did not like Alena for making us leave the palace, but I disliked Mother's idea of Modein even more.

Mother clung to my hand and wept as she walked. Beside me, Kissa carried a basket of dried meat and bread. On her head she wore a turban that could suffice if we needed a blanket. Behind us, Alena's servants led an ox-drawn wagon and stepped gingerly through the rutted streets, visibly shying away from travelers in soiled garments or with open sores.

"Maybe it won't be so bad," I heard Alena tell a woman who walked near her. "Once we get out into the country, we can glean the fields and orchards. We might even find a stray lamb or calf."

"If we need meat, we'll butcher your ox," the woman said, eyeing the animal and the wagon. "Because you can't possibly believe the enemy left any livestock for us. As for crops, the harvest ended weeks ago, so anything still in the field has been rotted by the rain."

My uncle's edict had tossed the wealthy, poor, old, and young alike into the streets. The clamoring, complaining throng passed through the gates of Jerusalem and spilled into the open area between the walls of Jerusalem and the Seleucid army. By the time the sun stood directly above our group, we were within sight of the enemy camps and the line of warriors defending them.

I tugged on Mother's sleeve. "Will they let us pass? Will they make a way for us to move through?"

Mother didn't answer, but Alena did. "Of course they will," she said, tossing me a confident smile. "Only a little while and we will be past the army and on the open road. Then we will be fine."

"Perhaps we can find an inn," Mother suggested, her tone cool. "Or you could come with us to Modein, if you think you can walk that far."

As my young head filled with images of sleeping under a cozy blanket in our old house, I realized we were barely moving. Finally we halted.

"Why did we stop?" Kissa whispered.

Murmurs rippled through the crowd like a snake. I shifted my weight from foot to foot, growing increasingly uncomfortable in the heat and the press of so many bodies. At last I sank to the ground, choosing to risk being trampled rather than continue standing in the oppressive heat.

Then the answer came to us in a wave of anguished shouts. *They will not let us pass.*

"Wh-what?" Mother stammered in surprised horror.

"How dare they!" Alena lifted her chin. "How can they keep us here, trapped like cattle? We are not animals."

"They mean to starve us," Mother said, her voice strangely flat. "The enemy will not let us pass because they mean to pressure the high priest. When we begin to die, he will have to surrender."

Alena shook her head, but what could she say? We were caught like wasps in a web, each of us pressed against her neighbor. The longer we waited, the more people poured out of the city and into what had become a corral for us all. We could move neither forward nor backward.

"Whatever made you think they would let us through?" Mother asked Alena, her voice sharp with scorn.

Alena peered toward the enemy lines, her face a study in frustration and fear. "We are not soldiers," she said. "We are women, children, and old men."

"Bah!" Mother lifted her hand as if she would smack our benefactor's wife, but then she moved closer to the wagon and crossed her arms.

I lay down on the earth, wedging my shoulders between Mother's legs and a stranger's. But when Mother shifted, she stepped on my shoulder. "Shelamzion!" she snapped, glaring down at me. "Get to your feet this instant."

"But I'm tired."

"We're all tired. Still, we're going to stand here until someone has mercy and lets us move forward."

Grumbling, I pulled myself upright, then let my forehead drop to Kissa's shoulder. She bore the extra weight without complaint, but from the look in her eyes I could tell she wasn't happy, either.

Especially not with me.

CHAPTER NINE

Kissa

I knew it would happen—I only wondered about when and how, and if people would start fighting in the midst of it. Fortunately, Alena did not resist when a group of men approached our wagon and eyed the ox. I think the poor animal had been even more miserable in the heat than we were, and he could not forage with so many people about. Alena had been keeping her eye on the beast, and I was certain she regretted bringing the animal out of the city. But who could have foretold that we would be trapped like flies in a bottle?

I think Alena was relieved when the men asked for the ox. She agreed to hand him over, and they cut the poor creature's throat immediately after freeing him from the harness. As hot blood steamed on the sand, one of the men took charge and slit the animal from chest to tail, then pulled out the stomach bag and other parts. As Shelamzion squealed and hid her eyes, I observed quietly. This was no worse than what I had seen many times when I went to Egyptian temples with my parents.

After gutting the animal and leaving the entrails for the buzzards, the butcher began to hack off pieces of meat and give them to eager groups of people. Right away I could see that the process was unfair. For those at the front of the line received generous portions, while those coming from a greater distance would receive little. But at least some of us would eat.

As for Alena, she received a large hunk of meat from the flank, which she quickly wrapped in cloth and hid under a blanket. "For later," she said, glancing at Shelamzion's mother. "Once the crowd has dispersed."

I looked at the cloudless sky, where the sun shimmered in a wide bowl of blue. The Jews were highly religious, as were most Egyptians, but their devotion to one God only seemed irrational to me. When things were bad, as they were now, who could you blame? In Egypt, if one god disappointed, you could always appeal to another, or go to yet another for help. But with the Jews, all things, good and bad, came from the hand of HaShem, and they had no other source of aid.

I considered my mistress, who lay faceup beneath the wagon, staring at the rough boards above her. She must have felt the pressure of my gaze, for after a moment she turned and looked at me. "What?"

I inclined my head toward an open area some distance away. Understanding, she crawled out from under the wagon and walked with me.

When Alena or other adults were nearby, I rarely spoke, for slaves were supposed to serve, not converse. Though Shelamzion and I had talked freely since our first day together, we had learned to keep our conversations private.

Once we were far enough away that the others could not hear us, I said to her, "What I want to know is why you are not furious with your HaShem."

Shock flickered over my young mistress's face. "Why would I be furious?"

"Don't you pray every day?"

She nodded.

"Don't you ask your God to keep you safe?"

Another nod.

"Then *why* isn't he answering your prayers?"

She ran a hand through her damp hair and sat down, radiating puzzlement. "I don't know," she said after a moment.

"Don't any of your people get angry with your God?"

"I don't know."

"What do you have to do to convince him to act on your behalf? In Egypt, we give our gods sacrifices. What do you give yours?"

"We give sacrifices, too," she replied, her voice small and uncertain. "And sometimes we do other things."

"Like what?"

"Like . . . we obey Him. That pleases Him."

I crossed my arms. "I don't understand your HaShem. And if he keeps us out here much longer, I don't think I want to."

Shelamzion didn't respond but instead propped her chin on her hand and looked at me as if I were a puzzle she needed to figure out. I sat with her, glad that we weren't sitting under the wagon in a puddle of ox blood.

"I don't know the answers," Shelamzion finally said, "but I will find the answers and explain everything to you. My father said all the answers can be found in the Torah."

Having spent my ire, I lifted my gaze to the heavens. "When you have solved all the mysteries of the universe, come to me and explain all."

"I will," she said, assuming a pose of mock solemnity. "If not today, then tomorrow, and if not tomorrow, then the next day. And if not that day, then the day after that—"

"Enough." I playfully swatted her shoulder. "I suppose it is enough that you are willing to listen to my questions."

CHAPTER TEN

Shelamzion

A nd so began a season of suffering unlike anything I had ever experienced. Years later I would dream of that horrific event—of sliding through the crowd of those evicted from Jerusalem, searching for a morsel of bread, a green leaf, a puddle at the base of a rock. In my dreams I am thin and weak and my skin is so burned I cannot stand to touch or be touched. My mother, Alena, Kissa, Gaia, and the other servants have made a rough camp by the side of the road, and we are all starving. Alena tries to console me by saying that at least we are aiding the high priest in his effort to save our Holy City, but what good is a city if all of its citizens are dead?

Our wagonload of supplies, meant to feed us for at least a week, lasted only an hour. The trouble began when Kissa opened her basket and gave me a piece of dried beef. Almost at once we were surrounded by grasping hands and open mouths. Kissa tried to turn and hide, but Alena commanded her to share what she had brought. When Kissa's basket had emptied, Alena instructed her servants to unload the wagon, so that everyone in the vicinity could receive a cup of water and a handful of food.

Confident that the stalemate would end in a few hours, Alena climbed onto her wagon and waited beneath a curtain Gaia had stretched over her head.

But it did not end. And the men came for the ox, which might have fed us for a long time.

I tried not to complain as the days stretched on, for everyone suffered alike—master and slave, adult and child, Jew and Gentile. We were caught between two armies and completely without supplies. Hunger and thirst waited for us like patient birds of prey, ready to swoop down and take the weakest among us. Most of the time we were so depleted we could not even spit. Our tongues stuck to the roofs of our mouths, and speech became difficult. Our lips cracked, and our voices, when we could use them at all, were hoarse and brittle.

Sleep, when it came, brought nothing but nightmares. I dreamed of my father lying dead on the ground and saw Ketura's lifeless eyes staring at me from a purpled, mangled face. "I was the pretty one," she said, her voice breaking in a rattling gurgle. "I was the one who would bring honor to the family."

I was not the only one who suffered from nightmares. Kissa cried out in her sleep, and when I woke her and asked what she dreamed of, she would not look at me.

"I was marching with the slave caravan again," she whispered. "You cannot know what it was like. I was stumbling forward, my eyes glazed over, my ears filled with wind. My feet cracked and bled. Sand blew into my nose and ears, scraped the skin of my feet, and irritated the flesh beneath my tunic." She offered a small smile. "Compared to that, this is not so bad."

I blew out a breath. "How can you think so?"

"We have some water," she said, "though we have to work for it. And we can always eat birds, rats, insects. And rabbits, if we can catch one."

"*You* can eat rats and insects and rabbits," I countered. "We cannot, for they are unclean."

"Why does HaShem forbid you to eat the food that is most plentiful in this place where you are starving?"

I watched her pull another squeaking rat from the trap she had fashioned. "I don't know."

I have to admit—sometimes my stomach growled in envy as I watched Kissa eat her roasted rats and grasshoppers. I would have eaten them too, if not for the Law and the dozens of watchful eyes around me.

And we *did* have water, though the spring of Gihon was always crowded and difficult to reach due to the crowd. We could roast pigeons and other small birds, if we were fortunate enough to capture them.

But we were not accustomed to working so hard for so little.

Years later, when faced with decisions that would impact lives other than my own, I would remember our suffering in the days of the siege. During that time I learned how it feels to be hungry and thirsty. I learned about the frustration and anger of helplessness, and I saw how desperate people can easily set aside their most devoutly held beliefs in order to survive.

One afternoon, while Kissa roasted a rat and observed the expression on my face, she silently offered me a mouthful and I ate it.

Later I begged HaShem to forgive me for breaking His Law, and there too I learned a lesson: nothing could taste as good as being forgiven felt.

On the first day of Tishrei, the seventh month, my mother announced that the day of Judgment had come. It was Rosh Hashanah, the head of the year, when HaShem sat on His throne and determined the destiny of each individual in the next twelve months.

"May HaShem determine that I die in peace," she murmured, closing her eyes as she lay beneath the wagon with me, Alena, and Kissa.

"Do not say so," Alena said and fanned herself with part of a palm branch. Now thin and sharp-featured, she looked nothing like the soft, pretty woman who had led us away from the high priest's house. "HaShem may feed us with manna and water us with rain. Or John will relent and let us back into the city."

"Why should he relent now when we are nearly dead?" Mother glanced at Alena. "Be realistic, Alena. Do not encourage those with foolish hopes."

On the tenth day of Tishrei, the day of Yom Kippur, I wondered if our high priest was thinking of us as he entered the Holy of Holies. When he killed the goat and bull for the sacrifices, when he ate the priestly meal, did he think of his starving family outside the gate?

"I think," I said to Kissa, "my uncle must have a heart of stone."

She bit her lip, then moved closer. "I have heard a story," she whispered, "and it concerns your uncle. It may help you understand him."

I moved closer, eager to hear. "What story?"

Kissa shook her head. "Not here."

I nodded and made a turning motion. Kissa rolled out from under the wagon, and I crawled after her. Without a glance behind me, I followed her away from our group, desperate to hear what she could not share in front of the others.

―――

Kissa waited until we stood in the shadow of the city wall, far from any listening ears. "I have the story straight from the cook," she said, lifting her chin as though I might challenge her. "She was traveling with your uncle's men before he became high priest, so she was witness to all I am about to say."

I nodded, silently urging her to continue.

"I shall put it in simple words," she said. "She told me that for years the kings of other nations have wanted to kill the remaining Maccabees. You are a kinswoman of the Maccabees, are you not?"

The question caught me off guard. I had never thought of myself as such, but would I be living with the high priest if I were not part of his family?

I nodded again.

"Well." Kissa leaned closer. "After Mattathias and his sons made Israel an enemy to be feared, Jonathan and Simon led the country. Both of them conquered lands that used to be ruled by the Seleucids and the Ptolemies of Egypt. The kings of those nations vowed to destroy any remaining Maccabees—or, as they say now, any of the Hasmoneans."

"They wanted to kill my uncle?"

"They wanted to kill him, his father, his brothers, and his children—if he had any. Last year, the Seleucids and Ptolemy, Simon's son-in-law, conspired to kill him and his children, too. They murdered Simon and his two oldest sons, but your uncle escaped. The enemy kept Morit, Simon's wife, and put her in prison."

"I have heard some of that story," I whispered. "But I did not know about Uncle's mother."

Kissa's eyes went dark and grave. "Your uncle hurried back to Jerusalem, where the Sanhedrin proclaimed him high priest and ruler. They poured holy oil on his head, and the next thing he did was assemble an army and ride for the fortress where his mother was being held." Kissa paused. "I am not sure I ought to tell you more. You are still so young."

I crossed my arms and strengthened my stance to show her I was not afraid. "If I am part of this family, I need to know what happened."

Kissa pressed her lips together, then drew a deep breath and nodded. "The fortress stood on a mountaintop, and your uncle's army couldn't reach it with arrows or catapults. John Hyrcanus ordered his men to climb the cliffs. But then Ptolemy brought out your uncle's mother and began to"—she shook her head— "torture her. And though the woman cried out in agony, she called down to her son and begged him not to be moved by her screams. She told him to let her die, because death at the traitor's hand was better than a long life, so long as her son avenged the wrongs that had been done to their family."

I felt sorrow like a huge, painful knot inside my chest. I did not know the people in this story, but I knew Uncle, and I had a mother. And I could not imagine what I would do if someone took my mother and hurt her, killing her little by little in front of me . . .

I met Kissa's troubled gaze.

"Have I said too much?" she asked, her face grim. "I should not have told the story to one so young."

I looked away and swallowed hard. "I do not want to think about it," I said. "Thinking about Uncle's mother makes my chest hurt."

"Then I was wrong—"

"You were *not* wrong. If this happened to my family, I ought to know about it. If it happened to my uncle, I need to understand. He is my guardian. Now, tell me—what happened after that?"

Kissa hesitated, then continued. "Your uncle spent days at the foot of the mountain, listening to his mother scream. While he waited for a miracle, he received word that the Seleucid army, under Antiochus Sidetes, was marching toward Judea.

He'd been caught in a trap much like this one. Sidetes meant to draw your uncle and his men out of the city so that Jerusalem could be captured."

I frowned. "But Jerusalem *wasn't* captured."

"No." Kissa's eyes filled with tears. "Because your uncle left his mother to die alone. He led his army back to Jerusalem, placing duty before family. And that"—her voice lowered to a whisper—"is the sort of man your uncle is."

After hearing Kissa's story, I understood why Uncle was allowing the old and the very young to die outside the gates of the Holy City. He was not unfeeling, but he placed the security of Jerusalem above everything else, including family obligations.

As, I supposed, a ruler should.

On the fifteenth day of Tishrei, the first day of Sukkot, the Feast of Tabernacles, we stirred as the gates of the city grumbled amid the clanking of chains. We sat up, unable to believe our eyes, as Judean soldiers rode out on horseback with a white flag of truce. We watched with hope in our hearts as the procession approached the enemy line, which parted so the emissaries from John Hyrcanus, our high priest, could speak to Sidetes.

By the time the sun began to drop toward the west, the leaders had finished their talking and we were preparing to reenter Jerusalem. Not only were we allowed to return to our homes, but Sidetes, a pagan, sent several wagons ahead of us, each carrying a bull with gilded horns. A gift, he said, for our festival. Cups of gold and silver accompanied the wagons, each of them filled with spices for the sacrifice.

"Who could know?" Mother asked aloud, "that an enemy could be pious toward HaShem?"

We could see that the enemy forces had stopped battering

our gates and launching stones at our walls. The Seleucids had called a halt to warfare and feasted to honor our festival.

"This pagan is not like Antiochus Epiphanes," Alena said as she slipped her arm around Mother's shoulder. "That one killed a swine upon our altar and sprinkled pigs' blood around the Temple. But this one—perhaps we should call him Antiochus the Pious."

A few moments after the delegation from Antiochus had passed into Jerusalem, dozens of carts came out of the city, those manned by soldiers and physicians who had been sent to provide help for the weak and dying. They offered water and shade to those in the worst condition and took them straightway back into the city.

The household of John Hyrcanus had suffered like the others, but we had been more fortunate than most, because we had enjoyed an abundance of food and comfort before the siege began. As we joined the flood of people reentering the city, I looked around and spotted Uncle standing on a watchtower. He wore a look of grim satisfaction, and he was not alone. With him were the three men I had met at his banquet—the three he had sent to Rome.

Not until years later did I learn that those men had returned with a letter from the Roman Senate, a letter intended to remind the Seleucid king of Rome's alliance and friendship with the Jewish people. That reminder was enough to convince Sidetes that peace would be a far better choice than continued war, which would eventually involve sending the Roman military to Judea.

Yet the war did not end with the Sukkot celebration. The Roman proclamation vanquished Sidetes's dreams of conquering Judea, yet the antagonist was determined to appear victorious. He and my uncle spent several days negotiating a peace.

Antiochus Sidetes asked for the return of the port city of

Joppa and other towns Simon had captured from Seleucia, and the placement of a Seleucid garrison in Jerusalem. My uncle refused to allow the garrison. Instead, he offered three hundred hostages and five hundred talents. Sidetes accepted, but countered with a demand for the demolition of Jerusalem's walls, a treaty of military alliance, and a payment of tribute.

My uncle accepted the Seleucid king's offer but found himself impoverished. After debating the matter, he decided he had no choice and ordered his men to plunder King David's tomb. Though this sacrilege greatly disturbed the citizens of Jerusalem, it was a small price to pay for ending the war. Furthermore, my uncle recovered more than enough treasure to pay Sidetes's tribute and hire a mercenary army to protect Jerusalem in the future.

The priestly warriors of my family had become leaders through bloodshed, and Uncle must have known that bloodshed would continue to be a necessary and regrettable part of his life.

But as Kissa and I climbed the stone staircase to return to my comfortable and much-missed bedchamber, I knew only that we had been hungry and thirsty, that people around us had died, and Sukkot would always be the happiest of holy days for me.

And as I climbed into my bed after a bath and a light supper, I realized I had learned one other thing: that no man who led a nation could win without also suffering losses.

CHAPTER ELEVEN

Shelamzion

The next year finally brought peace and safety to Jerusalem. For the most part, John Hyrcanus remained at home with his wife, and I admired her more than ever. To me, Alena was the most beautiful, intelligent, and capable woman alive. Uncle did more than love her—he respected her and frequently asked her opinion about how to handle situations that arose with foreign dignitaries. It was unlikely, however, that he sought her guidance on matters dealing with the Temple. And while members of the Sanhedrin, the ruling body of Sadducees, were more than willing to share their learned opinions, many times at dinner Uncle would ask Alena for advice on how to handle the quarrelsome merchants of Jerusalem, the disgruntled envoy from Egypt, and unruly Samaritan traders.

My mother did not seem to think much of Alena during the siege, but in the end, Alena was proved right—Uncle did open the doors and let us return once he knew Jerusalem would be safe. So while I did my best to honor my mother as the Torah commanded, when Kissa began to bleed, I took her to Alena for an explanation. There we received instruction on what happens to a girl when she becomes old enough to consider marriage and her future children.

"You may have noticed that sometimes I am not at dinner or present in other rooms of the palace," she said. "That is because once a woman begins to bleed, for the next seven days she should remain in her room lest she defile the house. Neither can she go to the Temple but should remain in one place, with her own bed and her own chair. These are the laws of *niddah*."

My head swarmed with questions, then one escaped: "Why?"

Alena laughed softly. "Because the Torah tells us that life is in the blood. Blood is sacred, not to be treated as if it were of no importance. Blood is what must be shed to atone for our sins. Blood is what the high priest carries into the Holy of Holies and sprinkles on the altar. So as long as a woman is bleeding, she should be thoughtful enough to confine her bleeding to one place so that others in the house are not made unclean, as well."

Alena had changed over the past months, her belly swelling like a ripe apple beneath her tunic. When I asked what had happened to her, she smiled and told me she was expecting a child.

"One day this bleeding will happen to you, Shelamzion," Alena said, dropping her hand to my shoulder. "And when it does, we will find you a suitable husband so you can have children, too. The high priest has already given much thought to your future."

I frowned, unable to imagine how any future could be better than the life I enjoyed at the high priest's house. I had Alena to admire, Kissa for companionship, and freedom to roam and explore.

Alena's hand rose to my cheek. "One day you will be an important woman, Salome Alexandra. You are a Hasmonean. Because your ancestors are greatly respected and highly honored, people will expect great things from you." She paused and smiled. "I think the time has come for you to have a tutor."

I blinked. Sons had tutors, not daughters. Sons learned at their fathers' knees and then went to school to study Torah. When they were old enough, they were apprenticed to a trade. But I had never heard of a girl being taught anything other than how to cook, sew, weave, and keep a house.

"Yes, a tutor," Alena repeated, as if reassuring herself. "I will ask my husband tonight, and we will find the perfect teacher for you."

"What will I learn? I already know how to grind wheat and fetch water—"

Alena laughed. "You will learn far more important things than that, dear one. You will learn how to speak proper Greek, how to add numbers, and how to identify the stars in the sky. You know how to read, but you must learn how to write. You will also learn how to buy and sell, and how to conduct business for a household."

I looked at Kissa in bewilderment. "My head is not big enough to contain all that knowledge."

Alena brought her fingertips to my chin and turned my face toward hers. "Your head is more than big enough. You are a bright girl, Shelamzion, and you will do well. Never doubt it."

CHAPTER TWELVE

Kissa

Though I was no Jew, and though they did not stop me from eating what I pleased during the siege, Alena insisted that when I was a niddah, or unclean, I would have to remain in one place. Fortunately, Shelamzion was kind enough to insist that I pass my seven days in her room, on the mattress where I slept. Since touching anything I touched made her unclean as well, she insisted that we be unclean together.

I did not mind. Only one thing concerned me during those days: when we went to see Alena about my bleeding, she had hugged Shelamzion and promised that one day they would find her a husband, but she did not say the same thing to me.

I knew why, of course. Slaves were property, and while I saw several who had clearly formed an attachment to another, slaves did not officially marry unless their master first freed them. So I would not marry, and given that I spent most of my hours with my mistress, neither was I likely to find a match among the other slaves.

Since I had never known love, save that of my parents, I was not greatly troubled by this realization. Still, I considered it when

I compared my life to my mistress's. Like me, she had lost her father, and though she still had a mother, Sipporah remained so aloof from her daughter that I barely counted her as a loving influence. Both my mistress and I benefited from life in the high priest's palace, and Shelamzion shared so freely with me that I could not be jealous of her.

When I was bleeding, Alena had one of the servants deliver our food on a tray and leave it at the door, and for one week out of every four my mistress and I were free to avoid work and laze about in our bedchamber. During those restful weeks we talked, laughed, and told each other stories, some true, some invented.

I told her about growing up in Egypt. About how our king and queen were not really Egyptian, but Greek, and how they lived in Alexandria, a city less Egyptian than any other in the kingdom. I told her about our gods and goddesses and about the legends associated with each. I told her about the stone statues of our gods and how some of them would travel by boat up and down the Nile, visiting the farming villages each year. About how the priests would clothe the idols of the gods on special occasions, and about how the idols were fed sumptuous meals three times a day—delicious dinners no one else could touch because they had been dedicated to the god.

As I spoke, I realized that the gods of Egypt had done nothing for me. They had not worked a miracle to win my freedom and return me to my parents. They had not heard my prayers, and I had no way of knowing if my parents had prayed at all for my return.

Perhaps they were glad I was gone. Life would certainly be easier without another mouth to feed. I had never been a perfect child, so perhaps they had been relieved, even eager, to send me away.

Shelamzion's mother scolded me when she heard me describing our gods to her daughter. "You ungrateful, evil girl!" Her eyes flashed. "Shelamzion will worship HaShem and no other. You should not be tempting her with the notion of idols!"

"She is not tempting me," Shelamzion replied, surprised by her mother's rebuke. "And Kissa is not evil. She is teaching me about Egypt."

"That place is well named the Black Land," Sipporah went on, "for all sorts of evil comes from there. You are not to speak of it again, do you hear? Not a word!"

I pressed my lips together and did not say anything else until Sipporah had gone downstairs. Then I reached out and touched my mistress's arm. "I am sorry to have offended your mother."

"You are *my* handmaid," Shelamzion replied, though her eyes remained troubled. "I don't know why Mother does not understand that I can make up my own mind about things."

I propped my head on my hand and studied my young mistress. We had been together well over a year, but in all that time I had never seen Sipporah demonstrate any sort of kindness for her daughter—no hugs, no caresses, no words of appreciation. Some of the slaves said Sipporah was unpleasant because she still grieved the loss of her husband and eldest daughter, but why should those losses prevent her from treasuring the daughter who remained? Shelamzion was an exceptional little girl, wise beyond her years, well-mannered, and much more clever than I. Yet Sipporah seemed not to care for the child at all.

I wanted to ask Shelamzion if her mother's inattention bothered her. Clearly she noticed it, because several times she had made passing comments about her mother's preference for the daughter who had died. But my mistress seemed perfectly content with the way things were.

How could that be?

I opened my mouth, about to pry, then decided to remain silent. For all I knew, the situation troubled Shelamzion deeply, and if that were so, I would not probe the wound and make matters worse. I liked my mistress, and she had been good to me. I would not hurt her, even if my life depended on it.

CHAPTER THIRTEEN

Shelamzion

After beginning her monthly courses, Kissa started to lose interest in playing games. She would play if I insisted, of course, as was her duty, but her attention soon wandered, and I would often catch her looking at the other slaves, looking with particular curiosity at the young men. Her face sometimes wore a distant look, and when I began to tell one of my stories about my famous relatives or life in Modein, at some point I could tell that her thoughts had wandered to a place I could not go.

Exasperated by her inattention, one afternoon I stalked away and went in search of something more interesting. I left the high priest's house and wandered down the twisty street, dodging carts and pack mules and women carrying water jugs. I found myself at the Temple and walked into the wide open space where the animals were kept in pens until purchased for sacrifice.

What I saw in that place made me sick. A man had pulled a young calf from an enclosure. With no rope to secure the animal, he was chasing it through the area, beating the animal about the head with a stick whenever he could get close enough to land a blow. The terrorized calf bleated hoarsely, a pitiful sound unlike anything I had ever heard—

"Stop!" Not thinking about anything except helping the panicked animal, I ran toward the man, my sandals skimming the stones. "Stop that! You are frightening him!"

The man scowled at me, then turned. "Whose child is this? She shouldn't be here."

No one claimed me, for I had come alone. I shrank back, suddenly aware of how vulnerable I was. In truth, I frequently took liberties that would not have been proper for an ordinary girl, knowing I would be excused on account of who my uncle was. But I had never gone into the Temple alone, and never had I acted so impetuously.

I forced myself to calm down. "That is wrong," I said, pointing to the stick in his hand. "The Torah says an animal offered to HaShem must be perfect and without flaw."

The man glared at me, then gestured to the bleating calf that stood with its trembling legs splayed, head hanging low. "Do you see any fault in this animal?"

"I do." I pointed to the animal's face. "He is bleeding about the eyes on account of your cruelty, and he is terrified. How do you know you have not hurt him in other ways?"

The question had been birthed from desperation, but it was enough to make the gathering onlookers pause for debate. "How does he know?" one Levite murmured to another. "Perhaps the animal *does* have a fault from this rough handling."

The man who had purchased the calf was not disposed to discuss the matter. Instead he came toward me. "Get out of here," he said, his voice a low, angry whisper. "Go home to your mother."

"I will go home and tell this story to everyone." I lifted my chin. "I live in the house of *Yoḥanan Cohen Gadol.*"

The use of John Hyrcanus's Hebrew name and title was

enough to elicit consternation from the circle of observers. But just as I was about to walk away, a priest came over, grabbed my arm, and dragged me from the courtyard.

～～～～～

Uncle narrowed his eyes and peered over the top of the scroll he was reading. He seemed to be studying me, and for a moment I was certain he was wondering if he had invited a demon into his home, for surely only an imp would have run into the Temple courtyard and stopped a man from offering a sacrifice.

The Levite who served as my escort had relayed the entire story, omitting no detail. So I waited—half afraid, half indignant—for the high priest's judgment.

"Shelamzion," he said, leaning forward as he lowered his scroll, "what makes you think the calf's eyes bled for some reason other than the stick? If the bleeding occurred in the act of stunning the beast, the stick could be considered a tool of mercy."

I gave him a look of horror. "What I saw was not a *stunning*; it was torture."

Too late I realized I should have chosen a better word. My uncle had seen enough torture in past years, and he did not need a reminder.

But he did not scold me. "Is it not merciful to stun the animal before cutting its throat? Would HaShem have us be deliberately cruel?"

"HaShem is compassionate and merciful," I said, reciting one of the lessons Father had taught me. "But beating an animal, especially one so young and frightened, is neither. The man I saw was chasing the calf, laughing and beating it whenever he could, as though it were a game for pleasure. My father taught me that hunting was wrong, for it brings terror to the beast and renders the meat forbidden. Is not the same thing happening in the Temple courtyard? Do we offer forbidden meat to HaShem and give the same to the priests?"

My uncle leaned back, cleared his throat, and sent a pointed look to the priest who had brought me. The man lowered his head and stepped back.

"Who *are* you?" Uncle murmured, resting his cheek on his hand as he studied me. "Such a grown-up mind in such a small body."

I answered his question the only way I could. "I am Salome Alexandra, daughter of Ittamar and Sipporah."

Uncle smiled. "Perhaps you have a point, Shelamzion. I shall study the matter and see what can be done. We must not torture the creatures destined for sacrifice. You are right—such a thing would not please HaShem."

I felt my heart turn over in happiness. "Truly? You will do this?"

"I will. Now run along. Do not leave the house again without an escort. And no more going to the Temple alone. Ever."

I sighed in relief and slipped out of the room, a little amazed that a mere girl could say something important and have a man pay attention.

No one was more surprised than I the next time Mother, Kissa, and I went to the Temple. As we entered the courtyard, I tugged on her sleeve, about to show her the awful spectacle of men beating the sacrificial calves. To my amazement, however, the livestock area had been changed. New wooden posts stood in the open area, and small circles had been etched around the posts. One man stood with a calf within the circle. I watched as he tied the animal to the post, and then with one swift blow he stunned the animal so that it fell to its knees. The man bound it and carried it to the altar.

I turned to Kissa. "Did you see?"

The heavy lashes that usually shadowed her cheeks had flown up. "Your uncle listened."

That was the miracle of it all. Not only had Uncle paid attention, but he had also considered my words and acted on them. A thrill shivered through me. Maybe I could make a difference. Maybe one day I could be important to creatures more appreciative than sacrificial calves.

Overcome by a heady rush of satisfaction, I clapped in delight.

"Stop daydreaming, Shelamzion." Mother pulled me toward the steps. "We must go inside."

Mother and I went inside, yet my thoughts wandered as the Temple musicians played. My uncle had tremendous power, and everyone knew it. I had no power of my own, but my father had set my feet on a path of knowledge, and that knowledge had spurred Uncle to act on behalf of the sacrificial animals. If I knew more, I might be able to convince Uncle to act on behalf of others . . . even girls who were not the most beautiful daughter in the family. If I could learn more, I might be able to give Kissa answers to her many questions about HaShem.

Though Alena had mentioned finding a tutor for me, no tutor had yet come to the house. I would have to find a tactful way to remind her that I wanted to learn. Perhaps after her baby came . . .

A girl might not be able to do much alone, but an educated girl who had her uncle's ear might be able to do a great many things.

CHAPTER FOURTEEN

Shelamzion

L ife in the high priest's house changed dramatically once
Alena began to have children. Judah Aristobulus was her
first, born when I was eight. My happy uncle allowed
me to visit the new mother, and I was amazed to see how a
woman's rounded belly could produce a fat, happy baby with
pink gums and chubby fingers. Three years later, when I was
eleven, Alena gave birth to her second son, Antigonus.

Uncle was not present to celebrate his second son's birth.
Bound by the terms of his treaty with Antiochus Sidetes, he
had to participate in that king's military campaign against
Parthia.

The Parthians were known to be fierce, bloodthirsty warriors,
with an empire so vast that not even the Romans had been able
to conquer it. But Antiochus Sidetes, my uncle explained, was
determined to attack the Parthians because they had captured
his brother, Demetrius III.

With great reluctance, Uncle said farewell to his pregnant
wife and left Jerusalem. I stood between Mother and Alena as
Uncle departed the palace with his generals. Though I tried to

be calm and steadfast, I was terrified he would be killed and never see his new baby.

No one was happy about my uncle's participation in the Parthian campaign. In order to raise an army, he had to hire additional mercenaries and conscript hundreds of Jewish citizens. In addition to the hardships this venture placed on the people of Judea, spies reported that Sidetes was not prepared to undertake such a dangerous campaign. According to reports, his military procession was more suited for sight-seeing than fighting. For in addition to fighting men, it was also comprised of three hundred thousand camp followers, including cooks, bakers, and actors. Rumor had it that Sidetes's wagons carried so much gold that common soldiers used golden nails in their leather boots, and so much silver that the cooks used silver pots for boiling water. One Judean captain told my uncle, "It is as if they are marching to a banquet rather than to a battle."

Fortunately for the army of Judea, the Festival of Pentecost fell during the Parthian campaign. Uncle saw to it that Sidetes—who was largely ignorant of Jewish laws and practices—was informed that the Jews were not allowed to travel or fight during their religious festivals.

Like many pagans, Antiochus Sidetes was desperate to avoid offending the gods—*any* gods—on a military expedition. Well accustomed to studying the entrails of goats and cattle before a battle, he did not question my uncle's devotion to HaShem or his insistence on remaining in camp to celebrate the completed harvest.

So on the sixth day of the Hebrew month of Sivan, while Sidetes and his men marched ahead, Uncle and his men remained in camp to observe *Shavuot* and remember the ritual taking place in the Temple. Because the Sabbath followed the festival, they remained in camp yet another day after that.

On the eighth day of Sivan, when the Seleucids had marched

a good distance toward the east, Uncle and his men packed up their tents and returned to Jerusalem.

Antiochus Sidetes died, we later learned, while fighting a Parthian general. If my uncle had been with him, he would likely have been killed, too. And for what? Nothing that mattered to Judea.

I approved of my uncle's actions and made a mental note for myself: do not waste your time or risk your life on a foolish venture.

I welcomed Uncle home with a big embrace, then took his hand and led him upstairs to meet his new son.

~~~~~~~~~

Though my uncle was circumspect enough not to publicly celebrate Antiochus Sidetes's death, I knew he was relieved that the Seleucid king would not be calling on him again. Judea no longer owed tribute to Sidetes, we would never have to fight in his wars, and he would never again conspire with the Egyptians to murder Hasmoneans.

With Sidetes gone, Judea had no formal obligation to any nation save Rome—and our treaty with them was one of friendship.

To mark the occasion of Judea's liberation, the high priest's family, a few Levites and several merchants gathered in the palace triclinium to enjoy a lavish feast. Alena wore a new tunic, fine jewels glittered in her hair, and the necklace at her throat might have cost a king's fortune. Even my mother dressed for the occasion, donning her best tunic and a silk himation in the Greek style. Kissa helped me choose a tunic, then braided my hair in a style that involved curls, needles, and thread.

When all the guests had assembled, my uncle stood in the center of the dining couches and blessed the bread:

Baruch atah A-donay,
Elo-heinu Melech Ha'Olam Hamotzi lechem min
  haaretz.

Blessed are You, Lord our God, King of the Universe,
Who brings forth bread from the earth.

He thanked HaShem for allowing Judea to be an independent
and free nation again, which it had not been since the time of
Solomon. "Keep Your hand upon us," he finished, "and may
Israel reflect Your glory among the nations."

At the conclusion of his prayer, he sat and smiled around the
gathering. The guests reclined on their couches and made quiet
conversation as servants brought in trays of food and allowed
each guest to take whatever he or she pleased.

If anyone thought it odd that a child should be present, no
one mentioned it. In fact, I was nibbling daintily at a honeyed
pear and feeling quite at home when I overheard one man say,
"Your niece is becoming quite lovely, John. I assume you have
plans for her."

"But of course." Uncle nodded. "And they will commence
soon."

"My other daughter"—Mother turned to the bald man who
had spoken—"was the family beauty. She would outshine any
girl in Jerusalem."

Uncle showed his teeth in an expression that was not a smile,
but I did not take time to analyze it. My mind had latched on
to his words: he had *plans* for me? I leaned toward him, eager
to hear more, but he only took a spiced chicken breast from a
tray and tore at it with his fingers. I shifted my gaze to the bald
man, hoping he would ask for clarification, but he seemed to
have lost interest.

Finally I gathered my courage and spoke during a break in
the conversation. "What plans do you have for me, Uncle?"

My voice, high and thin, floated above the murmur of adult voices and halted the other conversations. The other guests looked at me, their faces filled with surprise.

My uncle finished swallowing his chicken and dropped the bones onto the floor. He glanced at the man who had asked about me. "Have you ever seen such boldness in such a small girl?"

As the man chuckled, Uncle turned to me. "Salome Alexandra," he said, using my Hebrew and Greek names, "has anyone told you about Cleopatra Thea of the Ptolemies?"

I shook my head.

"That is a mistake," Uncle said and folded his hands in his lap, "for she is a woman worthy of emulation."

I leaned back, eager to hear more. Several guests stopped eating and listened, as well.

"Like you, Cleopatra Thea comes from an important family. She was tutored as a child, taught philosophy, history, and languages. When she was of age, her father betrothed her to Alexander Balas, the ruler of Seleucia. Jonathan of the Maccabees attended the wedding as an honored guest and sat between the groom and the bride's father on the royal dais. He was present not only to celebrate the wedding, but also to seal a pact between the Hasmoneans and the Seleucid Empire. Balas wanted the support of our legions, so he allowed Jonathan to anoint himself as the first Hasmonean high priest. You should know that history—just as you should be willing to marry whomever your family chooses for you."

I stared, trying to work out his meaning. "Are you—am I about to be married, Uncle?"

He laughed, his face brightening with humor. "No, little one. You are about to become educated. Tomorrow I will introduce you to your tutor."

"Salome, I would like you to meet Josu Attis."

The thin young man standing beside my uncle clutched a scroll to his chest and bobbed his head toward me. Then he turned to Uncle and arched his narrow brows. "I was under the impression, sir, that I would be educating one of your sons."

"My eldest is only four and not quite ready for a tutor," Uncle replied, chuckling. "But Shelamzion was born ready for learning. You will find her a bright and willing pupil."

"But . . ." The tutor faltered, a melancholy frown flitting across his features. "She is a girl, sir."

Uncle smiled at me. "Clearly."

"I am not equipped to teach cooking and sewing and how to drape a himation."

Annoyance struggled with humor in Uncle's expression as he turned to face the tutor. "Her mother will teach her those things. I want you to teach her about history, philosophy, and ethics. I am certain you will find her quite receptive."

Feeling awkward, I stepped closer to Uncle and lowered my voice. "Will he teach me Torah?"

Uncle bent to my level. "We have to be very careful about who teaches Torah," he whispered. "This Josu Attis is very bright, but I have not yet found the proper Torah teacher for you."

When Uncle straightened, the young man extended his arm toward a small space off the central hallway. "The high priest has said we may study in here, so long as the door remains open. Will you join me?"

I bobbed my head in a quick nod and hurried into the room.

CHAPTER FIFTEEN

Kissa

My mistress came bounding up the stairs, her face alight. "He was wonderful," she said, the words flowing on a tide of enthusiasm. "He brought a stylus and leather, and taught me how to write my name in Hebrew letters. And then he demonstrated Greek letters and said I would learn how to read and write both."

I gave her a tentative smile. "That is good, mistress."

"Tomorrow he will bring a scroll for me to keep as my own. He says it is simple writing, and soon I ought to be able to read it myself. Won't that be wonderful? Soon I will be able to write letters and lists and—oh! I might even write a book!"

I lifted the stack of himations I had folded and put them in a trunk. "Very good, miss. I am happy for you."

Shelamzion sat on the bed and peered at me. "You do not look happy."

"I am."

"No, you are not. What is wrong?"

I closed the trunk and blew out a breath. How could I verbalize my feelings? How could I explain that lately I had been depressed by the realization that I would never live anywhere but by her side, I would never meet anyone unless she allowed it, and I would never know anything unless I learned it from her?

"You are going to learn," I began, "and that is good. People will expect the ward of the high priest to know things."

"Why does that displease you?"

"It does not displease me. But . . . being a slave does not mean I don't want to learn. I would love to know how to read and write. I would love to know more about many things."

Shelamzion sucked at the inside of her cheek, her brows twitching like a pair of inchworms. "Why do you want to know how to read? You have no scrolls."

For a bright girl, my mistress could be surprisingly blind. The world in which I had found myself was one of letters—people sent messages, read scrolls, studied manuscripts, and wrote receipts. If I was ever going to find my parents in Egypt, I would need to know how to read and write. If I was ever going to be more than my mistress's hands and feet, I would need knowledge.

"I could read to you," I continued to explain, sitting on the edge of the trunk, "if perhaps you were too tired to hold a scroll. I could write letters for you, if you needed a scribe. Don't you see—I could be a much better servant for you if I knew how to read and write."

Shelamzion nodded slowly. "But how are you to learn? My uncle would not want you to be in the room with me and the tutor." She crossed her arms. "And the tutor might think it odd if my handmaid was present during my lesson."

"Then you could teach me," I said. "When you come back from your study time, you could share what you learned. If that pleases you, of course."

"That might work. But you could not fall behind on your duties. The laundry, the cleaning—you would still have to do your regular work. Mother would be upset if you fell behind."

"I won't. I promise."

"Then it's settled." Shelamzion's face brightened. "Make sure your work is finished by the time I leave Josu Attis. I will come here then and share what I have learned—most of it, anyway."

I smiled. "Thank you, miss. I promise I will be a good student."

"You had better." She lowered her brows in a stern expression. "Or I will have to punish you severely."

For an instant I felt a twinge of fear, but then Shelamzion released a peal of laughter. I laughed too, though the moment had been extremely uncomfortable.

In the six years we had been together, my young mistress had learned one lesson without being formally taught—how to maintain the dignified distance between master and slave. The young, innocent girl had grown into a sophisticated little lady. She still talked freely with me at night, and she still allowed me to sleep beside her bed, but in public she rarely spoke to me. By observing the high priest, his wife, and other important people, she had quietly absorbed all she needed to know about the relationship between slaves and masters.

So I was not surprised when she hesitated at my question. Masters were supposed to be educated, but slaves definitely did not have tutors. But as long as Shelamzion could control what, when, and how much I learned, she would be content to teach me.

I understood, for I too had been learning.

Chapter Sixteen

Shelamzion

T ime passed, months in which I studied and learned and left my childhood behind. As I developed a woman's sensibilities, I began to see the world around me through different eyes.

Mother, I saw clearly, would never stop grieving for her first-born daughter. She still mentioned Ketura at least once a day, usually after someone had said something to compliment me.

"Don't take it to heart," Kissa told me one afternoon as we sat on the floor outside my bedchamber. "She placed all her dreams on that girl, and when she lost your sister, she lost everything."

"But she still has me," I whispered. We were watching Mother through the stone railings on the balcony. "She has me and this house and a fine life in Jerusalem."

Kissa shook her head. "Some people can never escape their grief. They are like bugs caught in a spider's web. They cannot seem to free themselves, no matter what."

I watched Mother move to the window, where she stared out at the courtyard and sighed heavily. "I don't think she wants to be free."

In that moment I determined that I would never become stuck in my circumstances. No web would paralyze me with inertia, and no sorrow would break my heart beyond repair. Mother had given all her love to Ketura, so I would not love anyone but HaShem with my whole heart.

During my thirteenth year, Alena and I were walking through the garden when she told me I had become a beautiful girl. I was so startled I almost pressed my fingers across her lips. I didn't want to hear false words, especially from her.

She must have seen something in my face, because she caught my wrist and held it tight. "Do not listen," she said, her tone fierce, "to what your mother says. She cannot see the beauty in you because she has given all her love to her dead daughter. But you *are* attractive, Shelamzion, and you need only to look at yourself to know it."

That afternoon I sat at my dressing table as Kissa arranged my hair for dinner. The face reflected in the looking brass was not that of a raving beauty. Even at my uninformed age, I saw that my nose was too long and my front teeth too big. But when Kissa let a few curls dangle in front of my ears, my nose did not seem so long. And who did not look a hundred times better with a smile?

Perhaps Alena was right. With a few cosmetics and a suitable gown, I might be presentable. But even if I were not, I would be what my father and Uncle wanted me to be—knowledgeable, clever, and wise.

As Kissa finished her work, I casually mentioned what Alena had told me in the garden. Kissa grinned and put her box of hairpins away. "Watch out," she said, "as she may be considering you for a daughter-in-law. She has two sons, and those sons will need brides one day."

"Marry one of the babies?" I glimpsed my reflection—my face had gone idiotic with surprise.

98

Kissa nodded. "Important families frequently marry their cousins. It keeps the bloodline pure. And the age difference is not so great. You are, what, eight years older than Judah Aristobulus?"

I burst into laughter. "Surely you cannot be serious. He is *five*."

"When he is fifteen, you will be twenty-three," Kissa said. "You will be more mature . . . and perhaps you will be able to teach him a few things."

I whooped with laughter, rocking back and forth at the thought of being married to the little boy whose greatest delight in the world was chasing lizards in the courtyard. "The very idea!" I said.

Kissa stepped back and sighed. "All right, forget what I said. But one day you may find your cousin more handsome than you imagined possible. Look at his parents—they are both handsome people."

I sat up as my mirth died away. Kissa had a point—Alena was certainly beautiful, and Uncle was handsome, in his way. But Judah Aristobulus! Really!

"Do me a favor," I said, making a face as I wiped tears from my eyes. "Do not ever mention that idea to anyone outside this chamber. I would not want Uncle to think I was pining for the love of his little ones."

"Do not worry," Kissa said, her voice dry. "I will never mention it again."

<hr />

In the summer of my thirteenth year, Uncle stopped me as I came out of a meeting with Josu Attis and told me to prepare for a journey. He and my mother would be taking me to Antioch, where we would meet with Cleopatra Thea, the Seleucid queen I had heard so much about. I would also meet her fourteen-year-old son, Antiochus VIII.

The thought of a distant journey thrilled me, and with great enthusiasm I ran back to the house to share the news with Kissa. Yet she did not share my eagerness, and when I asked why, she only shrugged. "The last long journey I took was not pleasant. I have not forgotten it."

"This will be nothing like the slave caravan," I assured her. "You will travel with me, and you will never leave my side. And we will visit a queen! You will stay in a palace, not a slave market. Surely it will help you forget that other journey."

She moved toward my trunk, then turned and lifted a brow. "Your uncle said this queen has a son?"

"A youth my age," I said, my cheeks heating as I smiled. "Well, almost. He is fourteen."

Kissa blew out a long breath and sank to a bench by the bed. "Do you not see what the high priest is planning? The boy is fourteen; you are thirteen. He is a queen's son; you are the ward of Israel's ruler. I believe your uncle is planning a betrothal."

For a moment I could only stare at her. Only when I released a long exhalation did I realize I'd been holding my breath. "He wants me to be *married*?"

"Why else would he take you to meet a queen's son? If he wanted you to have a male friend, he could introduce you to the butcher's boy."

"But . . ." My protestations died on my lips. Uncle had always said he had plans for me, but he had never given me any idea what those plans might be . . . until now. Even a girl like me could understand that if he united the Hasmoneans with the royal family of Cleopatra Thea, he would benefit from the political and social advantages that came with the Seleucids and the Egyptians.

I sat on the opposite end of the bench as my heart began to pound against my breastbone. "Do you . . . do you think he would want me to marry the prince right away?"

Kissa lifted one shoulder in a shrug. "I know nothing about kings and queens, especially those in other lands."

"Married." I whispered the word, then gripped Kissa's hand. "If I am married to this prince, I must have you with me. I will not go anywhere without you, do you understand?"

For an instant, fear darted into Kissa's eyes. "Has your uncle not said that I belonged to you? Is it possible he would change his mind?"

"I do not think so." I swallowed. "No, he would not—he has no reason to change his mind about you."

Her fearful expression softened as she placed her free hand over mine. "Then I will go with you," she promised, speaking in an odd yet gentle tone. "And not only because I am your slave. I will go because you are my friend."

CHAPTER SEVENTEEN

Kissa

My young mistress walked thoughtfully away, leaving me alone in her bedchamber. I tidied up the scrolls and parchments she had brought with her, then sat on the edge of her bed and stared at the floor.

A trip to Antioch . . . a betrothal . . . a nightmare.

By all the gods, my mistress was naïve! She spoke of the upcoming trip as though it would be some sort of merry party, but she had never traveled such a long distance before. She said she would keep me by her side, yet how could she guarantee such a promise? Slaves did not travel with their owners. They either walked or were chained into wagons. Sometimes they had to carry water jugs or guide the donkeys loaded with food and water.

And when the caravan stopped at night, Shelamzion would sleep in a tent with her mother while I would be left to find a safe spot beneath a wagon or a palm tree. I would be vulnerable to every slave, merchant, and passing stranger who saw me. I would have to fend off the advances of strange men or die in an attempt to defend myself.

But Shelamzion would not think about these things. Neither would she consider the changes we would both face if she married the son of a Seleucid queen.

If she married this foreign prince, she might realize that she was as much a slave as I. We would move to Seleucia. We would live in a different palace, we would have new masters, we would eat new foods and have to accustom ourselves to new rules, ranks, and rituals. Everything Shelamzion knew would change, even the worship of her God. The foreign queen might let her continue to worship HaShem, but if Shelamzion made a mistake or angered one of her new relatives, that freedom could disappear. If Shelamzion refused to obey, she could be killed . . . and then what would happen to me? I would become one of hundreds of slaves in another foreign land.

I lowered my head into my hands. I had not lived long, but I had traveled from one world to another, and I had been forcibly taken to a place where everything was different. I had been beaten and violated, and though the gods smiled on me when they brought me to Shelamzion, no slave was ever truly secure.

My time in Judea had been bearable because Shelamzion was kind and not so very different from me. She saw herself as the pampered, fortunate niece of a great man, and to some extent she was right to think of herself that way. But her sheltered childhood was about to end, and once she was betrothed, she would realize just how much of a slave she was. Shelamzion might be called a *bride*, but she would be chained to whatever circumstances her uncle decreed for her.

My mistress was simply too young to understand the risks of such a venture, and these were not the sort of issues her tutor would address. These were things she would learn from experience, and for the first time I found myself wishing that Shelamzion could remain ignorant for a long time to come.

CHAPTER EIGHTEEN

Shelamzion

Uncle insisted that we ride in his new conveyance on the journey to Antioch—a wooden box on wheels with a curved roof and openings at the front and side to let in the air.

"Is that a chariot?" Mother asked.

"It is called a coach," he answered. "I saw a picture of a Roman coach and had my carpenter duplicate it." He watched as the slaves loaded our trunks into a wagon. "Traveling by coach appears to be quite comfortable; its walls will shelter us from the sun."

"And also the dust," Mother added, stepping onto a stool a slave provided for her. After another step she was through the doorway and sitting on a pillow inside the vehicle.

I approached the stool, then remembered my promise to Kissa. Since Mother would never allow a slave inside the conveyance, I made certain she could ride with the driver. "Under no circumstances," I told the man, "should my handmaid be forced to walk."

I entered the coach and sat next to Mother. Uncle followed and sat across from us.

As we departed, Uncle told me more about the queen I would soon meet. "Cleopatra Thea is a remarkable woman," he began, taking in the passing landscape through the open window. "Twenty years before you were born, she was married to Alexander Balas. Then Demetrius, the fourteen-year-old son of Seleucia's previous king, launched an uprising and seized the throne. Cleopatra Thea's father annulled his daughter's marriage to Balas and gave her to Demetrius, and then he set out to kill her first husband. Both Balas and Philometor died in the ensuing struggle."

I tried to disguise my horror at the mention of uprisings and deaths. Was this the sort of life Uncle wished for me? I cast about for something to say—something that would not offend him—and settled for, "She had to marry a youth of fourteen?"

Uncle nodded. "But her new husband was foolish, and the people despised him. He made a treaty with your great-uncle Jonathan, but then betrayed us. Around the same time, Cleopatra Thea birthed a son, which gave the people hope that one day they would live in peace and safety. Unfortunately, a general called Diodotus stole the child from its nurse and proclaimed him king."

"A baby king!" The words escaped my lips before I could stop them.

Uncle gave me a tolerant smile. "The child became a boy soon enough, though he only served as a puppet for Diodotus. Your great-uncle Jonathan championed the cause of the young king, and for a while Diodotus gave Judea great honors. But Jonathan's military success intimidated him, so he kidnapped Jonathan and demanded a ransom. My father, Simon, tried to gather enough wealth to ransom our kinsman, but Diodotus murdered Jonathan before my father could pay it."

Uncle fell silent as his face grew somber and his thoughts wandered. I waited as long as I could, then asked, "What happened to the boy king?"

Uncle sighed. "Cleopatra Thea received word that her son had developed a kidney stone. He died during surgery to remove it, and many people, including me, have wondered if Diodotus didn't invent the story of illness so he could kill the boy. After the boy's death, the usurper claimed the crown and called himself 'Tryphon the Magnificent.' In truth, he had been successful only because his followers were loyal to Cleopatra Thea's son."

I blew out a breath and turned to stare out the window. Kissa had to be right—we were making this trip to investigate a betrothal between me and another of Cleopatra Thea's sons. I wanted to please my uncle and honor my mother, but I did not want a life of murder and rebellion and sadness and being handed to one man, then taken back and given to another. I did not want to worry about my children's safety or wonder if someone would try to steal my baby from its nurse.

If marrying Cleopatra Thea's son meant I would face similar horrors, I would happily choose to remain unmarried.

My uncle's gaze came to rest on me. "Judea owes its existence to what happened next. Demetrius, still married to Cleopatra Thea, realized he needed the Jews to defeat Tryphon. He told my father he would promise anything in exchange for the Jews' help, so Father asked Demetrius to recognize him as high priest, exempt the Jews from all taxes and tributes, and allow us to build new fortifications in Judea. Demetrius agreed."

I closed my eyes, trying to remember what my tutor had taught me about the beginning of Hasmonean leadership. "So . . . we are free from foreign rulers because of the baby king?"

"In so many words, yes. HaShem used the baby king, Cleopatra Thea, and my father to bring us freedom."

I digested this information, more than a little awed that HaShem could orchestrate such a complicated chain of events. "And this queen . . . what is she doing now?"

The grim line of my uncle's mouth relaxed. "Cleopatra Thea was married to Antiochus Sidetes, the king who had my father killed and held Jerusalem under siege. But after he died, her husband, Demetrius, returned to claim his throne—and his wife. So she now rules Seleucia with Demetrius as her husband. And through it all she has been a loyal supporter of the Jewish people."

"She had another son, after the boy who died?"

"She had two others—Seleucus V, and the son we are going to visit, Antiochus Epiphanes Philometor Callinicus." The corner of Uncle's mouth lifted in a half smile. "The people refer to him as *Grypus* because he has a hooked nose."

I laughed, but then stopped when Uncle lifted a warning finger. "Never forget that Grypus and the queen are powerful people," he cautioned. "We are going to see them in view of a betrothal. A marriage between you two might benefit both our nations."

"If he will have her," Mother said dryly. "She is not a great prize."

I ignored her comment. "I never thought I would meet a real prince."

"Neither did I." Mother folded her arms. "Your sister should have married a king."

I looked at Uncle, who rolled his eyes toward the ceiling, then offered me a small smile. "You are a bright girl," he said, "and quite pretty. Grypus would be fortunate to marry you."

"But . . . what if I do not like him?"

"Do you think Cleopatra Thea liked all her husbands?" My uncle shook his head. "Liking matters not. Power is what matters—holding it, keeping it. I would not have arranged this trip if I did not believe you capable of being a wife worthy of a king. So now we will see what the queen thinks of you, Salome Alexandra."

We leaned back against the pillows in the coach and did not speak of marriage for the rest of the journey.

~~~~~~~~~

After long days of bumping over rough roads and sticky nights in which Mother, Kissa, and I jostled one another in a small tent—Mother had tried to keep Kissa out, but I would not allow her to be abandoned—we finally neared our destination.

Nothing could have prepared me for the sight of Antioch. Leaving the arid, dusty landscape of Judea behind, we entered a green land, heavily forested, with swift blue streams that ran beside the coach and sparkled in the sun. Eventually we followed a wide, paved road that flowed alongside a river my uncle called Orontes, and then we glimpsed the stone walls surrounding Antioch.

"It's beautiful," I whispered, poking my head out the window. "So green and lovely."

We entered the city through a gate named after Daphne, one of the Greek gods, and traveled down a street lined with tall colonnades. Compared to the haphazard construction of Jerusalem, where masons were always repairing walls and buildings destroyed in war, I had never seen anything so perfect.

"The palace and the circus are situated on an island," my uncle said, leaning toward me as he took in the sights. "I am sure you will be impressed. I've been here before, yet the sight of the palace always takes my breath away."

After traversing the length of the city, we turned and crossed its breadth, and only then did I see the stone bridge that led to a walled settlement within the walled city. When we crested a hill, I could see many tidy stone houses, neatly bordered by paved streets. Behind the houses we spotted the massive circus, which Uncle described as a place for entertainments and athletic exhibits. Next to the circus, rising like a vision in stone and marble, we beheld the royal palace.

We drove through the palace gate and stepped out of the carriage, accompanied by a salute from trumpeters announcing our presence with long blasts. I blushed to think my arrival would merit such attention, but then I realized the true state of affairs when dignitaries rushed past me and knelt before my uncle. He was the guest of honor, while Mother and I were afterthoughts.

But if the marriage was arranged as Uncle hoped, those dignitaries might one day be rushing toward me . . .

I turned away from the courtiers and took a few slow steps in the courtyard to stretch the stiffness from my legs. Mother did the same, pressing a hand to her lower back as she grumbled about the uncomfortable coach. We did not have much time to ourselves, for the courtiers immediately motioned us forward.

As we walked from the courtyard to the guest quarters, I found I had never before seen more statuary in a single place. I knew art, of course, for my tutor appreciated it and often sketched details of sculptures he had seen in Egypt or one of the Philistine cities. Jerusalem had no statues, however, for graven images were a violation of HaShem's Law.

"Josu Attis would love to visit this place," I whispered to Kissa as we walked through the palace entry. Statues of men, women, and beasts adorned every pedestal, and each step of our walk brought us in view of another pedestal.

After making sure we were comfortable, the courtiers left us in our rooms. Mother, Kissa, and I were given one set of rooms; Uncle and his servants settled in chambers nearby. "Make ready for your meeting with the queen," Uncle told me as we parted. "A servant will come to fetch us when she is ready."

Kissa went immediately to work. Because we had been traveling for days, I desperately wanted a bath and clean hair. Kissa was about to pour water from a pitcher into a bowl when Mother tapped her on the shoulder and pointed to a large marble basin beneath a window. "For Salome's *mikvah*."

"A bath!"

After bathing in the luxurious tub and donning a clean tunic, I sat at a dressing table and let Kissa work on my wet hair. Not knowing if we'd have time for my hair to dry, she tied a blue ribbon around my head to hold my riotous curls in place. She attempted to shape them with a heated iron, and finally, as a finishing touch, she pinned several pearls into the still-damp curls.

"I'm so glad Alena loaned these to me," I said, turning so I could see my reflection in the looking brass.

We had barely finished dressing when a servant knocked and said the queen was ready to receive us. We found Uncle waiting in the corridor, so Mother and I fell into step behind him as courtiers led us to the queen. We were not taken to the throne room—a disappointment, as I desperately wanted to see it—but to a private chamber, where we found Cleopatra Thea and her son.

I prostrated myself on the floor as instructed, but when I lifted my head I could not take my eyes from the powerful queen's face.

Cleopatra Thea, about whom I had heard so much, was not particularly tall or beautiful, but she had a firm jaw, resolute eyes, and a thin red line for a mouth. She wore a surprisingly plain tunic, simple in style. A sheer veil covered her graying hair, and on her long hands she had unpainted nails and a conspicuous absence of jewelry.

I had expected to behold some sort of royal personage. The woman I saw before me, however, appeared as if she could be a seller of linen at our neighborhood market.

"John Hyrcanus," she said, extending her hand to my uncle. He took it and bowed deeply, then stepped back and gestured to me. "My niece, Salome Alexandra, part of the Hasmonean family. And her mother, Sipporah."

"Rise, my friends, and be seated beside your high priest."

Feeling awkward and shaky, I rose and sat on the upholstered bench directly across from the queen and her young son, whom I assumed was the royal prince. Our gazes met and held.

His eyes were attractive enough, though I could not scrutinize them without also seeing the nose—a king of a nose, if ever one had existed. My uncle had warned me that his subjects called him "hook nose," but he had not mentioned the sheer size of it. The youth's eyes seemed small by comparison, for the nose occupied the center of his face like a misshapen sculpture affixed by putty or mortar . . .

When Uncle cleared his throat, I realized I had been staring. I quickly lowered my gaze.

"Salome Alexandra," the queen said in Greek. "A lovely name for a lovely girl."

I glanced up at her, my cheeks burning, and managed to stammer, "Thank you, O queen."

"Have you a tutor, my dear?"

"I do."

"What do you most like to study?"

I folded my hands in my lap. "I read the Torah, of course, and do my utmost to follow HaShem's Law. I have read many books from the Library at Alexandria—Uncle has them sent to Jerusalem. I have read Euclid of Alexandria, though I do not understand much of geometry and have no head for numbers. I have read Pythagoras, and I disagree with his assertion that man exists simply to observe the heavens. Observing the heavens leads one to contemplate the Creator of the heavens, and is it not more profitable to marvel at Adonai than His works? I have decided I like poetry more than geometry, and oratory more than history."

The queen gave me a smile that barely spread her lips. I wondered if she were capable of smiling more freely, or if all the sorrow she had experienced had permanently affected her mouth.

She arched a brow. "If we do not understand history, are we not bound to repeat the mistakes our fathers made?"

"Some would say we will make those mistakes in any case," I answered, "for the same passions that motivated our fathers motivate us, and young people are prone to ignore their elders' advice. We still love and hate, covet and desire. So we kill and maim and steal—not me, of course, but men who do not love HaShem's holy Law."

"Only men?"

"Women too. In truth, women would surely be as prone to sin as men, if only they were given a chance."

The queen laughed, a throaty chuckle that brought heat to my cheeks and made my mother squirm.

"You have been well educated indeed," the queen said. "Tell me, dear girl—have you ever considered the possibility that you might one day be a queen?"

I frowned. I had never dreamed of such a thing before this trip, and after hearing Cleopatra Thea's sad history—

"In truth, O queen, I do not think I would like it."

"Why not?" She smiled, but all traces of humor had vanished from her eyes.

I drew a deep breath. I didn't want to insult the woman, but surely she could not deny that she had experienced myriad sorrows and trials resulting from her position. If she had been a merchant's wife, would someone have stolen her baby? Would a tyrant have murdered her son?

"I am not sure what I want," I said. "I have been assured that HaShem has a special plan for me, but I do not know what it is. But just as our father Abraham waited to see his descendants become as numerous as the sand in the sea, I am content to wait in faith that HaShem will bring His will to pass."

"Abraham is dead." The queen directed her dark gaze toward my uncle. "Surely you do not think your God will make something of your life when you are in the grave."

"I beg the queen's pardon, but HaShem can do anything He wills to do. He created the world in seven days. He hung the stars in their places. He created life and light out of nothing, so death is nothing to Him."

"You have a gift for conversation, but you have not answered my question. Why would you not like being queen? You could have power. You could have wealth. You could have anything you desired, and men would spring to do your bidding."

I looked at the floor and slowly shook my head. "If only it were so."

"Explain yourself."

I lifted my chin to boldly look her in the eyes. "I am not unfamiliar with your life, O queen. You have power, but you have paid dearly for it. You have wealth, but it brings you no joy, for you are dressed even more simply than my mother. You can have anything you desire, and hundreds of servants obey your command, but you cannot retrieve the things you have lost—like your son. Your family."

I glanced at my uncle, whose back had gone as straight as a spear. While he might be displeased with me, I would answer honestly.

"I have heard that people once spoke of making Judas Maccabaeus king, but he would have none of it. I think he was wise as well as strong. I think he may have been the wisest of all the Hasmoneans—save for my uncle, of course."

The queen looked at Uncle with burning eyes, then gestured to the youth at her side. "I should introduce my son, Prince

Antiochus VIII, my heir. Son, let me present Salome Alexandra, from Judea's Hasmonean dynasty."

Not sure what to do, I stood and bowed before him, then lifted my head. A frown had crept between his brows, though I could barely see it due to the shadow of that monumental nose.

"Perhaps you two would like to walk in the garden," the queen said, "while I talk with John Hyrcanus. We have matters of business to discuss."

After an instant of hesitation, the prince stood and looked at me. I moved to stand beside him, then followed him out of the room and into a fragrant rose garden.

⁓⁓⁓⁓⁓

What should a common girl say to a prince, especially one from a bloody dynasty like his?

For several minutes we walked through the garden without speaking. I followed the graveled path and paused at each bush, taking care to inhale the fragrance and exclaim over its sweetness, beauty, or perfection. In truth, my mind was far from flowers, and yet I had no idea what I was supposed to talk about with this young man.

Fortunately he had an interest in plants. "Did you know," he said, nodding at a tree I had stopped to admire, "that seeds from that specimen can be sewn into a band and worn around the arm? The seeds will ward off snakebite."

I blinked. "I did not know that."

"And here." He walked on and pointed to a small bush. "The crushed leaves of this specimen will relieve fever if tossed into a hot bath with the sufferer."

"That is amazing." I gave him a genuine smile. "I had no idea."

"I study, too—but not like you. I have no use for Jewish Law, and even less for Jewish history."

I folded my hands and tried to remain pleasant. Though I did not want to marry this youth, neither did I want to insult him. "I think your knowledge about plants is incredible. You could do a great deal of good with such knowledge."

He snorted softly and kept walking until he came to a shrub with wide green leaves. "This plant, when boiled, can bring worms out of a man's belly. But the roots"—a sly smile spread over his face—"if boiled in water and allowed to cool, the roots can make a man vomit blood and die."

My smile wavered. Was he trying to shock me or impress me with his knowledge?

"I know little about plants," I admitted, turning down another path. "Perhaps we should speak of something else."

"What would you have me speak of?"

I stopped walking. "What I want to know is this—do you want to be married?"

He looked at me as if I had suddenly spoken in a foreign tongue. "What do you mean?"

"I have been brought here to meet you, and my uncle is hoping to announce our betrothal. Were you not informed of this?"

"Of course."

"So? Do you want to be married or not?"

He shot me a sidelong look I didn't like nor understand. "It is something I must do. I have not decided whether or not I will find pleasure in it."

I hesitated and considered his answer. "My uncle seems to find pleasure in his marriage. He is fond of his wife, and she admires him. And I believe my mother loved my father before he died."

The prince snorted. "Common people can marry whomever they please, whenever they want. They can marry for love or money or position, it matters not." He nodded when I lifted a questioning brow. "Yes, I know about you. I know you were born poor and without position, until John Hyrcanus lifted you from poverty. I know the Hasmoneans were simple priest-shepherds until Judas Maccabaeus fought his way out of obscurity. Now you're practically a princess."

I sputtered in protest, but my feelings were too confused to respond properly. He had spoken the truth, and what of it? I could not change the circumstances of my birth.

"I am who I am," I finally said. "If I have been elevated, HaShem did it. If I am lowered tomorrow, it will be HaShem's doing. No man can decide his fate, for Adonai is over all."

The prince's features hardened in a stare of disapproval. "What nonsense you speak! Of course man can decide his fate. If he wins a war, he has made himself a conqueror. If he falls on his sword, he has made himself a martyr. Only a woman would speak such foolishness."

"If a man loses a war," I said, lowering my voice, "he may make himself a prisoner. If he falls on his sword and the blade slips, he has only injured himself. HaShem controls the outcome of these things. As our King Solomon wrote, 'Man may throw the dice, but HaShem decides the outcome.'"

The prince frowned again. "*The name*? Why do you not speak your God's name?"

"Because His name is holy," I answered, "and not to be invoked lightly. Do you not treat your gods with respect?"

The prince snorted through his horn of a nose and put a nesting dove to flight. "Apollo, Hephaestus, Dionysus—we have so many gods we must say their names to differentiate between them. Sometimes I think there must be as many gods as there are mortals."

"We are not confused. Adonai is one. We are forbidden to worship any other."

"I've heard that about your people. But how can one God do everything? He would have to be huge, and he would have to be everywhere at all times—"

"He is," I replied. "'If I go up to heaven, He is there, and if I make my bed in the grave, He is there, too. If I take the wings of the dawn and settle on the other side of the sea, even there His hand will lead me, and His right hand will lay hold of me.'"

The words of the psalm had sprung easily to my lips, and the prince's countenance softened as I recited them. He nodded when I paused. "Go on," he said. "They are beautiful words."

I studied his face, afraid he was being cynical, but I saw no malice in his features. "'His eyes saw me when I was unformed, and in His book was written the days that were formed—when not one of them had come to be.'"

"Are you saying that your God knows your thoughts? And the things you will do tomorrow or the day after?"

I nodded. "He discerns my thinking from afar. He observes my journeying and my resting, and He is familiar with all my ways."

The prince laughed. "Then he is a foolish God, for what God would trouble himself with the affairs of a woman? Powerful gods are concerned with powerful people; the others are like ants scurrying to and fro. The gods watch mortals from on high and give their attention to kings and princes. In time you will see that it is so."

I inclined my head in what I hoped was a respectful posture. I did not want to argue with this youth, especially since I was his guest, but neither could I be false.

"Yet you are an educated woman." The prince leaned back on his heels and fingered the bit of dark fuzz on his upper lip. "Clearly you have a mind for learning."

I attempted to smile. "Clearly your mother the queen has been tutored. Anyone can see that she is intelligent and well informed."

"She is a queen."

"But she was once a girl like me."

"Not like you." He shook his head. "She was a princess of the Ptolemies."

"And I—" my voice trembled, for never had I voiced the claim aloud—"am a daughter of the Hasmoneans."

He lifted his hand, conceding the point, and turned toward the chamber where we had left the others. "Come," he said and extended his hand. "Let us go tell my mother that I find your company agreeable. It may be that she will make you my wife."

Certain that my uncle would never allow such a thing, I nodded and took his hand.

CHAPTER NINETEEN

Shelamzion

I sat next to Mother with my arms folded, my eyes on the shifting horizon outside the coach. I had not spoken since we parted from Cleopatra Thea and her son, hours and hours ago.

The wagon behind us now held more than our trunks; it also held gifts from the queen—fine gowns for Mother, a golden stylus and several richly embroidered tunics for Uncle, a trunkful of garments, and a Greek-speaking parrot for me. As we prepared to depart, the queen had ordered her servants to fill our carriage with aromatic flowers, and I was sick of their overpowering scent.

I wanted nothing to do with any of it, but I had no choice in the matter.

"I don't understand," I finally said, knowing my mother and uncle were already aware of my position. "I do not mean to be disrespectful, but I must ask why you agreed to this betrothal. The prince is a pagan. How can this marriage honor HaShem if my husband worships false gods?"

Mother's satisfied look shifted immediately to surprise, and

Uncle's brows shot up to his hairline. "How can you question my authority?" he asked, his jaw tightening. "I am not only your kinsman but also your high priest."

"Daughter!" Mother's rebuke held a thread of warning. "After all your uncle has done for us, how can you challenge his judgment?"

I stared, taken aback by her change of attitude. Until this trip, she had never uttered a hopeful word about my future, but apparently she had come to see me in a new light.

"I am not challenging," I said. "If you want me to marry the prince, I will obey. But I would like to know the reason behind such an unequal union."

"Such a question demonstrates willfulness and ingratitude," Uncle said, his face brightening to the color of a berry. "Consider this—out of all the royal women in the world, Cleopatra Thea, who hails from a long line of exalted Egyptian kings, chose you! You, who have no royal blood at all."

I stared at him, opinionated words rising to my tongue. *But neither do you!* I wanted to shout. *And how can you pretend otherwise?*

My studies had taught me that Israel *did* have a divinely ordained royal line, but it sprang from David and the tribe of Judah, not Levi. Yet my uncle had behaved like a king before Cleopatra Thea. He had accepted gifts from her like a king and had discussed uniting our nations. He allowed people to bow before him, people who were not Jews and need not show any sort of obeisance to a high priest. He was the spiritual leader of Israel, but HaShem was our King. How could Uncle have done those things?

I curled my hands into fists and refused to meet his gaze. Judas Maccabaeus and his brothers had given their lives to prevent Israel from becoming like the nations around us, but here we were, behaving just like the kings and queens of pagan nations. How could that be?

Did my uncle aspire to become king of Israel?

He did not fit the qualifications laid out in the Torah, but perhaps the tribe of Judah had no suitable candidates. After all, my uncle was high priest, and though he was a *cohen*, a descendant of Aaron, he was not a descendant of Zadok, as all high priests had been since the time of Solomon. The line of Zadok had been replaced, my tutor had explained, but not everyone in Judea thought it appropriate for other Levites— like my uncle—to be elevated to the high and holy position of high priest.

"If you will not answer my question about the marriage," I asked, frowning, "will you tell me why my kinsmen are high priests when they are not descended from the line of Zadok?"

Uncle folded his hands across the bulge at his midsection and studied me, his eyes narrowing. "Has your tutor been saying I should not be high priest? If he has, perhaps I should find someone else to teach you."

I shook my head, not wanting to get Josu Attis in trouble. In truth, I had learned much from him and appreciated his honest view of the world. "I read it for myself in the writings of the prophets."

"Then you should let a proper Torah teacher explain the situation. Reading the holy Scriptures without someone to adequately explain it could be . . . confusing."

"I don't find it confusing. Not often, at least. The other day I read the writings from the prophet Zechariah, who wrote that HaShem was going to send His servant, the Branch. Will He be our high priest or our king?"

Uncle glanced at Mother, then sighed and rested his elbow in the open window. "We are waiting for a king who was prophesied. One will come, a man who will sit on the throne of His father David, but until then, how are we to function in a world of kings and queens? Someone must speak for our people. Judas

Maccabaeus would not, but Jonathan did, and my father, Simon, as well, in the role of high priest. But these pagan nations do not understand what a high priest does, nor do they know HaShem. So yes, Shelamzion, I believe Israel must soon have a king."

"Will that king be you?"

"It will be as HaShem wills. And if HaShem wills that you marry Cleopatra Thea's son, then you shall, for the sake of your people."

I would, but in that moment I didn't feel at all willing. I shivered in revulsion as a spasm of disgust rose from my core.

I thought Uncle cared about me, but he had taken no thought for my feelings in the arrangement of this betrothal. I thought Uncle was proud of me, yet apparently he had given me a tutor because I would be a more valuable bride if I could converse about life outside my home. I thought Uncle loved me, and yet he was willing, even eager, to send me to a place far from my home and family.

Had I become as much a slave as Kissa?

I looked at him, wordlessly begging for some assurance of his affection. Instead he pressed his lips together and shifted in his seat to gaze out the window.

I knew he would not say anything else on the subject.

〰〰〰

The steady creaking of the carriage, combined with the dullness of the return journey, conspired to make my eyelids heavy. I leaned against the wall of the coach and allowed my weary mind to wander in the hazy state between wakefulness and sleep.

While in this shallow doze, I heard Uncle speak to my mother. "This betrothal serves its purpose for the moment," he said, his voice a low rumble, "but the girl is right—to actually give her to that prince would cause an uproar among our people. She is a Hasmonean, and he is a pagan."

122

"But Shelamzion is not well known among the people," Mother said. "She is not your daughter, so the news could be kept quiet. If sending her to Antioch serves a purpose for you, you should not be concerned about idle gossip. At least she will be a queen."

"Only time will tell what purpose it might serve," Uncle said. "Until your daughter begins to bleed, do what you can to prepare her for a life under public scrutiny. We will see what HaShem wills."

"John . . ." Mother hesitated.

"Yes?"

"If you had a daughter, would you betroth her to a Seleucid prince?"

I peered through the quivering lashes of one eye to see my uncle's response. He regarded Mother with a bland look, but the twitch at his right temple assured me that her question had rattled him. "If I had a daughter—" he paused and cleared his throat—"if I had a daughter, I would . . ." Trailing off, he shook his head. "Perhaps this is why HaShem has blessed me with sons only. But I would dearly love a daughter."

He sighed heavily, a false display of regret, for anyone could see how Uncle doted on his sons. He adored little Judah Aristobulus and Antigonus, and even now Alena was expecting another child. And though I was not experienced in the ways of the world, I knew that if Alena gave birth to a daughter, that little girl might be betrothed to another of Cleopatra Thea's sons, or a prince from some other kingdom.

In the end, I was not happy with the outcome of our trip to Antioch, but the venture opened my eyes to the width and breadth of the high priest's work. After our audience with Cleopatra Thea, I began to understand that Uncle's most urgent concerns lay not with the affairs of the Temple or even the administration of Judea, but with maintaining Judea's security in the world. Though he did not possess a crown or the title of king, he acted as our political representative before kings, queens, and emperors.

I understood now why dignitaries from Egypt and Tyre and Rome came to visit him. They were not coming to worship at the Temple; they were coming to negotiate. And the gifts that arrived at the palace were not offerings to HaShem; they were enticements to sweeten the political negotiations.

How could I have missed such an obvious reality? The trip to Antioch introduced me to a realm outside Jerusalem, a sphere of nations and kingdoms to which I had given little thought. And while I did not doubt that Uncle invited us to live with him because he sincerely wanted to care for his relatives, at that moment I also understood that he had seen an opportunity in our helplessness: Mother was a Hasmonean widow with a daughter. And daughters, once properly educated, trained, and groomed, could be valuable negotiating tools.

That was why I had been betrothed to a man with a trumpet of a nose. And why I would marry him once I began to bleed . . . unless HaShem had other plans.

I could only wait and see what HaShem would do in the months ahead. Being a young woman, I had no other choice.

CHAPTER TWENTY

Shelamzion

Kissa had just finished dressing me when we heard a shout from the palace courtyard. Hurrying to the window, we looked down and saw Alena's handmaid running toward the well, barking orders as she went.

"Her time has come," Kissa said, a wistful note in her voice. "All the servants will spend the day rushing to and from the mistress's bedchamber."

I looked at her, curious to know if Kissa yearned to be part of all the excitement, but another thought quickly shoved that notion aside—what if Alena birthed a girl? If John Hyrcanus finally had a daughter, to whom would she be promised as a bride? Betrothals sometimes took place when the girl was barely weaned, and marriages could occur as soon as the girl began to bleed.

I backed away from the window and imagined the reception hall, where Uncle was meeting with his advisors. Which kings needed placating and from whom did he need help? He might be considering the terms of his daughter's marriage even now. Perhaps he was even contemplating marrying his daughter to *my* betrothed prince.

I grabbed Kissa's arm. "Go help them," I said, ignoring the delighted smile that splashed across her face. "The minute the child is born, come back and tell me whether it is a boy or a girl."

She took a step toward the door, then turned back. "Are you sure you don't need me for anything?"

"I am going to practice my reading." When she hesitated, I lifted my arms and shooed her away. "Go! But don't forget—I need to know as soon as possible."

She left, and I picked up a scroll and tried to read the text. My Greek had greatly improved, though I could not keep my thoughts focused on the handwritten words.

Fortunately, at that moment Josu Attis came through the doorway. "It is good to see you reading," he said and greeted me with a respectful bow. "Your mother tells me you have been promised to a prince."

I lowered the scroll and made a face. "Forgive me if I am not exactly thrilled by the idea. The most impressive thing about Prince Grypus is his nose."

A smile flickered across the tutor's face. He pointed to the scroll. "What is that? Something useful, I hope."

"Plato." I lifted the scroll again. "I am trying to concentrate, but the house is filled with excitement today. My uncle's wife is giving birth to her third child."

"That explains why the doorkeeper was distracted." Josu sat on a stool and folded his arms. "What is Plato teaching you?"

"He says there are three kinds of people in any society, because people are tripartite. What does that mean?"

"Comprised of three parts. Plato believes humans are appetite, spirit, and reason. But I am not certain HaShem would agree. The Torah tells us that man is body and soul."

I considered his answer, then shrugged. "In any case, Plato says there are three types of people in a society—those who produce, like slaves, carpenters, masons, and farmers; those who protect, like soldiers; and those who govern. He says the producers align with the appetite of man, the protectors with the spirit of man, and those who govern with the reason of man."

Josu lifted a brow. "But is that absolute? Does not a farmer protect his crop? Does he not have a spirit? And does a mother, who produces children and food for her table, not protect and govern her children? I am not certain, Salome, that men can be so easily divided into categories."

"And what about women?" I tilted my head. "Where do women fit into all this?"

A smile flashed in his brown beard. "If only you could ask Plato. I would like to hear his answer."

A cry rang from the courtyard, and I hurried to the window. My uncle stood outside, both arms raised, his face turned toward heaven. "May HaShem be praised!" he shouted for the world to hear. "I have another son!"

Something inside me—I know not what—shriveled at his display of joy. What sort of announcement would he have made if Alena had delivered a girl?

I turned back to my tutor. "Another son for Uncle. That makes three."

Josu nodded. "The high priest is blessed indeed. May God bless his sons as he blessed the five courageous sons of Mattathias."

"I do not think," I said, settling onto a stool, "the five sons of Mattathias would have betrothed me to a pagan prince."

Josu made a face but held his tongue as I wearily considered Plato's treatise on the three types of men.

Chapter Twenty-One

Kissa

From the courtyard I glanced up and saw Shelamzion's face at her window. So she had heard the news. Another son for John Hyrcanus.

I would not go upstairs to tell her, for I had seen Josu Attis enter the house. Shelamzion was studying, which would distract her from her preoccupation with betrothals and marriages. Later, if she felt agreeable, she might share what she had learned or let me read one of her scrolls.

I stopped in the courtyard and looked around, searching for some task I could perform while I waited for the tutor to leave. The master did not like to see idle slaves, and neither did his foreman. I could always fill water jars and leave them by the back door. Or I could fetch a few honey cakes from the kitchen and set them on Shelamzion's bedside table. She always said that reading worked up an appetite.

I walked toward the kitchen but slowed my step when the front gates opened and a group of men entered, led by the master's foreman. The four men behind him were bound together with chains and rope. They had the look of Egyptians. I watched, clenching my hand until my nails bit into my palm.

Dropping into a well of memory, I saw myself in a similar line of slaves, hungry, stumbling forward, staring numbly at my surroundings. Until the day I was tied to another girl and led away, Egypt had been my world, my *home*, yet now it seemed nothing more than a collection of hazy images that ebbed and flowed like the Nile.

My gaze ran over the four new slaves. The first three were adults, strong and in the prime of life, while the fourth man was bent and had grizzled short hair. I squinted to bring him into better focus—the man was *old*. Had he been sold into slavery as an old man, or had he spent his life in service to someone else? If the latter, he must have done something to greatly offend his master.

My attention shifted to his skeletal shoulders and arms, then . . . his chest. A single eye stared back at me, an elongated eye with a narrow brow and a black pupil. The all-seeing eye of Horus.

I breathed deep and felt a jolt of memory, an image from my past life. My father had worn the eye of Horus on his chest.

I ran toward the new slaves, my heart racing as I approached the older man. I peered into his face and struggled to speak, but I could barely remember any of the words I had used as a child. "You—" I stammered, pointing at him. "Where from?" My gestures and baby talk elicited no response. "Me," I said, frantically tapping my own chest. "Kissa. I am Kissa."

Again, no response. The man only glanced at me, then lowered his gaze and continued trudging behind the others.

Engulfed by a wave of weariness and despair, I stopped walking and let them go. I was behaving like a crazy person. What were the odds that an enslaved father would end up in the same house as his daughter? The eye of Horus was a common image in Egypt; thousands of men tattooed it on their chests. That man could not be my father. The slave was far too old, and

surely my name would have elicited *some* spark of recognition
if I had once been his daughter . . .

I took a deep breath and felt a dozen emotions collide, chief
among them jealousy of my mistress. Her father was dead, but
she knew what had happened to him and she knew he had loved
her. He had not sold her into slavery and disappeared, leaving
her to wonder about him for the rest of her life.

I wandered to a shaded corner behind the house, leaned
against a stone wall, and went thoroughly to pieces.

After washing my face, I adopted the blank expression of
a slave and went into the house. The murmur of voices from
upstairs told me that Shelamzion was still studying with her
tutor, so I cast about for some work to do.

I knew I had been wrong to be jealous of Shelamzion, for
despite the differences in our station, we had much in common.
We were both fatherless girls, both helpless to control our situations, and both indebted to the high priest. Now that we were
approaching maturity, the five-year age difference mattered less
with every passing day.

I thought I would see if I could serve my mistress by serving
her mother. I found Sipporah sitting on the floor in her bedchamber, surrounded by mounds of fine linen. She was carefully
pulling threads from an edge of raw fabric. I didn't understand
what she was doing, but she looked like she needed help.

I entered the room and bowed. "Can I be of assistance, mistress?"

She glanced at me, then shook her head. "Ketura needs a
chiton," she said. "John Hyrcanus is hosting important people
at a banquet, and my daughter needs a new gown."

"You mean Shelamzion," I said, folding my hands. "I am
sure she would appreciate a—"

"Not her," Sipporah snapped, glaring at me. "Shelamzion has more than enough, while Ketura gets nothing! And she is the one who deserves more."

I should have quietly backed out of the room. I should have left the woman to her solitary undertaking and said nothing. But for so many years I had watched the woman belittle, ignore, and demean my young mistress, and in that moment I forgot my station.

"What is *wrong* with you?" I said, hissing the words through clenched teeth. "Why can't you see the value of the daughter who lives upstairs? She is a good girl, a clever girl, and the high priest adores her! More than that, he respects her, or are you so blind you cannot see it?"

Outside the house, a horse whickered, a child shouted, and water splashed in the fountain. Those sounds rushed to fill the astonished silence as Sipporah lowered the fabric and gaped at me like a woman who had just been knocked over by a charging ram.

I closed my eyes and prayed—to any god who would hear me—that she would not have me beaten.

"What did you say?" Her voice had gone soft with disbelief.

I adjusted my tone to sound more conciliatory. "Shelamzion is a good girl, a daughter you should be proud of. Yet you seem to ignore her at every opportunity."

The woman's hands began to tremble, and her eyes went damp with pain. "Shelamzion," she whispered, not looking at me, "was a mistake."

I stepped closer to better hear her. "What did you say?"

Sipporah's expression changed, memory making her eyes hard and her mouth tight. "I will tell you," she said firmly, "and then you will understand."

CHAPTER TWENTY-TWO

Shelamzion

C ome in, Salome."

I pushed the door open and stepped inside Alena's chamber. The new mother, as lovely as ever, sat in her bed, a swaddled infant in her arms. On the floor, six-year-old Judah Aristobulus and three-year-old Antigonus played with a set of wooden blocks.

As I walked past the older boys, the memory of my mother's suggestion that I marry Aristobulus made me groan. The boy had just stolen a block from his brother, and Antigonus was searching for it. In a moment he would scream.

"Come closer." Alena beckoned me with a smile. "See? Isn't he perfect?"

I stepped closer to the bed and leaned forward, trying to imagine those pinched features in an older child's face. The baby—what I could see of him beneath the wrappings—was as red as a rose, with small bumps on his forehead and a sharply pointed nose.

"Oh." I couldn't think of anything else to say.

"He's a good baby," Alena volunteered. "Hardly cries at

all—unlike those two over there. I think they cried for the first three months of their lives. But this one just sleeps and smiles. And eats. My, how he loves to eat."

I looked at the infant's little lips, which quivered in apparent anticipation of another meal. "Have you thought of a name?" I asked.

"Alexander Jannaeus," Alena answered. "*Alexander*, which is Greek for 'defender of man.' And *Jannaeus*, Hebrew for 'gift of God.'"

"And what will you call him, since he has such powerful names?"

Alena laughed. "Whichever name he likes best."

The baby lifted his pink eyelids, and his eyes seemed to focus on me. While Alena and I watched, his lips curved in a smile. Or was it a yawn?

"He likes you," Alena said and reached out to squeeze my shoulder. "I think he's going to love playing with his cousin Salome."

I bit my lip, unable to understand when I would ever have an occasion to play with this baby. I was fourteen, old enough to be married, and Uncle would soon send me to Antioch. This baby would probably grow up without knowing me at all.

But I was not so poorly mannered as to contradict Uncle's wife. So I smiled and patted Alena's hand. "If HaShem wills, perhaps we will become good friends."

In the summer of my sixteenth year, I awakened to find a smear of blood between my legs. I released a choked, desperate laugh at the sight—no longer could I argue that I was not ready to be married. I was no longer a girl but would soon be expected to marry and bear children.

I stepped over my sleeping handmaid and wet a piece of

linen, then sat on a stool and sighed as I washed my thigh. I knew I should tell Mother. She would tell Alena, who would tell Uncle, and he would make Cleopatra Thea aware that the promised fruit had finally ripened. Even if I said nothing, they would all figure it out when I did not go to dinner or join them in the garden. I would have to remain in my chamber for the next seven days, the time when I would be unclean.

Kissa woke when she heard me stirring. She sat up in the dim light of early dawn, and sympathy filled her eyes when she realized what I was doing. She took the soiled cloth from me, then pulled a basket from a trunk and showed me what she had prepared—short wooden sticks, not quite as long as my little finger, tightly wound with soft bits of lint and cotton fabric.

"Some women use pads made of wool," she said, her voice gentle as she handed me one of the sticks. "But Greek women wear these inside their bodies—I think you will prefer them."

I studied the item she placed in my hand. "Do you—?"

She nodded.

That morning I ruefully accepted my status as a mature woman. I spent the day studying in my chamber, then sent word that I would not be joining Uncle, Alena, and Mother for dinner for the next several nights. The women would understand why, and they would explain things to Uncle.

He would send a letter to Cleopatra Thea, discreetly telling her that I was ready to accept my promised husband.

<hr />

A few months later, my stomach clenched when a caravan from Antioch passed through the gates of the high priest's palace. The riders at the fore carried the Seleucid royal standard, so they might be bringing representatives from Cleopatra Thea . . . or even the queen herself.

And this visit might concern me.

I had been betrothed for three years, and I had not wasted those months. In addition to my regular studies, I asked Josu to find scrolls about Seleucia. I became an avid student of the empire's history, though what I read often horrified me. I learned that Seleucus, founder of the empire that bore his name, had been one of Alexander the Great's generals. Seleucus founded his capital city by ritual: a pagan priest gave an eagle, the bird of Zeus, a bite of sacrificial meat and set it free. The priests followed the flying eagle and established the capital at the point where the bird landed to eat.

I could not imagine living in a city founded on the whim of a bird.

Worse by far were the actions of Antiochus Epiphanes, the Seleucid king who had invaded Jerusalem, killed thousands of men, women, and children, and sacrificed a pig to Zeus. Not satisfied with defiling our Temple and the holy altar, he then commanded that we Jews could no longer refrain from eating pork, circumcise our children, or observe the Sabbath. He wanted us to become Greek—speak Greek, worship like Greeks, and even think like Greeks.

Would Grypus expect that of me if we were married?

Kissa knew of my misgivings and would often try to comfort me by appealing to my appreciation for creature comforts. "Think of the fine garments you will have as queen," she would say while doing my hair. "Think of living in that wonderful palace! You will have more than one handmaid; you can have as many as you want."

"What would I do with more than one? And how many tunics and himations does a woman need?"

"Princess Salome," she said, teasing me. "Queen Salome. You should get used to that name."

"Hush," I said. "That is not useful."

I knew Uncle had written the queen to say I was ready for

marriage. We had heard no response, unless this caravan brought her reply. Had she sent courtiers to escort me to Antioch?

I gripped Kissa's hand and bade her sit with me until we knew something certain. Until then I would have to wait until Uncle welcomed the riders, saw to their comfort, and entertained them in an official audience. Then he might send for me, or he might wait until the next morning when his head would be clearer and his thoughts untainted from wine.

While we waited, I looked through my belongings and considered which things I should take with me to Antioch and which I should leave behind. I would take all my scrolls, for I did not think I would find any Hebrew writings in Cleopatra Thea's palace. I would leave my tunics, for they were not fine enough for a prince's wife. I would give the few pieces of jewelry I owned to my mother. And I would take Kissa, for I could not imagine life in a strange land without a friend by my side.

We did not hear anything from my uncle that night or the next day. I spent hours pacing in my chamber and sent Kissa to wait outside the reception hall in hopes that she might overhear some news. Every hour I'd send for her, only to hear that she had heard nothing about the representatives from Antioch.

My mother was nearly as tense as me. During our years of waiting she had resurrected the hopes she cherished for Ketura. The weight of them now rested on my head, and the burden made me uncomfortable.

My unease shifted to a different kind of anxiety when Kissa and I watched the Seleucid riders depart, presumably traveling back to Antioch. What had transpired, and why hadn't my uncle kept me informed? I was betrothed to the prince, yet I had not heard a single word from my guardian.

An hour after the Seleucid contingent departed, a slave came to invite Mother and me to dinner with Uncle and Alena. The formal invitation made my heart congeal into a small lump of terror. I dressed carefully and tried to remain calm beneath Kissa's ministering hands.

As we reclined at dinner, my knees trembling beneath my tunic, Uncle cleared his throat and announced that Demetrius of Seleucia was dead. Cleopatra Thea now ruled the empire as a widow.

"She intends to remain unmarried," Uncle said, looking directly at me. "She has named her son as her co-ruler."

I stared at the food on the table and tried to sort through my jumbled thoughts. Seleucia no longer had a king? The kingdom that had once dominated and terrorized Judea would be ruled by a woman?

I saw bewilderment in my mother's eyes and knew she longed to ask the question uppermost in my mind. "What happened to the king?" I asked, knowing I would be forgiven the blunt query.

Uncle gave Alena a pointed look, then drew a deep breath. "After returning to Cleopatra Thea, Demetrius announced his intention to invade Egypt, overthrow his queen's family, and become pharaoh." He gave me a rueful smile. "The sordid tale is not fit for your young ears, but the king was killed in his foolish effort. The queen sent emissaries to apprise me of the situation, along with a message. In short, she said she was no longer willing to be handed from one man to another. She will rule without a husband, and she believes the people will support her."

"Why did she make her son a co-ruler?" Mother asked, her voice unusually shrill. "She doesn't intend to marry *him*, does she?"

Uncle blew out a breath. "I have heard of such strange marriages in other lands, but no, she does not intend to marry her son. Yet a pretender to the throne, one called Zabinas, tried to instigate a revolt, and she knew some of her people would demand a king who could fight if necessary. So she named Grypus co-regent, aware that he was skilled enough to pick up a sword and satisfy her people."

"I have heard," Alena said, reaching for bread as a servant offered a tray, "that Egypt is ruled by a queen, her brother-husband, and their daughter."

Uncle nodded. "The woman you mentioned is Cleopatra Thea's mother, and the daughter is Cleopatra Thea's sister. That sort of union is unprecedented, even for Egypt. Such marriages would never be allowed in Judea."

"Tripartite," I murmured.

Uncle arched his brow. "What did you say?"

I felt a blush heat my cheeks. "Tripartite—three parts. It's something I learned."

"Indeed." Uncle cleared his throat again. "Which brings me to other news, Salome Alexandra."

His use of my full name set off alarm bells in my head. I glanced at Mother and saw that her hand had risen to her throat.

"In order to improve relations with her Egyptian family," Uncle said, folding his hands, "Cleopatra Thea arranged for her niece to marry Grypus. Part of the marriage contract included much-needed military support for the queen's defense against Zabinas. Apparently it was a successful bargain, for Cleopatra Thea is secure and Zabinas is dead. It seems the hook-nose prince has poisoned him."

I stared into empty space. The prince . . . *my* prince had married an Egyptian princess. *She* would be his queen, not me. I didn't know whether to shout for joy or weep with my mother.

"What about the other son?" Mother asked. "The elder son, Seleucus?"

Uncle's expression went grim. "Dead."

Mother gasped. "How?"

"The courtiers did not say this, but I have heard rumors. They say the queen killed him because he was conspiring against her."

Mother sank back to her couch, her face darkening with unreadable emotions.

"So you are free, my dear." Alena reached out to pat my shoulder. "We will soon find you a better husband."

I swallowed the lump that had lodged in my throat. "I am not disappointed." I looked up to assure her. "I did want to please all of you, but I did not like him, and I could not see how the marriage would bring honor to HaShem. But did he not want to marry me?" My voice rose in an unflattering squeak. "Did he find some fault in me?"

"No, child," Alena said. "Not at all."

"She is not beautiful," Mother said. "Ketura was far more suited—"

"Ketura is not here," Uncle interrupted, his voice curt. "HaShem called her to be with Him, and then He blessed Salome Alexandra with beauty, cleverness, and a heart that seeks after righteousness. Do not question the sovereign plans of Adonai."

Mother snapped her mouth shut and lowered her gaze.

"The fault does not lie in you, Salome," Uncle said, turning to me. "The fault lies in those who cannot be happy with the territory HaShem has allotted them. Ambition and power poison their minds, and they will do anything to attain more— even break an honorable betrothal."

A thought, disloyal but apt, raised its head. What right had my uncle to accuse Cleopatra Thea of political manipulation? He had arranged a dishonorable betrothal in an attempt to gain political favor, yet HaShem had thwarted him.

I looked down and wiped my damp palms on my chiton. For three years I had waited . . . for nothing. By the time Cleopatra Thea received Uncle's message about my readiness for marriage, she was likely too embroiled in putting down a revolt and murdering her son to do anything about it.

In any case, HaShem had spared me from that bloody palace. Blessed be the name of the Lord.

And yet . . . I had been rejected. Abandoned. And now I was well past the age when girls were promised to bridegrooms. What was I supposed to do with my life if I did not find a husband?

I had trusted Uncle, who kept insisting that he had plans for me. His first plan had not come to fruition, so he would have to come up with another.

And I would have no choice but to trust him.

"I am happy," I said, looking around the circle, "to wait until you find someone more suitable. But the life of a queen"—I shuddered—"is not a life I would freely choose."

I smiled so they would not think me upset at this abrupt change in my future, then bit my lip and forbade myself to shed any tears.

Chapter Twenty-Three

Kissa

Shelamzion did not need to tell me what had happened at dinner—I had heard everything from the hallway where I eavesdropped with several other slaves. I heard the uncertainty in her voice when she said she would be content to wait until the high priest found another man for her to marry. I heard her uncle reprimand Sipporah, and I had heard love and comfort in Alena's words to my young mistress.

I helped Shelamzion prepare for bed, removing the pins from her hair and then combing through the wavy strands that had been braided and sewn into the elaborate style noblewomen favored. When her long locks hung freely down her back, I helped her into the linen tunic she wore to bed, then waited until she was snug beneath her blanket.

Ordinarily I would have blown out the lamp and lain down to sleep on my pallet, but not tonight. Instead, I sat on the edge of the bed and regarded my mistress, who had been unusually quiet since returning from dinner.

Now, unwinding in the anticipation of sleep, she regarded me with heavy-lidded eyes. "You know what my uncle told me tonight?"

I pressed my hands together. "Yes, I heard everything."

"Part of me is glad to know we will not be going to Antioch, while another part—"

"You should not feel hurt," I hastened to assure her. "From what I have seen and heard, royal families marry for political reasons, not for love. Perhaps this is your God's way of preserving your life, or perhaps he will bring you a better man—one you might actually favor."

Shelamzion's mouth twisted in wry amusement. "All my life I have heard stories about how deeply Jacob loved Rachel even before they married. Yet I was betrothed to a man I don't think I could ever love—not like that, in any case. How could I love a man who did not love HaShem?"

"You see?" I smiled. "Surely this is for the best."

"You will not miss living in a king's palace?"

I laughed. "I will not. Nor will I miss having to weave a crown into your hair every day."

Her smile faded. "Mother was disappointed by the news. Finally her daughter was about to become a queen, but then . . ." Tears glistened in her eyes as she shrugged the words away.

As I sat there, watching my mistress deal with an undeserved pain, I realized that Shelamzion's God had shown her great mercy by giving her an aunt and uncle who provided the things she should have received from her parents. She had always hardened her heart against her mother's indifference, but perhaps it was time she knew the truth.

"Mistress," I said, choosing my words with great care, "for years I have watched you with your mother. Many times I have heard her say cruel things, but mostly I have suffered with you when she remained silent. So many times she should have complimented you, encouraged you, or congratulated you for earning praise from your tutor and the high priest—"

"You need say no more." She turned away, rolling onto her side to face the wall.

"I have learned something that might help you understand your mother better . . . and I will tell you if you wish to hear it."

A Sabbath stillness filled the room, with only the quickened beating of my heart to disturb it. After a seemingly endless interval, my mistress turned from the wall and sat up, her wide eyes meeting mine. "I would know . . . what you know."

I glanced down at my hands, searching for a way to ease into the conversation. "One day I found your mother in her room—she said she was making a gown for Ketura. Something came over me, and words flew off my tongue. I don't remember exactly what I said, but I wanted to know why she favored your sister and ignored you."

Shelamzion stared at me, her face a blank mask.

I hesitated, afraid she would tell me to be quiet, but she remained upright, her arms wrapped around her knees, her eyes intent on my face.

"Your mother told me she was working in the field one day," I went on, "because when they were first married, she and your father were poor, so she had to glean the corners of the fields. A man came from out of nowhere and attacked her. She tried to run, but she could not get away. She screamed, but there was no one to hear."

I averted my eyes, unable to look directly at my innocent mistress as I told the rest of the story. "Your mother already had one daughter, and a few weeks later she knew she would have another child. Finally, months later, you were born. And every time she looked at you, she was reminded of the man in the field."

"Why?" Though Shelamzion's face remained blank, the word came out ragged. "Did I—do I *look* like him?"

"I do not know the answer to that. But your mother said

the greatest tragedy was that your father loved you even more than your sister. He made much of you, parading you around the village on his shoulders, despite . . . despite everything."

Shelamzion frowned and looked away. "She told him?"

"I asked your mother the same question. She said she did not, for what good would it have done? But every time she looked at you, she remembered that afternoon, and she would never forget."

Shelamzion nodded, her expression grim. I remained silent, allowing her time to consider the implications of this unfortunate truth.

Finally she turned to me. "She can't be certain that the other man is my father," she said, her eyes hardening. "Two sisters can look completely different in any family."

"They can," I agreed. "Your mother cannot know for certain whether or not you are the child of the man who attacked her."

"But she believes I am," Shelamzion said, her voice breaking. "She will always believe I am."

CHAPTER TWENTY-FOUR

Shelamzion

What can I say of the years that followed? I became a woman-in-waiting. Every time the gates of the high priest's compound opened, I looked out the window to see if one of the visitors might be a young man of marriageable age. Several were, but never did my uncle send for me or otherwise make an introduction. As far as I knew, no marriage contracts were presented to him; no one broached the subject of a betrothal or wedding.

I was beginning to wonder if Uncle had forgotten that an unmarried virgin lived beneath his roof.

My mother did not forget, but neither did she hold any hope for me. Within a few months of learning that the Seleucid prince had married someone else, Mother returned to mourning Ketura. Armed with new knowledge about her emotional background, I tried to be sympathetic and understanding, but her devotion to the dead went too far.

Despite the prohibition against graven images, and probably inspired by the statues we had seen in Antioch, Mother commissioned a sculptor to create a statue for the vestibule of our small house. "But, mistress," the sculptor protested, "how will I know what your daughter looked like?"

Mother gave him a demure smile. "Your task is simple—create the most beautiful face you can imagine, and you will have Ketura."

Three months later, a life-sized and—I thought—idealized statue of my dead sister greeted visitors to our home. Fortunately, we did not receive many visitors. If anyone was taken aback or offended at the graven image occupying the entry, they said nothing of it. Even my uncle, who paid the sculptor's bill, did not rebuke or deny my mother.

One afternoon I asked Josu Attis why Uncle had become tolerant of what had once been considered intolerable. "People often soften as they grow older," he said. "I do not know the high priest well, but it is possible he wants your mother to be content. If the statue comforts her, perhaps it is easier for him to allow it than to endure perpetual mourning."

"Jacob said he would mourn his son Joseph until he went to the grave," I said.

Josu smiled. "The Torah has set limits for every stage of grief: three days for weeping, seven for lamentation, and thirty for abstaining from laundered garments and from cutting the hair. The sages say that one should not grieve too much for the dead, and whoever grieves excessively is really grieving for someone else." He narrowed his eyes. "For whom does your mother really grieve?"

The answer came to me at once. "For herself."

The year after Cleopatra Thea assumed control of her kingdom, Alena gave birth to Absalom, a chubby and ruddy baby with the thick black hair of his historical namesake. She smiled down at her baby and gently smoothed a cowlick at his hairline. "My sister has just had a child, as well." She looked up at me. "A little girl. They are calling her Salina Alexandra."

"Pretty name," I said. "But I am sure she does not have as much hair as Absalom."

Alena laughed. "I am sure you are right."

Three years later she gave birth to a fifth son, whom she named Philo Elias. When I visited the infant for the first time, I thought I had never seen a baby so small or with skin so pale. The boy's flesh seemed almost translucent, and his cheeks were as white as alabaster.

Elias eventually gained strength and grew into a robust boy. And just as Aristobulus and Antigonus were as close as a tree and its bark, Elias and Absalom became inseparable.

One afternoon another group of riders from Seleucia arrived at the high priest's house. From my window, Kissa and I recognized the fluttering banners the horsemen carried, except the design had been altered slightly.

At dinner that night, I learned the purpose of the Seleucid delegation. "King Antiochus VIII—Grypus—has sent word of his mother's death," Uncle announced.

"Sad," Mother said. "She seemed such a strong woman. Was she ill?"

Uncle shifted on his couch. "The official cause of death is illness. But I paid one of the messengers twenty pieces of silver for the truth."

Alena arched a brow. "And that is . . . ?"

His glance shifted to me. "You should be thanking HaShem that you are not married to that pagan. Do you remember how he walked with you in the garden?"

I nodded, my memories of that unpleasant hour still crisp and clear.

"The courtier told me Grypus had begun to plot against his mother. Realizing that her son was conspiring against her, Cleopatra Thea prepared two servings of wine, one containing poison. She invited her son to drink, but he switched the cups. His mother drank the poisoned cup and died within minutes."

I couldn't stop a gasp. That clever, powerful woman had fallen victim to her son's plotting?

Alena pressed her palm to her chest. "I can't imagine anything more horrible than being betrayed by your own son."

"Our sons are nothing like that prince." Uncle reached for her hand. "Grypus has no heart and no pity. A tragic situation, indeed, but still a cause for praise because our Salome Alexandra was not involved."

He looked at me and lifted his cup. "Let us praise HaShem for keeping you here with us. His ways are marvelous, and today we have learned just how wondrous they are."

I smiled, lifting my cup as well, though something in my soul shriveled when my mother did not.

In the summer Cleopatra Thea died, I entered my twentieth year . . . and realized I was far too old to be a blushing bride. My mother grew thin with fretting over whether I would ever be allowed to marry, but whenever she put the question to my uncle, he would clear his throat and make excuses, finally resorting to a simple answer: "I am saving her for the perfect man, and I have not yet found him."

Was I upset by this? Not in the least. My unfulfilled betrothal to Grypus of Seleucid had taught me that contentment in the unmarried state was vastly preferable to marrying someone who might poison me to marry his sister.

I had no reason to complain about my life. Some women might have perished from boredom if they found themselves in my situation, but I had Kissa for company, my teachers for enlightenment, and Jerusalem for my home.

And oh, how I came to love the Holy City! Jerusalem prospered mightily during that time. The difficult days of hunger and war drifted into distant memory, and we dwelt in peace and safety. Most mornings Kissa and I would rise early, cover our heads with a himation, and slip away from the high priest's palace, venturing into various districts to explore the city. We loved the Valley of the Cheesemakers, where homes leaned against each other as if the newer buildings had forced their elders to jostle up against one another. The pungent odors of ripening cheese made us hold our noses, and we frequently had to refuse generous offers from merchants who, supposing us to be wealthy housewives, begged us to try their wares. We reveled in our anonymity and wandered as carefree as butterflies.

The fabric district had its own unique sights and scents. The colors of richly dyed fabrics—deep blue, ripe red, stunning yellow, and royal purple—never failed to thrill. We would linger at the booths and run our hands over the fabrics, admiring textures and close weaves. "You are so skilled," I told more than one woman at her loom. "I could never weave something like this."

My praise was always sincere. I had learned many things in my uncle's household—how to converse with learned scholars, how to appreciate sumptuous foods, and at least thirty-three ways to drape my himation. Alena had taught me the names of more than fifty different styles in wearing one's hair, all of them made popular by fashionable Greek ladies. And Josu Attis had taught me to appreciate the thoughts of Plato, Socrates, Euclid, and Juvenal, a young Roman poet. I particularly liked Juvenal for posing the question of who could be trusted with authority and power. "Who will watch the watchers?" he asked.

Who, indeed?

Of all my studies, I loved Torah study best. Most girls were not able to study at their father's knees, for they were expected to help their mothers keep house. Older boys could sit before the Great Sanhedrin, which, when it was not functioning as a *bet din*, or house of judgment, was a *bet midrash*, a house of study. But women could not sit before the Sanhedrin, so my uncle finally kept his promise and hired an esteemed Torah teacher, Simeon ben Shetah, to teach me.

At our first meeting, Simeon ben Shetah surprised me with his appearance. He was far younger than I expected, probably only a few years older than me. He was also attractive, with piercing eyes, but unlike most religious scholars, he had a quick smile and a relaxed demeanor. If he had been disappointed to learn that his pupil would be the high priest's ward, he disguised his feelings well.

"But why," he asked when we met, "does a young woman want to study Torah?"

"Because I have no husband to teach me," I answered, "and no father. So you, Simeon ben Shetah, must be as a brother to me and teach me the Law of the Lord."

He smiled at that, and may have been quietly relieved to know my interest had nothing to do with a desire to marry a scholar. Indeed, by that time I had little desire to marry at all.

One afternoon Simeon brought me several scrolls—sacred writings from a group of Jews in Alexandria. They had translated the Hebrew Torah into Greek and called it the *Septuagint*, the Translation of the Seventy. He explained that many Jews in Egypt could not speak Hebrew, as Koine Greek was the language of that city.

"I think you will enjoy reading these Scriptures," he said, placing one of the scrolls in my hand. "The sacred writings take on a different flavor in Greek."

I frowned. "Are the words trustworthy?"

"Do you think seventy devout teachers would give us anything less?"

And so I read . . . and discovered he was right. The sacred words did have a different flavor in Greek, but they were still like honey to my soul.

Simeon taught me to do more than read and memorize the Torah. He pointed out patterns and analogies and waited for me to discover others on my own. After he pointed out the similarities between Abram's and Israel's sojourns in Egypt—they both went down due to famine, they both witnessed plagues upon the Egyptians, and they both left Egypt with great wealth—he asked me to find others within the first book of the Pentateuch.

Within moments I spotted a pattern in the stories of Noah and Moses. "They were both saved from drowning by an ark," I said, my excitement growing with every word. "Both arks were impervious to water, and both men saved their families."

Simeon smiled. "*Ma'asei avot, siman l'banim*," he said. "The deeds of the fathers are a sign to the sons." He chuckled at my obvious enthusiasm for learning. "And they say women are temperamentally light-headed."

My education continued on other fronts, too. Through my uncle and the emissaries who regularly visited him, I became aware of important events in other parts of the world. I learned that the Romans had built two walls at the outer reaches of their empire—the Antonine Wall in a faraway place called Caledonia, and Hadrian's Wall, across a section of a distant land called Britannia.

My uncle and I would often discuss these things at dinner while Alena listened, Mother dozed, and the boys fidgeted on their couch. One night I told Uncle that I found the Roman system of government intriguing. In a world of kings and high priests, they were governed by a Senate and two consuls, men who were elected each year.

"The Romans have had their problems," Uncle said. "Men are fallible, and some men are corrupt."

As are some priests, I wanted to say, but I did not want him to think I was referring to anything he had done. In truth, I never asked about Temple activities because I did not want to meddle in his affairs. Knowing that many priests were strongly opposed to women studying Torah, I was content to study quietly.

I shared what I had learned with Kissa, who would listen as I read or wrote out a lesson for my teacher. Her hands were always about some bit of housework—mending, cleaning, or rolling cotton around twigs—and I was never sure how much of my scholarly babbling she retained. Occasionally she would sigh and ask, "And this is important—why, exactly?"

I would laugh and explain that I found joy in learning. If no one ever asked me about Plato's three types of men or patterns in the Torah, I did not care. Knowledge itself was a secret treasure made all the more precious because most women did not possess it.

In my twenty-seventh year—the twenty-second year of my uncle's tenure as high priest—he undertook a military campaign in the north. Since his two eldest sons did everything together, he placed twenty-year-old Aristobulus and seventeen-year-old Antigonus in charge of the siege against Samaria.

Our dinner conversations shifted away from Torah and toward plans for war, and the frequent talk of tactics and siege warfare made me shudder. Were the Samaritans not our relatives? Why were we warring against them?

But the campaign commenced, and the sons of John Hyrcanus led the siege. The Samaritans should have been easily defeated, but they received support from the Seleucid king, Antiochus Cyzicenus, half brother to Grypus and ruler of half the empire. After a year, the Seleucid army withdrew, and the high priest's army overran Samaria and destroyed the Samaritan temple at Gerizim.

Notably, for the first time in history, the people of a conquered territory were forced to adopt our Jewish customs and worship. Those who would not convert were enslaved.

The situation bothered me a great deal. Was this not what happened to us when Antiochus Epiphanes overran Judea? He profaned our Temple and demanded that we worship Zeus and abandon our Jewish Law. Those who refused were executed.

I began to think I had been spending too much time with Simeon ben Shetah, for the pattern was all too easy to spot.

I did not agree with my uncle's decision, and yet it was not my place to question him. I could think of only one reason why he felt compelled to attack Samaria in the first place: territory. Judea had been a small nation when Judas Maccabaeus led the revolt. Later, his brother Jonathan conquered lands to the east and west, enlarging our territory from the Great Sea in the east to Perea in the west. After Jonathan died, Simon conquered additional territory, but not nearly as much as his predecessor.

Now my uncle was doing his best to claim additional territory for Israel, and I suspected his motivation was the promise HaShem gave Abraham: *"I give this land to your seed, from the river of Egypt to the great river, the Euphrates River."* Adonai had promised that we would possess the lands presently occupied by Philistines, Idumeans, Nabateans, Pereans, Phoenicians, and Itureans. Uncle seemed determined to reclaim every inch of land promised to Israel by HaShem, going back many generations before him.

Of all the things I learned in my time of waiting for marriage, perhaps most important were the stories I learned about my ancestors. Mother would often be overcome with nostalgia for the life we had known in Modein, so Uncle would entertain her by telling stories about "the hammerhead" Judas Maccabaeus; Simon, the wise brother; Eleazar, the son who had been crushed by an elephant; Johanan, the eldest who bred fine horses; and Jonathan, the son who had married Eleazar's widow. I learned how the Maccabees purified the Temple after the desecration wrought by Antiochus Epiphanes. As Uncle told the story, he mentioned how the Maccabees had refused to wear Greek hats or wrestle naked in the gymnasium like so many others who adored all things Greek.

When I heard this, I looked around in confusion. When he was not wearing his ritual vestments, Uncle dressed in the Greek style, as did everyone I knew. He did not visit the gymnasium or wear a Greek hat, but he embraced other Greek entertainments with enthusiasm, as did his sons. As did Mother, Alena, and I.

"Why do we wear Greek clothing and read Greek writers when Mattathias and his five sons would not?" I asked.

Uncle thought a moment. "In those days," he finally said, "to love the Greeks meant despising your heritage. Some men even went so far as to attempt undoing their circumcisions. But now it is clear that we can admire certain Greek attributes *and* still keep the Law. If we can be true to the Law in spirit, then what we wear and do matters little."

While I understood his reasoning, I knew others would disagree. I had met a group of men who came regularly to visit the high priest. They wore simple white robes, grew long untrimmed beards, and refused to curl their hair in the Greek style. They called themselves Essenes, "the Doers."

"We are the doers of Torah," I heard one of them say. "We not only hear it and talk about it, we *do* it."

Though I could not help but admire their wholehearted devotion to the Law, my uncle had little patience for the Essenes. "They are too literal," he said when I mentioned them at dinner one night. "They do not understand that the world has changed, and we must change with it. Judas Maccabaeus said we should not keep the Sabbath if we had to defend ourselves from the enemy, so we made an exception to the Law. If we had not, we would not be alive today."

"I understand," I said, "yet I cannot help but admire the Essenes. They are resolute in their devotion to HaShem."

"As am I," Uncle said, smiling at me. "As are you. And one day that devotion will be your reward, Shelamzion. You will see."

⌇⌇⌇⌇⌇⌇

One afternoon Mother and I met Alena and Uncle in the courtyard to welcome a delegation from Alexandria. Uncle said the caravan was certain to be flamboyant and colorful, so we sat beneath a pavilion while servants kept the air moving with wide, plumed fans.

Uncle was correct. A line of trumpeters came through the gate first. As soon as they stepped into the courtyard they halted, planted their feet, and released a string of shrill blasts that startled the livestock and delighted us. Though I knew the Alexandrians were as Greek as Aristotle, they wore the pleated linen kilts and striped headdresses of ancient Egypt. Seeing them attired in such a manner reminded me of Joseph, who had risen from the darkness of that pagan kingdom and saved Israel.

My pulse quickened. Could I find a parallel story in the Scriptures?

Uncle stood as a smaller wagon entered, this one filled with little girls who tossed pink-and-white petals in his direction. The sight made me smile and brought a glint of pleasure to my uncle's eye. I leaned toward him, about to inquire about the girls, and saw his mouth twist, his eyes narrow, and all color leave his face as he clutched at the neckline of his robe. I peered into the courtyard, certain that some assassin had suddenly sprung from the approaching wagon, but all I could see was the group of wide-eyed girls.

"Uncle? What is it?"

Alena was at his side in an instant. "Sipporah—send for the physician!"

Mother hurried away as Alena and I supported the staggering high priest. We would have helped him to a chair, but

155

his legs gave way, causing him to crumple and fall. I sent Kissa for water and a basin, then commanded the slaves to fan my uncle, for large drops of sweat had pearled on his forehead and upper lip. His hands were wet too, as were his arms, and even the skin at his throat.

A moment later, Kissa ran to us with linen and a basin. I dipped the cloth in cool water and applied it to Uncle's forehead and face. He did not look at me but kept his gaze fixed upward, as if he expected the roof of the pavilion to blow away and HaShem to be waiting on the other side.

Recovering from her shock, Alena ordered several servants to carry Uncle to his bedchamber. Knowing that he was in good hands, I walked out to welcome the delegation from Alexandria and told them the high priest would receive them another day.

Then I joined the family upstairs in the hallway. Judah Aristobulus and Antigonus had come to the house and taken over the business of fussing over their father. They ordered servants about and made a great show of shouting at each other, but in the end, all any of us could do was wait.

After the physician conducted a private examination, he stepped into the hallway and announced that John Hyrcanus had suffered pain in his heart and lungs. "He needs rest," he said, looking at Alena. "He must remain inside, out of the heat, and his strength must not be taxed."

While Uncle's sons shouted questions at the physician, I glanced at Mother and wondered what we would do if Uncle died. Would we have to leave our home? Would we go back to Modein?

Mother's lips went thin as she turned toward Judah Aristobulus, Uncle's firstborn. If my uncle died, Judah would likely become the high priest and leader of Israel. Antigonus would undoubtedly assist him, for I could not imagine one without the other.

But neither could I imagine Judea without John Hyrcanus.

CHAPTER TWENTY-FIVE

Kissa

While the high priest's family fretted over his health, I went down to visit members of the delegation from Alexandria. They had set up tents in the courtyard, and the cook had provided them with food. The little girls were playing games on the paving stones while the adults paced, talked, and searched the sky for omens.

One man recognized me as a member of the priest's household. "Is there any word?" he asked, lifting his voice above the others'. "Is the man dying or will we be able to see him?"

I shook my head, unwilling and unable to give him an answer. I walked on by and soon spotted a woman alone—probably mother to some of the girls. She was sitting on a blanket, chewing on the ends of her hair and watching the girls play.

I knelt down beside her. "Greetings," I said in Greek. "I wanted to see if you need anything from the house."

She blinked in surprise, then smiled. "Kind of you to offer. If you have any soft beds, they would do."

I blew out a breath. "I'm not sure about beds, but I'll see if I can find some pallets and pillows. Is everything else as it should be?"

The woman shrugged. "We weren't supposed to stay overnight, but the gods are going to do what they do, right? If they decide to strike a man down, nothing can be done about it."

"I suppose not." Why couldn't I get to the point? I had left my mistress to come here, and now I didn't know what to say. "You are from Alexandria, correct?"

The woman blinked again. "Yes."

"Did you ever live in Memphis?"

"That's Egyptian territory."

"I know. I was born there."

Her painted brows shot up to her hairline. "How did you get here?"

I sighed. "Slave caravan."

She smiled, displaying a gap where a front tooth should have been. "I'd say you have done all right, ending up in a grand place like this."

I forced a smile. "I was wondering . . . I know it is unlikely, but do you know anyone from Memphis?"

The woman's mouth twisted. "Come now, slave. Memphis is a world away from Alexandria."

I drew a deep, shaking breath and nodded. "I know. Still, I thought perhaps—"

"I might know your lover? Your brother or sister?"

I shook my head. "I thought perhaps HaShem had heard my prayers. But I should have known better."

She snorted with the choking glee of a woman who seldom laughs. "You thought—ho, that's rich."

I stood and gave her a friendly wave. "I'll ask about the pallets. I'm sure the overseer will be out shortly to offer whatever help he can."

I walked away, painfully aware that the woman was still laughing at my foolishness.

CHAPTER TWENTY-SIX

Shelamzion

Over the next few weeks I did not see much of my uncle. He spent many days either in his bedchamber or his reception hall. When I did spot him, he moved like an old man—hunched forward, head down, his usual broad gait reduced to mincing steps as servants supported him, one on each side.

He slept late every morning, often not accepting visitors until the sun had passed its zenith. The visitors he did see were fellow priests and leaders of the community. He had no time for me, and little for his wife and sons.

I told myself he was not trying to snub me—after all, he had been extremely ill, and the sudden attack had frightened all of us. He was trying to follow his physician's recommendation and rest as much as he could. When he had time for family, it was only natural he would want to see his wife and his sons before anyone else. Who would expect him to take time for a niece who was not really a niece?

But one afternoon Uncle sent for me. My heart lifted at the news, for surely this meant his health had improved. I wore a new tunic for the occasion and had Kissa arrange my hair in a style I knew he liked. I was eager to discuss the latest commentaries I had read and get his opinion on the authors' views. Perhaps he would invite me to dine with him and Alena, and we would debate and laugh as we had in former, happier days.

When I stepped into the reception hall, I found that we would not be speaking alone. Alena sat by Uncle's side, and my mother stood a few steps away. All three of them wore small, tight smiles and focused intently on my face.

"Salome Alexandra," Uncle began, "have I not said that I would not give you in marriage until I found the perfect man?"

"You have said so many times, Uncle. So many times that I am perfectly content to remain in your household as long as you wish me to stay."

"I have found the man, and it is time for you to be married."

I blinked hard and glanced at the women. Mother's smile looked as tight as a bowstring, while Alena's had gone soft with pleasure. Uncle was no longer smiling but appeared completely sure of himself.

"I am your servant," I said, dipping my head in a sign of respect. "May I know who this man is?"

Uncle lifted his chin. "Our own Alexander Jannaeus. I have already written the *ketubbah*, which specifies the amount you and your mother will receive in the event of divorce or our son's death. You will be well provided for, Shelamzion. And you will be good for him."

"Jonathan?" The boy's pet name rolled across my tongue in a slip of surprise. Uncle's third son was barely fifteen.

I turned and looked at my mother through narrowed eyes. Had she been so desperate for me to be married that she proposed this idea? I did not want to marry a boy. I had nothing against the lad, but at twenty-nine, how could I respect a man who had barely reached manhood? I could understand why

Uncle and Alena might desire such a marriage—we were from the same bloodline and I was unquestionably a virgin, having spent every night of my life under a family member's chaperonage. I might have been less surprised had Uncle wished me to marry his firstborn.

"What of Judah Aristobulus?" I asked. "He is a mature man and is only seven years my junior."

"Judah has been betrothed already," Uncle said. "To Salina Alexandra."

I clamped my mouth shut, stung by what clearly amounted to a rejection. I knew Salina from family gatherings; she was the great-granddaughter of Maccabees warrior Jonathan and his wife, Ona, and her mother was Alena's sister. Apparently Uncle thought Salina was more suited than I to being a high priest's wife. Furthermore, she was younger and more beautiful, not having spent more than twenty years waiting for a husband.

I covered my mouth and turned toward the back wall, unwilling for any of them to see the storm of humiliation and resentment that had to be evident on my face.

"Daughter," Mother said, a touch of irritation in her voice, "you have lived twenty-nine years unmarried, and the high priest is offering you his son. Take the offer and be happy. Marrying a youth is better than living alone."

"Shelamzion," Alena added, her tone smooth and cajoling, "you know how much we love you. We have asked HaShem for wisdom, and He has guided your uncle to this decision. Salina will marry Aristobulus, Antigonus will marry Abigail Philomena, and you will marry Alexander Jannaeus."

So Antigonus had also been betrothed to a younger cousin. Twice I had been passed over.

And why were Uncle and Alena suddenly so focused on betrothing their sons?

"Salome?"

Slowly I turned to face my uncle.

"After the wedding, I am sending you and Jonathan to live in the Lower Galilee. Only a few Jews live there now, but if you live among the Gentiles, you may lead them to favor our administration and accept our leadership. There, you and Jonathan will enjoy a peaceful life away from the hustle and hurry of Jerusalem."

"But I love Jerusalem!"

"You will love Galilee as well. It is a beautiful, well-watered region."

I lowered my gaze, for I did not wish to look at him. Not only was Uncle marrying me to a mere youth, he was sending me away from the city that had molded me into the woman I was. I would be leaving my Torah teacher and my tutor. I would be leaving the life I had come to love.

And where would I go? To Galilee, a recently annexed, raw territory that teemed with Gentiles. An area filled with fishermen and farmers and women who dyed fabrics with plants and fish guts.

I pressed my lips together, feeling my uncle's will like a fist around my heart, squeezing the joy from it.

But what could I do? I was only a woman, with no power or authority of my own.

My wedding to Alexander Jannaeus was part of a week-long celebration in which three sons of John Hyrcanus, high priest of Israel, took wives, feasted, and stole covetous glances at the seat occupied by their father.

At dawn of the first day, Judah Aristobulus and Antigonus set out with their friends to fetch their betrothed virgins. In marked contrast, Alexander Jannaeus donned his best tunic and walked across the courtyard, knocked on my door, and bade me come out to be married.

I looked down at him—the youth barely came up to my shoulder—and sighed. "If it is truly your will, I will marry you."

I was certain it was no more his will than mine, but both of us were bound to obey the high priest.

I glanced at Mother and Kissa, who stood together with their hands clasped in an overflow of earnest hope for my happiness. While Mother looked content, Kissa's mouth had taken on an unpleasant twist.

I left the house and followed my betrothed husband. Mother and Kissa trailed after us, then joined the small crowd waiting for the other brides and grooms.

When the other two couples finally arrived, Uncle stood and blessed our unions, praying that we brides would be as fruitful as Rachel and Leah. To the grooms he said, "Remember that the Lord God said, 'It is not good for man to be alone.' So a man should love his wife as himself and honor her more than himself."

Then he gave his sons a sly smile, for we all knew what would happen next. Tradition dictated that we go to a bridal chamber to consummate the marriage, then we would return to the courtyard for the marriage feast.

My cheeks burned when Alexander Jannaeus took my hand. I should have been overjoyed to finally have a husband, but instead I felt like a mother to an inappropriate and awkward boy. Hadn't I held this youth as a baby? Hadn't I watched over him when Alena was busy? Hadn't I scolded him for disturbing the chickens, chasing the servants, and throwing stones at his older brothers?

I closed my eyes and breathed the only prayer I could sincerely offer: *HaShem, only you can help me see this youth as a husband. Help me behave like the overjoyed bride I have always hoped to be.*

My youthful husband led me into the bridal chamber, where he fumbled with his tunic and gestured for me to lie on the bed. I sat on the edge, placed my hand on his chest, and looked directly into his eyes. "Wait." I kept my voice low, for anyone could be listening at the door. "I will no longer call you Jonathan, because that was the name of the boy. From this day until my last I shall call you Jannaeus, the name of my husband."

A line crept between his brows, then he smiled. "I will no longer call you Shelamzion, but Salome, my wife."

I nodded. "That is fitting."

My husband performed a hurried act that brought me more pain than pleasure. When he had finished, he helped me up and led me to the wedding feast, where the men drank and congratulated each other while we brides ate quietly and wondered what our futures would hold.

CHAPTER TWENTY-SEVEN

Shelamzion

Compared to the pace of life in Jerusalem, our life in Galilee was simple . . . and I cannot say I despised it. I had no tutor there, and scrolls were nearly impossible to procure, but life was uncomplicated and we ate well.

We had departed for Galilee after the conclusion of the wedding feast. Mother and Alena stood in the courtyard and waved farewell as our wagon pulled away. From the back of the wagon, Kissa reached up and squeezed my arm in silent compassion. Guarded by a small group of mercenary soldiers, we traveled north through Samaria for several days, always watchful lest some Samaritan decide to vent his ill will toward John Hyrcanus on us. When we finally arrived in Sepphoris, a small town in the Galilee region, I was relieved to climb out of the wagon.

Uncle had arranged for us to have a small house near the center of the town. I liked the place immediately and knew that Kissa and Notus, Jannaeus's manservant, would have no trouble meeting our needs. Stately steps led visitors to a wide piazza that ran along the front of the structure. Inside the front doors, a tiled vestibule opened to a rectangular atrium that provided fresh air and sunshine. The open space was well suited for dining and entertaining guests.

While I had little demands on my time in Sepphoris, Jannaeus represented his father, so he frequently received local officials and merchants who wished to pay their respects and curry favor. Most of the time my husband murmured pleasantries while these guests welcomed him, complimented his father, and told him how grateful they were to know he had come to the area. The job was not at all demanding, and Jannaeus was clever enough to know that if he managed this position well, his father might offer more responsibility in the years ahead.

With the people learning we were newlyweds, they brought appropriate gifts: a bed carved of cedar, fragrant oils, bath salts, and fine robes. The visiting dignitaries' wives gave me fruit and nuts rumored to be aphrodisiacs and vials of oil designed to aid fertility. Many of them claimed to be Jewish, but from their offerings I could tell they had been only recently converted from paganism. "If you eat this and dance in a cedar grove beneath a full moon," one woman confided, pressing a gnarled root into my palm, "you will have nothing but fine, strong sons."

I found it easy to forgive the people their lack of knowledge. I gently attempted to correct this sort of ignorance when I could, but the women's superstitions were deeply rooted and I had not yet proven myself worthy of their trust. Few people had access to copies of the Torah, and even fewer people could read. If they were literate, most Galileans spoke Aramaic, not Hebrew, so even if they procured a Torah scroll, they wouldn't be able to read it.

As for my husband, his ignorance of the Law appalled me. As the third-born son of Judea's high priest, he had enjoyed access to all sorts of sacred writings, but the teachings of the

Sanhedrin had apparently gone no deeper than his ears. "While the high priest drank deeply at the fountain of knowledge," I told Kissa one day, "Alexander Jannaeus only gargled."

But he was not a complete fool. When the people asked him to render judgment and adjudicate their conflicts, more than once he glanced at me for advice. What could I do but help the lad? I would offer advice in the guise of womanly helpfulness: "Husband, surely you will want to do what Moses did in a similar situation . . ."

After the second or third such occasion, I began to understand why my uncle had made me such a baffling match. He had betrothed me to Jannaeus because he knew the lad lacked wisdom and scholarship, qualities I had always sought. And the high priest sent us to Galilee because he knew that in this secluded, recently acquired territory, Jannaeus would be able to make mistakes without spoiling his future prospects. He had also married me to this fifteen-year-old because the youth was one of his beloved sons.

I cannot say I loved the young man I married . . . not even when I realized I was carrying his child. But as Kissa placed the squalling infant in my arms, I knew I had finally found someone I could love utterly and completely. This small human, a flesh-and-blood miracle from Adonai, had been entrusted to *me*. I was to love him, cherish him, and raise him to godly manhood. Through his perfect tiny fingers and toes flowed the same blood that had inspired Judas Maccabaeus and filled the veins of John Hyrcanus, the high priest of Israel. *This* boy would receive anything and everything I had to offer.

I would always respect my husband—I owed that much to my uncle, who had lifted me from obscurity and allowed me the freedom to develop my mind and soul.

On the baby's name day, when we circumcised him, I named him Hyrcanus, after my father-in-law.

"Mistress."

I looked up from the blanket I was embroidering when I heard a warning note in Kissa's voice. "Is something wrong?"

She gestured toward a pile of freshly laundered linens. "You did not bleed this month."

I frowned as my thoughts flitted back over the past few weeks. "Are you certain?"

"I last prepared the woods for you during the full moon. Tonight the moon will be full for the second time since I last made preparation."

Kissa was inordinately careful about preparing for my monthly bleeding. Our monthly courses usually coincided, so we would remain in my chamber together in order to avoid spreading impurity throughout the house. But she was right—last month she had remained in my chamber alone.

I shrugged. "I am still nursing Hyrcanus. Perhaps that is why I have not bled."

"You have never missed an entire month." She arched a brow as she began folding the linens. "You should start counting."

I smiled as Hyrcanus toddled by, mouthing a wooden block one of the servants had carved for him. Could I be pregnant again? Sometimes I wondered if my husband's frantic couplings were enough to result in anything, but he had already given me one son. If Adonai chose to send me another baby as delightful as Hyrcanus, I would not mind being pregnant again.

I nodded and resumed my embroidery. "If you are right and I am carrying a girl, I will name it Kissa."

She snorted. "Your husband would never allow that. And if you have another son?"

I lowered my needle. "I have always liked the name Ittamar. That was my father's name."

Kissa stacked the linens and set them in a basket. "The people will think even more highly of you if you bear another son. A woman who bears girls is weak; a woman who bears sons is strong. Everyone knows it to be so."

"Do not count my sons too quickly," I said, "for we are not certain of anything."

I looked up as a servant stepped into the doorway and bowed. "A letter for you, mistress." He extended a sealed scroll. "A rider brought it from Jerusalem."

"For me?" I glanced at Kissa and saw the same surprise in her eyes. I had never received a personal letter. All correspondence usually went to Jannaeus, who then would give it to me.

"Thank you," I said, taking the scroll. The servant waited while I broke the seal and unfurled the parchment. I glanced at the signature and smiled. "It's from my uncle."

Greetings, Shelamzion:

I hope this letter finds you well. Jannaeus writes that you and your son are doing well in Sepphoris, and the region is thriving under his supervision. I daresay you are guiding him in his endeavors, and for that I am most grateful. Of all my sons, Jannaeus needed the most guidance and the firmest hand, and you are the best suited to that task. You are slow to anger, quick to learn, and you have a most pleasant demeanor. Of all my acquaintances, you are the most qualified to tame a headstrong youth.

I had another reason for betrothing you to my son, one I have kept hidden from Jannaeus because I did not want to spoil the love between brothers. I married you to my third son and sent you to Galilee because I want to keep him away from Aristobulus and Antigonus. His older brothers are ambitious young men, and in their bold eyes I have recognized a lust for power, especially of late. They watch me like birds of prey, and I fear I cannot die soon enough to please them. They are close—a good thing—but I do not believe they will make room in their plans for another brother, especially one who could pose a threat.

I have sent Aristobulus and Antigonus to subdue an area near Mount Carmel, along the sea. We have Jewish settlements in that region and wish to connect them to our territories in Samaria. My sons may visit you and Jannaeus in due time.

I trust you are content. As long as you and Jannaeus are in Galilee, you are safely away from my elder sons' thoughts.

I hope you are growing in experience and wisdom, and finding Adonai's blessing.

May HaShem continue to bless you both.

John Hyrcanus

I read the letter silently, then slowly rerolled the scroll.

"Is there a response?" the servant asked.

I shook my head. "Nothing written," I whispered, "but please convey my thanks to the courier. Have him spend the night under our roof, then tell him to return to my uncle. Ask him to tell the high priest that I am most grateful for his letter . . . and his wisdom. That is all."

I waited until the servant left the room, then looked at Kissa. "My uncle says he sent us here to keep us away from Aristobulus and Antigonus, who have grown far too ambitious for his liking."

Kissa frowned. "Will we never go back to Jerusalem?"

"Not for a while, I fear. We are to stay here so we can grow older and wiser." I laughed. "My uncle seems to think that in ten years, Jannaeus will be closer to my age."

Kissa snorted. "I doubt your husband will ever match you in knowledge or wisdom. He is neither pious nor studious."

"But he has given me a son." I looked over at my sleeping baby, content to know that HaShem had honored my obedience to my uncle by giving me a son.

⌇⌇⌇⌇⌇⌇⌇

Seven months later, Jannaeus insisted we name our second son Aristobulus, after the baby's uncle. I reluctantly agreed and could not help wondering if he chose that name to curry favor with his elder brother.

For John Hyrcanus was a mortal man and would not live forever. When Judah Aristobulus inherited his father's position, who knew what he might do?

I found it odd that although Judah Aristobulus and Antigonus were leading a campaign only a short distance away, they did not visit us, send greetings, or even ask for supplies. But soon we heard that the fighting had finished and the high priest's sons had returned to Jerusalem. Both Jannaeus and I felt much relieved.

In those days I found my greatest joy in watching my sons grow. Hyrcanus, the firstborn, had inherited my disposition. He was a quiet child, reserved and undemanding. He entertained himself easily and loved being outdoors, collecting leaves, flowers, and unusual rocks. At the end of each day, when I went into the boys' bedchamber to say good-night, he would happily show me the objects he had discovered on his walks.

Aristobulus, however, was clearly his father's son. Rough and loud, the child came screaming out of my womb and woke the entire household at sunrise each morning. Aristobulus did everything with great energy and volume, just as young Jannaeus had, and was as active as his brother was calm. My second son could not entertain himself and was constantly tugging at me or Kissa, demanding that we read to him, feed him, or carry him. Each night, after putting Hyrcanus to bed, I would turn to embrace Aristobulus, yet he would wriggle free of my grasp and force me to give chase until I caught him.

"One night," I told Kissa after the exhausting bedtime ritual, "I am going to chain that child to his bed."

Every morning, after I had given my boys bread spread with honey, I would attempt to seat them next to me so that I could tell a story from the Torah. Hyrcanus always sat perfectly still, his eyes intent upon my face. Aristobulus would sit only until I began the tale, and then he would slip down and run through the garden, forcing Kissa to hurry away and catch him. In the beginning I was tempted to chase him as well, but Hyrcanus wanted to hear the story his brother ignored. So I shared my love of the Torah with Hyrcanus while Aristobulus squealed in the delight of evading Kissa's grasp.

Long before my sons were born, I vowed I would never love one child more than another. HaShem knows I intended to keep my word, but when one child loves what you love and the other spurns wisdom, how can your heart keep from favoring one more than the other?

Jannaeus, of course, adored Aristobulus. Anyone could see why. I loved the boy, too, but at times I found it difficult to enjoy his company.

Sometimes I would look at my second son and try to recall what Jannaeus had been like as a child. I did not spend much time with Alena's children, though I do remember that young Jannaeus was forever running away from his nurse and doing whatever he could to catch his older brothers' attention.

If only my Aristobulus had been a little more like his brother.

I knew my feelings were not good. I knew a mother should be fair and not enjoy one child more than the other. I knew about the trouble unequal favor could produce. The Torah warned that discord resulted from unequal loving, for Jacob loved Joseph above all his brothers, and Rebekah favored Jacob more than Esau. And oh, the bitterness of the unloved brothers!

I tried to hide my feelings. I did not bestow favors on Hyrcanus without bestowing the same on Aristobulus. I did not compliment the elder without finding some praise for the younger. Yet the heart, deceitful and wicked though it is, will love whom it loves.

I could only pray that HaShem would change my heart . . . or keep my children from ever realizing my secret.

My husband matured a great deal while we lived in the Galilee region. He cultivated friendships with leaders of the Jewish villages, and when raiding Gentile invaders struck their vineyards and farms, Jannaeus took great delight in assembling an armed company and chasing the marauders back to their own territories.

After developing a taste for law-keeping, my husband had little patience with the Jews who came to him for the adjudication of smaller matters. He delighted more in action than in legal debate and did not possess the experience or wisdom to judge complicated cases. He frequently asked me to dispense judgment in his absence. I agreed to do so, and before long he became absent more often.

By the beginning of our seventh year in Galilee, we had effectively divided our responsibilities. With Kissa caring for the children, Jannaeus rode out with his army while I received petitioners every morning but the Sabbath.

The people came to me with problems great and small. Some dilemmas were easily settled by referring to the Torah; others required an application of common sense.

Two women came to me because they had been betrothed

to the same man and he refused to marry either of them. A father came because his daughter had been raped in the field and found herself with child. A pair of quarreling neighbors came because one had stolen the affection of a village dog. The animal remained in the first man's house day and night, frustrating the second man, who wanted the dog to guard the lambs in his courtyard. My ruling? Since the dog had been born in the wild, it should be free to make its home where it was most wanted. Both men were to keep their gates open at all times.

"But I cannot!" the second man blurted out. "My lambs would escape!"

"Then let the door contain your livestock and not the dog," I answered. "And be at peace with your neighbor."

As I suspected, some men were reluctant to bring their cases to me—after all, I was a woman. But after I reminded an audience that HaShem told Abraham to listen to the voice of his wife, my reputation grew. Those who sought an audience with me came to understand that I was not young and uneducated, nor was I foolish.

One morning I was startled to see a man standing before me with a firm grip on his young wife. He complained that she refused to sleep with him because she had found a younger man she preferred. "I know what she is doing," he said. "She thinks that by denying me I will divorce her, and she will be free to marry another."

My husband, even my uncle, would rarely speak to a woman in a public gathering, but I had no compunctions about conversing with someone of my own gender. "Does your husband speak the truth?" I asked, giving the woman a stern look. "Are you refusing to lie with him because you want to marry someone else?"

A blush brightened the young woman's face. "He comes home dirty from his work and never bathes. He expects me to lie with him when he's filthy."

I shifted my attention back to the petitioner. "Do you wash before you take your wife to bed?"

A tide of dusky red crawled up his throat. "Why should I? A wife should be glad her husband comes home soiled from honest work."

"You should wash," I told him. I looked at the wife. "And you should have a basin and pitcher waiting. Help him get clean, then you can sleep together. Keep your attention set on your own man, and not on another. Care for him, and he will become precious to you."

"Is that what you do?" the young woman asked. "Care for that youth you call a husband?"

The question caught me off guard. "My husband . . ." I paused and changed my approach. "The issue here is not my marriage but yours. Be tender with your husband, and he will treat you well. The Torah commands us to be fruitful and multiply, so go home and obey."

When they had finally departed, I leaned back in my chair and exhaled in contentment. How things had changed in seven years! I would always be older than my husband, and Jannaeus would always be more concerned with his desires and ambitions than mine. But he had given me two beautiful children, and he seemed to respect me. Indeed, he was probably grateful for me, because my willingness to accept some of his responsibilities gave him the freedom to pursue the things he enjoyed.

The young woman's personal question might have embarrassed me . . . if I had not accepted my situation as an unusual blessing from HaShem.

Kissa mouthed words as her finger moved from right to left across the scroll. "'Then he believed in Adonai,'" she read aloud slowly, "'and He reckoned it to him as righteousness.'"

She looked up. "Abram believed?"

I lowered the scroll I'd been trying to read. "Yes."

"What did he believe?"

I blew out a breath. Kissa had made great strides in reading Hebrew, but she struggled with understanding why we Jews felt so strongly about keeping the Law. "He believed Adonai's promise to make him a great nation and give him the Promised Land."

Kissa's gaze returned to the scroll. "And your God was happy with simple belief?"

"Yes. Abram was counted as a righteous man."

"If belief makes one righteous, then why do you live by so many rules?"

"Because later Adonai gave Moses the Law. Those who would be righteous keep the Law."

"But do they believe?" Kissa lifted a brow. "Because I am your handmaid, I have lived by your laws for years. I remain inside when I am bleeding, I rest on the Sabbath, and I do not eat forbidden foods. Am I righteous?"

Something in her tone made me stop. Was *she*? She did keep the Law as I did, but she did it to avoid offending me, not Adonai.

I bit my lip and looked at her. "Do you believe in Adonai?"

She stared into space for a moment, then shrugged. "I do not know."

I floundered, not knowing what else to say. If she did not believe in Adonai, then keeping the Law was of no benefit to her. "I am glad you keep the Law," I said, carefully feeling my way, "though I know you do it for me and not for Adonai."

"There is so much I do not understand," she said, turning to face me. "I have read your Torah three times, and each time I am more confused."

I straightened, confident in my years of Torah study. "Please explain. I don't understand why you are confused."

"Here." She pointed to a section of the scroll. "Moses gave

Israel the Law and said they would break it and go into exile.
You have told me that your people *did* go into exile in Babylon."

"That is right. Moses was a prophet as well as a leader."

Kissa shrugged. "If your God knew the Law would be broken,
why did He give it to you?"

I closed my eyes and fervently wished that Simeon ben Shetah
were sitting beside me. He would have an answer.

"The Law was broken," I said, "and Israel was exiled. But
at the end of the seventy years prophesied by Jeremiah, we
were allowed to return. Now we live in the land promised to
Abraham—not all of it, but Uncle is working to reclaim the
rest of Israel's territory."

Kissa lifted both brows and nodded slowly. "So now you all
endeavor to keep the Law even though you could not keep it
when it was first given to you."

"That is true." I was dismayed to hear a note of uncertainty
in my voice. "Because if Israel keeps the Law perfectly, HaShem
will bless us. We will also be counted righteous enough for
HaShem to send His Messiah and usher in His kingdom."

"So you think every Jew can keep the Law *perfectly*?" Kissa
made a face and returned to the scroll. "Who is this Messiah?"

"The Anointed One who will come in the last days."

Kissa shot me a frightened look. "The last days of *what*?"

"The last days of this cursed earth," I answered, though I felt
more uncertain than ever. "Can these questions wait? I would like
to consult with Simeon ben Shetah before answering further."

Kissa tapped the scroll. "So you don't know."

"No, but I will find out."

<hr />

I would not have objected if we remained in Sepphoris for
the rest of our lives. Though I would always love Jerusalem, I
came to appreciate the quiet beauty of the hills beside the Sea

of Galilee. The Gentiles of the area looked at us with curiosity, and I hoped Jannaeus and I could be examples of righteous Law-keepers who had earned the blessings of Adonai.

Spurred in part by Kissa's penetrating questions, I began to correspond with Simeon ben Shetah. I asked him about the last days, and he wrote to tell me that in the Torah, Moses mentioned the last days four times.

"First," he wrote, "when Jacob called his sons together for a blessing, he said he would tell them what would happen to their descendants in the last days. When Balaam tried to curse Israel, he foretold what would happen to Israel in the last days—a star will come from Jacob, and a scepter will arise from Israel. In Moses' final song, he prophesied that Israel would do evil, and evil would fall on our people in the last days. Moses also said that when we were in distress, in the last days we would return to Adonai and listen to His voice. He would not abandon us or destroy us or forget the covenant with our fathers.

"So do not despair, Shelamzion," Simeon added. "We did forsake the Law and go into exile. But we have been restored, so surely we are entering the days in which our Messiah will come."

My question must have stirred something within him, for a few weeks later I received another letter in which he called my attention to a prophecy of Isaiah:

> He treated lightly the land of Zebulun and the land of
>   Naphtali,
> But in the future He will bring glory—
> By the way of the sea,
> Beyond the Jordan—
> Galilee of the Gentiles.
> The people walking in darkness will see a great light.
> Upon those dwelling in the land of the shadow of death,
> Light will shine.
> You will multiply the nation.

You will increase the joy. . . .
For unto us a child is born,
A son will be given to us,
And the government will be upon His shoulder.
His Name will be called
Wonderful Counselor,
Mighty God
My Father of Eternity,
Prince of Peace.
Of the increase of His government
And shalom there will be no end—
On the throne of David and over His kingdom—
To establish it and uphold it
Through justice and righteousness from now until
forevermore.
The zeal of *Adonai-Tzva'ot* will accomplish this.

"You are living in Galilee," Simeon concluded, "the territory allotted to the tribes of Zebulun and Naphtali. The prophet foretold that one day the land will be filled with the glory of Adonai. So I must know—have you seen it?"

Had I? The question puzzled me, and for several days I looked at my husband's petitioners with new eyes. Could one of them be the Anointed One? Was one of them destined to sit on the throne of David?

Or—more daring still—could the prophet have been speaking of one of my sons? Surely they were more likely to be chosen than one of the Galileans. Perhaps Hyrcanus would be the Anointed One . . .

If so, HaShem had already answered my prayer. Had I not told Kissa more than once that the thing I wanted most in life was to be important to someone? If Hyrcanus became Adonai's Messiah, then as his mother I would be a part of the man who would bless all of Israel.

I wrote my Torah teacher and told him I had not seen any glory save that of my own beloved children. "They are HaShem's blessing to me," I wrote, "and perhaps one day they will bless the people of Galilee, but not yet."

~~~~~~~~

In the summer of our seventh year, I ordered the servants to prepare a lavish banquet for important guests. Simeon ben Shetah had come from Jerusalem, and I was eager to introduce the esteemed Torah teacher to the Jews of Galilee.

"I don't understand why you are so excited to entertain this Pharisee," Jannaeus said, scowling as the cook walked away with her instructions. "And I don't know what he has in common with Diagos. This might well be the most boring banquet I have ever attended."

Jannaeus had invited Ezra Diagos, commander of his law-keeping force. Jannaeus thought highly of the man, saying Diagos had proven himself to be quick, clever, and courageous. Though Jannaeus's militia lacked numbers, the skill and daring of its members more than compensated for its small size.

My husband may not have been the brightest of John Hyrcanus's sons, but he was clever enough to realize that he owed his success to an excellent commander.

"Simeon ben Shetah," I said, "is an intelligent and devoted Torah teacher. He is an expert on the Law and actually keeps it—the sort of man who would have made the sons of Mattathias proud. But more than that, he has been my teacher for years. I am pleased to call him my friend."

Jannaeus blew out a breath. "Fine. But make sure I am seated next to Diagos, so we can talk. Keep the Torah teacher and his wife at your side."

I bowed my head. "As you wish, husband."

We greeted our guests in the vestibule, where I met Simeon's wife, Naava, with an embrace. "Tell me about events in Jerusalem," I said, squeezing her hand. "I feel as if we have been away for a lifetime."

She tugged at a wayward curl that had wandered onto her forehead. "The talk is all about the high priest," she said, then cut a glance toward Jannaeus. She lowered her voice. "A Pharisee called Eleazar stood up at a banquet and said he had heard the high priest's mother was a captive during the reign of Antiochus Epiphanes."

I frowned. "What did he mean?"

She moved closer to whisper in my ear, "A woman who has lain with a man is forbidden to marry a priest, and if they *do* marry, their children are disqualified from the priesthood."

I gasped as the full meaning of the comment became clear. "That is not true! I am from Modein, as was the high priest's mother, and no woman from that village was ever taken captive by the Seleucids."

"The truth hardly matters," Naava said. "Eleazar is one of many who believe John Hyrcanus should not be high priest because he is not descended from Zadok. The Essenes have protested that point for years, but this is the first time the Pharisees have made it an issue. Once Eleazar's claim became public, the high priest demanded the Pharisees punish him for that terrible slander."

"But why would they raise this complaint now? John Hyrcanus has been high priest for nearly thirty years."

She sighed. "I am not certain, but my husband thinks it may be an attempt to seize power. John Hyrcanus is not well, so if they can discredit him, they discredit his heirs, which opens the door for a high priest from another family."

My mouth fell open—I had not realized Uncle was sick. "Is the high priest dying?"

Naava shook her head. "He is old and frail, so many have

turned their thoughts toward his successor. My husband says many of the Pharisees are angry with Hyrcanus because he forced the Samaritans to become Jews. Eleazar and many others—even my husband—disagreed with the high priest's action, and now they are making their voices heard."

I, too, had not understood why Uncle would force the Samaritans to become Jews. And criticism, once voiced, frequently spurred others to find fault where none had been noticed before. Perhaps Jerusalem would be more peaceful if the dissenters remained silent . . .

I caught Naava's hand. "Did the Pharisees punish this Eleazar?"

"They whipped him, but the high priest was highly offended and said Eleazar should have been executed. So John Hyrcanus declared he was no longer a Pharisee, but a Sadducee. His sons have become Sadducees, too. I suppose all the Hasmoneans now count themselves among the Sadducees."

I thanked her for the information, then turned away to sort through my jumbled thoughts. Uncle, a Sadducee? What would possess him to make such a decision? If he were not old and unwell, he would never have done such a thing. As to Naava's assertion that all the Hasmoneans had become Sadducees, she was wrong. Even if Jannaeus declared for that group, I could never consider myself anything but a devout Pharisee.

I would have to discuss this development with Simeon ben Shetah.

Our guests of honor had already found their seats, so I walked over and made myself comfortable on a couch between Simeon and Ezra Diagos. I nodded to the gentlemen at my right and left, then picked up my cup. Though I was eager to talk to Simeon, I thought I should at least introduce myself to my husband's commander. Surely Jannaeus would not mind if I learned if he belonged to any particular sect.

I plucked a bunch of grapes from the table, then tossed a

question to the military man. "So what do you think, Ezra
Diagos, of our oral traditions?" I asked, barely glancing at him
as I smiled at Simeon and his wife. "Should they be as binding
as the Torah?"

"I must confess to being surprised you would ask such a
question."

I swiveled in time to see the commander check a fish for
bones, then pop a piece into his mouth. A reluctant grin tugged
at Diagos's lips as he swallowed and leaned toward me. "Most
women—especially wealthy women—are content to center their
thoughts on their husband and children."

"I am not like most women," I replied with a smile. "And I
was not born into a wealthy family. But I would very much like
to know what you think. Do you believe our oral traditions are
to be obeyed in addition to the written Law?"

The man bowed his graying head, then looked up at me.
Something in his powerful eyes made my heart constrict. The
commander was an unusually attractive man and did not seem
offended by my admittedly blunt questions.

"Should the traditions invented by men be followed with the
same reverential obedience as the laws written by HaShem?"
he asked. "I think not."

"Then I take it you are a Sadducee."

"I don't like organized sects. I prefer to be true to my own
understanding."

"So you are . . . uncommitted?"

He chuckled. "I am a warrior. I obey your husband and lead
my men. If I can do that faithfully, I will leave Torah debates
to the scholars."

From the couch on my other side, Simeon ben Shetah cleared
his throat. "I see no fault in the commander's answer, so long
as a man has diligently studied the Torah, writings, and the
prophets. Ezra Diagos is correct when he says men's words do

not have the authority of HaShem's. But the Sadducees place far too much emphasis on free will, believing that men have the ability to control their own destinies. Does not the psalmist tell us that every day of our lives has already been written?"

I realized Simeon was attacking the Sadducees—and speaking loudly—in order to influence Jannaeus, who was talking with others on the opposite side of the room. But Diagos, apparently unaware of the rabbi's hidden motive, continued with the discussion. "Our lives have already been recorded, because HaShem knows the future," the commander countered. "He allows men to make choices. Just as He allows nations to rise and fall according to their actions."

Simeon shook his head. "Can anyone truly do whatever he wills? Can you step outside and fly over the sea of Galilee? Can you create bread from stones? You cannot. Those who maintain that man is free to do whatever he wants are only deluding themselves."

I glanced at Diagos, hoping he would not take offense at the Torah teacher's comment. Though he had declared himself neutral, the commander was making an adequate defense of the Sadducees, even as the volume of the discussion continued to rise.

"'Man tosses the dice,'" I quoted, smiling at both men, "'but Adonai determines the outcome.' Man and God act together. Surely we can all agree with Solomon."

Both men nodded politely, yet the Torah teacher had not finished.

"What about life after death?" Simeon asked. "If my kind hostess will allow, I would remind my friend that when his child died, David said he would go to him one day. How can we go to the dead unless there is an afterlife?"

"David meant he would go to Sheol," Diagos answered. "And yes, we will all go into the grave. You Pharisees have been too influenced by the Hellenes and Egyptians, who babble about the afterlife and judgment after death."

"While the Sadducees refuse to believe in angels." Simeon leaned closer to me. "How many times does the Torah mention ministering angels? They visited Lot, Hagar, and Abraham. They walked with Hananiah, Mishael, and Azariah in the Babylonians' fiery furnace. And as to the anointed guardian cherub—did Ezekiel not describe his fall from heaven?"

Diagos snorted. "I do not claim to know what the prophet was thinking as he wrote. Perhaps our hostess would like us to speak of something more . . . easily understood."

"Please continue." I folded my hands and glanced at Jannaeus to make sure we had not caught his attention. "I have no problem with ambiguity."

"With your permission, then." The commander smiled, his neck brightening to an intense shade of red. "The Pharisees are waiting for God's anointed Messiah to rule as king over Israel. Well, where is He? The Pharisees say a son of David will take the throne in Jerusalem, but the closest thing we have to a king is John Hyrcanus, and he is from the house of Levi, not David. From where will this savior come? The house of Hasmon has enough sons to continue their line for several generations, so how will this son of David knock the sons of Mattathias from their positions of power?"

"The prophets speak of a Messiah who is the begotten Son of HaShem," Simeon said. "And if they truly spoke for HaShem, then He *is* coming, just as the prophets foretold. From where is He coming? HaShem knows, and when it is time, He will send Him."

I pressed my lips together, quelling a sudden urge to share my thoughts about the coming Messiah. This was clearly not the time or place to suggest that my son might be the Lord's Anointed One.

"You had better hope this Messiah doesn't rebel against all the rules and regulations you Pharisees have added to the Torah," Diagos said. "HaShem said the Sabbath was to be a day of rest, but you have made it so complicated that a man could exhaust himself determining how he should rest. We can pull a donkey from a well, but we cannot light a fire to warm our frozen hands. We can walk two thousand cubits in any direction outside our city, but since any house next to another is considered part of the city, you could walk from Jerusalem to Samaria if the road was covered with houses." The commander tugged on his beard and laughed. "Moses would roll his eyes if he could see how you have mutilated HaShem's Law."

The conversation had become loud, and from the corner of my eye I saw Jannaeus move toward us, his eyes narrowing.

Time to call a halt to this enjoyable exchange.

"Gentlemen." I thrust my cup into the center of the debate. "Each of you has made valid points, but it is time to consider another subject."

"Not all points can be valid," Simeon muttered. "One of us has to be wrong."

Diagos was opening his mouth to say something else when I lifted my hand and cut him off. "I'm not sure we can settle the debate tonight."

"Another time, another place." Simeon lifted his goblet toward me and then toward the commander, a sign of good grace.

The gesture pleased me. I would have conversed more with both men, yet at that moment my irritated husband asked Simeon to lead us in a blessing.

As the Torah teacher stood, I pulled my himation over my head and wished for a more private opportunity to talk to Ezra Diagos. While many people in Jerusalem did not declare for the Essenes, Pharisees, or the Sadducees, rarely did I encounter anyone who openly proclaimed neutrality. Conventional wisdom would recommend aligning oneself to the sect of one's employer, but though my husband would now undoubtedly declare himself a Sadducee, I had to respect a man who had considered all sides of a situation and chose to remain above the fray.

When Simeon had finished his prayer, I uncovered my head and smiled my thanks at the teacher. "Thank you for the invitation," he said as his wife joined him on the couch. "It is not every day we are invited to travel."

"I was hoping you might be able to open a school in the area." I smiled, thinking of Kissa and her bold exploration of the Tanakh. "Few of the Galileans have a proper understanding of the Law, and they are not far removed from pagan superstition."

"I would not be able to teach here myself," Simeon said, "but I have students who might be willing to come. I will broach the matter as soon as we return to Jerusalem."

The servants entered, bringing additional trays of steaming meat. Amid the murmurs of pleasure coming from the guests, I counted the serving trays to make sure the servants had brought enough food. Then for no reason I could name, a sudden shiver raised the hair at the back of my neck.

Drawn by some inexplicable force, I turned . . . and felt Ezra Diagos's eyes upon me. I stiffened, momentarily abashed, but the commander lifted his cup, smiled, and drank, relieving my awkwardness.

I turned away, hoping no one noticed the blush that had heated my cheekbones. What was wrong with me? I was not a young girl, nor was I prone to indulge in silly fantasies.

I smiled at a server and took a piece of cheese from a platter, then stole another glance at the commander. Though Jannaeus had leaned toward him and was filling his ear, the commander was watching me.

I turned toward Simeon and his wife, determined not to look in Diagos's direction again.

CHAPTER TWENTY-EIGHT

Shelamzion

In the spring of the next year, when our sons were four and six, a rider from Jerusalem brought urgent news: John Hyrcanus was dying. If we wanted to see him before he died, we would have to depart immediately.

The news filled me with sadness, for Uncle had given me opportunities few girls ever received. I thought Jannaeus would be sorrowful as well, yet he received the news with an eagerness that seemed vulgar. "We shall leave for Jerusalem at once," he told the messenger. "Thank you for bringing us the news."

After the rider departed, a strange light gleamed in my husband's eye. "Finally we can return to Jerusalem," he said, hurrying to our bedchamber. He paused to give me a heartfelt smile. "I know you have suffered in this primitive region, but our time of travail is nearly at an end."

I stared in confusion because, apart from having two babies, I had neither suffered nor travailed. Jannaeus's words only proved how little he knew me, and how rarely he paid attention.

I sent Kissa to gather the things my sons would need while I oversaw the packing of food, water, and supplies for the journey.

I did not know how long we would remain in Jerusalem, but I was beginning to suspect that Jannaeus would not willingly return to Galilee. He had come to this region only because his father commanded it. If Judah Aristobulus offered him a place in his administration, Jannaeus would undoubtedly take it.

The gangly adolescent I married had grown into his name, surpassing me in height as well as weight. He was now twenty-three, with a young man's ambition, passions, and interests. When he joined me in the courtyard where the servants were loading wagons, I could see that the prospect of returning to Jerusalem had lit a fire within him.

I caught his arm as he strode by and studied his face when he halted. "You're eager to return home," I said, stating the obvious. "Be careful that you don't appear eager for your father to die."

"And why shouldn't I be eager?" His dark eyes narrowed as he shook my hand from his arm. "The old man has led a full life. His time is finished."

My eyes filled with tears—whether from sadness at my husband's attitude or the thought of losing my uncle, I could not say. "He loves us," I said, my voice breaking. "Both of us. And I will miss him dreadfully."

"So be it." Jannaeus stepped away, then lifted his arm to catch the eye of a passing servant. "Saddle the stallion for me," he called. "My wife and children will ride in the wagon." He turned. "Anything else, Salome?"

I shook my head and turned, arranging my himation like a cowl about my face, so he would not see me weep.

⁓⁓⁓⁓⁓

John Hyrcanus, high priest of Israel, beloved of man and HaShem, must have waited for us. After arriving at the palace where I had spent so many happy years, we hurried into Uncle's bedchamber. I tapped my sons' shoulders and gestured for them to kneel at his bedside. As Alena watched, Uncle placed his hands on their dark curls and blessed them, his lips moving in an inaudible whisper. When he had finished, Kissa took the children away while Uncle took my hand.

My heart broke to see a tremor in those once-strong fingers. "Uncle, we have come to be with you."

Alena stepped forward. "We are glad you have come, but do not encourage him to talk. He has trouble drawing breath, and speech is difficult. But *you* may say whatever is on your heart."

I sat on the edge of the bed and wrapped my hands around his. "I shall miss you, Uncle," I told him. "Every day we have been away, I have thanked HaShem that you set me on a path I could never have walked on my own. When you came to Modein and offered your hospitality and guardianship, you changed my life for the good."

His gaze softened, and the corners of his eyes crinkled as he gave me a wavering smile. He did not speak, but his fingers trembled in my grasp.

"Shelamzion." Alena gestured toward the hallway. "Would you like to oversee the unloading of your wagons? You can make yourself at home—"

"I will wait." I tightened my grip on Uncle's hand, remembering that it was forbidden to leave a dying person lest he die alone.

An hour later, amid the flickering of the oil lamps and in the company of many of his fellow priests, John Hyrcanus drew his last breath. And only when the hired mourners began to wail did I look up and realize that my husband had not followed us into the sick man's bedchamber.

⌇⌇⌇⌇⌇⌇

After the funeral, the high priest's family, members of the Sanhedrin, and dozens of Levites crowded into the palace reception hall. One of Uncle's assistants picked up a scroll and read the preamble.

Aware that his health was failing, John Hyrcanus had written a will months before his death. The statement of most interest to those gathered at the funeral was this:

> Some have boldly stated that the offices of priest and civic leader should not be vested in the same man. Though I did my best to represent the nation of Israel before man and Adonai, perhaps I should now submit to those who have protested the arrangement. I decree therefore that the office of high priest shall go to my eldest son, Judah Aristobulus, who meets the qualifications established in the Torah. Responsibility for ruling as the civil authority will go to my wife, Kefira Alena, for she has labored by my side and knows what should be done to govern Judea. Like Deborah, wife of Lappidoth and the fifth judge of Israel, she possesses the knowledge and experience to oversee the nation. She can be trusted to seek HaShem's wisdom as she makes decisions for Israel.

An audible gasp filled the room at the mention of Alena's name. John Hyrcanus had accomplished many noteworthy achievements in his lifetime, but perhaps he would be most remembered for leaving the leadership of the nation in his wife's hands.

After the initial shock, I couldn't stop smiling. Uncle's decision, while unexpected, did not surprise me because I knew how much he admired the female sovereigns of neighboring kingdoms. He had spent years observing Cleopatra Thea, and he knew strong women had a talent for weaving peace from the raveled strands of a war-torn empire.

I turned to look at the others in the room and saw dismay on my kinsmen's faces. Judah Aristobulus, who apparently expected to step into his father's dual position, was glaring at his mother with burning, reproachful eyes while Antigonus's nostrils flared with fury.

I looked for Jannaeus, spotting him leaning against the wall, his attention focused on his older brothers. Absalom and Philo Elias, the two youngest sons, were red-eyed and weeping, their faces a study in anguish.

My heart brimmed with compassion for them. Ambition had not made its home in their young hearts, so they had room to grieve the father they had lost. Not so with Judah Aristobulus and Antigonus.

And Jannaeus? I studied my husband. His face was utterly blank, a perfect mask of indifference.

The Levite who had read the will rolled the scroll back onto its spindle, bowed to the assembly, and left the chamber. Every eye swiveled toward Alena.

"I know we are still mourning our high priest," she said, her voice wavering as she stepped forward, "but on the morrow we must move forward with new hope for Judea. John has entrusted us with the safekeeping of a nation. We must continue to work for the goals he established, and we must serve HaShem as faithfully as he did. For now, let us depart to our homes and mourn him, but tomorrow we will rise to the challenge before us."

A sudden movement caught my eye, and I turned to see Judah Aristobulus whirl and leave the room. Antigonus followed.

Alena stammered in the sudden silence. "I . . . I am afraid my husband's wishes have come as a shock to some," she said, glancing at the doorway through which her sons had disappeared. "But we are a family. We will work together for the good of Judea."

People began to exit the chamber in groups of twos and threes, heads together as the mourners whispered their reactions to the astonishing news. I walked over to Alena and embraced her, then motioned for my sons to join me as we climbed the stairs and escorted her safely to her chamber.

Chapter Twenty-Nine

Shelamzion

I lay beneath a thin blanket in a silence so thick that the only sound was the annoying whistle of Jannaeus's breathing. We had been given one of the upstairs chambers, and though my husband lay sleeping by my side, my thoughts centered on my sons, who slept next to Kissa in my mother's house. Were they safe? I could not think of any reason someone might want to harm them, but the expression on Judah Aristobulus's face had made my stomach tighten. As he left, he wore the expression of a man who would do anything to achieve his goal.

I mentioned my concern to Jannaeus, and he laughed at my fears. "You are worried about my brother? You might as well worry about the moon swooping down to harm us. We are family; we do not hurt each other."

And most mothers did not kill their sons, yet Cleopatra Thea killed one and was murdered by another. The allure of power could destroy familial bonds and turn God-fearing individuals into executioners.

Feeling restless and anxious, I slipped out of bed and padded in bare feet to the balcony, where a soft breeze fluttered the linen curtains. I stepped through the gauzy fabric and shivered in the moonlight, bracing my hands on the balustrade and peering into the empty courtyard. The moon had gilded the paving stones with silver, and a pair of horses in the corral stood motionless beneath their saddles.

I frowned. Why did the horses wear saddles at this hour? Uncle's proud mounts were always brushed down and put away at night, led to plush stalls with fresh straw. Either some servant had grown lazy, or the regular routines had been abandoned in the aftermath of the funeral.

I breathed deeply of the cool night air and closed my eyes, relishing the silence. The wind whispered in the palm branches, but nothing else stirred, except . . .

My ears alerted me to a sound in the distance—a soft, rhythmic thumping that grew stronger as the moments stretched. What was it? In all my years of living in the high priest's compound, I had never before heard that sound. Then came silence, followed by a faint chink of metal as a dark figure emerged from the barn.

I leaned forward as a sense of unease sent prickles up my spine. Who was this, and was he planning to take the horses? The man moved toward the gate, then vanished into shadows thrown by a massive terebinth tree. I pressed my hand to my forehead, trying to make sense of what I was seeing. Then I heard the gates creaking as they parted, and the strange sound began once more.

Rows of armed soldiers marched from the street into the courtyard, their rhythmic tread abruptly shifting to quick steps. They spread out like hungry ants, darting toward the stable, the servants' quarters, even my mother's house, their drawn swords glinting in the moonlight.

Who were they? Had someone sent a squad of Temple guards to protect Alena and Aristobulus?

Realization shattered my unlikely notion. Temple guards would have no reason to approach stealthily in the dead of night, nor would they enter the premises with swords drawn. These men, whoever they were, intended evil for the occupants of this house.

I flew back into the chamber.

"Jannaeus!" I gripped my husband's shoulder and shook him awake. "Armed men have entered the house. They are downstairs even now."

He blinked at me and frowned, clearly irritated. "What are you—? If there is trouble, it has nothing to do with us."

No sooner had the words left his lips than the doors to our chamber burst open. A half dozen soldiers entered the room, swords drawn, their attention focused on my husband. I retreated toward the balcony, desperate to keep an eye on the building where my sons slept.

"Alexander Jannaeus," one of the men called, his voice echoing in the high-ceilinged room. "You will come with us."

Jannaeus sat up, a scowl darkening his face. "What is the meaning of this?"

Without answering, two of the men dragged him from the bed, tied his hands behind his back, and hauled him out of the room. As I cowered in the corner, I heard my husband's demanding questions: "Why are you doing this? Where are you taking me?"

A moment later I heard Alena's shrill scream. I rushed onto the balcony, crouched behind the balustrade, and peered through the gaps in the stone pillars.

John Hyrcanus's heirs were being rounded up like cattle—Alena, still wearing her nightdress, along with Absalom, Elias, and Jannaeus. The four of them stood in the center of the courtyard while watchful soldiers encircled them. I froze when I heard the gruff voice of a commander, afraid I was about to witness my family's execution. I squeezed my eyes shut, but after an interval of uncertainty I opened them in time to see four of the people John Hyrcanus loved most being dragged into the darkness.

Who had done this? Months ago, Simeon's wife had said that a certain Pharisee wanted to discredit Uncle and his heirs, but that sort of slander should not involve violence. If the Pharisees wanted to name a new high priest, they simply had to raise the issue in the Sanhedrin . . .

Understanding overcame my panic and asserted itself. All of Uncle's heirs had been sleeping beneath this roof except for Aristobulus and Antigonus. The two eldest were missing . . . because *they* had instigated this action. They would return, probably at sunrise, to declare their victory.

I did not want to be present when Aristobulus claimed the high priest's palace as his own, nor did I want my sons to be anywhere in the vicinity.

I hurried back into the chamber and pulled a tunic from my trunk. I dressed quickly, then grabbed my himation, cloaked my head, and slipped out a side door. I ran to a back door of Mother's house and let myself in.

As I ran, I couldn't help remembering the murderous plot that had eliminated Simon and his two eldest sons on the same night. The murderers had also searched for John Hyrcanus that night, but by HaShem's grace they were unable to find him.

I would find Kissa, my mother, and my sons, and we would go into hiding. I did not know how far Aristobulus had cast his net of destruction, but I would not allow it to snag my sons.

~~~~~~~~~~

We escaped the high priest's house without being noticed, thanks to Kissa, who led us through a servants' passage and out a gate that had been partially hidden behind vines and shrubs.

Mother refused to go with us at first, believing that Aristobulus would never harm anyone. Only when I insisted I needed her help with the boys could I persuade her to leave.

After making it past the walls of the high priest's palace, we slipped down the streets of the Temple district, slinking through shadows while I tried to think of a safe place to hide. I then remembered my tutor, Josu Attis, who lived with his family near the Valley of the Cheesemakers.

Because I did not know exactly where the tutor lived, the five of us slept in a doorway until sunrise. The boys woke early and peppered me with questions: "Where is Father?" "Will we sleep here tonight?" "Can we go home soon?" "Can I have bread and honey?"

I tried to soothe them as best I could, but I had only gentle words to offer. True to their natures, worry clouded Hyrcanus's eyes, while Aristobulus thought our frantic journey through the darkened city was quite the adventure. Happy to see his enthusiasm, I maintained that fiction and told the boys we were playing a game, the goal of which was to find a kindly scholar named Josu Attis.

"We will ask people for clues about where he lives," I explained, holding tight to Aristobulus's hand. "But we must not tell them who we are or why we want to find him."

By the second hour of the day, we had found someone who directed us to the tutor's home. We were tired and thirsty when we finally knocked on his door, and when he opened it I nearly collapsed into his arms. After hearing my story, he and his wife agreed to let us stay until we could learn what had happened to Jannaeus.

Within two days, everyone in the city had heard about the aftermath of John Hyrcanus's death. Judah Aristobulus had left the reading of the will and gone immediately to take command of the Temple guard. He had the high priest's house surrounded—his house now, by right—dragging his mother and three youngest brothers off to the Baris. The next day, as an assembly of Levites and members of the Sanhedrin watched in astonishment, Aristobulus sat in the high priest's reception hall and proclaimed himself king, momentarily trading the high priest's miter for a golden crown. He rewarded his brother's loyalty by appointing Antigonus as commander of the Judean armies.

The new king's final announcement was about a reward. One hundred talents would be given to anyone who could locate the two sons of Alexander Jannaeus. They had become lost in the confusion, Aristobulus explained, and he wanted to keep them safe at the Temple fortress.

"He would keep them imprisoned," I whispered when Josu Attis gave me the dire news. "He wants to make sure they are not free to lead an uprising against them."

Josu nodded. A current of fear stirred in his eyes, and I was sure he saw the same dark current in mine. "He has captured his opposition," he said. "And you can be sure none of them will be freed so long as he sits on his throne."

"HaShem be merciful," I whispered, remembering how I had once considered John Hyrcanus my savior. Where was he now that I needed saving again? I could think of no one who would or could step forward to rescue my husband or my sons.

The streets of Jerusalem buzzed with the news of such astonishing developments, yet no one dared stand against Judah Aristobulus. He commanded an army of mercenaries, he controlled the Temple guards, and he occupied the high priest's palace. He had also taken everything without spilling a single drop of blood.

Still, the people were not happy. Jerusalem had not been home to a king since Zedekiah, whose reign ended when Nebuchadnezzar carried the city's inhabitants away to Babylon.

When I realized how thoroughly Judah Aristobulus had prepared and how long he had waited, I saw that Uncle had been more than a wise man; he had been a prophet. He knew his eldest sons would cause trouble for the younger ones, so he sent us to Galilee and kept the two youngest by his side. If we had remained in that area, out of Aristobulus's sight, we might have spent many happy years in that region.

"How long?" I asked Josu. "How long do you think Aristobulus will keep Jannaeus in the Baris?"

My former tutor sat across from me with his little son on his knee. "Until he decides to kill him," he replied, his voice sober. "Because as long as your husband lives, he is a threat. So are Absalom and Elias. And so are you and your boys, Salome, if you do anything to encourage support for any other Hasmonean heir. You would do well to live quietly, even obscurely, as long as Aristobulus is in power."

"What if he remains in power for years?"

Josu shook his head slowly. "We will pray it will not be so. Because things will not go well for Judea with such a ruthless man as king. To think he is also the high priest . . ." He shuddered. "HaShem will not be mocked. And the righteous will not tolerate a usurper in the Temple."

I sat in silence, studying my sleeping sons. Why had I ever allowed Jannaeus to name our second son after his brother? The name would forever taste like gall on my tongue.

"What do you think will happen?" I asked. "What should I do? My innocent sons are my most important concern. I need to know whether we should stay in Jerusalem or find some other place to live quietly."

"I can tell you what will happen next," Josu said, his eyes narrowing. "Aristobulus has been fortunate so far, but blood is always shed when power is forcefully seized. People are going to die. Some will draw their swords in defense of Alena,

Hyrcanus's choice to lead the nation. Others will draw their swords for Aristobulus, because he will promise riches and power in return for their support. Men will fight to the death, and the winner will rule Jerusalem and Judea. The loser will not be shown mercy."

His somber eyes met mine. "Has history not taught us this? You know these truths from your studies; now you will know them from experience. Consider the kingdoms around us, and you will see that we have become like them."

A ghost spider climbed the length of my spine as I realized how right my former tutor was. In the next few weeks, either Alena or Aristobulus would die, and all traces of the love that used to exist between them would vanish.

"A son plotting against his mother," I said, looking at my innocent boys. "I can think of nothing more horrible."

"I can." Sadness filled Josu's eyes. "*Two* sons plotting against their mother."

<hr />

Josu and his wife helped me find a small house where I could live with what remained of my family. The place was near Josu's home, and every day Kissa and I helped his wife with her daily work—grinding grain, drawing water, mending clothing. I had not done such menial labor since childhood, but Kissa was a patient teacher.

Because we needed an income, Josu suggested that I work as a copyist. "I know people who need copies of important documents," he said. "I receive so many requests that I cannot possibly handle the work by myself. But I could take these jobs and pass the work to you. You have a fine hand and could probably earn a living as a scribe. No one needs to know that a woman is doing the copying."

"Kissa also writes well," I said, suddenly grateful that I had taught my handmaid how to read and write. "With her help, surely we could make enough to meet our needs."

So it was settled. Josu began to bring us documents, some in Greek, some in Hebrew, and a few in Aramaic. While my mother oversaw the care of the children, Kissa and I procured the supplies we needed, set up desks in the front of the house, and began our work as copyists. I determined to follow Josu's advice and live quietly, not revealing my identity or my association with John Hyrcanus's family. I would not even go out in public unless absolutely necessary.

Every morning Kissa visited the marketplace to buy food, supplies, and hear the latest gossip. Every day she came back with new reports of skirmishes, riots in the Temple courtyard, and protests outside the high priest's palace.

Three weeks after Aristobulus's violent takeover, she came into the house and slammed the door behind her, her face streaked with tears and her breath coming in quick gasps.

"What's wrong?"

She shook her head, then looked pointedly at the boys. Realizing she would not speak in front of them, I gestured for her to step outside with me.

Once we were alone in the courtyard, she took my arm. "Alena," she said, her eyes filling again. "She is dead."

"Did he . . . did Aristobulus execute her?"

"Indirectly," Kissa said. "Since that first night, Alena was not allowed to leave her room. Aristobulus gave orders that she be given no food and only a cupful of water a day. She died yesterday."

I turned away, the news too much to bear. How could any son allow his mother to suffer such an agonizing death? Alena had been the kindest, most capable and sophisticated woman in Jerusalem. I had never seen her do anything cruel, and if the situation were reversed, she would have treated her sons with kindness and mercy.

"So the resistance is over. Aristobulus is king, and no one remains to challenge him. Judea has a king."

"And a high priest," Kissa added.

I turned back to her. "What of Antigonus?"

"He commands the army. He has already won his brother's approval by defeating the men who fought to free Alena from the fortress. More than forty died in that effort."

I sank onto a nearby bench. "And my husband? Is Aristobulus feeding Jannaeus?"

Kissa sat by my side. "They say that Jannaeus, Absalom, and Elias are alive and well as they can be in that place. Aristobulus probably knows the people would turn on him if he starved them as well."

"Why didn't he worry about public opinion concerning Alena?"

Kissa shook her head. "I don't know, mistress. Perhaps . . . perhaps he dared starve her because she was a woman and not likely to win the approval of the religious leaders. I heard one man say that Aristobulus won his position just as John Hyrcanus won his—at the cost of his mother's life."

I had nearly forgotten the tragedy that overshadowed Uncle's early days as high priest. Now, however, the memory of it resurfaced with fearful clarity. Uncle had abandoned his mother to a tyrant in order to claim his place as the high priest and leader of Judea. But Uncle had to leave his mother, because an army was threatening Jerusalem. The Holy City was not under any threat when Aristobulus abandoned Alena.

Bending beneath a load of grief, I folded my hands and stared at my interlocked fingers. What would Uncle say if he could see his family now? His beloved wife dead and his sons—three locked up in the Temple fortress, two rising to power after a bloodbath. He had suspected something like this would happen, so why hadn't he done something to prevent it?

A sudden thought occurred to me. "What about Salina Alexandra?" I asked, turning to Kissa. "Does she support her husband in this, or did she protest?"

"No one knows," Kissa answered. "Although when has a woman been able to stop a man from doing what he wants to do? She is queen now and living with Aristobulus at your uncle's palace—probably sleeping in Alena's bedchamber. But she has not been seen in public. Perhaps she is ashamed of what her husband has done."

"Or perhaps she is having someone make her a few more richly appointed tunics," I countered, dismayed to hear sarcasm in my voice. "Could this be what she wanted?"

Kissa stared at a stunted olive tree in our garden. "Perhaps. After all, she may be the mother of the next Hasmonean king."

"Or she may be dead within the year. With Aristobulus sitting on the throne, who can say? Still, Salina is a cousin, and we have been friendly in the past. I should write her."

"Careful." Kissa's eyes widened. "Josu counseled you to remain hidden. If Aristobulus knows you and your children are still in Jerusalem . . ."

"I do not think Salina would betray me," I said, standing. "And if she does, we will set out at once for Galilee. I have friends there, and a house."

Kissa lifted a brow. "You had better pray we can get away in time."

⁓⁓⁓⁓

Dear cousin and friend, greetings!

I hope this letter finds you well. I am sending it with my trusted handmaid in the hope you will receive her in my name. How distressed I was to hear of Alena's tragic death! My heart breaks to think of the anguish wrought by your husband, my kinsman. I do not blame you for the outcome, for the power of life and death lies in HaShem's hands, but I am sure you must ask yourself if there was anything you could have done to save her.

I know I am taking a liberty in writing you, but necessity demands that I extend these words with the courage of Esther. I have two sons, young boys I love more than life, and I must have the truth from you.

Are we safe, or should my sons and I take measures to safeguard our lives? We remain in Jerusalem, but if the king's attention should turn toward us, or if his face should cloud in disfavor when our names are mentioned, I would take my sons and flee the Holy City. Please, I do not count it a small thing to ask a wife to circumvent her husband, yet I know you would not do anything to destroy an innocent woman and her precious children.

Thank you. Please send word via my handmaid, or if that is not possible, please seek out the tutor in the Valley of the Cheesemakers. He will know how to reach us.

I remain forever in your service,

Salome Alexandra

Slipping into the high priest's palace through a servants' entrance, Kissa found my kinswoman sitting in the garden. When she told me she had been able to place the letter into Salina's own hand, I thanked HaShem for giving my handmaid knowledge of every inch of that grand house.

"I waited while she read it," Kissa told me, breathless from her dash through the twisting streets. "And though I expected an answer, she rolled up the scroll and said she could not reply yet, but I should tell you to remain quiet and safe. She said she would make things right when she could, but she would have to be careful. Then she bade me leave before I was spotted."

"What does she intend to do?"

Kissa shook her head. "I don't know. The queen may not know. But when her mind is settled on a plan, she will act in your favor, I am sure of it. She looked quite distressed as she read your letter."

Since I had no idea what Salina might do, I had no choice but to continue living in quiet obscurity. Every night my sons and I prayed for Jannaeus, that he would remain healthy and strong despite the privations of his makeshift prison. Privately I prayed that public opinion would remain firmly set against Aristobulus, who had murdered his innocent mother and imprisoned his brothers.

I also prayed for Salina, that HaShem would give my quiet, beautiful cousin the courage to do whatever was necessary to free my husband and guarantee my sons' safety.

CHAPTER THIRTY

Kissa

I paused at a fabric booth and ran my fingers over a length of silk.

"Very fine, very expensive," said the woman behind the counter. "From the East."

I quickly withdrew my hand. "I was just looking for my mistress."

"Ah." The woman's face brightened. "Your mistress is a fine lady?"

"She is . . . from a good family."

"She can afford such things?"

I smiled, uncertain of how I should answer. Shelamzion had been a wealthy woman, but now we barely earned enough to buy food and supplies for our work as copyists.

I lifted my chin. "My mistress has no need for silks, but you have lovely fabrics. Good day."

I lowered my head as I walked toward the merchants who sold fruits and vegetables. The rising sun had swallowed up the strong wind that rattled our windows last night. The boys had been frightened, and my mistress was anxious too, though she tried not to show it. Every rattle of the window or door quickened our pulses. Was it the wind, or was it someone who wanted to eliminate any challenge to Aristobulus?

Months had passed since I had delivered her letter to Salina Alexandra, and we had heard nothing from the high priest's wife. I was beginning to think that Salina had decided to do nothing, yet every night Shelamzion prayed that deliverance would soon come from Salina's hand.

I stopped by a booth and fingered the leather on the counter. The material was far softer than the leather we had been writing on, and I wondered how it would hold the ink.

The merchant stepped forward and waggled his brows. "Do you like?"

I nodded. "It is very soft. And probably very expensive."

The merchant laughed. "Yes, it is costlier than the usual leathers prepared with quicklime. This is prepared by the Persian process that uses dates. The leather is much more flexible and will last longer."

I touched the leather again. Shelamzion had recently been asked to copy a document containing a *pesher*, or commentary, on a section of the Torah. She would probably want to use the finest leather possible for that task. "How much?" I asked.

"For two lengths, four drachmas."

I bit my lip. We usually earned four drachmas in a day, so was the finer quality worth a full day's work?

"I will take it," I said and pulled the silver coins from my purse. "We will see if my mistress feels it is worth the extra expense."

"Think of it as an investment," the merchant said as he wrapped two lengths of the leather. "Your mistress will appreciate the quality when she sees the finished writings."

I paid him, took my package, and dropped it into my basket. When I turned to leave, my gaze crossed that of a man standing across the way. He was not shopping but examining my face with great concentration.

I averted my eyes, unease washing over me. I took two steps, then pivoted and returned to the leather merchant. I glanced over my shoulder and saw that the stranger was still staring at me.

"Sir?"

The merchant came over. "Ah! Do you want more skins?"

"No—do you see an odd man behind me? He is standing in front of the booth that sells sandals."

The merchant craned his neck. "There are so many people out today . . . wait." He hunched forward and looked at me. "Do you mean the man in the red cloak? The one looking this way?"

"Yes. Do you know him?"

The merchant peered behind me again, then leaned closer. "I do not know his name, but he works for the high priest. Aristobulus has employed several men who roam throughout the city."

"What do they do?"

The merchant shrugged. "They look for spies and infidels—or so I've heard. And they are still looking for the two grandsons of our late high priest. But no doubt that is a red cloak, so the man there belongs to the king."

I thanked him and clutched my basket more tightly. I had done nothing wrong. If one of the king's men was following me, then I had been recognized.

Aristobulus and Antigonus knew me well—not only had we grown up next to each other, but I used to watch over them when they were small. Aristobulus could have given a detailed description of me to his men, knowing Shelamzion would send me out to buy supplies, and knowing I would lead anyone who followed right back to Shelamzion and her boys.

I kept my head lowered as I hurried down the lane of booths, then ducked into an egg merchant's shop. "Hey!" the seller called, but I waved her away and rushed into an alley, quickly increasing the distance between myself and the marketplace.

After glancing behind to be sure I was not followed, I broke into a run and took the long way home.

〜〜〜

"What do you mean, a man was watching you?"

My mistress's face, usually calm and reserved, had gone blank with concern.

"In the marketplace," I repeated. "I asked the leather merchant if he knew who the man was, and he said he served the king. Apparently he has an army of red cloaks who spy for him."

Shelamzion went straight to her children, who were practicing their letters on the table. With a hand on each boy's shoulder, she looked at me with fear and confusion in her eyes. She lowered her voice. "Do you think he knows where we are?"

I knew who she meant, of course. Neither of us wanted to speak the king's name in front of her sons or do anything to frighten them.

I moved to the window, peered out at the street, and closed the shutters. "I don't know. I only know what I saw and what the merchant told me. I know the man saw me, but I don't think he followed me. He doesn't know where we live."

"But next time, Kissa—next time the spy will not be wearing a red cloak. Next time he will look like an ordinary man, and you won't notice him." Shelamzion released her boys and paced the length of the room, her hands fretting at her waist. "What do we do now?"

I certainly didn't know. I sat on a bench and watched my mistress pace the floor nervously. "I will ask Josu Attis," she said, nodding. "I will ask him for advice. Perhaps instead of going to the market, you could watch his children while his wife goes in your place. We should avoid being in public at all costs, both of us."

"For the rest of our lives?" My voice came out as a hoarse croak. "We cannot hide for the rest of our lives."

She gave me a stern look. "Aristobulus will not be king for the rest of our lives."

I pressed my lips together. Had she forgotten that the king was younger than we were? We were not likely to outlive him.

"Perhaps we should change our names," she said, still pacing. "We could move to a village outside Jerusalem and call ourselves something else."

"But how would we live? We are able to work because we are in Jerusalem, where scholars can afford to pay copyists. Few scholars live in small villages."

"Josu Attis could visit and bring us work. He could come once a week, and we would have the previous week's scrolls ready for him."

I gave her a reproachful look. "Is it fair to ask him to go to all that trouble? He and his family have already done so much for us."

Her brows rushed together. "Are you determined to thwart me? I am trying to save our lives—"

I held up my hand. "I know. I only wish to help you find the best solution."

A rapid knock at the door cut into the heavy silence around us. Shelamzion looked at me. "Could that be Mother?"

"Why would she knock? She usually walks right in."

My mistress went over and opened the door a crack, then widened it. Josu Attis's wife stepped into the room, then lowered the himation she had wrapped about her head. "A soldier," she said, her voice breathless, "came to the house looking for a tutor. When I said my husband was a tutor, he asked where he could find Salome Alexandra."

A tiny flicker of shock widened Shelamzion's eyes. "You—you didn't tell him, did you?"

"Of course not. I told him that many tutors lived in the Valley of the Cheesemakers, and that we did not know a Salome Alexandra."

My mistress grasped the woman's hands. "Thank you! Go back home now, but make sure you are not followed. And may HaShem bless you for your kindness."

Once the woman had left, Shelamzion sank onto the bench, her face a study in resignation. "She was not happy with me, and I don't blame her for being upset."

I nodded. "No woman would be pleased to find one of the king's men at her door."

Shelamzion pressed her hand to her flushed cheek and shook her head. "You are right, of course. I cannot ask more of Josu. But I don't know what else to do."

I blew out a breath. "You are always saying that HaShem cares for us. If that is so, you should ask Him to hide us from the king."

CHAPTER THIRTY-ONE

Shelamzion

I pulled the fabric of my himation forward on my head, hiding my face within a cowl. I had spent two days worrying about the stranger Kissa described, and I would not worry anymore. I would go to the marketplace myself and see if anyone followed or even noticed me.

As I walked, I thanked HaShem again that I had not been born to John Hyrcanus. Because I was not the former high priest's daughter, I had not lived in the public eye, and few people knew of my association with what had become Judea's royal family. I felt a wry smile tug at my lips as I thanked HaShem that I had not been born as beautiful as my sister. If I had been, I might attract attention, and attention was the last thing I wanted so long as Aristobulus called himself king.

I wound my way through the Valley of the Cheesemakers, then skirted the Essene Quarter. An impromptu market always appeared near the Essene Gate on Friday, so I approached with the air of a woman gathering the items she would need for the Sabbath meal. As I sorted through vegetables and fruits, I kept glancing over my shoulder, alert for anyone who might appear unduly interested in my activity.

I was studying the cages of chickens when a nearby commotion made me turn around. A man had stumbled over a woman studying a rug on the ground, and she was not happy about being flat on her belly in public. "Why do you not watch where you are going?" she said, pushing herself to her knees. "Did you not see me down here?"

"Um, no." The man glanced at me, and my uneasiness swelled to alarm when our eyes met. He had no reason to look in my direction. Considering his circumstance, he ought to be focused on the woman he had knocked to the ground.

My heart stopped dead when he looked at me, but an instant later it resumed beating, thumping in my chest like a warning—*run, now!*

Dropping my shopping basket, I spun on the ball of my foot and fled, but not even the powerful pounding of my heart could disguise the sound of footsteps in the distance.

When I thought I had finally lost my pursuer, I ran home and barred the door behind me.

Kissa spun around, her eyes filled with alarm. "Did you—?"

I nodded. "As I thought, he wasn't wearing any kind of uniform, but he chased me when I ran. I've been running—" I grabbed the back of a chair as my knees went weak—"I'm sorry, let me catch my breath."

"Sit, sit. I will get you some water."

As Kissa poured water from a pitcher and Mother gaped at me, I sank into the chair and leaned forward to inhale great gulps of air. My sons looked at me, confused.

"Why were you running, Ima?" Hyrcanus asked.

Somehow I managed to smile. "Ima was shopping and decided to hurry home."

Hyrcanus looked at Aristobulus, who went right on eating his stew.

Kissa handed me a cup of water. "So," she said, "what do we do?"

"We stay inside. We keep the door barred. And we think about moving to Modein."

"We wouldn't have this problem in Modein," Mother said. "You should forget your husband and go to Modein, where you can find someone else to marry. That would solve all your problems."

When the boys had finished eating, Kissa and I filled our bowls and discussed the problem in low voices. I wasn't sure how we could survive in Modein, but we could live on the kindness of distant family members until it was time for planting. Perhaps one of my relatives would agree to take us in.

I had just put my sons to bed when someone knocked on the door. A thrill of fear shot through me as I looked at Kissa. The sun had already set, and the street was quiet outside. Who came knocking at a woman's house after dark?

Kissa gestured for me to step away from the door. She walked toward it, but then stopped to pick up a wooden spindle she could grip in one hand. She lifted the bar and peered through a sliver of an opening. "Who knocks?"

"Salina Alexandra." A soft voice, female. "Let me in, please. The king does not know I have come."

Salina? I caught my breath and hurried forward as Kissa opened the door. The queen, her slender form enveloped by a disguising cloak, stepped into the room and opened her arms to me. "Cousin!"

I embraced her with grateful relief. "How did you know where to find us?"

"I have had a man looking for you. He says he had great difficulty—"

"That was one of your men? Oh!" I sank into the nearest

chair to prevent my knees from giving way. "We thought he was from the king."

"You were wise to be wary." While Kissa stood guard at the door, Salina sat next to me, then reached out and took my hands. "I used to think I would enjoy being a queen and the high priest's wife. Now I see the wisdom of John Hyrcanus—Alena would be far better suited to rule Judea, for my husband is not a good king. And being the king's wife is not something I want to be."

"What makes you say so?"

Looking sad, pale, and utterly young in the glow of the lamp, Salina released me and shook her head. "Aristobulus is not well, not steady in his mind. He sent Antigonus and his troops to fight in the northern region of Galilee, but now he wanders about the palace sick and forlorn because he feels abandoned by his brother. He is despised by the Pharisees and criticized by the Sadducees with whom he is aligned, because they cannot forget how he treated his mother. The Essenes are opposed to his forcible circumcision of the Galileans. And the people! While none have dared denounce him within his hearing, they remain silent when he appears in the Temple. No one shouts for joy when he ends his prayers, and no one shouts praises when he has finished a sacrifice. He knows he is not liked, and he wants to be as beloved as his father was."

I exhaled a deep breath. I had no answers for her, but perhaps she would feel better after unburdening herself. "I am sorry to hear this."

Salina lifted her head, a weight of sadness on her thin face. "I have come up with a solution—some might say it is madness, but I believe it is my only way out. And I hope, Shelamzion, that my action will please you."

"Say what you mean, child," Mother scolded from the corner where she sat. "You speak in riddles."

Ignoring my mother, Salina leaned forward and looked into my eyes. "You were always kind to me, and I am grateful for it. I am sorry your husband is in prison and I am sorry for . . . well, you will see when the time comes. Now I must go."

"Stay," I begged, not wanting to send her away while she was distraught. "Surely there is something we can do to ease your mind."

She shook her head and moved toward the door. When she opened it, I saw her handmaid waiting outside in the moon-cast shadows.

"May HaShem bless you," Salina said, stepping out into the night. "If we do not meet again, know that I am doing what I must do because I am not as strong as you are."

I stood on the threshold, shivering beneath my shawl, and watched Salina and her handmaid hurry down the street, moving toward the high priest's palace. What had possessed the queen to come to me? And what could she possibly be planning?

I went back in the house and barred the door, then bent to stir the embers smoldering in the fire.

"That woman is crazy," Mother said, not caring to lower her voice. "As crazy as a mad rooster."

"Perhaps," I whispered. "But we shall see."

Not long after Salina's visit, Kissa and I were shopping and overheard a conversation between two merchants speaking Aramaic. I heard them mention a man called Judah, a well-known elder among the Essenes.

I held up my hand, warning Kissa to remain quiet. I had heard of this Essene—some said he was a prophet. Simeon ben Shetah did not believe so, but he said Judah occasionally predicted the future as HaShem gave him knowledge.

"The old Essene may not know what he is talking about," the first merchant said, "yet he claims the king's brother will die before Sukkot. He even named the place—Strato's Tower."

The second man laughed. "How can that be? The king's brother is already in Jerusalem for the feast. I saw him myself, parading through the Temple courtyard in shiny new armor. Strato's Tower is six hundred fifty furlongs from here; he could never reach it before the feast begins."

"They say old Judah has never been wrong," the first merchant countered, elbowing the second man. "If I were him, I would hate to be wrong about the king's brother. If either of them hears that Judah says he will die . . ." The man made a face and lifted his hands, then turned away.

I looked at Kissa, my thoughts spinning. Could this have anything to do with Salina's plan? Surely not. Salina had nothing in common with an elderly Essene, and the Essenes were even more opposed to Aristobulus's kingship than the Pharisees. None of them would even be willing to speak to her.

"What do you think?" I asked Kissa as we made our way through the marketplace. "Antigonus, dying? That is highly unlikely."

"Salina talked as if the king had gone mad," Kissa replied. "I have heard it whispered that the king has locked himself up in a room in the Baris and won't come out. Apparently he believes Antigonus is going to turn the army against him."

I halted. Aristobulus, at the Baris with his brothers? Not in the same chamber, certainly, but in the same structure. The walled tower at the Temple had been a last refuge for kings, priests, and the Maccabees during times of war and siege.

But Judah Aristobulus was not under attack, nor was he under siege. And I could not imagine Antigonus turning against his brother. They had been as close as a man and his shadow since childhood.

"Who would tell the king such a thing?" I asked. "It can't be true."

"I don't know, but Aristobulus has been barricaded inside a chamber at the Baris for more than a week."

We finished our shopping and carried our baskets home.

My thoughts were still preoccupied with the problem at midday. "No one in the military would tell the king that Antigonus wanted to betray him," I said, thinking aloud as I poured grain into a bowl. "No warrior would dare come between those two. I wish *my* sons were as close as they are."

"The king does not trust many people," Kissa pointed out. "So it would have to be someone close to him."

"Someone . . ." I gasped as the pieces fell into place. "Someone who had something to gain from a rift between them. Someone who does not think Aristobulus is a good ruler. Someone . . . like his wife."

Kissa's face lit with understanding. "Of course! But what could Salina hope to accomplish by coming between them?"

I brought my hands to my head as my mind vibrated with a thousand thoughts. "She has already managed to isolate the king. He is afraid, suspicious and mistrustful, and he has locked himself away—with no counselors, no brother, no father to guide him. He has only Salina."

Kissa's gaze rose to meet mine, and neither of us dared to predict what might happen next.

<hr />

I imagined all sorts of scenarios for Aristobulus and Antigonus, whom I had once loved as younger brothers, but could never have imagined what actually happened just before Sukkot. I learned the details from Kissa, who heard them from a servant at the high priest's house. As the streets of Jerusalem echoed with the cries of mourners, Kissa came home to tell the story.

The marketplace rumors were true. Judah Aristobulus had locked himself away in the Temple fortress because he believed his brother was preparing to overthrow him. He had even given his guards a standing order—if Antigonus appeared in his armor, they were to execute him immediately.

When Antigonus arrived in Jerusalem to celebrate the Festival of Tabernacles, Judah Aristobulus sent a message as a test of his brother's loyalty: *Come to me, but unarmed.*

Salina—or one of her servants—intercepted the courier and substituted a different message: *The king yearns to see your new armor. Wear it when you visit him in the Baris.*

So, fully armed and armored, Antigonus went to the Temple. Happily, or so the rumors reported, he trotted down the stairs leading to the underground passageway that ended at the Baris. When the guards at the entrance saw a fully armed warrior approaching, they killed him without hesitation.

The news of Antigonus's death spread throughout the city like a contagion. Judah the Essene was among those at the Temple to celebrate Sukkot, and when he heard where Antigonus died, he was perplexed . . . until someone pointed out that the underground tunnel was known as Strato's Tower.

My heart twisted as Kissa told me the story. "Oh, those poor boys," I whispered, seeing their young faces in a flash of memory. "I am glad Uncle and Alena are not alive to hear this. What a terrible tragedy."

"The story gets worse," Kissa said. "But if you would rather not hear it—"

"Tell me." I looked her in the eye. "I would know everything."

Kissa drew a deep breath. "After hearing that Antigonus was dead, Aristobulus fell ill. They say he became sick with pain in his gut and lost his mind. He wandered about the Baris and pounded on the door of the chamber that held Jannaeus and the other two brothers, but he would not speak to them. Then he began vomiting great quantities of blood."

I made a face even as some speculative part of my brain summoned up a recollection of Grypus walking with me in his garden. He had pointed at various plants and mentioned one that could make a man vomit blood.

"A servant came to clean up the mess," Kissa went on, "and as he was leaving, the slave slipped and spilled the king's blood on the very spot where the blood of Antigonus had stained the stones. When the king heard about *that*, he cried out, saying he would not be able to escape the wrath of Adonai but would have to pay for his brother's murder. Though his wife and servants tried to calm and console him, he would not be comforted. He sank onto his bed . . . and died."

As Mother wept quietly in her corner, I closed my eyes. Salina had been desperate when we last saw her. Desperate enough to use poison? Perhaps.

But had her desperation been motivated by a desire to be rid of a troublesome husband or an eagerness to rule Judea on her own?

<hr />

Judah Aristobulus's reign over Judea lasted only one year.

I was not surprised to receive a summons from the high priest's palace the day after his death. The two brothers had been quickly buried—side by side, as they had lived—in a Hasmonean tomb. Since Salina had no children, all Jerusalem waited anxiously to hear who would be the next high priest and king.

The king's widow would not make them wait long.

I went to the high priest's palace alone, sauntered through the courtyard gates, and looked at the buildings I had once called home. I could almost see Mother sitting on the porch of our small house and hear the clatter of Uncle's coach over the paving stones. Alena used to look out of that upper window, her face alight whenever she saw her husband approaching . . .

I blinked the images of the past away and forced myself to move forward. I crossed the threshold and found myself in that beautiful vestibule. I was about to turn into the reception hall when a priest stopped me. "Salome Alexandra?"

I nodded.

"Salina Alexandra would like to see you privately. Come with me."

I found Salina in the high priest's bedchamber, sitting on the bed and wearing a simple tunic with her hair down. Like a proper grieving widow, she had not adorned herself with cosmetics or jewelry.

"Shelamzion." She stood to embrace me, then gestured to a padded bench—a bench I had used many times when I visited Alena in the same room. "Please," Salina said, sitting again. "I need to tell you what will happen next."

I took the seat she offered, folded my hands, and studied her face. She did not look like a murderous conspirator, but neither did she look like the wild-eyed girl who had visited me days ago. I had never seen a woman so calm and self-possessed.

"Before you say anything," I said, "I know about the poison. I know you told Antigonus to wear his armor because you knew the king had given an order to kill any armed man who approached the Baris."

Her brows rose, delicate arches above bold eyes. "John Hyrcanus always said you were clever."

"If you want my approval—"

"I am not asking for anything, cousin. I am not explaining anything. But I will say this—I saw the situation in Judea more clearly than anyone, for I knew Aristobulus better than anyone. Someone had to do something." A smile flickered over her lips. "I have no time now for idle chatter. What you need to know is this: Aristobulus's will declares that I will become queen and rule Judea."

I nearly choked on the bitter laugh that rose in my throat. Somehow I clamped it down, even though I wanted to stand and leave the room as quickly as I could. I wanted nothing to do with murder or the clear-eyed, manipulative woman before me.

"I know what you're thinking"—a corner of her mouth twisted—"and you are wrong. I brought you here because my first act as queen will be to release your husband and his brothers from prison. My second act will be to relinquish the throne and crown your husband king. The Sanhedrin will anoint him as high priest shortly thereafter."

I sat completely still, blank, amazed, and shaken. "You—Jannaeus. Why him?"

"Because," she said, "he knows his place."

I did not know what she meant by that, but she gave me no time to question her further.

"Soon," she finished, "you will be queen. I hope you can find some joy in it."

She stood and abruptly dismissed me as a wall of whispering approached us. A group of guards came into the room along with Jannaeus, Absalom, and Elias—all of them thin but alive and well.

Without looking at me, Jannaeus stepped forward and knelt on one knee before Salina Alexandra. She gave him a small smile, then took a step back and lowered herself to the floor in a formal bow.

I looked around. Behind me, the servants, guards, and even Absalom and Elias were doing the same. Though my mind spun with bewilderment, I commanded my limbs to obey and sank to the floor.

Jerusalem was about to receive a new king.

Chapter Thirty-Two

Shelamzion

Queen.

I walked up the stone staircase of John Hyrcanus's former home, past the reception room where I used to observe him, and past the curious servants watching from the vestibule.

I never wanted to be queen. In all my thirty-seven years, I never dreamed I would be. But here I was, married to Alexander Jannaeus, the twenty-three-year-old king of Judea and high priest of Israel.

I entered the chamber where Uncle and Alena had slept. I saw the bed where Alena had proudly presented her new baby, Alexander Jannaeus, to a fourteen-year-old girl called Shelamzion.

The same bed Salina sat on when she told me her plan.

"I hope, Shelamzion, that my action will please you," she had said when she visited our home.

How could it? How could I live in this house as queen when that title rightly belonged to Alena? If not for the avarice of Judah Aristobulus, this would still be her home. If not for

Salina's conniving and Jannaeus's ambition, this house might belong to someone far more deserving.

"Oh, Adonai," I whispered, standing at the doors that opened onto the balcony, "give me wisdom and grant us grace. For the man I have married is not wise enough to be king."

I had hoped my husband would mature during the months of his confinement. I had hoped he would develop a tender affection for his younger brothers and a deeper reverence for Adonai.

But after only a few weeks, I saw that he had done none of those things.

Within a year, both Absalom and Elias had joined Aristobulus and Antigonus in the family tomb. Elias had the temerity to attempt a coup, which Jannaeus easily put down by executing his youngest brother. Absalom was wise enough to stay away from the palace and its politics, but several months after Jannaeus claimed the throne, Absalom died under mysterious circumstances.

With four of John Hyrcanus's five sons gone, only Jannaeus remained.

The night we received the news of Absalom's death, I looked at my husband and realized we had become just like the Gentiles who ruled the empires around us. As a young girl, I was appalled to learn how the Ptolemies married their kin and murdered their siblings, but had we not done the same things? Had we not become like the pagans who did not know HaShem?

Uncle once told me that as long as we did not despise our Law, we had the freedom to adopt new ways and attitudes. Yet the more I considered the kingdom of Judea, the more resolute I became in my determination to serve Adonai and honor every jot and tittle of the Law.

In that moment I made HaShem a promise: I would send

for Simeon ben Shetah, and I would devote myself anew to my Torah studies. I would study the Scriptures and the oral laws, and I would do my best to please Adonai and be an example to my husband and my precious sons. How else could I live in a family who only pretended to seek HaShem's blessing?

Simeon would help me observe even the smallest portions of the Law, written and unwritten, and I would allow these to define every aspect of my life—how I ate, how I walked, how I worshiped, and how I dealt with Gentiles. I would observe the Sabbath faithfully. So long as my monthly courses flowed, I would remain apart from others and end my time of separation with a proper mikvah. I would do all this and more in order to demonstrate righteousness in a palace where righteousness had become rare.

At home I would be a virtuous mother to my sons. I would teach them the Law of the Lord, and I would encourage them to seek wisdom above all else. I would tell them stories of our forefathers, those who followed Adonai and those who did not, so my sons could learn from their examples.

I would be a virtuous wife to my husband. Though he did not seek my bed as often as he once had, I would be faithful to him and modest in my speech, dress, and conduct. I would encourage him to love HaShem and seek righteousness, and I would offer to help as I had in Galilee. Jannaeus was not a man who liked to sit and listen, so if I could listen to the problems of the people in his stead, I would.

Because my year of living among the people had taught me that they were not happy with the events of the past two years. Most of them missed John Hyrcanus, and Aristobulus's bloody reign had left them disturbed and disgusted with the Hasmoneans. If a new candidate appeared on the horizon, a righteous man from the tribe of Judah, they would fall to their knees and beg him to be their king.

Israel wanted a savior. The people's longing for a fresh start was almost palpable in the city streets.

A new appreciation for the Pharisees and the Essenes bloomed in my heart. I had heard that many of the Essenes were planning to establish a community in the desert to prepare for the coming of the Messiah. Like me, they were no longer content to merely acknowledge the Law; they vowed to *perform* it and become living examples.

In stark contrast, my husband was a Sadducee, who cared nothing for talk of the coming Messiah, and he cared even less about the idea of an afterlife. His thoughts centered on living each day and taking pleasure where he could find it.

Yet I knew life did not end with death. David spoke of living after this life, and so did Job. Enoch and Elijah had been taken away, and where did they go? Surely they were with HaShem.

One day I would also be with Him. Until then, I would do my utmost to live a holy life. Every day I would ask HaShem to help my husband be the king he could and ought to be.

A king ought to be an example for his people. Likewise I would have to become an example for my king.

⁓⁓⁓⁓⁓

I do not know what my husband did to pass the time in prison, but eventually I realized that he must have whiled away the hours planning his first actions as high priest and ruler. I said as much to him at dinner one night.

"Husband," I said, turning on my couch to better see him, "you have been so decisive since becoming king—one would almost think you knew you would be released."

He gave a half smile. "I knew it would go one of two ways. Either I would die or I would sit on the throne. Aristobulus had no other options."

"He could have freed you to come home to your family."

Jannaeus shook his head. "He could not. So long as I lived, I could have led an insurgency against him, and he would have been a fool to take the risk. Live or die—the only two choices."

And the reason he killed his two younger brothers.

"I am glad you were not executed," I said, leaving a host of words unspoken. I could not hope to win my husband if I spent all my time berating him.

"Of course you are. Without me, you would be nothing."

He was correct, and yet my spirit flared at his assertion. Kissa, Mother, and I had nearly chosen to move to Modein and live in poverty, but even as poor farmers we would never have been *nothing*.

Becoming king changed my husband in ways I could not have foreseen. He still had no patience for dealing with the problems of common people, and his vision for territorial expansion now extended far beyond Galilee. Not content to be a capable ruler, he aspired to the particular renown of Alexander the Great.

"I *am* Alexander," he frequently boasted, reminding all who listened of his formal name. "I have his character and his genius." He commanded the Jerusalem mint to produce coins that on one side displayed the lily, a symbol of Jerusalem, and on the other side an anchor, a symbol of the coastal territories he desperately desired to conquer.

Within a few months of his investiture, Jannaeus summoned his military chiefs. His first conquest, he informed me as a servant helped him into a new suit of armor, would be Ptolemais, a Galilean port city controlled by the Seleucids. "I have dreamed of capturing Ptolemais for years," he said as the servant slipped a heavy coat of mail over his tunic. "When Ezra Diagos and I would ride through the Galilean hills, I would see that city gleaming on the western horizon. It is the perfect port, and we shall claim it for Judea."

I smiled in wifely agreement, but my thoughts had been distracted at the mention of Jannaeus's commander. "Will Diagos lead your army?"

"Who else is as cunning and brave?" Jannaeus flexed his arms, testing his freedom of movement. "I have sent for him. He is bringing five thousand mercenaries to Jerusalem, and we will leave for Ptolemais as soon as possible."

"Diagos is coming here?"

My husband nodded absently, then raised his arms while his servant adjusted the belt. "The gold-handled dagger," Jannaeus said, pointing to a selection of blades on a table. "And the sword."

The servant slid these onto the belt, then fastened it and stepped back. Jannaeus put on his new silver helmet, shaped close to the head and topped with a red plume, then turned and admired his reflection in the large slab of polished granite he had installed in his bedchamber, a large space at the back of the house . . . and as far away from my room as it could possibly be.

"You look handsome," I told him, hoping to say what he wanted to hear.

He smiled at his reflection, resting his hand on the hilt of his sword. Then he turned to face me. "Tonight I will be out. If Ezra Diagos arrives early, you must keep him company at dinner. I will join you if I can."

He moved toward the door, then paused to pour himself a glass of water, gargled, and spit into a basin. He then left the chamber, his red plume bouncing with every step.

With startling clarity, I realized where he was going. The gargling and spitting was a breath-cleansing ritual he used to perform just before climbing into my bed. If he was gargling in the middle of the day, he was off to see another woman.

I considered that revelation as if it were a stone in my hand.

I studied it, marveled at it, searched my heart for some reaction to it . . . and discovered that I simply did not care.

~~~~~

Determined to remain above reproach despite my husband's dalliances, I planned a dinner for myself, my sons, Simeon ben Shetah, and Ezra Diagos. I had the servants arrange the couches in the shape of a half-moon with the long side open for the servants. I would sit in the center and would not favor anyone with more attention than any other. I would definitely *not* favor Ezra Diagos, though I had thought about him many times since our first meeting in Galilee.

I cannot say why I thought about him. I was a married woman, a righteous woman, and I had no wish to betray my husband. But the commander was handsome, intelligent, and more clever than any man of my acquaintance. More than that, he laughed at my little jokes, which Jannaeus never understood, and he actually seemed to *hear* when he listened to me. A light filled his eyes when we talked, a gleam that led me to believe he might feel the same pleasure in my company that I felt in his.

Before dinner, I sat at my dressing table and tried to remain calm as Kissa did my hair. While my thoughts scampered about like squirrels, I took deep breaths and pretended that this dinner would be like any other.

Kissa pinned the last pearl into my hair. "Would you like to wear the blue gown?"

"The rose, I think." I forced a yawn. "I was saving it to surprise Jannaeus, but I doubt he would even notice."

Kissa pulled the new garment from the trunk and ran her fingers over the silky fabric. I rarely wore this shade, but the pink hues might bring out the color in my skin and lips. Perhaps I would look younger than my years.

My thoughts took a sharp detour at the thought. Jannaeus

was probably with a young woman now, celebrating her beauty because mine had faded even before he took me as his wife.

"Kissa"—I fingered the garment's modest neckline as Kissa adjusted the fit—"you hear all the rumors being spread among the servants, do you not?"

She chuckled as she drew several himations from a basket. "Even rumors I would rather not hear."

"So tell me—who is my husband with tonight?"

She froze, himations in hand, and reluctantly met my gaze. "The daughter of a salt merchant." She looked away and spoke more rapidly. "I hoped you would never know. I do not want to see you hurt."

"Is everyone in the palace aware of his new infatuation?"

She hesitated before dipping her chin in a slight nod.

I reached out and selected a white himation from her offerings. "Thank you for telling me. I am not hurt, although my pride is a little wounded."

"Who told you?"

The corner of my mouth twisted. "Jannaeus. Not directly, of course, but I think he meant for me to know. Life will be easier for him if I am aware of his infidelities. He won't have to make such an effort crafting his lies."

"Even so," Kissa said, "I am sorry for it. You deserve a husband who loves you alone."

I caught her hand and squeezed it. "So do you. But here I sit, and there you stand, and apparently neither of us was meant to find happiness in marriage. Yet HaShem brought us together for His reasons."

I picked up the bouquet of roses she had placed on the dressing table. "And now, while my husband dallies with his mistress, I will go entertain his guests."

"How do you find your life as queen?" Ezra Diagos asked, leaning toward me.

I lowered my gaze and wiped my fingers on a piece of linen. "Adonai does what He wills. I never meant to be queen—"

"But here you are," Simeon ben Shetah interrupted. "And have you considered how much good you may do in your position?"

I tilted my head, surprised by the question. I was about to answer, but a piece of flying citron peel distracted me. Hyrcanus had tossed it at Aristobulus, and my younger son was preparing to throw a handful of grapes at his brother.

"Children!" I caught the eye of a servant at the door, then gestured to the boys. "My sons are ready to retire. See to it, will you?"

The boys did not complain, nor did I expect them to. At five and seven years, they would rather play in their bedchamber than sit quietly during a banquet.

Once they had left the room, I drew in a breath and looked at my esteemed Torah teacher. "In truth, since becoming queen, I have been feeling—" I searched for the right word and could only come up with one—"guilty."

Simeon lifted a brow. "Why is that?"

I shook my head, not knowing how to explain without implicating others. "I have become aware of failings . . . in my family. As a child, I thought John Hyrcanus the most righteous, most noble man in Judea, but now I see things differently. I have seen what his eldest son did to his mother. I have seen what my own husband did to his brothers . . ." I bit my lip, afraid I might say too much. Speaking one's mind could be dangerous in the high priest's palace, even for me. "Let me say this: I have been feeling a strong desire to return to the study of Torah. I want to lead others by example. I want my sons to understand that I am committed to obeying the Law. I want the righteousness of Adonai to shine from me."

I glanced at Ezra Diagos to see how he would react to my statement. If he was not equally committed to following HaShem, he might not be interested in continuing our friendship . . . and I could slam the door on the unrighteous yearnings of my heart.

Diagos's eyes warmed as he looked at me, the hint of a smile either appreciating my pursuit of righteousness or mocking it, I could not tell which.

But Simeon leaned closer, his face alight with eagerness. "This is good news indeed. HaShem, blessed be He, will reward you enormously."

I had expected him to approve, but his level of enthusiasm surprised me.

"Shelamzion," he continued, "many in Jerusalem feel the same way. They have seen the corruption of our leaders, and they know the current high priest—excuse me, my queen, but it is true—does not honor Adonai. We have turned our backs on everything Judas Maccabaeus and his brothers fought to defend, and we have forgotten how to live according to the Law."

Diagos shook his head. "Not everyone has forgotten. Many still follow the Law and worship at the Temple."

Simeon waved the commander's words away. "They follow a form of the Law, but it does not touch their hearts. Yet there are devout men and women who want to understand the Torah, who are studying the writings and the prophets, and are preparing for what is to come."

I snatched a quick breath. "What do you mean? And who are these people?"

"They are the faithful." Simeon rested his elbows on his knees. "Some, mostly men, have gone out to the desert. Those who have families are still in Jerusalem, worshiping in homes, not the Temple. They have established *haverim* throughout the city of Jerusalem."

Not familiar with the word, I looked at Diagos, but he appeared equally puzzled.

"A *havurah* is a fellowship," Simeon explained. "Those who want to join must repent of transgressing against the Law. They must take an oath to accept the havurah's rules of ritual purity and eat only food that has been properly tithed. After a year of studying Torah, if the prospective member has not transgressed in any way, he or she is examined and allowed to participate fully in the fellowship."

"Wait." Diagos swallowed the bit of quail he'd been chewing, then lifted a dark brow. "You mentioned something 'to come.' Are these people organizing an insurrection? Do they want to overthrow the king?"

Surprise blossomed on Simeon's face. "They are expecting the arrival of Messiah. And the birth pangs that will precede Him."

Diagos and I stared at the teacher, waiting for an explanation.

Simeon sighed, clearly dismayed by our ignorance. "The Teacher of Righteousness speaks often about the age of tribulation and the birth pangs of the Messiah. We hope to emerge from the age of tribulation into the age of messianic perfection."

I had a hundred questions, so I chose one at random. "Who is the Teacher of Righteousness?"

"What is the age of tribulation?" Diagos asked.

I smiled. "Perfection? What do you mean by perfection?"

Simeon lifted his hands. "This is why you should join one of the haverim. You will find answers to these questions and others you did not even know you had."

I turned to Diagos. "Will *you* consider it?"

He shook his head. "My place is with the king. In fact, tomorrow I must go with him to Galilee."

I shifted my gaze to Simeon. "Perhaps I will join one of your fellowships—if they will have me."

"A willing and repentant heart," he said, folding his hands, "they will not turn away."

~~~~~~~~~~

And so Jannaeus's reign began, progressing in the same pattern our lives had taken when we lived in Galilee. My husband went out to conquer cities and left me to care for the children and fulfill many of his duties. Yet this time we were managing the affairs of a nation, not only a region, and the stakes involved millions of lives.

Jannaeus did not return to Jerusalem during those early years, but frequently sent Ezra Diagos to inquire of matters concerning the Holy City. I would speak to Diagos in the reception room while scribes took notes, and then I would entertain him at a banquet with other leading officials. I understood the importance of maintaining the appearance of propriety, so I made sure the chief priests and other members of the Sanhedrin heard Diagos's glowing reports from the battlefield.

One night, however, after a banquet had ended, Diagos motioned for me to step onto the balcony where we could talk privately. "I must tell you the truth about the battle for Ptolemais," he said, keeping his voice low. "I don't know if you have heard other reports from the battlefield—"

"Nothing other than what you have told me," I interrupted. "No one else speaks to me of war. I have no idea what is happening outside Jerusalem."

As he stood in the moonlight, his face transformed, the handsome and polished veneer peeling back to reveal the frustration beneath. "I am not surprised. I am sure the king does not want you to know everything that has happened. But the war is coming to you, and you should be prepared for it."

I stared, tongue-tied, as Diagos told me that Jannaeus had not only failed at capturing Ptolemais, but might have doomed

Judea in the attempt. His siege of the port city had gone well until the people of Ptolemais sought help from Ptolemy Soter, a deposed Egyptian king and son to Cleopatra III. Eager to command a force large enough to unseat his mother and his brother, a co-ruler of Egypt, Soter sailed from Cyprus to Ptolemais. But by the time he arrived, the citizens of Ptolemais had realized that by inviting Soter to defend them, they might antagonize Cleopatra III of Egypt, and no one wanted to ruffle the feathers of that fiery queen. When Soter arrived, they refused to let him enter their city.

"Jannaeus," Diagos continued, leaning on the balcony railing, "realized he had inadvertently become involved in a war between Egyptian royals. So while he talked peace with Soter, he sent a negotiator to pacify Cleopatra."

I recognized my husband's error at once. "Surely he didn't think he could keep his double-dealing from—"

"He realized his mistake soon enough. When Soter learned that your husband had played false with him, he vented his wrath on Judea, beginning in Galilee. He and his army have killed hundreds of Judeans."

"Sepphoris," I whispered, thinking of the town and the people I had grown to love. "Did he—?"

"He tried to attack that city. But he could not breach the walls, so he crossed the Jordan in hopes of picking up allies from the Seleucid towns. His plan, I believe, is to sweep through Judea, capture Jerusalem, and threaten Cleopatra from a position of power."

My throat, which had tightened, suddenly went dry. "And what was my husband doing during this rout of our territory?"

Diagos's jaw tightened. "The king is fighting. Your husband has brave warriors, but Soter's troops overcame them. In one battle, Soter's mercenaries chased the army of Judea until their swords were blunt from killing. We lost more than forty thousand men."

I clung to the balcony railing for support. Forty thousand? Diagos was not describing a battle but a bloodbath.

"That is not the worst of it."

I stepped back, not wanting to hear anything else, but Diagos was determined that I should know all.

"Soter came upon several small Judean villages filled with women and children. He commanded his soldiers to strangle them and cut their bodies into pieces, then to fling the remains into cauldrons over the cook fires. He wanted any Judean who escaped the battle to come home and assume that Soter and his men were cannibals. Soter intends to terrify our people into submission."

I closed my eyes against the horrific image of butchered women and babies. "Please." The word came out strangled. "Stop."

Diagos lowered his voice. "This is the nature of war, my queen, and you must face this reality. Now Soter controls Ptolemais and the regions to the north. Your husband will be unable to halt the enemy's advance toward Jerusalem, and Soter is determined to wreak even more havoc in the days ahead."

I turned and stared at the commander, who was looking at me with a cold, hard expression. Why had he shared these horrible stories? My uncle, who had seen more than his share of war, had never brought home such bloody tales. How could I have ever called this man a *friend*?

"Why are you being so cruel? You should not have shared these things with me."

"Someone must speak the truth, and your husband will not. He is too afraid of the inevitable, but you, Salome, have backbone. You have courage; I have seen it flash in your eyes." He stepped forward, so close I could see the mingling of brown and gold flecks in his eyes. "Of all the people in Jerusalem, you and I know the king is a fool. But hope is not lost, for you can influence him like no one else. I watched you in Galilee. I saw you solve problems and allow Jannaeus to take the credit."

"Much has changed since then," I said, turning away from his powerful gaze. "My husband no longer cares for me, but for his concubines."

"I do not care who sleeps in his bed. I care about who he respects, and he does respect you. You must make it your job to know everything happening in Judea so that you can counsel him. If you do not save him, he will be overthrown, and some other family will rise to power, though not without war and struggle and much unnecessary bloodshed. Our lives—the fate of Israel—depend on your efforts."

The thought was so ridiculous I almost laughed, and yet I saw nothing humorous in his statement. Could Diagos be right? I had been the guiding hand behind Jannaeus in Galilee, but he had been little more than a boy in those days. Now he was a man and even less inclined to listen to me.

I looked at the commander. "You do not know what you are asking. Jannaeus has withdrawn from me. He has changed; he is now much more ruthless and ambitious."

"Then you must draw close to him. Take his part, become indispensable. Because Cleopatra has sent her son and co-ruler, Ptolemy Alexander, to our territory in pursuit of Soter. Her army and Soter's are fighting each other on Judean soil, and our people are suffering for it. You can be sure that the victor in this struggle, whomever it may be, will claim Judea."

I recoiled, stepping backward until my legs hit a stone bench, then I staggered and fell onto it. "What . . . what are we to do? What am I to do?"

Diagos locked his hands behind his back and stared into the gathering darkness. After a long moment, he dipped his chin in a decisive nod. "You must convince your husband to go to

the victor and beg for his country. They have been fighting for
months, and the struggle cannot continue much longer."

"I cannot imagine Jannaeus begging."

"But he must. Call it what you will, paint it in any terms you
like, but if you would save the Holy City, the king will have to
go to the victor as a supplicant. If he does not, all will be lost."

Diagos turned, and something in his dark eyes softened when he
saw the expression on my face. "Fear not," he said, "for if HaShem
smiles on you, the battle will go to Cleopatra, who respects the
Jewish people. She may accept the king's plea for mercy."

I buried my face in my hands. "You have no idea what you
are asking. I have not seen Jannaeus in months."

"You must go to him. Like Esther, who went to the king un-
bidden, you must put away your fears and seek his company."
Diagos bowed slightly. "In truth, that is why I came to Jerusalem.
I came here to ask if you would allow me to escort you to the
king, so you can convince him to save Judea."

After a long interval, during which I prayed for courage and
wisdom, I rose on shaky legs and gave the commander a stiff
nod, then turned toward the banquet chamber. "I will depart
with you tomorrow," I said, my voice breaking. "But now you
must leave me to my prayers."

～～～～～

The War of the Scepters, as it would later be called, raged
for nearly three years. Jannaeus and the remainder of his army
tried to defend the people of Judea as opposing Egyptian armies
waged war on the land HaShem had promised to Israel.

As Diagos suggested, I left my children in Kissa's care and
traveled with him to the battlefield. I found the Judean army
dwelling in tents in the region of the Galilee. I did not visit Jannaeus when I arrived but went immediately to the tent Diagos
had set aside for my use.

I knew I would have to approach Jannaeus carefully. If he suspected the reason for my arrival, he would have settled into obstinacy and refused to see me. I would have to convince my husband that I had come because I longed for his company—an idea that would please him even if the feeling were not reciprocated. I would have to be as persuasive as Eve, as charming as Esther, and as determined as Jael when she hammered the tent stake into Sisera's skull.

After three days, Diagos entered my tent and announced that the king wished to see me. "Does he know why I have come?" I asked.

A smile flashed in Diagos's beard. "He was informed of your arrival on your first day in camp. I am sure he was curious, but he did not ask. Yesterday he asked if you were well, and I assured him you were. Today he asked why you had come, and I suggested that he ask you himself. So if you are ready . . ."

I stood, smoothed my tunic, and touched the fragile curls I had pinned in my hair. Dressing was not easy without a maid, but I would rather Kissa care for my boys than bring her to a battlefield. On the other hand, Jannaeus cared deeply about physical appearances, so I could not risk looking less than my best.

Ezra Diagos led the way to the king's tent, but I entered alone and bowed before my husband. "Salome," he said, his voice seeming to come from a great distance. "Why have you left the safety of the city to come here?"

I lifted my head and gave him a sincere smile. "Can a wife not wish to see her husband?"

"Are the children well?"

"Yes, my king."

"And the affairs of Jerusalem? Are the chief priests causing trouble?"

I shook my head. "Not at the moment. I am happy to report

that even the Pharisees and scribes seem to be at peace with one another."

"A momentary peace, to be sure."

I nodded. "I am certain you are right."

"You may rise."

I nodded and stood, then gestured to an empty chair. "May I sit?"

Jannaeus's brows rushed together, but then he nodded and sat as well.

I smoothed my gown and met my husband's eyes. "I have heard, husband, of many deaths in Judea. I have heard that this Ptolemy Soter has terrorized our people and waged war against his mother on our land."

Steadily holding my gaze, Jannaeus nodded.

"I also know that Cleopatra III has always been a friend to Israel. She has Jewish commanders in her army and has always been kind to the Jews residing in Alexandria. Having her as an ally would be good for Judea—as I am sure you are aware."

He nodded once more. "I know all this."

"I knew you would." I smiled, remembering several Egyptian caravans that had arrived at the high priest's palace. Egyptian dignitaries often visited John Hyrcanus, though young Jannaeus had never seemed to pay them any attention.

"Ptolemy Soter will never be a friend to Israel," I continued. "I am sure you have realized that it is in our best interests to meet with Cleopatra. Promise her whatever you must in order to win her affection. Only then, I fear, will Judea be safe from Egyptian domination."

The line of my husband's mouth tightened, and a muscle flicked at his jaw. The idea had to be repugnant to a man who saw himself as Alexander the Great, but surely he would realize that capitulation was the only way to achieve any sort of victory.

"Egypt was once our taskmaster," he said with a credible attempt at calm, marred only by the thickness in his voice. "How can the high priest of Israel willingly kneel before an Egyptian queen? What would the people say?"

I smiled. "The people do not need to know what happens between you and Cleopatra. What they will know is that you negotiated a peace, and Soter left our land. They will be grateful for your skills as a diplomat, and they will revere you as high priest and king."

"Do you think I care about what the people think?"

I closed my eyes lest he glimpse the storm raging in my soul. Jannaeus did not care if the people thought him a murderer, an adulterer, and a blasphemer, but he would care a great deal if they despised him enough to overthrow him. And they would surely reach that point if he did not convince the Egyptians to leave Judea.

"The time has come," I announced, firming my voice, "and you must visit Cleopatra. Any delay gives her more time to see how pleasant this land is, and how easily she could expand her territory."

"I cannot do it." He spoke through clenched teeth. "How can I lower myself to beg for what is already mine?"

"Because tomorrow it may not be yours," I said. "I have heard that some of the queen's counselors are urging her to annex Judea. What would become of our Promised Land if she did? The blasphemies committed by Antiochus Epiphanes would pale in comparison to the blasphemies of an Egyptian queen and her pantheon of foreign gods."

"Out!" I flinched as Jannaeus lifted his arm and pointed to the guards stationed at the doorway of his tent. "All of you, out!"

The guards and servants bowed and hastily retreated, leaving us alone.

"You must gather gifts for her," I said, softening my voice, "and you must have your servants polish your armor. You will take gold and silver and pearls—the finest you can procure— and you must not wait. Delay could be fatal . . . for all of us."

Jannaeus leaned forward in his chair and covered his face with his hands. For a moment I thought he might weep, but then he lifted his head. "Alexander was never brought so low," he said, staring at something beyond my field of vision. "His wife never told him what to do."

I could have said so many things. I could have chided him for coveting a Gentile city, for misleading Soter while negotiating with Cleopatra, and for not adequately protecting the ravaged villages of Galilee. Instead, I thought it wiser to soothe him.

"Alexander's generals told him what to do," I said. "And your general, Ezra Diagos, has already sent a message to the queen. Together we will go to Scythopolis in Samaria, where Cleopatra waits for you."

"The Samaritans hate me," Jannaeus mumbled. "They have not yet forgiven my father for destroying their temple."

"If you want to retain your position," I said, reminding him that the stakes were personal as well as national, "you will kneel before her and offer your gifts. Then you will go home to Jerusalem and rule your people well."

He pressed his hands together and sighed, then looked up at me. "It will be as you say, Salome. I have no other choice."

I bowed and gave him a genuine smile. "Honor HaShem, husband, and know that I support you now even as I did in Galilee. When this is over, you will be as beloved as you were in those days."

Offering him hope and the promise of adulation, I left my husband alone in his tent.

CHAPTER THIRTY-THREE

Kissa

A report reached us by messenger: Ptolemy Soter and his mercenaries had sailed back to Cyprus, the island to which his mother had earlier banished him. Jannaeus, king of Judea, met with Cleopatra III, and that queen allowed him to keep his throne largely because a Jew named Ananias, one of her generals, told her that to do otherwise would antagonize the Jews of Egypt.

In a personal note delivered into my hand, Shelamzion wrote:

> *How fare my sons? The worst part of all this, my friend, is realizing that Ptolemy Soter was Cleopatra's own dear son. I will never understand how the bonds of familial love can become so feeble that a son would make war against his mother and a mother fight against her son.*
>
> *I trust my children are well, for how could they be otherwise in your care? Kiss them for me and tell them I will be home soon. The king and I will return together. According to the terms of the treaty with Egypt, Jannaeus must not wage war against Egypt again, so I am filled with hope and peace.*

Shelamzion's letter should have brought me great joy, but instead my heart ached as I rolled up the scroll. Her sons had done well during the weeks she remained away, but her mother . . . Sipporah was gone.

Shelamzion had not spent much time with her mother since becoming queen, yet the fault was not entirely hers. Day by day, Sipporah had retreated into a private world of her own, a place inhabited by dire memories and the ghost of her daughter. The servants took care of her, making certain she was bathed, clothed, and fed, while Sipporah, when she spoke at all, credited these kindnesses to Ketura, not Shelamzion. I became convinced the woman thought Ketura was queen, not her younger daughter, and many times I stepped into the woman's house and found her talking to Ketura. She would often stare at the space where the statue of Ketura had once stood—it vanished during Aristobulus's reign—and speak as if her daughter's ghost were in the room.

In her last days, however, Sipporah did not leave her bed. She had fallen, one of the servants told me, and after getting up she did not have the use of her right arm or leg. Even the right side of her face seemed ineffective, so eating became difficult.

"What will we tell the queen?" one of the anxious maids asked when I stopped by the house where Shelamzion and I had become fast friends. "We have not failed in our duty—"

"The queen will understand," I assured them. "Her mother has been . . . unwell for some time."

Now she was dead.

I moved to the balcony and looked past the courtyard, into the busy street where Shelamzion and Jannaeus would soon appear. I had hoped to understand the Jewish God one day, but certain situations left me more puzzled than ever. HaShem, it seemed to me, did not allow His people to experience joy unless it was accompanied by a commensurate portion of sorrow.

CHAPTER THIRTY-FOUR

Shelamzion

Amid great celebration, Jannaeus and I returned to Jerusalem. People lined the streets waving palm branches as we entered the city, and the cheers continued until we passed through the gate at the high priest's palace. Even our servants were jubilant, apparently believing their king had won a great victory over the Egyptians.

Only a handful of us knew that Cleopatra had gone back to Alexandria because she was a wise woman who prized peace. No one outside the king's inner circle knew that Jannaeus had groveled before the Egyptian queen and promised to send her an annual tribute of gold if she would allow him to retain his position and power.

Cleopatra had looked at me as my husband knelt at her feet, and from her expression I could see that she understood more than she would admit. Like me, she stood as an older wife behind an impetuous young co-ruler. "Alexander Jannaeus," she said, her throaty voice rolling like thunder through the room, "I will let you keep your kingdom if you agree to this treaty. You will not engage any Egyptian army in battle. You will not infringe upon our territory, and in the spring of each year you will send us one hundred pounds of gold."

Jannaeus bowed his head. "I will agree to your terms."

I gave the queen a look of relieved thanks, which she acknowledged with the smallest softening of her eyes. Then I folded my hands and waited for my husband to stand and put his signature on the document.

Cleopatra and Jannaeus had signed the treaty, and I could see great value in it. One hundred pounds of gold was but a token gesture to remind Jannaeus that he remained in Cleopatra's debt. The treaty gave us a secure western border and would keep my husband from the battlefield. Jannaeus's pride might have suffered in his encounter with the Egyptian queen, but Judea would survive, and that mattered more than anything else.

Only after disembarking from the coach did I spot Kissa with my sons. I knelt and greeted the boys with open arms. I wanted to sit and listen to all their stories, yet something in Kissa's usually pleasant expression seemed off.

"I will find you later," I told my sons. "Run along while I speak to Kissa."

As I turned to face my handmaid, I noticed several hired mourners in the courtyard. They were not wailing but sat silently . . . as if waiting. Cold fingertips skipped down my spine. "Who died?"

Kissa lowered her head. "Your mother."

I blinked. "Was she ill?"

Kissa sighed heavily. "You have been away many weeks. Your mother grew weaker and could not get out of her bed. In the end, she could not—would not—eat. She died on Shabbat, several weeks ago."

I nodded as the world spun slowly around me. "Is she . . . can you take me to her?"

"Come with me," Kissa said.

Not knowing when I would return, Kissa had asked an embalmer to prepare my mother's body. Mother now lay on a table in an empty storage room, her only company the statue of my dead sister.

I blew out a breath when I saw it. "Where did that come from?"

Kissa folded her arms. "One of the slaves found it at the bottom of a trash heap. He remembered your mother having it when—"

"I remember." I gazed at the carved stone and wondered if its perfect face would ever match that of an actual human girl. "When Mother was sick, did she call for me? Tell me the truth, please."

Kissa drew a deep breath, then exhaled in a rush. "Your mother called for Ketura. She spoke to her as if she were in the room. She slipped away, a little more each day, until she breathed her last."

I swiped at the tears clinging to my lower lashes. My tears did not spring from a sudden realization that I would no longer have my mother's love, for I had never really possessed it. She had given all her love to Ketura and had none left for me.

But HaShem had not left me wanting. My father had loved me dearly, and Uncle had always spoken to me with respect and affection. Alena had been fond of me, and Kissa had remained by my side for years.

"Have her placed in the royal tomb," I said. "And you had better return *that*"—I nodded to the statue—"to the garbage heap. Others would not understand."

Kissa nodded. "I will see to it."

I left the storage room and realized I was crying only when I felt full, round drops running over my cheeks. I did not weep for myself. Long ago I had learned how to make my own way in the world. I wept for my mother, who wanted more than anything to see one of her daughters grow up and marry a wealthy man with power and position. She had pinned all her hopes on Ketura, and so great was her blind obstinacy that she was not aware when her dreams and yearnings were fulfilled in a totally unexpected way.

"Good-bye, Ima," I whispered as I wiped the wetness from my cheeks. "Thank you for teaching me to always keep my eyes open to the workings of HaShem in the world."

CHAPTER THIRTY-FIVE

Shelamzion

For the next few years, Jannaeus set aside his territorial ambitions and focused on nonmilitary pursuits. Privately, I told Kissa that he had shifted his focus to what the Greeks called *hedone*, or pleasure. Though my husband openly indulged in concubines and mistresses, I could not be his conscience. I could only be his wife.

Sometimes, as I sought to settle an argument between our sons or stared at Jannaeus's empty couch at a banquet, I wondered why he bothered to remain my husband. The Pharisees were quick to divorce a wife for any cause, while the Sadducees, the group with whom Jannaeus had aligned himself, did not allow divorce except in the case of sexual infidelity. Since Jannaeus knew I had not been unfaithful, he had to remain married to secure the Sadducees' approval. He could have changed his allegiance to the Pharisees and divorced me, but then he would have had to adhere to the Law, which would have disallowed his pursuit of pleasure.

Therefore we remained married in the eyes of God and men.

Did he regret marrying me? Probably not, for I had proved

useful on several occasions. And whenever the Pharisees condemned his unrighteous manner of living, Jannaeus always
pointed to me, as if my obedience to the Law could atone for
his disobedience.

Knowing that I could not force my husband to repent of his
unrighteous practices, I decided to focus on my own spiritual
life. I asked Simeon ben Shetah to find a suitable havurah in
Jerusalem, then I eagerly joined. I took an oath of obedience
to the group's rules of food and ritual purity, and Kissa and
I attended meetings whenever we could. We left the palace in
plain clothing and wore veils to obscure our faces. If any of the
other members knew who we were, they were kind enough not
to draw attention to us.

During the meetings of the havurah, a Torah teacher would
explain the reasons behind some of the oral traditions—laws
that went far beyond the six hundred thirteen laws given to
Moses at Mount Sinai and written in the Torah. Animals, for
instance, could not righteously be sold to non-Jews lest they
be used for pagan sacrifices. Untithed produce could not be
sold to non-Jews lest it then be resold to a Jew who did not
know the produce had not been properly tithed. Slaves who
expressed a desire in knowing Adonai and following the Law
could not be sold lest their spiritual desire be quenched by
uncertain circumstances.

"Ritual purification," one Torah teacher explained, "is a sign
of spiritual purification. But no amount of washing or ablution
will purify anyone who remains an unrepentant transgressor
at heart. Ritual purity is simply a manifestation of the state
of the individual."

"But why," a man in the crowd asked, "do we make purity harder than the written Law demands? If the Law says I
must wash before eating, why do *you* say we must wash three
times?"

"Ah." The Torah teacher bobbed his head. "The Law is so sacred that it must be protected by a hedge, or fence, to keep us from offending inadvertently. If you wash three times before eating, have you not obeyed the Torah?"

The questioner considered a moment, then nodded.

The Torah teacher smiled. "So you have protected the sacred Law. If the written Law says not to take more than ten steps on Shabbat, and I tell you not to take more than five, have you broken the Law if you slip and take six? That is why we make purity more rigorous than the Law demands. Our *halakhah*, or way of living, guards the Law and protects it."

Why, I wondered idly, did the Law need protecting? Was it a living thing that could be wounded or killed?

Because I was a woman, I did not ask my questions in public. I determined to offer them to Simeon ben Shetah when I had opportunity. But until I knew the answers, I would be scrupulous regarding the Law. I had to set an example for others.

One night I stepped into the triclinium, where servants were preparing food on silver plates. One of the young girls had a red spot on the back of her tunic, and I suddenly realized she was a niddah, a menstruating woman and therefore unclean. Everything she had touched—plates, linens, trays, and food— would have to be destroyed.

"Stop!" I shouted. The servants froze in place. I looked directly at the girl and told her to go outside the kitchen and wait for instructions. When she had left, I had the other servants throw out the food, linens, and the trays. The silver plates could be saved, if they were melted down and remade. The fire would purify them.

I was exhausted by the time the banquet ended. As Kissa helped me prepare for bed, she asked why I had gone through such trouble to have the servants make more food, find more linens, and use other plates and trays.

"The first group was unclean," I mumbled as she pulled my chiton over my head. "I could not have my guests touch unclean items or they would be unclean, as well. If that girl had touched the furniture, I would have brought in other couches."

"And you would have destroyed the unclean ones?" Kissa shook her head. "It is a wasteful practice."

"That girl should never have been working during her time of impurity," I said, holding out my arms so Kissa could pull up my nightgown. "Just as you and I do not go out when we are bleeding."

Kissa made discreet clucking noises as she fastened my gown. "I do not understand your rituals. You burn what could be washed. At the end of the bleeding, you require a woman to bathe in running water when even your Torah does not require it."

"What?" I turned. "Of course the Torah requires it. Bathsheba was in a mikvah when David saw her bathing."

Kissa shook her head. "I read that story. But your Law says only that a woman is unclean for seven days. It says nothing about a bath or running water."

I turned away so she could remove the pins from my hair, but her question troubled me. In our desire to protect the Law, had we made it so complicated that no one could follow it perfectly?

I would have to ask Simeon the next time we met.

~~~~~~~~

"Why?" I asked as Simeon came into the room.

His puzzled expression reminded me that I had not explained myself. "Forgive me." I smiled. "Please, have a seat, make yourself comfortable. But I want to begin our time of study with a question."

Simeon nodded respectfully, then sat at a table with an open Torah scroll. "My queen, I am delighted to serve."

"You don't have to observe the formalities, just answer my question."

His smile was a blend of curiosity and indulgence. "As you wish."

I sat on the chair next to him. "Why is it necessary to protect the Law?"

He blinked. "Because if we don't protect it, we might accidentally offend."

"Offend who? Can the Law be offended? Is it a living thing that requires protection? We speak of it as though it breathes and lives."

Simeon tilted his head. "In a sense, it does. It was breathed by HaShem, written by Moses, and guides our actions—"

"Not all of it was breathed by HaShem. The oral laws were not written by Moses, but have been passed down by Torah teachers and the sages. But why? Why did Adonai give us the Law, knowing that over time it would become so complicated that Gentiles cannot understand it?"

"Is this about someone in particular?" Simeon asked.

I nodded. "For years I have tried to be a righteous example to my handmaid, Kissa. I have tried to explain HaShem and the Law, but she refuses to see the logic in my explanations. She finds the Law complicated, and sometimes I know she thinks I am being—"

"Overly righteous?"

"Silly." I exhaled a sigh. "Please, Simeon. She is pragmatic, and the Law makes no sense to her."

Simeon leaned forward and rested his arms on the table. "Do you remember how we talked about patterns in the Torah? About how both Abram and Jacob went into Egypt and came out with great wealth, and how both Moses and Noah floated in an ark and ultimately saved their people?"

"I remember *Ma'asei avot, siman l'banim.* The deeds of the fathers are a sign to the sons."

"Exactly." Simeon tugged at his beard. "There is another pattern in the Torah, that of Adam and Israel. Can you find it?"

I searched my memory. "Both Adam and Israel were . . . no, they were not both placed in a garden. They were both—" I shook my head—"I don't see it."

Simeon turned to the scroll and pointed his finger to where the first book began. "God established a covenant with Adam and Israel," he said. "First, God spoke to Adam. He blessed them and said, 'Be fruitful and multiply, fill the land, and conquer it. Rule over the fish of the sea, the flying creatures of the sky, and over every animal that crawls on the land.'"

Simeon looked over at me. "Blessing, filling the land, conquering it. Now let's look at Israel."

"I understand—HaShem did the same with Israel. He blessed them, said they would fill the Promised Land, and commanded them to conquer it."

Nodding, Simeon continued, "HaShem also gave commands. To Adam, He gave one commandment: no eating from the Tree of the Knowledge of Good and Evil. To Israel, He gave six hundred thirteen commandments at Sinai. To both Adam and Israel, HaShem promised that the land would be theirs as long as they obeyed. If they broke His covenant with them, they would be exiled."

The pattern was becoming clearer to me. Adam and Eve disobeyed HaShem's command, and so did Israel. The first humans were exiled from Eden, and Israel was exiled from their Promised Land. But now we had returned, and we had brought renewed passion to keep the Law . . .

Or had we? My husband, Israel's king and high priest, only observed the public rituals. In private, his heart turned continually toward power and pleasure, living as he pleased with no regard for eternity. Many Sadducees lived exactly as he did.

Our nation was as divided as I had ever seen it. Two generations ago, the Maccabees had stirred us to renewed zeal, but
even then the nation had been composed of Hellenes, who
followed Greek gods and philosophies, and the Hasidim, who
observed the Law. Now we were made up of three groups—no,
four groups—the Sadducees, Pharisees, Essenes, and those who
didn't care enough to choose an affiliation.

"What is the point?" I asked. "Why should we try to keep
the Law when we have already tried and failed?"

"Some would say we need to try harder, that we must build
walls around the Law so we cannot sin against it even accidentally," Simeon replied. "But perhaps you are right—making
the Law harder to keep does not seem to be the answer." He
tugged on his beard again, then shifted his position. "Lately I
have been talking to an elder of the Essenes. He has given me
much to think about."

I leaned forward. "And?"

"This elder believes that the Law was given to show us that we
could not keep it perfectly, that our human efforts are doomed
to failure. He says the Torah was not written to bring Israel
to the Law, but to lead Israel *through* the Law to the kingdom
of God."

I slumped in my chair, more confused than ever. "*Through*
the Law?"

"HaShem wants you to believe above all things." Simeon
gave me a brief, distracted glance and tried to smile. "Have
you noticed how many times the Torah tells us that Israel failed
because they did not believe?"

"Believe . . . what?"

Simeon did not answer directly, but a spark of some inde-
finable emotion lit his eyes. "Adam was HaShem's first king
on the earth. He was to have dominion over the animals and
plants. And one day another king will come, the other half of

the pattern. He is to exercise dominion, as well. As the Torah says, 'One from Jacob shall exercise dominion . . .'"

"Who is this?"

"Adam was also HaShem's first priest," Simeon continued, ignoring my question. "HaShem talked with him in the garden just as He talked with Moses in the Tabernacle. The same precious metals mentioned in the Garden of Eden were used in the construction of the Tabernacle. The One who is to come will be a priest who also talks to HaShem."

I felt the truth all at once, like a tingle in my stomach. "You are talking about the Messiah."

Simeon nodded like a dreamer in a trance. "He has been in the Torah all along, and yet I never saw Him. He is the coming Adam, a king. He is a priest like Moses. Even Balaam prophesied about Him."

"Balaam? The Gentile with the talking donkey?"

"The *Ruach HaKodesh* came over him, and Balaam saw the future with the eyes of Adonai. He said, 'I see him, yet not at this moment. I behold him, yet not in this location. For a star will come from Jacob, a scepter will arise from Israel."

I stared at Simeon, not knowing how to respond. The confident Torah teacher had vanished, leaving behind a man who had exchanged the absolutes of the Law for the uncertainties of prophecy. No wonder my uncle had been so cautious about finding the right Torah teacher for me. Scripture could be dangerous in the hands of a man with an improper understanding.

As the silence stretched between us, I leaned on the arm of my chair and looked deep into my Torah teacher's eyes. "You have not answered my questions, Simeon ben Shetah. I asked you what purpose the Law serves, and you have not given me a clear answer."

Something in my words snapped him out of his reverie. He

looked at me with an odd mingling of caution and excitement in his eyes. "Moses prophesied that we would break the Law and go into exile, and we did," he said. "Now the Law serves as our tutor to shield us from the consequences of unbelief until the Anointed One comes. When He comes, we will no longer need a tutor, for the Messiah will teach us all things."

"Are you saying we will no longer need the Law?" I tried to imagine a world without moral guidelines. "How will we know how to behave? It would be impossible to rule—to live in—a nation where every man did whatever he pleased."

"You are right, Shelamzion. The Law must be replaced."

"Replaced with what?"

Simeon folded his hands at his waist. "Remember the words of the prophet Jeremiah." In a soft voice, he quoted, "'Behold, days are coming'—it is a declaration of Adonai—'when I will make a new covenant with the house of Israel and with the house of Judah—not like the covenant I made with their fathers in the day I took them by the hand to bring them out of the land of Egypt. For they broke My covenant, though I was a husband to them.' It is a declaration of Adonai."

"I have read that," I said, "but I did not understand it."

Simeon held up a finger and closed his eyes. "'But this is the covenant I will make with the house of Israel after those days'—it is a declaration of Adonai—'I will put My Torah within them. Yes, I will write it on their hearts. I will be their God and they will be My people. No longer will each teach his neighbor or each his brother, saying, "Know Adonai," for they will all know Me, from the least of them to the greatest.' It is a declaration of Adonai. 'For I will forgive their iniquity; their sin I will remember no more.'"

Simeon opened his dark eyes and smiled. "Keep the Law, Shelamzion, until you find the Messiah. Believe that He is coming . . . though when or how I cannot say. But when He comes, you will not need to obey the Law, because it will be inscribed in your mind, your soul, and your heart."

I made a face, not understanding how such a thing could be possible. "How will we know what we have not been taught?"

Simeon shook his head and pressed his hands together. "It is a mystery," he said, his eyes meeting mine. "It is a miracle."

CHAPTER THIRTY-SIX

Kissa

My mistress was unusually quiet at dinner. I served the meal in the small family dining room, where Shelamzion, her sons, and the king ate on the rare occasions they came together.

Hyrcanus and Aristobulus were in high spirits, having spent the day hunting with their father, and I thought their talk of killing deer and a lion might have ruined my lady's appetite. For once the boys were not arguing, and they relived their hunting experience aloud, each of them describing his exploits as the king listened with amused approval. None of the three even glanced at my mistress, who reclined on her couch and only nibbled at the fruit and cooked meats on the tray.

How could they not notice Shelamzion's silence? She was usually the liveliest of the group, cleverly advising her husband while rebuking her sons' antics when they became too loud or spoke of something not appropriate for a family dinner. But the hours stretched on, the three men congratulating each other without once noticing their silent dining partner . . .

Finally, Jannaeus looked at his wife. "Salome," he said,

leaning toward her, "why haven't you congratulated your sons? Today Hyrcanus killed an eagle, and Aristobulus speared a lion!"

When my mistress did not respond, the king looked at me. "Is she ill?"

I stepped forward and nudged Shelamzion's shoulder. "Mistress? The king has spoken to you."

A deep flush rose up from her throat as she turned to him. "Apologies, my king. I was deep in thought."

"Obviously." He glared at her, his eyes hot with resentment, then forced a smile. "I asked why you have not congratulated your sons. Both boys snagged a kill during the hunt."

"Oh." She looked at the boys with indulgent pride. "Apologies to you as well, my sons. I'm sure you are both skilled hunters."

"I'm the best," Aristobulus said, grinning with the confidence of a young warrior. "I killed a lion with only a spear. Hyrcanus shot a bird."

"An eagle," Hyrcanus countered. "And they're strong and fast and not easy to kill. You couldn't kill one if you tried."

"You doubt me?"

"I do."

"Then let's go out again tomorrow." Aristobulus turned to the king. "Will you take us hunting again tomorrow? Perhaps we could go to a different place."

Jannaeus shook his head. "No, but I can ask Ezra Diagos to take you."

Hyrcanus scowled. "That old man? He cannot keep up."

"That old man," the king said, "could wrestle either of you to the ground in a heartbeat. He deserves your respect. If you want to go hunting tomorrow, it will be with him."

My mistress lifted her head and looked at her husband. "If you will grant me permission, my king, I would like to retire. I am in need of a good rest."

The king waved her away. "Go then."

I waited as my mistress stood, then followed her out of the room.

My mistress had not told the entire truth. She might have been tired of the dinner conversation, but she was not ready for sleep. I followed her to her bedchamber, but instead of going to bed, she went to the desk where she kept a Torah scroll.

"If you would light the lamp, Kissa," she said, sitting, "I would do some reading before bed."

I thrust a piece of straw into the ashes of last night's fire. When the end caught an ember and flamed, I brought it to the small oil lamp near the scroll. In the golden glow of the lamp, my mistress bent over the text and began to read: "'I will put animosity between you and the woman—between your seed and her seed. He will crush your head, and you will crush his heel.'" Shelamzion paused, then repeated the words, "'He will crush your head . . .'"

"Who is speaking?" I asked, aware that she was asking me to participate in her musing.

"Adonai Elohim."

"And who is He speaking to?"

"The serpent who enticed Eve into sin."

I tilted my head. "So Adonai will . . . what?"

Shelamzion looked at the scroll again. "The serpent will have descendants and so will the woman. A descendant of the woman will crush the serpent's head, but the serpent will crush his heel."

I sank to a nearby bench. "What does that mean?"

"I don't know," she whispered. "But here's another one." She turned back to the scroll, searching the text, and stopped. "'The scepter will not pass from Judah, nor the ruler's staff from between his feet, until he to whom it belongs will come. To him will be the obedience of the peoples. Binding his foal to the vine, his donkey's colt to the choice vine, he washes his garments in wine, and in the blood of grapes his robe.'"

"Who is speaking now?" I asked.

"Jacob," she answered. "When he gathered his sons to tell them what would happen to their descendants in the last days."

"The last days of what?"

She shrugged. "I don't know. But he seems to say that a king is coming from the tribe of Judah."

"A king for many nations," I said, "because many different peoples will obey him. Is that right?"

She picked up the lamp and held it closer to the scroll. "Yes. Many peoples, not just one. So not just Israel . . . I think."

"What else could it mean?"

She hesitated, lowered her head to the table, and sighed. "I only wish I knew."

"Maybe," I said, sitting on the edge of her bed, "you should think about something more pleasurable."

"Like what?" she mumbled.

"Like . . ." I smiled. "Ezra Diagos."

Her head rose at once. "What do you mean?"

I shifted to face her. "I know you want to deny it, but I have seen the way you light up when his name is mentioned. Even tonight, when your husband said Diagos might take the boys hunting."

Shelamzion groaned. "No. It cannot be that obvious."

"You always take extra care with your hair and dress if you know Diagos will be attending a banquet," I continued. "And your voice—it is lighter when you speak to him. You sound almost happy."

She groaned again, bringing both hands to her cheeks. "You cannot mean it."

I tossed her another smile, thinking she would return it, but my mistress's face had clouded. "Why, I thought you liked Diagos."

"I do," she murmured, then buried her face in her folded arms. "But I should not. I am a married woman."

I stared at her in dazed exasperation and crossed my arms. "You have not sinned against your husband. You admire Diagos, and he admires you. Or is HaShem so intent on destroying your happiness that you are not allowed to have a friend?"

"I have friends," she whispered. "But I wish Diagos were . . . more."

When a muffled sob escaped her folded arms, guilt coursed through my veins. "I'm sorry," I said, slipping from the bed. I walked over and placed my hands on her shoulders. "I should not have said anything."

"It is all right." She sniffed as she lifted her head. "It is good you mentioned it. If my . . . affection for Diagos is obvious to you, it will be evident to others. I cannot allow that."

"You have few friends, Shelamzion. You should not deny yourself the pleasure of a friend's company."

She sniffed again. "But what I feel for Diagos is not mere friendship. I . . . I will have to stop seeing him."

"Forever?"

She swiped at her eyes as she slumped into a chair. "I know my heart, Kissa. It can be desperately wicked, and I am trying to live a righteous life."

Shaking my head, I pulled the himation from her shoulders and tossed it in a trunk. Though I could see no sense in depriving herself of joy, Shelamzion had her reasons, and I would respect that.

CHAPTER THIRTY-SEVEN

Shelamzion

With each succeeding year I found myself marveling that Adonai saw fit to keep my husband on the throne of Israel. With Kissa and Simeon I quietly continued my Torah study and searched for clues about the coming king-priest. Would he come this year? Would he overthrow Jannaeus at once, or would he first raise an army? Would I recognize him if I saw him?

Simeon told me that the Essenes had begun to write about Jannaeus. The man they called the Teacher of Righteousness wrote openly about "the wicked priest" who everyone recognized as my husband. Jannaeus's arrogance and debauchery were now common knowledge, and even the common people realized he had murdered his younger brothers.

I did not understand how HaShem could tolerate a sinful high priest like Jannaeus. But when I caught myself thinking such things, I remembered that I was not HaShem and had no right to question His judgments. Perhaps HaShem was giving Jannaeus time to repent, or perhaps He was preparing the Messiah for the day He would take the throne of Israel.

As in so many situations, I could do nothing but watch and wait.

Five years after Jannaeus established a treaty with Cleopatra III, the Egyptian queen died. Now that she no longer monitored Jannaeus from Alexandria, my husband renewed his abandoned dreams of conquest and decided to increase his territory. He attacked several weak city-states east of the Jordan River and then set out to capture Gaza.

He would not have been successful at Gaza had two brothers, Apollodotus and Lysimachus, not convinced the city's citizens to surrender. Jannaeus entered the city in peace, then set his mercenaries free to loot, pillage, and take captives for the slave market. In the ensuing mayhem, the men from Gaza killed their wives and children to prevent them from being captured, while others burned their homes to prevent them from being looted. When more than five hundred people took refuge in the Temple of Apollo, Jannaeus battered down the doors and slaughtered them all. In the end, Jannaeus had conquered a city of blood, bodies, and burned ruins.

My heart constricted when I read Ezra Diagos's report of the campaign. Though I knew I ought to support my husband, I could not sanction wanton cruelty, especially when directed at innocents or those who were willing to surrender. Why did Jannaeus have to destroy others so completely? Not even Alexander the Great had been so brutal.

Shortly after that campaign, both of my sons married. Hyrcanus, who had become a quiet, thoughtful man, married a pleasant young girl and seemed to enjoy being a father to his two girls. Aristobulus married the daughter of one of the leading Sadducees, a young woman I disliked within minutes of meeting her. I could not deny her beauty, but she was also loud, arrogant, and manipulative—all the qualities I despised in other women.

But my boys had grown into men, and they did not ask me

to approve their choice of brides. That authority resided with their father, and Jannaeus was only too happy to cement relationships with other wealthy families.

In the twenty-second year of my husband's reign, the city prepared to celebrate the autumnal festival of Sukkot, always a time of rejoicing. I urged my sons to bring their families to the high priest's palace, so that we could all participate in the traditional family rituals. When both sons and their families had arrived, I led everyone onto the rooftop, where we constructed makeshift shelters out of palm branches and linen fabrics.

Aristobulus's firstborn, five-year-old Alexander, kept tossing citrons into the air and trying to make his younger sisters squeal. "Careful," I warned him. "We will need that fruit when we go to the Temple."

He held the citron close to his chest and gave me a winning smile. "Will we see grandfather the high priest when we are there?"

"I expect we will," I answered, my heart warming at his sincere expression. "And you will see many other things, as well."

With the children we collected palm, myrtle, and willow branches, then bound them together to create the *lulavs* we would wave during the festival. While we tied them, I recited the Levitical injunction we were obeying: "'On the first day you are to take choice fruit of trees, branches of palm trees, boughs of leafy trees, and willows of the brook, and rejoice before Adonai your God for seven days.'"

My sons' wives watched the proceeding without speaking. Hyrcanus's wife smiled as though she enjoyed the spectacle, but Aristobulus's wife paid more attention to the state of her nails than to her son.

When we had finished, I asked my sons if they would like to spend the night in their shelters. I doubted they would, as neither of them had ever freely chosen to experience a moment of discomfort.

As I expected, they declined. "Would *you* sleep outside?" Aristobulus asked.

"I used to sleep in our shelter when I was a child," I said, keeping my voice light. "Sometimes it is good to remember what our fathers endured."

"Enjoy yourself, then." Aristobulus kissed my cheek, scooped up young Alexander, and followed Hyrcanus and his family down the stairs.

I watched them go with a heavy heart. Despite my earnest love for my sons, my boys did not love each other. Hyrcanus had clearly inherited my scholarly temperament; Aristobulus possessed his father's excitable nature and unflagging ambition. They were oil and water, and each seemed to repel the other.

As a gift for their twenty-first birthdays, I had given each of them a large, splendid house near the winter palace I constructed near Jericho. I gave the builders explicit instructions—the two houses were to be absolutely identical lest one of my sons claim I had favored the other. The builders used the same marble, the same cypress, and the same carvings of olive wood for both structures.

The day I presented my sons with their princely palaces, they thanked me, looked over their new homes, and turned on each other. "He has the sunset views," Aristobulus complained.

"And he has the sunrise!" Hyrcanus countered.

I calmly suggested that they exchange palaces, since each seemed to favor a different direction, but they immediately dismissed my suggestion and resumed their argument. Their wives joined in a moment later, adding feminine voices to the distressing clamor.

"Let them be," Kissa whispered. "Wanting what the other has is part of their nature."

"I could do without that particular aspect of their personalities," I had replied, watching my sons quarrel. "They are determined to make me miserable."

But at least we managed to make lulavs together without destroying the Sukkot spirit of celebration.

~~~~~~~

Like the Feast of Unleavened Bread and the Passover Feast, the Feast of Tabernacles was a pilgrimage festival, requiring Jews from all over the world to come to Jerusalem if they were able. Thousands of people had streamed through the gates of the city, coming from Galilee, Egypt, Samaria, and other regions near and far. Standing in a recently constructed tower at the high priest's palace, no matter where I looked I saw temporary shelters crowding corners, doorways, and rooftops. Every unoccupied wall in the city had been partially or completely covered by some family's *sukkah*.

My heart lifted as I descended the tower stairs and went back to my bedchamber to dress. Kissa and I would enjoy the celebration today. My little grandchildren would wave their lulavs and hear how HaShem brought us out of the wilderness into a land flowing with milk and honey. Perhaps this would be the year they began to understand the miracle of it all.

With Kissa's help I dressed quickly, then led her and a few of the other servants from the house. Holding tight to each other's hands lest we be separated in the crowd, Kissa and I slipped into the throngs of people moving toward the Temple. The morning sacrifices were finished, so the people were now waiting for the water ceremony that commemorated the drawing of water from the rock at Horeb.

Today and each of the remaining days of the festival, a priest would take a golden ewer from the Temple and go out to draw water from the pool of Siloam. He would then carry the filled vessel back to the Temple, moving through the Water Gate and into the inner court. Once he had reached the altar, he would pour the water into a silver basin while ceremonial trumpets blew and other Levites chanted the words of Isaiah: "With joy you will draw water from the wells of salvation."

Any priest could conduct the ceremony, but on this first day of Sukkot, Jannaeus had elected to perform the honor, probably for the sake of the grandchildren. He informed me the night before, and I had been pleased to see him taking more interest in the Temple ceremonies.

Kissa and I slipped through the courtyard and made our way into the inner court. From where we stood I could see the bloodstained stones of the altar and the expectant faces around it. The trumpeters stood in their place, instruments in hand, and the choir stood opposite them, ready to sing HaShem's praises.

I smiled as I spotted several family groups among the crowd. Fathers raised their little ones onto their shoulders while mothers held on to the children's lulavs until it was time to wave them toward the north, south, east, and west.

One young girl held a citron close to her nose, happily breathing in the lemony scent. "Look at that one." I elbowed Kissa. "Isn't she adorable?"

Kissa smiled. "Perhaps you will have another granddaughter soon."

"If HaShem wills it . . . and I hope He does."

Finally we heard the roar that signaled the high priest's approach. Jannaeus had reached the Water Gate and would soon cross the Temple courtyard. We would have to wait only a few more moments . . .

There! I glimpsed the high priest's blue robe moving through the crowd. Though I could not say I loved my husband, as a wife and righteous woman I had to respect him. HaShem had placed him on the throne of Israel for reasons I did not understand, and so long as He kept Jannaeus there, how could I not honor the man?

I pasted a smile on my face in case Jannaeus should spot me. But as my husband walked past the line of Levites who kept the people from crowding the altar, I sensed a shift in the mood around me. The spirit of jubilation vanished once the people saw *which* priest would perform the rite. The faces that turned toward Jannaeus as he climbed the altar's stone steps were surly and filled with disdain.

I cannot say what went through my husband's mind in the moment he held the golden ewer above the silver bowl. He was supposed to pour water into the bowl, but as he looked out over the sea of disapproving faces, he adjusted his grip on the jug and poured the water onto his sandaled feet.

An audible gasp rose from those at the front of the assembly, followed by a rumbling growl that spread through the crowd. The angry faces flushed, and before I realized what had happened, men began to throw the only weapons they had—citrons. The yellow fruits flew through the air, pelting Jannaeus's shoulders, head, and body. The rain of citrons followed him as he hurried down the altar steps and struck him as he ducked and ran through the line of Levites, finally disappearing into one of the storage rooms.

I stood motionless, my hand at my throat, and only Kissa's insistent tug snapped me out of my paralysis. "Hurry!" she said, yanking on my sleeve. "It would not be good for you to be recognized in this crowd."

Unable to think of any other response, I lowered my head and fled with her.

❧

When Kissa and I reached the house, I went immediately to the reception hall where I paced and prayed that Jannaeus would return from his humiliation and ask himself why his people had been so angry. But though I prayed diligently, I knew the episode would not end as I hoped because my husband had no gift for introspection. HaShem had allowed this to happen for a reason, and an event as momentous as this had to have a significant reason behind it.

Two hours later, I heard a full report of what had taken place after my husband fled the crowd. When their citrons could no longer reach him, the people began to shout that Jannaeus was a bastard and unfit to be high priest. The taunts only inflamed my husband's temper, and he reacted by sending the Temple guards into the crowd, telling his men to "kill them all." The Levites who served as guards went after the crowd with the same zeal their forefathers had shown in the wilderness, striking left and right at brothers and friends and neighbors, whoever stood in their way.

After Israel danced around the golden calf, the Levites killed three thousand men. After Israel threw citrons at Alexander Jannaeus, the Levites killed six thousand.

I could not help but see a pattern, but to me the first killing was righteous, while the second . . . ?

Part of me wanted to say it was wrong. Jannaeus reacted in anger because the people hurt his pride. On the other hand, he was the Lord's anointed high priest, and to disrespect him was to disrespect Adonai. Or was it?

I could not settle the matter in my mind, yet Jannaeus had not finished. To further signal his displeasure, he had the Levites place wooden barriers around the Temple's inner chamber and the altar, declaring that henceforth only the priests would be allowed to observe the sacrifices—a sight that had once been available to any Jewish man, non-menstruating woman, or child.

So he denied his people access to the home of their God.

Disappointment and despair struck me like a blow in the

stomach when I heard the news. I had to turn away and choke back the bile that rose in my throat. This was too much! The wicked priest indeed! Just when I thought Jannaeus had gone too far, he strode further into wickedness.

"My queen?" The poor messenger who had delivered the news waited for me to release him, which I did with an anguished gesture. Then I collapsed in a heap on the cold tiles of the vestibule.

"Shelamzion!" Kissa knelt beside me an instant later, her hand on my shoulder. "You must rise. Do not let anyone see you like this. They might report your reaction to your husband, and that one must never think you are weak."

I lifted my blurry gaze to Kissa's face. "I have tried to respect him, even to love him, but how can I be a party to this? He murdered people *in the Temple*. In the presence of Adonai he struck out because they wounded his pride. And then, not content with bloody revenge, he barred them from HaShem's presence."

"Wipe your tears, mistress."

"And my sons! They were in the crowd, along with my precious grandchildren. The little ones saw the horror and heard the screaming. Will they ever be able to visit the Temple without remembering this horrible day? It is too much! I cannot bear it."

"Rise, Shelamzion." Kissa murmured soothing words as she helped me to my feet. She quickly escorted me to my bedchamber where I could mourn in private.

⚬⚬⚬⚬⚬⚬

Jannaeus did not return home after the massacre at the Temple. He went instead to the Baris Tower, where he summoned his generals and turned his ferocity toward the enemies of Judea.

I should not have been surprised. Whether or not he would admit it, I suspected that he was ashamed to face me. Either that or he had hardened his heart to the point that he wanted nothing to do with a woman who strove to live a righteous life.

Jannaeus erected barriers against me in other areas, as well. I would not have known anything of his military battles if Ezra Diagos had not faithfully written me. Every week or two I would receive a message informing me—in impersonal terms—of the Judean army's activities. As a parting note, Diagos would inquire about my health and assure me the king was well.

After reading his letters, I would wrap them back onto a spindle and hide them away. I was grateful I never had to tell Diagos I could no longer see him. Something in me wondered if he had sensed the dangerous attraction between us and decided to remain at a distance, but I found it more likely that HaShem had come between us.

From Diagos's reports I learned that Jannaeus had launched a campaign against the Nabatean Arabs who lived east of the Galilee. The Nabateans, overwhelmed by the size of the Judean army, petitioned the Seleucid king, Demetrius III, for help. Diagos wrote that Jannaeus should have lost that campaign, but six thousand Jewish soldiers who were fighting for Demetrius defected to our army. Alarmed to lose so many warriors, Demetrius fled the field.

Feeling invincible, and taking such events as signs that HaShem approved of him, Jannaeus returned to Jerusalem and the high priest's palace . . . and his wife. He did not seek me out, however, but was immediately beset by advisors and priests, who crowded the reception hall and reported increasing unrest and displeasure among the people of Jerusalem.

I did not feel the need to repeat what he was hearing from his most trusted advisors. I rarely spoke to him, even during the rare meals we shared, but every king has informants and Jannaeus had an army of spies. He learned about the Essenes, who had left Jerusalem and established a community in a secret location near the Dead Sea. He was not happy to hear that their writings referred to him as "the wicked priest," but as long as they remained far from Jerusalem, he was willing to let them stay in the desert.

The Sadducees, for the most part, were satisfied with my husband's rule, for they controlled the Sanhedrin and the Temple. They were the wealthy ruling class, and because they claimed to be descended from Zadok, Solomon's high priest, they lent an air of legitimacy to Jannaeus's priesthood.

But the Pharisees, who followed the Law and spoke out against everything from forced circumcisions to bloodshed in the Temple, were not content to merely protest my husband's actions. They met in covert groups and investigated ways by which they could overthrow Jannaeus and put someone else on the throne.

I was not happy to hear that some Pharisees were planning insurrection. History had taught me that the dethroned king and his family usually ended up dead or in prison, and I did not wish that fate for myself or my sons. But neither could I endorse Jannaeus's open persecution of righteous people.

Apparently forgetting that his father was once a devoted Pharisee, Jannaeus behaved as if he had been born a Sadducee and let it be known that he would not tolerate dissension. When he learned of groups that had formed against him, he had the organizers rounded up, arrested, and tortured until they confessed the names of their coconspirators. For six agonizing years he conducted a campaign of terror, searching out Pharisees in home meetings, outlying villages, and Jerusalem haverim.

What did I do while my husband killed more than fifty thousand righteous Jews? I retreated to my room and wept. I prayed. I fasted. I tore my garments and wore sackcloth—all because I could not be of one mind about the situation. I did not want to see godly people executed, but neither could I turn a blind eye toward those who would kill my sons and grandsons to prevent other Hasmoneans from ruling Judea.

In the early days of the persecution I feared for the lives of those in my havurah every time Kissa and I slipped away from the palace. I prayed with my eyes open, half expecting soldiers to burst through the door before the meeting ended. I finally realized that my involvement in such a fellowship endangered the lives of others.

Simeon ben Shetah continued to come to the palace for my Torah study, but he came less frequently and always appeared nervous when he visited. I told him I would understand if he chose not to come, yet he insisted that as long as I was willing to learn, he was willing to teach.

Did I fear for my life? No. Jannaeus knew I was a Pharisee, but he also knew I did not want him to lose his position. I believe he thought that having a devout, Law-obeying wife ratified his actions in the eyes of the people.

As time passed, I came to believe that Jannaeus did not persecute the Pharisees because they had conspired against him, but because their commitment to HaShem made him feel guilty. As high priest, he should have been closer to HaShem than anyone else, but how could he be holy with the blood of so many innocents on his hands?

Night after night I lay awake in my bed and wondered if I were also guilty before HaShem. Was I complicit in my husband's sin because I did not stop him?

Many times I thought of Grypus, who knew plants and their unsavory uses, and Salina, who had almost certainly poisoned Judah Aristobulus. She had done it for the good of the nation, yet her husband had not killed nearly as many as Jannaeus.

I had been taught to honor the Ten Words, and I obeyed them instinctively. I kept the Sabbath, I did not take the name of my God in vain, I did not worship graven images, and I did not steal or covet or bear false witness.

Would there ever come a time when HaShem would allow me to disobey *You shall not murder?*

I thought that time had come when my sons and I returned from a visit to the winter palace in Jericho. The streets of Jerusalem were quiet when we reentered the city, and I noticed that doors and windows had been shuttered or boarded up. I shot Kissa an inquisitive look and she returned it. "I am sure we will hear the latest news when we return home," she said. "If not from the servants, then from someone in the king's service."

Kissa and I had just stepped through the doorway when one of the kitchen slaves, a pale girl from across the Great Sea, ran into the vestibule and dropped to her knees in front of us.

I glanced at Kissa. "Is this some new form of greeting?"

"Excuse me, mistress," the girl said, folding her hands as her voice trembled, "but the entire household has been shaken by what happened last night."

I steeled myself to hear the dreadful news. "Tell me, please."

Tears welled in the girl's eyes and flowed over her cheeks. "The king . . . the king your husband—"

"Slowly now, collect yourself," Kissa counseled. "You need not fear your mistress."

"I know. But what we saw . . ."

"Take a deep breath," I told her. "And tell us everything."

The girl inhaled, then stared over Kissa's shoulder. Whatever she had seen last night, she was seeing it again.

"Eight hundred men," she said, her voice flat. "Eight hundred Pharisees."

I tried to keep my heart calm, for it had begun to race at the mention of so large a number.

"The king crucified eight hundred Pharisees," the girl said, "in the Valley of Hinnom. And while they hung on the execution stakes, the king's mercenaries murdered the condemned men's wives and children in front of their eyes. And while—" the girl choked on a sob—"while the air filled with the screams and cries of dying women and children, the king and his concubines sat and feasted on a platform overlooking the valley."

Grief drove me to my knees. The Valley of Hinnom lay south of the city. It was where pagan worshipers used to meet to sacrifice their children to Baal and Molech.

Jannaeus could not have chosen a more cursed spot.

As Kissa cried out and my sons came running from the courtyard, I beat my breast and wondered why HaShem had allowed such a terrible tragedy. Why didn't He remove Jannaeus from the earth? Why had He spared my husband so often on the battlefield? Why was this bloodthirsty king allowed to continue his murderous rampage?

Where was the Messiah, the Savior HaShem had promised?

Hyrcanus scooped me up and carried me upstairs to my bedchamber. Kissa put me to bed, where I lay in a dark stupor for several days, unwilling to face another day where I felt helpless and torn. I wondered if I would ever rise from my bed again.

But one morning I woke with a lighter heart—as if HaShem had planted within it a seed that sprouted in the middle of the night. The fruit of that seed? A psalm that kept running through my mind:

> Though the wicked spring up like grass,
> and all evildoers flourish,
> it is only to be ruined forever.
> But You, Adonai, are exalted forever.
> For behold, Your enemies, Adonai
> —behold Your enemies perish—
> all evildoers are scattered . . .
> The righteous will flourish like a palm tree . . .
> Planted in the House of Adonai,

they will flourish in the courts of our God.
They will still yield fruit in old age.
They will be full of sap and freshness.
They declare, "Adonai is upright, my Rock
—there is no injustice in Him."

Later that day, I would come across a scroll written by one
of the Essenes. It contained a prayer not unlike my own:

Rise up, O Holy One, against King Alexander Jannaeus
and all the congregation of Your people Israel who are
in the four winds of heaven. Let them all be at peace and
upon Your kingdom may Your Name be blessed.

Because Simeon ben Shetah would not come to the palace, I
wrote him a letter and sent it with a personal servant:

Greetings, highly esteemed teacher!

I have spent many days praying and studying, all to find
the answer to one particular question. Is it right to commit
murder in order to save many innocent lives?

You taught me that the Torah's laws are intended to
enhance life, never to cause death. So whenever observance
of the Law endangers life—such as allowing a killer to
live so he may kill again—the requirement to observe the
Law is suspended.

But you have said there are four instances where the
Law takes precedence over life: we shall not worship idols
or commit adultery, incest, or murder.

So, with great difficulty, I have put the thought of mur-
der out of my mind, even though I may have to watch
others die or even find myself and my sons in danger.

*If I have misinterpreted the Law, please write to me
at once. You need not sign your letter—I will know who
sent it.*

Pray for me, as I pray for you and your family.

S.A.

That afternoon a messenger knocked on my door and said
the king wished to see me at dinner. He was hosting important
men from the Sanhedrin, and he wanted his queen in attendance.

I told the messenger I would come and had Kissa begin to
dress my hair.

An hour later I found myself in the banquet hall, seated on
the couch next to Jannaeus's. He bowed his head when our
gazes crossed, and I sent him a chilly smile in acknowledgment.
A moment or two later, our guests streamed in—a half-dozen
Sadducees and their wives, all of them dressed in silks and
jewels and finely crafted leather sandals.

Mindful of the many eyes focused on us, I tried to maintain a
pleasant expression, though I wanted nothing more than to turn
to my husband and scream accusations. But when a king held
the power of life and death, a queen could not scream out her
frustrations, nor could she rebuke him without risking her life.

I was not foolish enough to trade my life for a fit of self-
indulgence. I also lacked confidence in my ability to sway
a stubborn fool with words from the Torah. Jannaeus had
counselors—members of the Sanhedrin—who were supposed
to counsel him in legal matters, but they despised the Pharisees
and Essenes as much as he did.

So what was I to do, except avoid him?

One bit of good news sustained me during that troubling
evening. I knew that most of the remaining Pharisees had fled
Jerusalem for Egypt, where they would remain until they were

sure they could safely return to their homes. When I heard how few remained in the city, I sent Kissa to inform their leaders that I would supply horses and wagons for any who needed conveyance. I would not let them remain in Jerusalem as long as their lives were endangered.

I reached for my goblet and sipped the sweet wine. Not only had Jannaeus denied the common people access to their God, he had also chased the Pharisees away from the Holy City.

As the king reclined on his couch and reached for his first bite, we followed his example. Then, looking around the gathering, he noted with some dismay that we had no Torah teachers in attendance.

Smiling wistfully, Jannaeus looked at me. "Would that we had someone to say grace for us."

I inclined my head in a gesture of respect. "I could send for someone, but you will have to swear you will not harm him."

His eyes narrowed for a moment, then he smiled, playing to his guests. "I swear it. Any Pharisee brave enough to remain in the city need not fear me."

I gestured to Kissa. When she came near, I asked her to fetch Simeon ben Shetah, who had been staying with Josu Attis ever since the king crucified the Pharisees.

When Simeon arrived, Kissa escorted him to the dining chamber where I introduced him to the gathering and seated him on the end of my couch. I gave him a smile. "Sit here and see how much honor the king pays you."

The corner of his mouth twisted. "It is not the king that honors me, but the Torah. For it is written: 'Exalt her, and she will promote you; she will bring you honor when you embrace her.'"

I glanced at Jannaeus, who had never given anything but perfunctory attention to Torah study. "Indeed."

Simeon stood and offered the blessing: "*Baruch atah A-donay, Elo-heinu Melech Ha'Olam shehakol nihiyah bed'varo.*" Blessed are You, Lord our God, King of the Universe, by whose word all things came to be.

When he had finished praying, I asked Simeon if he would like to stay for dinner. "No," he said, pitching his voice for my ears alone, "but I will remain until you are finished. I would have a word with you before I go."

I nodded, understanding his anxiety, and promised to meet him as soon as I could slip away.

When the last guest had gone, Jannaeus and I stood alone in the vestibule. He turned, caught sight of me, and bent at the waist in a respectful bow. "Good night, wife."

I bowed as well, having long found myself without words when facing my husband. What could I say that I had not already said? He knew I disapproved of his actions. He knew I did not love him. He ought to know that I worried about his eternal soul.

I was walking toward the stairs when a hissing sound caught my attention. Kissa stood in the shadows, gesturing for me to come closer.

"Your teacher is waiting to say good-bye," she said, pointing to a dark room off the vestibule.

I found Simeon waiting in the shadows.

"My heart nearly stopped beating when I received your summons," he said, the corner of his mouth twisting. "My wife fainted."

"I am sorry to have caused you distress. I hoped the summons would go out in my name."

"Given our long relationship, I would have suspected the king behind any summons from this house. The king would lie, I believe, to catch a Pharisee who opposed him."

He folded his hands at his waist—in an effort, I think, to

refrain from touching me during this difficult farewell. He took a deep breath and adjusted his smile. "As much as it pains me to leave the Holy City, I am leaving for Egypt. My wife and I will leave on the morrow."

Though I had been expecting such an announcement, I still felt the pang of loss. "The king swore he would not harm you."

"A king who will lie will not keep an oath. So we are going to Egypt and will return, if HaShem wills, if—when—Jannaeus is no longer king. Until then, Shelamzion, know that you will be in our thoughts and prayers."

I folded my hands too, though I wanted to draw him into an affectionate embrace out of simple gratitude for all he had taught me over the years.

"I would not be . . . I could not be the woman I am without your guidance," I said, my chest tightening with unexpressed emotions. "I am so grateful."

"It was not I who guided you," he replied. "It was the Torah. And though I am leaving, you will always have the Torah with you. If not on a scroll, then here"—he tapped his chest—"and here." He tapped his temple. "Blessings on your head, Shelamzion. I hope to see you again."

I stood silently and watched him go, my heart breaking. Over the course of my life I had lost my father, my uncle, and now my Torah teacher. To whom could I go when I needed godly guidance?

Not to my husband, nor to either of my sons.

Only to the Torah . . . and HaShem.

CHAPTER THIRTY-EIGHT

Kissa

I followed my mistress up the stone staircase, my heart as heavy as her slow footsteps. I knew her spirits were low—studying Torah with Simeon ben Shetah had been one of her truest joys, and she would miss him desperately. The sober Torah teacher would probably miss her too, for never again would he find a woman with such a thirst for knowledge and wisdom.

My mistress sighed as we entered her chamber. She pulled the himation free of her throat and let it flutter to the floor. "My world is closing around me, Kissa," she said, undoing the broach at her shoulder. "I have no friends but you and my sons. Though I don't see them often now that they are married with children of their own."

"You cannot lose me," I said and stooped to pick up the himation. "I will always be at your side."

She gave me a weary smile, then sank to the edge of the bed. "I think it is time for me to free you. When I was younger, I said Uncle wouldn't allow me to free one of his slaves, but that has not been a valid reason for a long, long time." I looked up and felt the weight of her gaze, dark and gentle like the sea at dawn. "What say you to becoming a free woman?"

I took a wincing little breath. "I . . . I don't know what to think."

Shelamzion ran her hand over the blanket on the bed. "You do not have to remain in this household if you would rather leave. I know you have always wanted to go back to Egypt—I will pay for your passage should you still wish it. You could even go with Simeon ben Shetah and his family."

The words hung in the silence like bait, tempting me. I did want to visit Egypt, but without Shelamzion? I would feel . . . unanchored. Adrift.

"We are no longer young women," Shelamzion went on, "but we are not so filled with years that we cannot enjoy the remaining time HaShem intends to give us."

I dropped to a stool and stared at the floor. How could I leave the household to which I had become so attached? And how could I leave Shelamzion? I tried to imagine boarding a ship without her, journeying to the land of my birth alone, but the images would not form. We had become intertwined, one beginning where the other left off. By deciding to become her friend so many years ago, I had given her my heart . . . and shaped my life around hers. And it was a *good* life.

"I know what your Torah says about slaves," I whispered, not willing to speak the words too loudly lest I wake myself from a dream. "If a master sets a slave free and the slave says, 'I love my master and I will not go out free,' then the master is to bring him to God, then pierce his ear and let him serve his master forever."

Shelamzion nodded. "Yes, that is right."

"I would not be your slave forever," I said, my throat tightening, "but if you would have me, I would be your friend forever."

Shelamzion stood and looked at me with eager tenderness,

then drew me into her arms. "Thank you," she said, squeezing me. She smiled into my eyes. "From this day forward you shall not be my slave but my hired servant. I will pay you a weekly wage, and if you desire to take a day for yourself, you must do it. And we will finish our days on earth together."

I nodded, happy with the deal we had struck, but needed one thing more. "I would like a document of manumission."

"Of course." Shelamzion turned to her desk. "I will write it, and you shall have it immediately."

She sat down, pulled parchment from a drawer, and began to write while I straightened up the fabrics in her trunk.

With a few written words and the stroke of a pen, Shelamzion set me free.

How ironic that I had no desire to go.

⁓⁓⁓⁓⁓

I walked carefully down the stairs, my hand on Alexander's shoulder. Shelamzion was carrying Aristobulus's youngest son on her hip, and with the other hand she gripped her son's youngest daughter, making sure the girl had a firm footing on each stone step before descending to the next.

"There," Shelamzion said, setting the other twin onto the floor. "It was so good to see you sweet children today."

Aristobulus stood in the vestibule, waiting for his offspring. I released Alexander and watched as the girls ran to hug their father's knees.

Shelamzion crossed her arms as she watched her grandchildren scamper out the doorway. Then she turned and dashed tears from her eyes. "What should we do next?" she said, her voice bright as she looked at me. "Do we have a meeting planned?"

"You don't have to pretend," I said, brushing past her as I turned to go back upstairs. "I know your heart breaks every time you have to let those little ones go home."

My mistress's chin wobbled as she fought back tears. "They are only little for such a short while. Sometimes I wish Hyrcanus and Aristobulus could be small again, just for the day. They were sweeter in those days . . . or maybe I was." A frown passed over her features, and she squeezed my arm. "Listen to me, going on about my family. I have not told you, but I have been preparing something special."

"Something for the grandchildren?"

Her smile deepened. "Something for you. Come into the reception hall and I will make my meaning clear."

I trailed behind her, my curiosity rising as she went to the large table Jannaeus had built some years before. An artist had painted a map of the known world on the tabletop, with Jerusalem at the very center.

"Here we are," my mistress said, lightly pressing a fingertip to a miniature painting of the Temple. "But here"—her hand swept over the surface, crossing the desert, the land of the Nabateans, and into Egypt—"is where we will be in a few weeks."

I frowned at the map. "Are you traveling with the king?"

She snorted softly. "You and I will make this trip alone— well, not completely alone because we will have a contingent of guards. But not so many as to draw unwanted attention."

I leaned closer to the map, in case I was missing a key part of a joke. "We are traveling to Egypt?"

"Yes."

"You must have an audience with King Auletes."

"I do. But we are going to Egypt on your behalf, Kissa. We are making the journey for you alone."

Stunned by the delight on my lady's face, I found myself unable to move.

Shelamzion moved around the table, her fingers trailing over the bright blue waters. "You once told me that if you could have anything, you would want to return to Egypt and find your parents. I have not forgotten your wish, so last month I wrote Auletes and asked if we might visit his palace. I told him the truth about the purpose of our visit, and he has agreed to help find your mother and father. If they still live, I am sure he will search them out."

Ripples of shock spread outward from my center, tingling the crown of my head and numbing my toes. "Impossible," I whispered.

"Nothing is impossible," Shelamzion said, her eyes sparkling.

Somehow I broke free of my paralysis and caught her arm. "You do not have to do this. I know you are no longer comfortable in this palace. I know you are lonely and your husband brings you nothing but sorrow. But you do not have to do all this—"

"It is the least I can do for one who has been so faithful." She smiled, her eyes serene and compelling as she took my hands. "Let me take you back to Egypt. For a few weeks, let us forget about the trouble in Jerusalem and explore a new land together."

What could I say? I cast about for a reason to refuse her but came up empty-handed. I sighed. "If it will please you."

"It will." A soft and loving curve touched her lips. "Jannaeus does not need me. My children do not need me. So pack a trunk, my friend, and dream of finding your family. We leave at sunrise tomorrow."

We traveled by coach, a stifling box with narrow windows that did little to ventilate the conveyance. Shelamzion kept saying that her uncle's coach had been far more comfortable, but then I reminded her that she had been traveling north on that journey and not across a desert.

During occasional glimpses through the windows, I saw thin clouds moving across the sky and barren trees stretching skeletal arms toward the heavens. The territory between Judea and Egypt was not fertile or beautiful, but sandy, with sterile dunes and broken rocks that marked the course of former waterways. An air of brooding desolation lay over the land, and I found myself wondering if Shelamzion had been so desperate to leave Jerusalem that she had traded unpleasantness for genuine discomfort.

When we finally reached the verdant plain watered by tributaries of the Nile, I begged the driver to stop so we could disembark and stretch our legs. We stood by ourselves near the shoreline, breathing in the sights, sounds, and rich aromas of Egypt.

"I remember this," I said as those scents opened the door on a host of memories I had tried to lock away. "You can smell the loamy soil. You can smell the water, too."

Shelamzion inhaled deeply. "There is nothing like this in Judea. Does it bring back memories of your home?"

I thought for a moment, then shook my head. "The last time I saw this water I was chained to a line of other slaves. It is not a memory worth reliving."

We climbed back into the coach and traveled farther down the king's highway, finally entering Alexandria through one of the eastern gates.

"At last!" Shelamzion rose on her knees to peer out the window, then settled on her pillow and smiled. "We are staying at the palace—the king has been most generous."

"Do you think he'll see us tonight?"

"I do not think so. He would not know when we were to arrive, so he will not be prepared. Perhaps tomorrow."

Before the hour passed, we arrived at the seashore. When we stepped out of the coach, armored guards pointed us to a dock where shallow boats waited to transport us to the palace. I walked behind Shelamzion, trying to imitate her calm and grace, though my heart was thumping loudly enough to be heard several paces away.

~~~~~~~

The next morning we rose, bathed, and dressed in our best. Servants brought trays of fruit, bread, and honey. We ate our fill and washed everything down with lemon water. "I must say," Shelamzion said, dabbing at her lips with a piece of linen, "the climate here is infinitely preferable to that of Jerusalem. The breeze is nearly constant, and the air feels so moist."

"We are at the seashore," I said, suddenly realizing that this region was nothing like the Egypt I knew. "Memphis is much farther south."

A small boy entered our room and rang a bell. We looked up, and my mistress nodded. "Yes?"

"The king will see you now," the boy said and bobbed his shaved head. "The queen and the royal children are eager to meet you."

"Wonderful." Shelamzion stood and brushed crumbs from her chiton. "Shall we follow you?"

The boy smiled, revealing matching dimples, and I stood to follow my mistress. She walked forward, a picture of calm and confidence, while I padded behind her, wondering if I had finally come full circle.

We followed the boy out of the building, down a marble walkway and through a beautiful garden of Greek design. We were led into an impressive marble building with columns as tall as four men standing atop each others' shoulders. The floor beneath our sandals gleamed in the morning light, and sweet incense perfumed the air. A quartet of armed guards snapped to attention at our approach. The little boy trotted between them, so we continued to follow his lead.

We entered an imposing chamber that appeared to be made

of gold. Gold leaf covered the walls, golden tapestries hung from the ceiling, and golden candlesticks stood in the room's corners. High clerestory windows allowed the sunlight to pour in, gilding the furniture and the carvings on the walls.

On an elevated throne in the center of the space sat a clean-shaven man who had to be Ptolemy XII, known to his people as Auletes the Flute Player, because he was inordinately fond of music. He wore a Greek tunic, his curled hair gleamed with oil, and in his hand he held a golden cup, apparently filled with wine. His wife, Cleopatra Tryphaena, sat on a smaller chair at his side. Before the king and queen, seated on small benches, were the royal children—three girls and two boys.

My mistress bowed deeply before the Egyptian king, and I did the same. He stood and extended his hand to Shelamzion; she accepted it, then rose and embraced the Egyptian queen, who did not appear to be thrilled by my mistress's warm greeting.

The royals exchanged formal salutations, though I barely heard the words, so anxious was I to see if the king had been able to find my family. Gift baskets were exchanged, accompanied by all manner of overblown compliments. Promises were made, enforced by false smiles and exaggerated posturing.

Shelamzion then gestured to me, and I choked back a gasp. I had been startled by the unexpected turn of events, yet the king paid no attention to my reaction. He smiled at Shelamzion and clapped. I heard the creak of a door and turned in time to see a pair of guards approaching with a wizened couple between them.

The man, who appeared to be a collection of bones wrapped in skin and a kilt, walked with his head forward and his gaze lowered. He wore simple papyrus sandals, as did the woman next to him. She wore a linen tunic and a black Egyptian wig into which someone had woven colorful beads. Their lined faces

looked up at me, and in that moment I realized they were supposed to be my parents.

Silence fell like spring rain as we stared at each other. The
king uttered a sharp command in Egyptian. In unison, the old
couple released a surprised cry, but they were poor actors.

What was *this*? Though I no longer retained any memories
of my parents' faces, this couple appeared no older than I.
And my parents were poor, with no prospects for wealth. Yet
this woman had beads in her wig, a luxury no poor person
could afford.

Comprehension seeped through my confusion. Shelamzion
had asked the king to search for my parents. He must have done
so, though he might not have expended much effort, and when
he could not find them he commanded these two strangers to
play the part rather than disappoint Judea's queen.

I could not disappoint Judea's queen, either. I could not denounce these two as imposters, nor could I be rude and accuse
the king of trickery.

So we each had a role to play. Forcing a smile, I stepped forward and knelt before the man and woman. Though I could
no longer speak Egyptian, in Greek I told them I was their
daughter, that I had come a long way, and I was happy to see
them well and prosperous.

I gestured to the Judean guards who had entered with us.
One of them brought over a basket containing honey, dates,
and expensive fabrics from the Galilee region. I laid these gifts
at the couple's feet, thanked them once again, and looked at
my mistress with a silent plea for release.

Shelamzion had always understood me. With a grace honed
through years of diplomatic experience, she thanked the king
and queen for their hospitality and asked if we could enjoy
their country a few days more before returning home. Though
Auletes pressed her to stay longer, Shelamzion replied that she

had important responsibilities in Judea and could not remain in the lovely land of Egypt as long as she wished.

We left the royal reception hall and did not speak until we reached the privacy of our own chamber. Then I sank to my bed, stared at the linen cover, and burst into tears.

"They . . . are not my parents," I said, my words strangled by sobs. "I am sixty-six years old. That woman was my age or younger. And the man, as well."

Shelamzion sat across from me and clucked in sympathy. "Auletes made an effort," she said. "That is something."

I nodded, not wanting to appear ungrateful. I met her searching gaze. "I would like to visit Memphis before we go. Let me look around to see if I remember anything. After that, we can return to Jerusalem."

"Are you sure?" Dewy moisture filled Shelamzion's brown eyes. "I want you to be happy. If that is your lifelong wish . . ."

"I think—" I hiccupped a sob—"for years I have labored under a delusion. I have been angry with my parents and I have grieved their loss. I promised the gods a thousand sacrifices if they would send me home, but they did nothing. I thought I no longer had a home, no place to belong. But this morning, when I looked into the faces of those strangers, I realized the truth."

"And what is that?"

I tried to control my emotions, but my chin quivered and my eyes filled despite my resolve. "My home is in Jerusalem, and you are my family, Shelamzion. You have been my family since the day we met."

My mistress's eyes softened. "I know you are free now, but promise you will never leave me."

"Where would I go?" I laughed, warmed by the realization that my restless spirit had quieted. Inexplicably exhausted, I stretched out across the bed and pillowed my head on my arm. "If you want to return home straightway, I do not need to go to Memphis."

Shelamzion, too, stretched out on her bed and yawned. "I am in no hurry to climb back into that wooden box. We can travel to Memphis, and if you do not mind, we can also visit the temple at Leontopolis."

"You wish to visit an Egyptian temple?"

She shook her head. "Simeon ben Shetah told me about it. It is a Jewish temple, built years ago by a Zadokite priest. He used to say Egypt had an illegitimate temple with a legitimate priest, while Jerusalem had a legitimate temple with an illegitimate priest."

I frowned. "What would—I mean, would it be troublesome for your husband if you were seen at this other temple?"

Lines of concentration deepened beneath her eyes. "You are right. I had not considered the consequences. I cannot go there, though I would dearly love to see it."

The idea came as easily as breathing. "I could go. You could wait in the coach while I go in to worship."

"Yes." A hopeful glint came to my mistress's eyes. "And you will tell me all about it?"

I nodded, thrilled to do this for her. "I will."

～～～～

Heliopolis lay only a day's journey north of Memphis, so Shelamzion decided that we would visit my birthplace first and stop by the temple on our way home.

When we arrived in Memphis, Shelamzion asked the driver to stop at a bazaar. We stepped out and tightened our himations to shield our faces from an abrasive wind.

"Where do you want to go?" Shelamzion asked.

I looked right and left, floundering in indecision. The place reminded me of the market in the Valley of the Cheesemakers, complete with merchants, haggling housewives, and children, who scampered around their mothers' feet. I breathed in the odors of open sewers, overripe fruit, and donkey dung, then looked away. "I could see this very thing at home."

Shelamzion smiled. "Let us walk on."

With two guards for company, we walked past the market-place and entered a wealthy area, which we quickly traversed. Four streets farther on, we found ourselves on an unpaved road lined with shanties and mud-brick huts. Women squatted outside the unsteady shelters, frying small bits of meat over burning sticks. The sight of a discarded bit of rat fur brought back memories of the siege outside Jerusalem, and I shuddered. Shelamzion must have experienced the same memory, because she put a hand on my shoulder and turned to face me.

"Does any of this evoke a memory?"

"Not of Egypt," I said. "Only of Jerusalem."

"Shall we continue, then?"

I did not need to be asked again. Before leaving, I bent and gave a poor woman a silver coin, then caught up with Shelamzion and hurried back to the coach.

<hr />

We traveled through the night and stopped at an inn in Leontopolis to wash and break our fast. When ready, we packed our things and returned them to the coach, then had the driver take us to the Jewish temple. The Sabbath had come and gone, so the temple was not crowded.

"Go," Shelamzion said, opening the door of the coach. "And be sure to make note of all the details. I want to hear about everything you observed when you return."

I nodded, stepped from the coach, and pulled my himation closer about my head and shoulders. I did not know if anyone at this temple would be offended by an Egyptian woman in the outer court, but I could always leave if someone voiced an objection.

The building was rectangular, similar to the Temple in Jerusalem, with white limestone steps leading up to pillars that outlined a small porch. The double doors stood open as if in invitation, so I swallowed hard and entered.

The beauty of the place, fully visible because so few people were present, nearly took my breath away. The long, narrow space was divided in two. The nearest section, I knew, was for worshipers, the second reserved for priests. The walls were paneled with fragrant cedarwood, the floor with cypress and inlaid with gold. Intricate designs of flowers, palm trees, and cherubim decorated the walls and crowned two massive pillars.

Behind a dividing rail stood the Holy of Holies, separated by a linen curtain. I could not see into the sacred space but knew the place was reserved for the high priest when he made the annual sacrifice on the Day of Atonement.

I turned slowly in the room, mentally recording the details—the gold, the detailed pomegranates carved into the wood, the petals on the flowers. Two cherubim with massive outstretched wings stood on either side of the holy place. They looked like sphinxes—lions with human heads. Had an Egyptian artist carved them?

I was about to leave when a priest entered and began lighting incense. I bowed and felt my breath being whipped away as a soundless voice overshadowed my awareness:

I am Adonai your God, who brought you out of the land of Egypt, to be your God. I am Adonai.

I glanced around, certain that others must have heard the voice. But the priest continued lighting the incense, and a woman at prayer did not move.

Then a second priest entered and walked to a platform where

he picked up a scroll. Without looking up he began to read the text in Hebrew:

> "In that day five cities in the land of Egypt will speak the language of Canaan, swearing allegiance to Adonai-Tzva'ot. One used to be called the City of the Sun."

Certainly the words referred to Heliopolis, the district where we were.

> "In that day there will be an altar to Adonai in the middle of the land of Egypt, and next to the border a pillar to Adonai. It will be as a sign and a witness to Adonai-Tzva'ot in the land of Egypt. For they will cry to Adonai because of oppressors, and He will send them a savior and defender—and He will deliver them . . . So Adonai will strike Egypt—striking yet healing—so they will return to Adonai, and He will respond to them and heal them.
>
> "In that day there will be a highway from Egypt to Assyria, and the Assyrians will come to Egypt, and the Egyptians to Assyria, and the Egyptians will worship with the Assyrians.
>
> "In that day Israel will be the third, along with Egypt and Assyria—a blessing in the midst of the earth. For Adonai-Tzva'ot has blessed, saying:
>
> > 'Blessed is Egypt My people,
> > And Assyria My handiwork,
> > And Israel My inheritance.'
>
> "It will also come about in that day, a great shofar will be blown. Those perishing in the land of Assyria and the exiles in the land of Egypt will come and worship Adonai on the holy mountain in Jerusalem."

The priest lowered the scroll, turned and left. I closed my

eyes and felt a trembling in my arms and legs. Was that message for me? The woman at prayer did not even lift her head, and the other priest had long finished lighting the incense. If the message was not for me, then whom?

And what did it mean? Shelamzion would undoubtedly understand it better than I, but one thing had been made clear: Adonai was not only the God of the Jews. One day the people from Assyria, or Seleucia, would know Him, as would the Egyptians. And we would all travel to Jerusalem, where we would worship on the Temple Mount.

But I would be there first.

I whirled and hurried away, eager to share the news.

I waited until the coach had settled into its rocking rhythm for the long journey back to Jerusalem.

"You look like a cat who has just swallowed a mouse," Shelamzion said, her eyes sparkling. "There is no one to interrupt us, so tell me everything."

I knew she wanted details of the construction, the decoration, and the artful embellishments. But other words tumbled from my mouth. "I heard a voice . . . that no one else seemed to hear. It said, 'I am Adonai your God, who brought you out of the land of Egypt to be your God.' It seemed to be speaking to me alone."

Shelamzion blinked, and her mouth dropped open before she found her voice. "To you?"

"I know Adonai brought your people out of the land of Egypt," I assured her, "but today He spoke to me. I felt it, here." I tapped my breastbone. "No one else seemed to hear anything at all."

"Others were in the sanctuary?"

"A woman and a priest. They did not even look up when the voice spoke."

Shelamzion looked away as her mouth curved in a wistful smile. "I do not doubt you, Kissa. I find that I am even a bit . . . envious, considering all the times I have yearned to hear the voice of Adonai for myself."

"Does He do this often? Speak to your people?"

"Not often." She met my gaze again. "But yes, He does speak to those who are willing to listen. Samuel. Daniel. Moses. All of the prophets. And others, too." Her graceful brow rose. "Now do you believe He is the Almighty God?"

I nodded. "That is not all. No sooner had the voice finished speaking than the priest began to read from the scroll. Fortunately I knew enough Hebrew to understand."

"What did he read?"

"Something about five cities in Egypt that would swear allegiance to Adonai. They would cry out to Adonai because of oppressors, and He would send them a savior and defender who would deliver them. And all the Egyptians would know Adonai, and the Assyrians would worship with the Egyptians and the people of Israel, and all of them would worship Adonai on the Holy Mount in Jerusalem."

Shelamzion's face rearranged itself into an inward look, and I knew she was searching her memory. "I believe that reading is from the prophecies of Isaiah," she said, looking at me as if I had suddenly shone a light on something she had never understood. "Imagine . . . my people worshiping Adonai with your people and even the Seleucids. In the Holy City."

I grinned. "Will it happen soon, do you think?"

"I don't know. I think the Savior will have to come first. When we are delivered from the wicked mess this world has become, perhaps then."

She reached across the space between us and caught my hand. "I can never thank you enough. You have helped me see the future of our beloved city."

CHAPTER THIRTY-NINE

Shelamzion

K issa and I returned to Jerusalem with a quiet confidence that surely must have mystified all who noticed it. That confidence, that faith, enabled me to endure the growing insolence of my sons, my unfaithful husband, and the strife that continued to rock Judea. The Pharisees may have fled, but plenty of others remained to oppose the hedonism of the Sadducees, though they remained hidden. The king railed against them all, yet he could not execute those he could not find.

In the twenty-fourth year of Alexander Jannaeus's reign, I returned from an outing with my grandchildren to urgent news: the king was ill and wanted to see me.

"Why didn't someone send for me sooner?" I asked. I uncovered my hair and handed the himation to Kissa, then hurried up the stairs to the king's bedchamber.

I found Jannaeus in bed, propped up on silk pillows. A physician sat by his bedside, and at my approach he stood and prostrated himself. "Forgive me, my queen, for not sending a message earlier, but the king would not allow me."

Of course he wouldn't; Jannaeus was too proud.

I gave the physician a perfunctory nod and went to Jannaeus's side. His eyes were closed, his hair wet with perspiration. His complexion, usually ruddy and robust, had gone a pale yellow.

"Jannaeus? Husband?"

His eyelids fluttered.

"The king is suffering from fever," the physician said, still facedown on the floor. "If the queen will allow me—"

"You may rise," I said, studying my husband's face. "Tell me what happened here."

With great effort, the aged physician got to his feet, then pressed his hands together. "It is a quartan fever, my queen. Every fourth day he suffers. Tomorrow he will feel more like himself, perhaps a bit weaker than usual, and the next day he will feel stronger still, but on the fourth day he will have fever again."

I pressed my hand to Jannaeus's damp forehead.

"He doesn't feel hot."

"He will—he chills, then he burns. It is the way of the fever."

I sat on the edge of the bed and took my husband's hand in mine. "Jannaeus," I said firmly. "Jannaeus, wake up. Your wife is here."

Again the eyelids fluttered, but this time they lifted. The dark eyes rolled in his head, lowered, and focused on my face. "Shelamzion?"

He had not called me by that name since his childhood. I gave him a curt nod. "I am sorry to hear you are ill. Can I get anything for you?"

"I need . . . your help."

I glanced down at his pale, waxy hand. How many nights had I thought about killing this man? Too many to count. But HaShem had kept him alive, and here I was, offering my help as his wife and partner.

Truly Adonai worked in mysterious ways.

I squeezed his hand. "Tell me what to do, and I will see to it."

A faint smile lifted the corners of my husband's cracked lips. "I am sick."

"So the physician says."

"I am sure I will get better—"

"If HaShem wills."

"But until I do, I need your help."

He seemed so childlike, so unlike himself, that I patted his hand. "Tell me what I can do to help."

"I need you to help . . . like you did in Galilee. Remember?"

I lifted both brows. "You want me to receive people in your name?"

His chin dipped in a barely perceptible nod. "And oversee the treasury. I am not certain my accountants are managing things . . . properly."

"And how do I explain why I am doing these things in your place?"

His face went blank as his eyelids closed, a curtain coming between us.

"He sleeps," the physician said, stepping forward.

I released my husband's hand and slowly left the room, my thoughts spinning in bewilderment. What had motivated Jannaeus to ask for me? I was far from young—sixty-two, by my reckoning—and no man would call me a beauty. Jannaeus had not slept with me since we lived in Galilee, so he certainly did not think of me as a lover.

But he had not forgotten that I had a good head on my shoulders. He must have remembered that I judged well during our days in Galilee, and he had always known that his father admired my desire for learning.

My husband did not love me, he would not call me a friend, but he did respect me.

And, considering everything that had passed between us, that was enough.

~~~~~~~

For the next two years Jannaeus and I ruled Judea together. When he felt strong, Jannaeus would ride out to oversee his army, which was busily engaged in a campaign to reclaim some of the cities he had lost when his health began to suffer.

True to my word, I took over the day-to-day affairs of ruling Judea. I received visiting dignitaries, resolved disputes between Judean cities, and sent and received tributes and gifts from other national leaders. I sent a kind message to the Ptolemies in Egypt and sent gifts to Philip II, the current ruler of Seleucia. On Rosh Hashanah I sent emissaries to Rome, assuring them that we valued our treaty with the Roman Senate and wished them a prosperous new year.

When I was not receiving visitors or sending gifts, I quietly held banquets for several of the leading Torah teachers, Pharisees, and Essenes. I paid little attention to the Sadducees, and because they sat at the top of the Temple's power structure and had the king's blessing, they paid little attention to me.

But I thoroughly enjoyed my conversations with the Torah scholars. Both the Pharisees and Essenes were eagerly awaiting the Messiah. I was astonished and encouraged to realize their hope for the future had been fueled by the very incidents that had driven me to despair. The more corruption and violence they observed at the Temple, the more tumult in the world, the more convinced they became that the Messiah was on His way.

Once the Essenes learned to trust me, they told me that a large group of their unmarried members had gone to an area near the caves of Qumran, near the Dead Sea. I had heard this, of course, but I had not learned the exact location or the details.

These Essenes called themselves "the community" and had submitted to the leadership of the Teacher of Righteousness. This man, they explained, had been given a special understanding from the Ruach HaKodesh, or Holy Spirit of God. He opened the Torah scrolls, the prophets, and the writings to his followers, and taught them the proper meaning of the Scriptures.

I found that the Pharisees and the Essenes had much in common. Both groups believed in a coming Messiah. Both groups believed in the afterlife, angels, and the importance of circumcision. Both groups believed that righteous Gentiles like Kissa would be included in the kingdom of God.

They disagreed on divorce, however. The Pharisees were all too quick to divorce their wives, citing the Law of Moses as their authority. The Essenes, on the other hand, believed that God's ideal was one man for one woman for one lifetime. "How can it be otherwise," one Essene told me, "when HaShem created one wife only for Adam?"

I smiled when I heard this, for though I had always considered myself a Pharisee, I agreed with the Essenes on that point. Jannaeus had caused me deep and abiding grief over the years, and while I had considered murdering him, I had never considered asking him to grant me a divorce.

When I mentioned that the Essenes and the Pharisees were much alike, the Torah teacher with the Essenes laughed aloud. "On the surface, yes," he said. "But we believe the Pharisees seek the 'smooth way' to godliness. We Essenes do not believe in an easy road. To join the community, a man must renounce the world, his family, and surrender his earthly possessions. He must repent of sin and present himself to the community, where he will be on probation for at least one year. Every detail of our lives is watched by the community. If a member bears a grudge against his neighbor, falls asleep during a meeting, or even burps during a meeting, he is punished. It is not easy to be part of the community."

I leaned forward. "I am most interested in matters that might affect Judea. What does your Teacher of Righteousness say about the coming Messiah?"

The teacher picked up a scroll and unrolled it. "'An oppression will come to the earth,'" he read aloud. "'A great massacre in the province. The king of Assyria and Egypt will rise, and he will be great on the earth. He will call himself grand, and by his name he will be designated. Then the Son of God will be proclaimed and the Son of the Most High they will call Him. Like the sparks of the vision, so will be their kingdom. They will reign for years on the earth and they will trample all. People will trample people, and one province another province vacate until the people of God will arise and all will rest from the sword. The people of God's kingdom will be an eternal kingdom and all their path will be in truth. They will judge the earth in truth and all will make peace. The sword will cease from the earth, and all the provinces will pay homage to them. Their dominion will be an eternal dominion.'"

I frowned. "I do not understand. What does it mean?"

The Torah teacher returned his gaze to the scroll. "I do not fully understand myself. But I know this: if we live in righteousness, if Israel commits to keeping the Law of Adonai, then HaShem will raise up the Anointed One, the Son of the Most High. He will have the Ruach HaKodesh upon Him, and He will defeat the wicked king."

My eyes wandered over the dining room—the ornate couches, the thick rug, the wall carvings inlaid with precious gems and metals. I enjoyed these comforts along with my husband, but might I be called upon to sacrifice them for a new king?

"Do you think," I said, lowering my voice, "my husband is the wicked king? Should I be expecting this Messiah to unseat him?"

The Torah teacher's eyes widened. "I . . . I cannot say, my queen."

I understood the anxiety filling his expression. "You may speak freely," I said. "I would never try to prevent or deny HaShem's truth."

The man swallowed hard, then closed the scroll. "The Teacher of Righteousness has called your husband 'the wicked priest,' but I do not believe he considers Alexander Jannaeus the wicked king described in the text. Your husband does not rule Egypt and Syria."

I sighed. "So we should not expect the Messiah until later?"

The Torah teacher pressed his hands on the table for a moment, then shook his head. "I do not know, my queen. I only know He is expected. Some say we are to look for two anointed messiahs—a king from the line of David and a priest from the line of Zadok. I do not know when they will come, but I am always watching."

I lifted my cup. "Then I will watch with you."

CHAPTER FORTY

Shelamzion

As the months passed, Jannaeus's good days became fewer and fewer. The yellow cast did not vanish from his skin, his eyes watered almost constantly, and his once-strong constitution weakened. He stopped visiting his military commanders and remained in Jerusalem, conducting business when he could. As he grew weaker, he spent more time in his bedchamber, usually accompanied by one or two of his favorite concubines, whom he housed in a new wing of the palace. He no longer visited the Temple, but allowed other *kohanim* to perform the sacrifices usually offered by the high priest. The wooden barriers blocking access to the inner sanctuary remained in place, and I knew he would not remove them during his lifetime. Any act to restore the Temple to the people would have to come from his successor.

Though he tried, he could not hide his illness from the people of Jerusalem. How else could he explain his absence from the Temple, the Sanhedrin, and his reception hall? For I handled all questions of state. I presided over banquets attended by delegations from other nations. I even met with the chief priests whenever they sought the high priest's advice. Jannaeus had become so frail, and looked so diminished, that he refused to be seen in public.

For their part, the people of Jerusalem did not seem to miss him. They could not forget the atrocities he had committed, and though the people who entered our reception hall always made solicitous inquiries about his health, I suspected they were patiently waiting for his reign to end.

I waited along with them, for every day I saw proof that my husband was dying. I dutifully visited his bedchamber each morning to offer my help and ask his opinion on certain matters. I followed his commands, when he made them, but as the days passed and he grew more incapacitated, more and more often he told me to do what I thought best.

Finally, the physician told me that Jannaeus would not live another week. "HaShem could always work a miracle," the man hastened to add, "but you should be prepared, my queen. I do not think the king will live to see another Shabbat."

He left me then, and I sat in the dying man's room, alone with him . . . and a troubling predicament.

We had two sons, neither of whom would make a good king. I loved my sons deeply, but though I had been quick to praise their virtues, I had never been blind to their faults.

Hyrcanus, our firstborn, had grown into a soft, gentle, intellectual young man . . . who, I had to admit, was inordinately fond of sensual pleasures. As far as I knew, he was faithful to his wife, but he loved fine food, extravagant garments, and fine furnishings. If he were to move into this house, he would toss out every stick of furniture and every curtain, replacing them with furnishings far more expensive and grand. If the Seleucids or Egyptians or Romans were to threaten Judea in the years to come, Hyrcanus would negotiate Judea into poverty and utter submission, for he preferred capitulation over violence.

On the other hand, if Aristobulus were faced with the threat of war, he would fight until the last citizen of Judea lay gasping for breath. As king he would not hesitate to attack whoever stood in the way of his territorial ambitions. He would conscript warriors from our people and tax the people to hire mercenaries until he had the largest and most fearsome army in the known world. He would push Judea's boundaries to the north, south, and east, and his reign would be remembered for its bloody battles.

Which son should inherit my husband's throne? By right, the throne should go to Hyrcanus, and yet I did not believe Aristobulus would accept his brother as king. Prodded by his own ambition and his pushy wife, he would seek to overthrow his brother and would almost certainly succeed. Which meant he would have to kill my beloved Hyrcanus, because the firstborn would always be a threat. He might as well kill me too, because I could not continue living if one of my sons had murdered the other.

That thought dredged up another, with a chill that struck deep in my heart: Alena. I had always thought her death a senseless tragedy, but perhaps I was wrong to think so. If she had not died in prison, how could she have survived knowing that Judah Aristobulus had killed Antigonus, and that her daughter-in-law had killed Aristobulus? Later, how could she live with the knowledge that Jannaeus had murdered Absalom and Philo Elias?

The grief at losing so many of her children would have destroyed her, and that same knowledge would devastate me, as well.

So what could I do?

I had been judging the cases of Jews for years, weighing facts and considering situations in the light of the Torah. But when it came to deciding between my two sons, I could not think clearly.

Each day I woke and considered the question of succession, one day favoring Hyrcanus, and the next day Aristobulus. And by the end of each day, I arrived at the same conclusion: choosing either of my sons would invite disaster upon my family and my people.

Desperately I sought someone who could help me. Josu Attis, who had long been a friend, knew little of politics, so he would be of no help. Simeon ben Shetah was in Egypt, too far away to be of service. I dared not go to any of the Sadducees, for those power-hungry men were wealthy enough to have my entire family killed.

In truth, I had no one to turn to. Kissa was always with me, ready to listen and sympathize, but she was a second mother to my sons, and as confounded by her emotions as I was.

One name came repeatedly to my mind: Ezra Diagos. He would have answers for me; he would consider the situation dispassionately and would not be afraid to give me the hard truth. Oh, what a lovely relief it would be to hand my responsibilities over to him! However, Diagos was not my husband or my king.

Each morning I rose and went into my husband's bedchamber, evicting the concubines so I could have a few private moments to converse with him. Jannaeus was rarely lucid on those occasions. He mumbled in his fever, calling out for his generals, his mistresses, and occasionally his sons. Each day I listened and grew ever more convinced that the physician was correct—these were the king's last days.

One morning Jannaeus did not mumble but lay silent and still. Only by lowering my face to his could I detect any sign of life. He breathed still, but not deeply and not often.

I bit my lower lip. The urge that had brought me to this room now had a sharper spur; I had to either make a decision or compel Jannaeus to make the decision himself. As I stood there, about to drown in waves of confusion, I knew the consequences of that decision would echo throughout Israel and Judea for generations to come.

Was it possible that my entire existence had come down to this moment? Had HaShem worked in my life—moving me from Modein to John Hyrcanus's house, marrying me to a boy, bringing me into contact with men like Josu Attis and Simeon ben Shetah and my teachers at the havurah—had He done all of that so I could make the right decision during this crisis?

The memory of an afternoon with Kissa brought a wry, twisted smile to my face. We had sat in my upstairs bedroom at this palace, and we had asked each other what we wanted most in the world. When pressed, I had said that I wanted to matter. To be important to someone . . . even lots of someones.

Oh, what fools children are! HaShem had honored my childish prayer, and what I did next would matter a great deal to millions in Judea.

I lifted my gaze to heaven and asked, "HaShem, will you honor my prayer for wisdom now?"

I heard no answer in the silent room but carried the problem with me as I went to bed.

~~~~~~~~

The next morning I awoke to find Kissa fussing with the curtains in my bedchamber. I bade her a good morning, then sat up and saw that she was watching someone from the window. "What do you see out there?" I asked, half afraid to hear the answer. "Some form of protest?"

"No, mistress. I see the circle-drawer. He is speaking to a group outside the courtyard. I believe they are Sadducees."

I tossed off the blanket and crossed to the window. A bearded man in a white tunic stood just beyond the courtyard gate, and a group of well-dressed men stood around him. They were listening to the bearded one with rapt attention.

I glanced at Kissa. "What did you call him?"

She laughed. "His name is Honi Ha-Meaggel, but people call him the circle-drawer because of what happened during the drought."

I pulled up a chair and sat. "I am not sure I heard about this. Remind me, please."

Kissa let the curtain drop and turned from the window. "During the last dry spell, a group of farmers sought out this Honi and begged him to intercede with HaShem to end the drought. So he drew a circle in the sand and vowed that he would not leave it until the skies opened with rain."

"And?"

"It rained—a lot. But though the farmers were happy, the local Torah teacher was not. He said it was not right that a simple man like Honi should have direct access to HaShem. But now the people say this Honi is closer to Adonai than any man in Judea."

Kissa went on, saying something about the man's family, but I did not listen because my thoughts had turned inward. Could this Honi really speak directly to HaShem? Could he draw on the wisdom of Adonai? If he did, and if he were willing, could he help me decide what to do about the succession?

I stood, squeezed Kissa's arm, and moved to the trunk that held my garments. "Go down to the guards at the gate," I said, "and have them bring this rainmaker into the house. I would meet with him."

Kissa hesitated. "Should I—do you want me to first make your hair presentable?"

I waved her off. "I care not for my hair. Fetch Honi at once. I would speak to him today."

She hurried away, and I quickly pulled off my nightdress and stepped into a chiton. My fingers trembled as I fastened the broaches at the shoulders. Could HaShem have sent this circle-drawer to guide me? I would not know until I questioned the man myself.

<p style="text-align:center">~~~~~~~</p>

I came downstairs and found Honi Ha-Meaggel waiting in the vestibule. "Good morning," I said, hoping my desperation did not show on my face. "I was delighted to see you outside the gate."

He bowed politely, then lifted his head and looked directly into my eyes. "I have heard many good things about you, Salome Alexandra. They say you are a righteous woman."

I looked away as my cheeks grew warm. I could not say why his words embarrassed me—perhaps because this stranger seemed to look right through me, as if he could weigh my motives and my desires.

"Come." I gestured to the large doors of the reception hall, and the guards opened them. I led the way into the room, but instead of walking to the grand chair in the center of the dais, I nodded at two chairs that had been placed beneath a window.

"Please, sit. Unless you are uncomfortable sitting with a woman who is not your wife."

Many religious men would have refused to meet with me alone, but apparently Honi had no such reservations. He dropped into a chair as I took the other seat and faced him.

"This morning," I began, "my handmaid related the story of how you brought rain during the last drought. Because I know how tales can be exaggerated, I would like to hear the account from your own lips so I can understand exactly what happened."

Honi gave me a half smile. "It is no secret."

"Good." I folded my arms. "Please proceed."

The small man smiled again. "It was the time of the early rains, but the clouds had not come. The people of my village asked me to pray for rain, so I told them to bring the clay Passover ovens inside lest they soften and crumble in the wet. I prayed, but no rain fell."

I nodded. "So your prayer didn't work."

His dark brows rose. "They had no faith. They did not bring in the ovens."

"Ah."

He lifted a finger and continued. "So I drew a circle, stood inside it, and said to HaShem, 'Master of the Universe, Your children have turned to me because they consider me a son in Your household. I swear by Your great Name that I will not move from here until You show compassion on Your children!' Then a cloud blew in, and a few raindrops fell."

My heart sank. "That is all?"

Again the uplifted finger. "So I commanded the people to take the ovens inside, and they did. Afterward I said to HaShem, 'I didn't pray for that kind of rain, but for rain that will fill the ditches, caves, and water cisterns.' And rain began to fall most violently, scattering all who waited outside. So I said, 'I didn't pray for that kind of rain either, but for good, pleasant rain that will be a blessing.' Then it began to rain normally, and it rained for so long that the villagers asked me to pray that it would cease." The little man smiled and shrugged. "And that, my queen, is what happened."

I stared at him, amazed at his friendly manner with the Master of the Universe. His manner of speaking was almost irreverent— why didn't HaShem strike him down for blasphemy?

"Do you always speak to HaShem in that way?"

He tilted his head. "HaShem is my God, but He is also my friend."

I blinked. "Your *friend*?"

The man leaned toward me. "I know what you are thinking. You are thinking that my manner is ill-advised and I am being irreverent. But doesn't the Torah tell us that Adam talked with HaShem in the garden? And doesn't the Torah say Moses was a friend of HaShem? As was our father Abraham."

I nodded, too stunned to speak.

"Why, then, cannot I be a friend of HaShem? I have what those three had."

"What . . . what is it you have?"

A smile sparkled in his eyes as he looked at me. "Faith. I believe HaShem is real, and I believe He means what He says. Few people truly do, you know."

For a moment I felt a surge of energy, a momentary flash of insight. Words sprang to the tip of my tongue, then vanished. Something I had remembered. Something I had forgotten.

"The religious leaders aren't happy with me," Honi went on, crossing one leg as he made himself more comfortable. "They are so filled with learning and laws that they forget they are speaking to a real God when they pray. But the Creator of the Universe, blessed be He, is always there, listening and wanting to commune with us."

"But—" I groped for words—"He has not spoken through His prophets in nearly four hundred years."

"Perhaps the prophets are not listening? Or perhaps He has already said what we needed to hear. Either way, one thing is clear—HaShem is with us. He is still working out His plan to redeem Israel and bless—not destroy—the Gentiles."

I held up my hand; I had heard enough for the moment. Any more and I would be too confused to ask the question that had spurred my invitation to this odd little man.

"You have given me much to consider." I forced a smile. "And I appreciate your thoughts. But I asked you to come here because I need wisdom from a righteous man."

Honi gestured through the window toward the courtyard, which at any time might be filled with priests, Sadducees, and

Torah teachers. "Are there no righteous men in the high priest's palace?"

"I need wisdom . . . from a man who talks with HaShem."

Honi chuckled. "I will listen, my queen. But you do not want my wisdom. You want the wisdom of HaShem."

"He doesn't speak to me!" The cry broke from my lips, harsh and raw, and Honi's eyes crinkled in sympathy.

"He doesn't speak to me, either," Honi said. "But He hears and He answers. Perhaps He will do the same for you."

I pressed my lips together, not sure if I should proceed. I had spoken of my conundrum to no one else—to openly discuss the succession could be interpreted as treason. I could not speak of it to my sons, nor could I speak of it to the king's advisors, for they would support the man most likely to advance *their* interests.

This Honi, however, seemed to have no particular interest in who inherited the throne. Now I would see if my instincts proved correct.

"I do not know what we will do when the king dies," I whispered. "Each of my sons has his virtues and his faults, but neither is ready to become king. I am afraid that any decision I make will result in unrest, bloodshed, and further corruption of our holy Temple."

Honi closed his eyes, nodded slowly, and pressed his hands together. He seemed to meditate for a moment. Then he opened his eyes and looked directly at me. "Salome Alexandra," he said, a note of exasperation in his soft voice, "for what purpose did HaShem fashion and prepare you?"

I stared at him, both amazed and perturbed by the question. "I—I don't know."

"We are HaShem's creations, and He sees the beginning and the end. He created you and brought you to this place, and I do not believe He would bring you unprepared."

"I have never been anything but a woman who liked to learn."

"And you have learned—from all those HaShem has brought into your life." The man's dark eyes sparkled. "Why must either of your sons rule Judea? You have another choice."

I stared wordlessly at him, my heart pounding. What was he saying? Was he suggesting that *I*—

Surprise siphoned the blood from my head, leaving me dizzy. I grasped the arm of my chair in an effort to stop the room from spinning.

Me, rule Judea? I was a woman. My place was at my husband's side, and the father's portion always went to the firstborn son, unless . . . it went to his wife.

"Israel has never had a queen," I said, speaking more to myself than to my guest.

"Yes, she has," Honi countered.

"Athaliah." I made a face. "An illegitimate queen and a wicked woman."

"I was thinking of Salina Alexandra," Honi answered. "And John Hyrcanus's wife. Alena lost her authority when her son ambushed her, and Salina gave her authority away. But you could accept the crown, Salome Alexandra. You could be a righteous ruler. You could fulfill your desire to help Israel while you prepare your sons for their future roles in Judea."

I sat in silence while I considered the idea from several angles. The circle-drawer was right—Alena had been chosen to rule, and so had Salina Alexandra, so the notion of a queen would not strike the people as preposterous. Furthermore, for generations the nations around us had been ruled by strong women who ably defended their nations' territories. If I held the reins of power, I could correct Israel's course. I could name Hyrcanus high priest, a job for which he was well suited, and place Aristobulus in charge of the military. My sons would feel valued and appreciated, they would grow in maturity and experience, and they would have responsibilities to keep them gainfully occupied.

If I were queen, I could right so many wrongs! I would permanently evict the concubines from the high priest's house. I would ensure that girls had an opportunity to study Torah as well as boys. I would remind the people of Israel that HaShem intended us to be an example to the Gentiles, and to bless them. I would remove the barriers from the Temple, allowing everyone to observe the sacrifices and participate in the worship of Adonai. I would not persecute Essenes or Pharisees or Sadducees, but would allow all of them an equal voice in the Sanhedrin.

I would take every opportunity to remind our people that the Law did not exist for its own sake, but to guide us to belief in a real God who heard our prayers and would soon send His Messiah—*that* was what I could not remember! Before the Law even existed, Abraham *believed* God, and HaShem reckoned it to him as righteousness.

Kissa believed.

So did I.

A thrill shivered through my senses as I looked up and caught Honi's gaze. "I will have to speak to the king," I said. "I could not do this without his approval."

Honi stood and bowed his head. "I will ask HaShem to guide you."

―――

The young concubine reluctantly slid off the bed at my approach. Jannaeus had rallied, for I found him propped up on pillows, his frame shrunken beneath the embroidered sheet. His cheekbones reminded me of tent poles stretched beneath canvas, and dark circles lay beneath his yellowed eyes.

His lips, which had kissed me and commanded the deaths of thousands of godly men and women, had shrunken into thin gray lines.

I sat next to him, in a spot warmed by the concubine. Jannaeus appeared to be dozing, a fact confirmed by the physician when I looked at him with a question in my eyes.

"He was speaking a moment ago," the doctor said. "You should find him coherent when he wakes."

I slipped my hand over my husband's, then drew upon all my stores of tenderness to whisper his name. "Jannaeus?"

Beneath the thin eyelids I saw movement.

"Husband? I have come to ask for your favor."

His eyes opened and focused on my face. "Wife?" His voice was barely audible.

"Yes, it is Salome Alexandra. I have come to talk to you about the succession." I had never dared broach the subject, so I knew my words might shock him. I did not know how forthright his physician had been, and I was certain the concubine had avoided the topic of death.

But I was his wife and his queen, and we had no time for illusions.

His eyes flicked toward the physician, then the concubine, who stood in the corner. Then his gaze returned to me.

"I must know, husband—who have you named as your successor? Who would you seat on the throne of Israel?"

His brows lowered, and his lips trembled as his eyes filled with question. I could think of only one question he would ask.

"Yes, husband," I said as gently as I could. "You will soon join your parents in the tomb. So we must know your choice to rule over Judea."

He stared at the ceiling as his face rippled with anguish. I knew he had thought about death—no man could be sick for so long without realizing that life was slipping away. But until that moment, apparently no one had confronted him with the inevitable truth.

I let him have the time he needed. While I waited, I wove my fingers between his, reminding him he was not alone.

Finally, his expression smoothed into resignation. His head turned and he looked at me. "You," he said simply, his fingers tightening around mine. "In my will, I have given Judea to you."

I said nothing but let my streaming tears speak for me. I listened as he continued to speak in halting words, and in his voice I heard regret for his sins. As he gave me final instructions regarding the transfer of power, I understood that he was finally coming to terms with all he had done and the consequences he would leave behind.

Despite the years of painful distance between us, I could not set aside my commitment to this man. I had been in the house when Alexander Jannaeus was born. I had loved his mother and respected his father. I had loved our children and appreciated the freedom he gave me to do things other women could not do.

So I would remain by his side until the end. HaShem had brought us together, and only HaShem could pull us apart.

Three hours later, as Jannaeus's breathing slowed and stopped, I wept genuine tears of loss—for my sons, who had lost a father; for a nation, who had lost a king; and for Jannaeus, who had never fulfilled the greatness that could have been his.

Then I nodded at the assistant priest, who had come from the Temple, and listened as he read prayers for the dying:

Yeetgadal v' yeetkadash sh'mey rabbah
May His great Name grow exalted and sanctified

B'almah dee v'rah kheer'utey
in the world that He created as He willed.

*v' yamleekh malkhutei, b'chahyeykhohn, uv' yohmeyk-
hohn,*
    May He give reign to His kingship in your lifetimes and
in your days,

uv'chahyei d'chohl beyt yisrael,
    and in the lifetimes of the entire Family of Israel,

ba'agalah u'veez'man kareev, v'eemru: amein.
    swiftly and soon. Amen.

Y'hey sh'met rabbah m'varach l'alam u'l'almey almahyah.
    May His great Name be blessed forever and ever.

    The day after Jannaeus died, I rose early and rode to Ragaba,
where Ezra Diagos was commanding the Judean forces involved
in a siege. I was a little embarrassed to face my old friend. I had
not seen him in years, and age had thickened my waistline and
slowed my step. My face, which had been smooth the last time
we met, had lately been etched by concern about my husband
and my sons.
    I alighted from my chariot outside the commander's tent. A
moment later my old friend appeared and lifted a brow when
he saw me standing with the military convoy. But he quickly
caught himself and bowed.
    "Rise, Diagos," I said. "I want to look at you."
    What I saw made me smile. He had aged as well, though his
dark and thoughtful eyes had not changed.
    "My queen," he said, opening the flap of his tent, "welcome
to Ragaba. I assume the king has sent you?"
    "The king is with me," I said, keeping my voice level. "And
you and I have much to discuss."

He looked around, but then I led the way into his quarters and took the proffered bench. Diagos sat across from me and spread a map on the table between us.

"My queen," he said in the manner of one who carefully chooses his words, "I hesitate to speak bluntly to you, especially when the king is so ill—"

"The king is dead, Diagos, and I am his choice to rule Judea. So please, friend, be as blunt as you like. I need to know exactly where we stand."

Diagos frowned as our eyes met. "I am sorry to hear it."

"I am sorry to bring you sad news. But we must finish our involvement here, so we can focus on important matters at home."

The soldier gave me a grim smile. "You are probably aware that Jannaeus knew the Seleucid Empire was crumbling, so in the last several years he attacked several of its cities at random. Some battles we won, some we lost, but now we are facing the consequences—the Seleucids are seeking revenge for the king's unprovoked attacks. We have had to surrender Moab and Galaaditis, a town beyond the Jordan, to Aretas, the Nabatean king."

"And why are we at Ragaba?" I asked.

"We have had the city under siege for months. It would be a valuable addition to our territory."

I stared at the map on the table. Ragaba was situated in a region that had belonged to the Seleucids. But since we had conquered the land north of this city, the surrender of Ragaba would give us a broad expansion in an area HaShem had promised Abraham.

"Thank you for the explanation." I drew a deep breath. "This is what we are going to do . . ."

~~~~~~~~

For the next week I had embalmers work on Jannaeus's body while Diagos and I increased the patrols around the city of Ragaba. I ordered one battalion of mercenaries to build a battering ram.

At the end of the week, Diagos entered my tent. "Excuse me, my queen, but the battering ram is ready."

"Good," I told him. "Tomorrow at sunrise we destroy the gate and enter the city."

"And after that?"

I swallowed hard. "We take Ragaba in the name of Alexander Jannaeus. Then you and I will travel to Jerusalem together. Upon our arrival, we will announce this victory . . . and the king's death."

He nodded soberly, then bowed. "As you wish, my queen."

Three days after the defeat of Ragaba, Diagos and I returned to Jerusalem. With the king's body in a simple coffin behind me, I stood before an audience of priests, Levites, and other influential leaders from all of the major sects. As I looked over the assembly, I closed my eyes and asked HaShem for strength lest I be trapped like Alena, and wisdom lest I commit folly like Salina.

I marshaled my courage. Only a few weeks before I would have trembled at the thought of standing before this sea of learned holy men. But all my years of womanly reticence fell away as I looked upon the faces of the men with whom I would now have to work, negotiate, and reason.

"Friends and citizens of Judea," I said, lifting my chin, "I would have you know that your king, Alexander Jannaeus, has died of his illness. The sickness troubled him for three years, but he would not surrender his efforts to claim the territories HaShem promised to Israel. We have just defeated the fortress at Ragaba, further reclaiming our Promised Land."

A murmur ran through the crowd, an undisguised ripple of

pleased surprise. Whether the pleasure came from the news of Jannaeus's death or his victory at Ragaba, I could not tell.

"I went to my husband before he died," I continued. "Among the things I asked him was, 'How can you leave us, knowing how much ill will your nation bears toward you?'"

Another ripple moved through the crowd, a murmur of agreement.

"Jannaeus told me I should conceal his death until we had taken Ragaba, and after that I should return to Jerusalem and put some of my authority into the hands of the Pharisees, for they would commend me for the honor I had done them. 'The Pharisees,' the king said, 'will reconcile the nation to you, for they have great authority among the people. Do this, and when you have come to Jerusalem, give my body to the Pharisees to use as they please. Then you will see if they dishonor my body by refusing it burial or do any further injury to it. Then you will see that I shall have the honor of a more glorious funeral from them than you could have made for me, and you will rule in safety.'"

I swallowed hard and looked toward the place where the leaders of the remaining Pharisees had gathered. "I believe my husband regretted his actions toward the Pharisees, and the violence with which he treated them. I also believe he counted on your forgiveness and your mercy. And so, learned teachers, I hereby place the king's body in your hands to do with it as you will. And I will make no decisions without consulting you, for I value your opinion and your dedication to the Torah. I have also studied Torah and am committed to living righteously before HaShem. This I promise you, and this I will do."

I glanced at the flushed faces of the Pharisees, who could not now mutilate or dishonor my husband's body without suffering a severe loss of reputation. If they did not give him the finest funeral Jerusalem had ever seen, and if they did not support me as their queen, they would be seen as unmerciful, unspiritual, and unrighteous.

"With the king's permission and blessing," I continued, "I am appointing our son Hyrcanus as high priest, for his heart is devoted to HaShem. Also with the king's permission and blessing, I am appointing our son Aristobulus as commander of the armies of Judea. From this time forward, we will use our army for defense only. We shall remain neutral in the disputes of other kingdoms, and we will do whatever possible in order to keep the peace."

"In closing," I said, "many of you have read the widely circulated *pesher* about the prince who will come. Just as during the Jubilee year, all debts are forgiven and we return to our ancestral homes, so let us look forward to the restoration of Israel to holiness. Let us forgive the debts of the past, forget the hurts and sorrows, and look to HaShem for restoration. For the anointed Messiah will soon come, and He will forgive our many sins and will be Israel's King and High Priest. When He comes, I will happily yield the throne to Him."

I stepped back and placed my palms on my husband's coffin. After whispering a Hebrew prayer for the dead, I looked again at the men who had not moved since I finished speaking. The Sadducees were clearly unhappy with this new turn of events, for they would lose power now that I had granted authority to the Pharisees. But the Pharisees and the Essenes should be pleased that I had expressed agreement with their view regarding the Messiah. How could I not, since the prophets had steadfastly proclaimed that HaShem would send His Anointed One in the latter days?

I gave a slight bow to the men who had listened so patiently, then left the reception hall and joined Kissa in the vestibule.

"It is done," I said, squeezing her hand. Without my pounding pulse to energize me, I felt suddenly exhausted. "Now we will see how they react to a woman on the throne."

"If they are wise," Kissa said, helping me up the stone stairs, "they will consider themselves blessed."

～～～～～～

The week after Alexander Jannaeus's funeral—truly one of the greatest Jerusalem had ever seen—I sent for Ezra Diagos. He appeared at the palace two hours later, dressed not in military garb but in a fine tunic, well-worked leather sandals, and a rich mantle.

He bowed deeply, an unnecessary gesture that caused me to blush. "Please, get up," I said, standing. "We are alone, so you need not do that."

He rose with an ease that belied his age, then took my hand when I offered it. "You are my queen. Why shouldn't I bow before you?"

"You are my friend." I met his gaze and felt my heart turn over the way it always did when I was in his company. "Apart from Kissa, you are my dearest friend, the one who seems to understand without benefit of words."

He smiled, but with a distracted air, as if something weighed on his mind. "I was glad to receive your message. I have been wanting to ask you about my future service."

"Then let us go into the garden." I tilted my head toward the open doorway, where we were less likely to be overheard by servants. "At this hour, the air is far cooler outside."

He walked with me into the garden and gestured to a stone bench. I sank onto it as gracefully as I could and was disappointed when he remained standing. "Won't you sit?"

To my surprise he lowered himself to the ground before me. "Salome Alexandra," he said, "I have come because I have wanted to ask you something for years, and only now am I at liberty to do so."

My heart swelled with a feeling I had thought long dead. "Diagos—"

"I hate to ask this," he went on, head bowed, "because some will say I am motivated by selfishness. But trust me in this—every man reaches a point, I believe, when he cares less about power and position than having a companion with whom he can be himself."

I knew where he was going, but I had to stop him. "Diagos—"

"Someone with whom he can share his days and nights, someone who speaks his language and appreciates his wit, small though it may be."

"Diagos, please stop."

He lifted his head until our eyes met. "I have adored you for years, you know."

"I spent those years begging HaShem to remove you from my heart."

"I kept silent—but there is no reason why I should remain silent now. Know that I do not wish to share your position or power. I wish only to be your husband."

I flinched and looked away.

"Is the idea so repulsive?"

"Diagos." I whispered the word like a farewell. "If I had met you earlier, before I was betrothed—"

"You would not have liked me." He laughed. "I was a rough soldier then, with no regard for women."

"I cannot marry." Though tears blurred my vision, I met his gaze. "I thank HaShem for bringing you into my life, for you have been a great blessing to me. But now I must be married to Judea, to Jerusalem, because I am not a young woman. If HaShem is willing, I have only a few years to prepare my sons and my people for the One who is to come."

Diagos lowered his head and sighed. "I thought that might be your answer."

"I am sorry. And I will freely admit that marrying you would bring me a great deal of pleasure. But so would your friendship, and I hope I will always have that."

"Of course." His mouth quirked with wry humor. "I had to try. I hoped I would catch you in a weak moment."

I took his rough hand and clasped it between my own. "You will always be dear to me, Diagos. And for this honor—something I would never have dreamt of—I will always be grateful."

And then, while he remained on his knees, I leaned forward and pressed my lips to the cheek of the only man who had ever completely understood me . . . and loved me nonetheless.

Kissa

My mistress did all she promised and more. Working with Simeon ben Shetah, who was among many Pharisees who had returned from Egypt after the death of Alexander Jannaeus, Queen Salome Alexandra decreed that all children, boys *and* girls, would be allowed to attend school.

Prior to Salome Alexandra's reign, a groom had been required to set money aside for the bride's family—not the bride. But Simeon, with the queen's blessing, required all bridegrooms to state in a ketubbah, or marriage contract, that in case of his death, his bride would receive all his property.

True to her word, Salome Alexandra hired soldiers and expanded Judea's army, but fought no wars to acquire new territory, only to defend her people.

She also made changes in the Temple administration. For the first time, Pharisees and Essenes were admitted to the Sanhedrin, the religious court that also taught Torah studies to young men.

Through negotiation and diplomacy, Salome Alexandra balanced Judea's relationships with Egypt, Seleucia, and Rome. In

Judea, she made and maintained a peace between the leaders of the Pharisees, Sadducees, and Essenes.

Ezra Diagos, the queen's advisor and nearly constant companion, came to the palace every day until he collapsed unexpectedly one afternoon and died in her arms.

I only wish my mistress had taken the throne earlier in her life. She was sixty-five when she told Israel that her husband had bequeathed the leadership to her, but her nine-year reign would later be described as Judea's golden age. Even her critics could find no fault in her piety and devotion to Adonai.

Years after her death, a Torah teacher would write, "In the time of Rabbi Simeon ben Shetah and Queen Salome Alexandra, the rain would fall on Friday nights, from one week to the next, until the wheat grew to the size of kidneys, the barley to the size of olive pits, and the lentils to the size of golden dinars." Judea had never known such peace and prosperity.

Such was the reign of Shelamzion, my mistress and friend.

But though she held high hopes for her sons, they could not escape their natures. As she grew ill in the last years of her life, she asked Hyrcanus to rule at her side, a request that embittered Aristobulus. And Hyrcanus, the son she loved most, was not trustworthy. Without Shelamzion's knowledge, he began to persecute the Sadducees, undermining my mistress's attempts to maintain the peace in Jerusalem.

Even before she drew her last breath, Aristobulus and his wife were conspiring to take the kingdom from Hyrcanus, Salome Alexandra's appointed heir. The violent rivalry between the two brothers grew into civil war and ultimately caused Rome to invade. Once Rome's Gnaeus Pompeius Magnus and his army arrived, Judea was no longer an independent nation.

The Romans' arrival brought strife and struggle back to Judea, and as I watched events unfold from my small house, I wondered if Shelamzion's zeal for righteousness had been wasted.

But one day when I visited the Temple, a priest stopped me. His name was Simeon, and though my aging eyes had trouble making out his appearance, my ears heard him clearly. "The Ruach HaKodesh is upon me," he said, his voice low, "and the Spirit has told me that I will not die before I see the Anointed One of Adonai." A smile filled his voice as he gripped my gnarled hand. "I thought you would want to know."

I carried that promise home with me, grateful that Shelamzion's devotion was about to bear fruit. The Messiah was coming, and those who followed her example would be ready.

Author's Note

In the few resources available about Queen Salome Alexandra, most writers report that she was the wife of Judah Aristobulus and later married Jannaeus in a Levirate marriage after Aristobulus's death. But in *A History of the Hasmonean State: Josephus and Beyond*, Kenneth Atkinson points out that it would have been impossible for Salome to marry Judah Aristobulus.

First, no ancient writer mentions an Aristobulus–Salome Alexandra marriage. No ancient manuscripts support this supposition.

Second, a man could not serve as high priest if he had married a widow, a divorced woman, or a prostitute—any woman with prior sexual experience: "He who is the *kohen gadol* [high priest] . . . should take a wife in her virginity. A widow, or one divorced, or one who has been defiled as a prostitute, he is not to marry. He is to take a virgin from his own people as a wife, so as not to corrupt his offspring among his people" (Leviticus 21:10–15).

Third, Josephus refers to Hyrcanus II as the son of Salome Alexandra and Alexander Jannaeus. If theirs had been a Levirate marriage, Hyrcanus II would have been the *legal* son of Salome Alexandra and Judah Aristobulus.

Finally, Josephus writes that Judah Aristobulus married Salina Alexandra, a different person altogether. Alexandra and Alexander were common names in the generations following Alexander the Great.

Readers always want to know how much of a historical novel is fact and how much fiction. First, the story about Salome Alexandra stopping a banquet because the dishes had been touched by a menstruating woman—this is true. She was held in high esteem because she once melted down silver plates in her quest for ritual purity. Her palaces all had mikvahs, where women could easily bathe in running water, and many stories about her piety were recorded.

The stories about Cleopatra III and Cleopatra Thea are true—in fact, the success of those two queens probably paved the way for Salome Alexandra's reign. If the Cleopatras had not existed, Jannaeus might have left the throne to one of his sons, both of whom were old enough to reign, but neither of whom would have made a good king.

We do not know much about Shelamzion's parents or if she had siblings, so I took liberties there. We do have reason to believe she was somehow part of the Hasmonean family, so it is likely she knew John Hyrcanus and his sons.

John Hyrcanus did change the way sacrificial animals were handled at the Temple.

The story about Judah Aristobulus and his role in his brother's death is historical, as is the information about the prophecy by Judah the Essene.

The people really did pelt Jannaeus with citrons during a water ceremony. And he did commit all the atrocities described in this novel.

If you are familiar with Herod's Temple (commonly known as the Second Temple, though it was actually the third), you may have arched a brow to read that Kissa and Salome were together in the Temple. But the "Court of the Gentiles" and the "Court of the Women" were not instituted until Herod's Temple. Before that time, Solomon's and Zerubbabel's Temples had only two courts—one for the people and one for the priests.

The ancient historian Josephus tells us that Jannaeus died in Ragaba, but contemporary scholar Kenneth Atkinson maintains that Jannaeus probably died at home. Josephus was related to the Hasmoneans and tended to portray them as more illustrious than they actually were. The story about how Jannaeus asked Salome to give his body over to the Pharisees comes from Josephus, so I mingled the two stories into an account that pays homage to both.

Much of what we know of Salome Alexandra is speculation, yet this much is true: she lived a devout life, she reigned over Jerusalem, and within a generation of her death the long-awaited Messiah was born and did live in Galilee, just as the prophets had predicted. Whether or not she realized it, her peaceful, pious reign did much to prepare the way of the Lord.

Discussion Questions

1. Had you ever heard of Queen Salome Alexandra before reading this book? Did you know Israel was ruled by a queen before it became a province of Rome?

2. After Sipporah dies, Kissa thinks: *HaShem, it seemed to me, did not allow his people to experience joy unless it was accompanied by an equal portion of sorrow.*

   Do you believe this is true? Why would God send joy as well as sorrow? Is it good for us to experience both?

3. When her mother dies, Salome thinks: *I did not weep for myself. Long ago I had learned how to make my own way in the world. I wept for my mother, who wanted more than anything to see one of her daughters grow up and marry a wealthy man with power and position. She had pinned all her hopes on Ketura, and so great was her blind obstinacy that she was not aware when her dreams and yearnings were fulfilled in a totally unexpected way.*

   In what way was Sipporah like the Jews a generation later? Who were they yearning for? What did they expect?

And when their long-awaited Messiah came, why did so many not recognize Him?

4. If you had been Salome Alexandra, which of the two sons would you have chosen to sit on Judea's throne? Do you agree with her decision to accept her husband's choice and sit on the throne herself?

5. Why do you think Alexander Jannaeus asked Salome to give his body to the Pharisees to whom he had been so cruel?

6. Did you identify with any of the characters in this story? Why or why not?

7. Salome Alexandra died sixty-seven years before the birth of Christ. Before reading this novel, were you aware that many of the Jews of that day were living in great anticipation of the Messiah's arrival?

8. Have you read the other books in THE SILENT YEARS series? How did this novel expand your knowledge of the Intertestamental Period?

9. Women in biblical times were often considered chattel with very few rights. Their husbands could divorce them for almost any reason, they could not vote, and in some cases they could not even leave the house without a male attendant. Why was Salome Alexandra granted such independence?

10. Salome often thinks about Kissa's status as a slave. But on a basic level, wasn't Salome as much a slave to her circumstances as Kissa was? Were any of the women in this story truly free?

11. Salome frequently looks for a savior, and God does send her a savior from her poverty and her unhappy marriage. How does this theme of a savior carry throughout the story?

12. The doctrine of God's sovereignty declares that He's sovereign over all His creation and implies that He works out a plan for each person. What were some of the events in Salome's life that enabled her to become the queen she ultimately became?

References

Atkinson, Kenneth. *A History of the Hasmonean State: Josephus and Beyond*. New York: Bloomsbury T&T Clark, 2016.

Atkinson, Kenneth. *Queen Salome: Jerusalem's Warrior Monarch of the First Century B.C.E.* Jefferson, NC: McFarland, 2012.

Charlesworth, James H. "Honi." In *The Anchor Yale Bible Dictionary*. Edited by David Noel Freedman. New Haven: Yale University Press, 1992.

Dąbrowa, Edward. *The Hasmoneans and Their State: A Study in History, Ideology, and the Institutions*. Krakow, Poland: Jagiellonian University Press, 2010.

Eastman, Mark. "Chapter Five—Messiah: Son of God?" In *Search for Messiah*. https://www.blueletterbible.org/comm/eastman_mark/Messiah/sfm_05.cfm, accessed August 14, 2017.

Green, Joel B., and McDonald, Lee Martin, eds. *The World of the New Testament: Cultural, Social, and Historical Contexts*. Grand Rapids, MI: Baker Academic, 2017.

Hagee, John. *His Glory Revealed: A Devotional*. Nashville: Thomas Nelson Publishers, 1999.

Postell, Seth D., Bar, Eitan, and Soref, Erez. *Reading Moses, Seeing Jesus: How the Torah Fulfills Its Goal in Yeshua*. One for Israel, 2017.

Rajak, Tessa. "Roman Intervention in a Seleucid Siege of Jerusalem?" University of Reading and Center for Hellenic Studies, 1980.

Regev, Eyal. *The Hasmoneans: Ideology, Archaeology, Identity.* Journal of Ancient Judaism. Bristol, CT: Vadenhoeck & Ruprecht, LLC, 2013.

Rich, Tracey R. *Torah.* http://www.jewfaq.org/torah.htm, accessed August 14, 2017.

Schiffman, Lawrence H. *Reclaiming the Dead Sea Scrolls: The History of Judaism, the Background of Christianity, the Lost Library of Qumran.* Philadelphia and Jerusalem: The Jewish Publication Society, 1994.

Stern, David H. *Jewish New Testament Commentary: A Companion Volume to the Jewish New Testament,* electronic ed. Clarksville, MD: Jewish New Testament Publications, 1996.

Telushkin, Rabbi Joseph. *Jewish Wisdom: Ethical, Spiritual, and Historical Lessons from the Great Works and Thinkers.* New York: William Morrow and Company, 1994.

Vermes, Geza. *The Dead Sea Scrolls in English*, 4th ed. Sheffield, UK: Sheffield Academic Press, 1995.

Yamauchi, Edwin. "722 צר." In *Theological Wordbook of the Old Testament.* Edited by R. Laird Harris, Gleason L. Archer Jr., and Bruce K. Waltke. Chicago: Moody Publishers, 1999.

Angela Hunt has published more than one hundred books, with sales nearing five million copies worldwide. She's the *New York Times* bestselling author of *The Tale of Three Trees*, *The Note*, and *The Nativity Story*. Angela's novels have won or been nominated for several prestigious industry awards, such as the RITA Award, the Christy Award, the ECPA Christian Book Award, and the HOLT Medallion Award. Romantic Times Book Club presented her with a Lifetime Achievement Award in 2006. She holds both a doctorate in Biblical Studies and a Th.D. degree. Angela and her husband live in Florida, along with their mastiffs. For a complete list of the author's books, visit angelahuntbooks.com.

Sign Up for Angela's Newsletter!

Keep up to date with Angela's news on book releases and events by signing up for her email list at angelahuntbooks.com.

More from THE SILENT YEARS

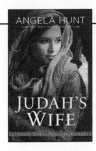

Seeking safety after a hard childhood, Leah marries a strong and gentle man of the nation of Judah. But when the ruler of the land issues a life-altering decree, her newfound peace—and the entire Jewish heritage— is put in jeopardy.

Judah's Wife: A Novel of the Maccabees
THE SILENT YEARS

BETHANYHOUSE

More from Angela Hunt

For a full list of Angela's books, visit angelahuntbooks.com.

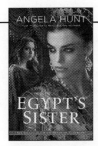

Chava, the Jewish daughter of a royal tutor, vowed to be true to her friend Cleopatra always. But after they argue, she is ripped from her privileged life and sold into slavery. Now, alone in Rome, she must choose between love and honor, between her own desires and God's will.

Egypt's Sister: A Novel of Cleopatra
THE SILENT YEARS

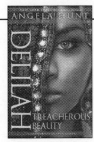

Abandoned and forced to beg for food to survive, Delilah vows to one day defeat the men who have taken advantage of her. When she meets Samson, she knows he is the key to her victory. To become a woman of prominence, she must win, seduce, and betray the hero of the Hebrews.

Delilah: Treacherous Beauty
A DANGEROUS BEAUTY NOVEL

When King David forces himself on Bathsheba, a loyal soldier's wife, she loses the husband—and the life—she's always known. Now, pregnant with the king's child, she struggles to protect her son and navigate the dangers of the king's household.

Bathsheba: Reluctant Beauty
A DANGEROUS BEAUTY NOVEL

◆ BETHANYHOUSE

You May Also Like . . .

Egyptian slave Kiya leads a miserable life. When terrifying plagues strike Egypt, she chooses to flee with the Hebrews. Soon she finds herself reliant on a strange God and falling for a man who despises her people. Will she turn back toward Egypt or find a new place to belong?

Counted with the Stars by Connilyn Cossette
OUT FROM EGYPT #1
connilyncossette.com

This powerful series captures the incredible faith of Ezra, Nehemiah, and their families as they returned to God after the Babylonian exile. These stories of faith, doubt, and love encompass the Jews' return to Jerusalem and their efforts to rebuild God's temple amid constant threat.

THE RESTORATION CHRONICLES: *Return to Me, Keepers of the Covenant, On This Foundation*
by Lynn Austin
lynnaustin.org

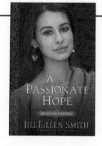

Two Old Testament women, Hannah and Peninnah, want to be loved by their shared husband—and to bear children. To what lengths will they go to get what they want most, and will either find her heart's desire?

A Passionate Hope: Hannah's Story by Jill Eileen Smith
DAUGHTERS OF THE PROMISED LAND #4
jilleileensmith.com

◊BETHANYHOUSE